The Sur

Linda Sawley

Linric Publishing

Published in November 2007 by Linric Publishing
18 Victoria Lodge
READ, Lancs
BB12 7SZ

British Cataloguing in publication data
Sawley, Linda
The Survivor
I. Title
Classification: Historical Romantic Fiction

ISBN 978–0-9557258–0-7

Cover design by David Eaves

Proof reading by Edward Habiak

Digitally Printed by Beacon DM
Unit 2, Valley Road Business Park
Gas Works Road
Keighley, BD21 4LY

Dedicated to my husband Jim,

who always says

'I hope you're not going to write another book.'

Also to Santa Montefiore, who told me to get on with writing it instead of talking about it!!!

With grateful thanks to my highly efficient but totally unpaid sales and marketing team

Judith Habiak

Jackie Hindle

Gladys Hughes

Sandra Nuttall

Charis and Christine Rowlands

Grace Sawley

The lifeboat was lowered quietly into the water from the side of the ship. The four-crew members started to row as quickly as possible, to prevent the lifeboat being sucked under by the larger ship. The passengers remained calm as the lifeboat gently pulled away. Desultory talk started between the occupants of the boat, mainly women and children. They had been reassured that as soon as the repairs had been done to the ship, they would be going back on board. It would only be a matter of time.

The girl sat in the corner of the lifeboat. She didn't join in the conversation, even though her neighbour tried to initiate some small talk. Her mind was racing: her thoughts reliving the last few minutes.

Suddenly, there was a sound from the large ship. All talk ceased and eyes were riveted towards it. The lights flickered off, and then briefly came back on again, before finally going out completely. There were a few more ominous creaking sounds and then the ship slowly but inexorably upended. It stayed in that upright position for several minutes, then slowly slid deeper into the water. Within a few more minutes, the ship had completely disappeared. This brand new boat, that was supposed to be unsinkable, had disappeared under the water.

After a few seconds of silence and disbelief, one or two women started to cry or moan. They were crying for their husbands. Children began to sob, unnerved by their upset mothers. Most of the men hadn't been allowed on the available lifeboats and the ship didn't have enough for everyone.

The girl sat staring at where the RMS Titanic had been. She thought not of a husband or lover, but of her guardian, her maid and her jewels. Her guardian was the only member of her family left and now he was probably gone. But it was the loss of her maid that was troubling her most. Not from a closeness of relationship, although she had served her for eight years. No, it was the fact that she'd sent the maid back to their suite of rooms just as they were boarding the lifeboat, to get her jewellery box. As it turned out, it was the last available lifeboat. And now the maid would probably be drowned along with many others for whom there was no way of escape. In effect, she had sent the maid to her death; all to satisfy her own greed and desire for possessions.

The girl pulled her coat round herself, trying to keep the cold out, but it only reminded her afresh that her maid had given her this warm coat just as they went to the lifeboats; her own coats too flimsy and impractical for a journey like this.

'Wear my new coat, Miss, it'll keep you warm. I'll wear my second best coat.' The girl felt even guiltier, that she had taken the maid's warmest coat, as well as sending her back for the jewels. How would she ever live with herself?

An elderly woman sat next to the girl and asked her questions. The girl stared at the woman but found that she couldn't speak. It wasn't that she was too emotional to speak, but she seemed to have lost the ability to speak at all. The girl turned quickly away from the woman, wondering whether she would ever be able to speak again, or ever want to. She knew that she would never assuage her guilt: not even if she lived to be an old lady.

Chapter 1

February 1912

Arabella Charlotte Sophie Montague collapsed on to the small chair in front of her dressing table. She was exhausted. Having danced until four in the morning, she had then been driven home by the chauffeur, politely refusing all offers to accompany her. Arabella peered into the mirror. The view was not as pleasant as it had been at eight o'clock last night, when she'd been setting out to the ball. Her sparkling blue eyes looked more cloudy than usual, and her skin looked pale. She looked critically at herself, but her maid entering the room soon disturbed her thoughts.

'Oh, Lizzy, there you are. Where've you been? I've been waiting for you to help me get undressed,' she said petulantly.

The tired maid replied, 'I was taking your slippers down to the boot boy. I wanted to get the mud off as soon as possible. I know you love those slippers and wouldn't want them ruined, Miss.'

'Well, I needed you. What does another pair of slippers matter? I could always buy another pair.'

'Yes, Miss Arabella,' replied the maid.

'Now get me undressed at once. I'm exhausted.' The maid started unlacing the back of Miss Arabella's dress.

'Aren't you going to ask me about the ball? You usually like to ask me lots of questions.'

'How was the ball? Did you have many dances?'

'Of course I had many dances,' replied Arabella scornfully, 'I was the belle of the ball as usual. I'm the richest heiress around here so all the men want to dance with me.'

'You certainly looked beautiful when you left here,' offered Lizzy trying to muster up some enthusiasm in her voice.

'I know, I find this shade of ivory suits me. It's much better than the pure white which young unmarried girls are expected to wear. I love the burgundy flowers that trim the dress too. All across the shoulders and neck. And the burgundy velvet lacing down my back just completes the effect.'

'That's why I wanted to get your slippers cleaned, Miss Arabella. The dressmaker struggled to get just the right shade of burgundy flowers to match your shoes.'

'Yes, she did. I suppose it'd be difficult to get another pair just like them,' said Arabella. The maid slipped the dress off and laid it carefully on the bed. She helped Miss Arabella into her nightgown, and started undoing the clips that were holding her hair. Lizzy started brushing Miss Arabella's blond curls, but was soon told to stop, when she caught the comb in a large red birthmark that Arabella had behind her left ear.

'Ouch! That hurt. Oh leave it tonight, Lizzy. I just want to go to bed. You can sort my hair out tomorrow. I want to go to bed now,' yawned Miss Arabella.

'Yes, Miss. I'll take your dress, then. Goodnight Miss.'

'Night,' said Arabella and turned over in the bed, and was asleep before Lizzy was out of the room.

Next morning, Lizzy was up early, even though she'd not got to bed until after five in the morning. She cleaned and tidied Miss Arabella's drawing room and did some ironing, making sure that all her clothes were ready for whatever activity she would be doing that day. It was after lunchtime when Arabella eventually sent for Lizzy.

'Has my uncle breakfasted yet, Lizzy?'

'Yes, Miss, and had luncheon as well. He went out with the estate manager about an hour ago. Do you want some breakfast?'

'Yes, I'm ravenous. It must be all the dancing that's made me hungry. Tell Cook I'll just have bacon, kidneys, eggs and toast.' Lizzy curtsied and left the room.

Down in the kitchen, Cook wasn't too pleased about the order for breakfast when she was trying to get the evening meal ready, but she knew better than to argue. She slammed the pots and pans around a little, but Lizzy ignored her – it was just Cook's way. Miss Arabella could be difficult at times, but they all felt sorry for her and made allowances for her petulance. Cook made the breakfast as requested and Lizzie served it to Miss Arabella. For the rest of the afternoon, Arabella lay on her bed remembering the ball and planning what she would wear for the next one, and deciding with whom she would condescend to dance.

Prior to the evening meal, Arabella's uncle was waiting in the library for her to come downstairs. He was enjoying a glass of whisky.

'There you are my dear,' he said beaming at Arabella. 'Let's go into the dining room and you can tell me all about last night's ball.' He took her arm through his and they walked into the small dining room. They only used the large dining room when they had guests, but there were only the two of them that night.

Arabella loved her uncle, who was also her guardian. She had been left an orphan at the age of nine, and her uncle had been childless. She chattered on about the ball whilst the servants carried dishes of food backward and forwards: enough to feed several families.

When the servants had served cups of tea, they retired, leaving Arabella and her uncle alone together.

'I have some news for you, my dear,' Uncle Robert started.

'Oh, is it good news? I do hope so,' interrupted Arabella. Her uncle laughed.

'Well, if you let me carry on, you'll find out. I've booked us passage on a ship as a treat for your birthday. You'll actually celebrate your birthday on the ship. It will be the maiden voyage and will sail from an Irish town called Queenstown to America. It's the biggest ship ever built and is called the RMS Titanic.'

'When are we going? Oh, I'll need a whole new wardrobe of clothes. I'll have to contact the dressmaker tomorrow. Or perhaps I need to have a visit to London or even Paris.'

'Now then, Arabella, there's plenty of time. We're not sailing until April. You have two months to get ready. Besides, you've far too many clothes already.'

'A girl can never have too many clothes, uncle. I wonder who else will be going? Are the Huntingdon-Smythes going? Or the Smethursts?'

'I doubt it. There are very few English people going. It is an American owned ship, but I am friendly with the owner, so I managed to persuade him to allow us berths. The ship is owned by the White Star Line. Here are the leaflets. It's said to be very luxurious and they are bragging that the ship is unsinkable.' Arabella quickly looked through the leaflets whilst he was talking.

'I can't wait. I love the sea. Will I be allowed to take Lizzy?'

'Yes, I have booked two large suites for us and two smaller rooms for Lizzy and Vickers.'
'I must tell Lizzy now. She'll be so excited. Oh thank you uncle. You are so kind to me. I know I'll have a wonderful time.'
'Perhaps you will meet a young man and then I can wash my hands of you, and have a bit of peace in my old age.' In reply, Arabella hugged him tightly and said 'You don't mean that, you would miss me.'
'I suppose I would,' he laughed, 'like toothache! Now off you go, tell Lizzy what is happening,' but he was talking to himself; Arabella was already running across the room and jangling the bell pull. Too impatient to wait for a reply, she jangled the bell again, just as Vickers, the craggy faced butler, answered the summons.
'Vickers, where have you been? I need to speak to Lizzie. Get her for me,' ordered Arabella.
There was a short silence.
'Lizzie has retired for the night. It's her evening off Miss Arabella.'
'Well, you'll just have to get her up. I need to speak to her now, tonight.' Vickers bowed and left the room. Some minutes later, a dishevelled Lizzie entered the room after knocking on the door.
'You wanted to see me, Miss Arabella?'
'Yes, why did it take so long?'
'I was asleep in bed, Miss.'
'Well, you're here now at last, so come to my room. I've a lot of planning to do.'
'Can't it wait until tomorrow? interjected Uncle Robert. 'Lizzie was asleep,'
'She's awake now, so it doesn't matter. And no, uncle, it can't wait until tomorrow. Come along Lizzie,' she said on her way out of the room, leaving her uncle shaking his head at the selfishness of his niece.
When they arrived in the bedroom, Arabella sat on the chaise longue. 'I need to look at all my ball gowns and day dresses and see which I can take and how many more I'll need to order.'
'All of your ball gowns, Miss?'
'Yes, I need to decide which I'm to take.'
'Are you going on a journey, Miss?'

'Oh yes, haven't I told you? I'm going on a new ship, the maiden voyage in fact. Oh and you're coming with me, Lizzie.'
'Me, Miss? Going on a big ship?' replied Lizzie, transfixed by the news.
'Yes, of course, I'll need you to help me dress won't I? What's the matter with you standing there staring? Just get my ball gowns out.'
Lizzie hurried over to the dressing rooms adjacent to the bedroom and opened the many wardrobes. Arabella followed her.
'I'm so happy, Lizzie, I really like going on ships, although my uncle is hoping that I'll find a suitor and then he'll get rid of me.'
'Perhaps you will, Miss. That would be wonderful, running your own home.' replied Lizzie.
'I'll get married when I am ready. I'm not in a hurry. But I am sure there'll be many eligible young men on board and I shall enjoy looking,' Arabella laughed.
'When's the journey, Miss?'
'In April.'
'April?'
'Yes, why do you ask?'
'But that's two months away.'
'I know. But there's so little time to get all my clothes ready.' Lizzie sighed and continued to retrieve the ball gowns. 'And I think that we had better order you some new uniforms, too. It won't do if you look shabby in front of all those Americans.'
'Americans?'
'The ship is owned by Americans, and the passengers will be mainly American. The ship is called the RMS Titanic.'
'I've never been on a ship before, Miss. I can't even swim.'
'You don't need to be able to swim, you goose. We're going on the biggest ship that has ever been built and it's unsinkable.'
'Good. I've always been frightened of water.'
'There's no need to be frightened. It'll be just like going to a luxury hotel, only we'll be floating. There will be bedrooms and lounges and restaurants, just like a hotel. Do you remember when we stayed at the hotel in London, when Uncle's house was being refurbished?'
'Yes, Miss.'

'Well, it'll be like that. It's supposed to be furnished in the height of luxury according to the brochures. Now, let me see. I can take several of these gowns as I won't have met most of the passengers.'
'Will you be taking the one you wore last night, Miss Arabella?'
'Probably. I do like that one. And I'll take the white satin one, and the cream silk, and the white with pink flowers. So that is, er, let me see, four. Is that right?'
'Yes, Miss. How many nights are you going to be on board the ship?'
'Six nights, so I'll need at least twelve evening gowns and twelve day dresses. It would be awful if someone wore one of the gowns I was going to wear.'
'Twelve Miss?'
'Well, yes, there is the homeward journey as well. And we are staying in New York for a few days before our return, so I will need some clothes for those occasions. Then I'll need morning dresses and sports outfits.'
'Sports outfits, Miss Arabella?'
'There is a gymnasium on board, with suitable sporting activities for ladies. There is even a swimming pool. Well, I'm obviously going to need a shopping trip very soon. I haven't anywhere near enough clothes to take with me.'
Lizzie surveyed the enormous pile of clothes decorating the bed, thinking that it would keep most women in clothes for several years, but she said nothing.
'I think we will go to Paris. That would be easiest. I'll tell my uncle in the morning. Oh dear,' yawned Arabella, 'I'm feeling quite tired. Now I know what clothes I've got, I think I'll go to bed. Just take these clothes off my bed, Lizzie. Put them in the dressing room until morning, then you can hang them all up again. I'm too tired for you to do them tonight.'
Lizzie started carrying the clothes into the dressing room, whilst Arabella stood and watched her.
'Hurry up Lizzie, I'm tired,' Arabella whined, but didn't offer to help.
'Being as fast as I can, Miss,' replied Lizzie patiently. Eventually the piles of clothes were transferred to the dressing room and both girls went to their own beds.

Next morning, Arabella was up early for once, pestering her uncle for a trip to Paris, but this time, he was reluctant to grant her wishes.
'There is absolutely no need for you to go to Paris. There are plenty of excellent dressmakers in this country. Go to York or Bradford or Leeds, or even London. But not Paris.'
Arabella pouted, sulked, cajoled and wheedled, all to no avail. Uncle Robert was adamant.
'You told me yourself that American women are far behind English women in fashionable garments, so there is no need to go so far afield.'
'You would have me dressed in sackcloth. How embarrassing. What will I look like? I'll be mortified.'
'Arabella, you have never looked less than beautiful in anything you have ever worn. Why you'd look beautiful if you did wear sackcloth. And judging by the amount of clothes allowance you get through, you already have plenty of clothes.'
'Won't you be going to get some new clothes? Won't you want to go to Paris?' she asked her uncle, trying a new tack.
'No Arabella. I have sufficient clothes for the trip.'
'But uncle, I have to have the right sort of clothes for a trip on a new boat. Surely you understand that? How will I meet the right sort of young man if I am not wearing the right clothes?' she wheedled.
'Oh, Arabella. I despair. You can turn anything I say to your advantage. If the young man is the 'right sort', what you are wearing will make no difference whatsoever. No, that is my final word. You can only purchase any necessary new clothes in England. And don't expect any birthday present this year. If you are having new clothes, as well as the trip, that is all you will get.'
Watching the grim look on her uncle's face, Arabella knew she was beaten. She remained sulky for the rest of breakfast, merely playing with her food, and her uncle was glad to get out of the house for some peace and men's company on the estate.
Arabella retired to the small lounge and, sitting at her writing desk, started to compile lists of what she would need for the journey. It took her all day.

Chapter 2

The chauffeur drove the Rolls Royce Silver Ghost carefully out of the old converted stable, which was now grandly called the garage. It was Robert Montague's second automobile, which he had bought in 1911. It was his pride and joy. At first the chauffeur, Arthur Marks, had been very wary of driving automobiles, but over the last five years, had come to love the freedom and speed that it gave. He checked over the seats, ensuring that they were as immaculate as they had been when he left the garage, only three minutes earlier. Arthur took as much pride and joy in the machine as his employer did, if not more.

He rang the bell on the front door, and returned to the automobile to await Miss Arabella's convenience. Eventually, Arabella, Lizzie and the housekeeper, Mrs Seeney, came out of the house. They all settled themselves in the seats, then checking that their motoring scarves and gloves were in place, settled back for the long journey.

Arabella and Lizzie listened to Mrs Seeney fussing about the journey with Marks. She was always like that when she had to go in an automobile and said that it wasn't natural: what was wrong with horses and carts like they had in her day? The young girls smiled, and looked out of the window at the woodlands and park surrounding Montague Hall. Eventually the automobile turned on to the main road towards York, and the girls admired the passing scenery.

As they approached the city centre, Marks asked Mrs Seeney where they wanted to alight.

'I think we'll start in Piccadilly. We'll be able to reach Goodramgate and Fossgate easily then,' she replied.

'No,' objected Arabella, 'drop us earlier, near the Assembly Rooms. I've a mind to have a cup of chocolate before we start shopping. Take us there, then wait for us, and you can take us nearer afterwards.'

'Yes Miss,' replied Marks, glancing at Mrs Seeney with a certain look on his face.

Arabella alighted at the Assembly Rooms and was soon enjoying the rich hot drink, whilst the other three waited in the automobile.

Eventually, she got back into the automobile, and Marks drove round to Picadilly.
'I think we'll get your uniforms bought first, Lizzie.'
'Oh thank you Miss Arabella, that's very kind of you, I'm sure.'
'Well, it won't take long and then I can concentrate on buying my new clothes. Better still, Mrs Seeney, you take Lizzie to Mason's on The Shambles and leave me here.'
'Certainly Miss. What shall I purchase for Lizzie?'
'Whatever you think necessary. I suppose she'll need dresses, aprons, underclothes, nightwear, and the like. You'll know best. Oh, and you'd better get her a coat. A good warm one. The ship is going to cold regions.'
'And hat and gloves?'
'Yes, whatever she needs,' replied Arabella irritably. 'Now I'm going in Juliana's. I shall wait here for you. I'll be quite all right on my own.'
'Thank you Miss Arabella, it's so kind of you,' murmured Lizzie.
'Oh, thank my uncle, Lizzie. I shan't be paying. Besides, he will probably deduct the money from your next quarter's earnings.'
'Yes, Miss,' replied Lizzie, trying to keep the panic out of her voice. Most of her meagre wage went to her family back home, so they would be the poorer for Lizzie having new clothes. Perhaps she could send some of her old clothes to her younger sisters, she mused. That would ease the burden on her family. Her mother could make the clothes into smaller garments for her younger sisters.
Lizzie and Mrs Seeney set off on foot to the servants' outfitters in the Shambles. Marks stood by the automobile, polishing the bonnet whilst looking lovingly at it.
Arabella walked in to Juliana's and sighed deeply as she entered. It would have been so much better to go to Paris, but she had to admit that Juliana's was good. They did seem to know what would suit her, and also kept an eye on the London fashions.
'Ah, Miss Montague. How kind of you to visit us. Do come and take a seat. How can we help you today?' asked the shop assistant.
'Is Miss Juliana in?'
'Certainly, I shall just get her for you. May I get you a little refreshment whilst you wait?'
'No, I've just had chocolate.'

The assistant bowed and left the room. Soon an older elegant lady came in to the room and the greetings began all over again.

'My dear Miss Montague. How are you and how is your charming uncle?'

'Both fine, Miss Juliana. And yourself?'

'Never better. Now what may I show you today?'

'My uncle is taking me on a voyage on a new ship called the Titanic. I will need several ball gowns and some day dresses. And a new fur wrap.'

'I will just send out a girl to the furriers, whilst we are discussing your needs, then they can bring some suitable examples.' She turned away from Arabella and called out 'Sally?'

A tiny girl scurried out of the back room and curtsied at both Miss Juliana and Arabella, without speaking or looking upwards. She was despatched off to the furriers with a note and another girl called for.

'Martha? I need you to model some garments for Miss Montague. Wear the new white dress that arrived yesterday, the one with pale blue silk trim, please.'

After a short wait, Martha entered the salon and walked graciously around the room. Arabella looked critically at the gown.

'Yes, that is quite nice. I'll look at all the dresses and make my mind up afterwards.'

Martha returned again and again with a different gown on each time. Arabella looked carefully, making notes from time to time, on a pad that she had taken from her reticule. Miss Juliana kept up a running commentary on the attributes of each gown, saying where the inspiration for each one was from.

'I'm sure you'll like this one best of all,' gushed Miss Juliana. Martha entered the salon and Arabella was impressed. It was a very low cut white satin gown, but it had an overcoat of lace from the neck to the hem, resulting in a daring but still modest gown for a young lady. The sleeves were made entirely from lace.

'You're right. I do like it the best.'

'It has been modelled on a gown that Queen Mary wore at the Lord Mayor's Ball recently. It's rumoured that it was made in Paris and brought over specially for her.'

'I'm sure that will be just fine for what I need. I shall wear it on the last night of the voyage.'

'Why not the first night, Miss Montague, if I may make so bold a suggestion? That way you will set the standard for the rest of the voyage.'

'Yes, I suppose that would cut quite a dash. And now I need to look at day dresses.'

'But which of the ball gowns will you be requiring, Miss Montague?'

'All of them, of course. Now do you have any sporting wear as well?'

'Yes, certainly,' replied Miss Juliana catching her breath. In one morning, Miss Montague had bought practically all of her stock of finest white and cream ball gowns. 'Martha will model some day dresses first.'

Martha returned wearing a neat two piece costume in lightweight fawn wool, with fur trimmings around the cuffs and collar. 'I thought this would be suitable for promenading on the deck during the day, if there is a cold wind.'

'A good idea. Yes, I'll take that. But I also need some dresses for inside. What do you have?'

'Martha will be back shortly. In the meantime, would you like to look at underclothes?'

Arabella chose some dainty underclothes and added them to her list of purchases. Martha soon returned wearing a pale grey wool dress, which ended just above her ankles, displaying her neat black ankle boots. The edge of the skirt and neck was trimmed in black also, making it a very fetching outfit.

As soon as this was approved, Martha returned wearing another dress, until seven day dresses and outfits had been approved. The tinkle of the doorbell announced the arrival of the furrier.

Several fur wraps, shawls and full length coats were displayed for Arabella. She chose a full-length mink coat with hat to match, and a sable wrap and muff. The furrier thanked her for her custom and left.

Arabella turned to looking at sports outfits. She chose two long white divided skirts, similar to cycling skirts, and some long sleeved cotton blouses to match.

Next she turned her attention to accessories. She chose bags, scarves, and many pairs of gloves in every colour, style and material.

Her purchases completed, she instructed Miss Juliana to send them all to her home, once they had been adjusted to her size and height, and she made to leave.

'Thank you so much for your custom, Miss Montague, it has been a pleasure to serve you.' Arabella just inclined her head and left the shop. Miss Juliana let out a long breath. Martha entered the room and was surprised that Miss Montague had gone.

'Which ones did she buy then, Miss Juliana?'

'Everything. Everything that we showed her. Plus the furs. Her bill will be a little over eight hundred pounds with the furs – just for one voyage.'

Martha shook her head disbelievingly. 'I bet that is as much as you make in a month usually,' she suggested.

'More like several months,' replied a grateful Miss Juliana. 'You will be receiving a bonus in your wage packet this week, Martha. You demonstrated the gowns well today. I'm very pleased with you.' Martha glowed with pleasure and hurried to the back room to tell Sally of all the goings on that morning.

Meanwhile, Arabella returned to the automobile. Marks jumped to attention and held the door open for her. Mrs Seeney and Lizzie were sat in the back seat, having completed their purchases ages ago.

'All that shopping has made me ravenous. I'll go to the tearooms across the road, Marks. You three can go to the pie shop if you like,' said Arabella condescendingly, and walked across the road for her lunch. By the time she came out of the tearooms, it was three o' clock. Marks was getting fidgety, as he was worried about driving home in the dark. The lamps never seemed bright enough, he felt, especially on the unlit roads in the countryside.

'I can't be bothered to go to the shoe shop now. Can we just call round there, Marks?'

'Yes, Miss. The usual one in Lendal?'

'Yes. No, on second thoughts, we'll try the new one in Fossgate.'

'Very good, Miss.' Marks turned the automobile round and faced in the opposite direction. He manoeuvred the automobile and parked outside the shoe shop and opened the door. Arabella got out and entered the shop.

'Good afternoon, miss, may I help you?'

'Yes, I'm Arabella Montague of Montague Hall. I would like someone to attend me at my home as soon as possible.'
'Certainly Miss Montague. Would you take a seat whilst we measure your foot to make a last?'
'Oh I suppose so. I was just going to ask you to attend me, but I suppose it will speed things up.' The proprietor quickly measured Arabella's foot to prepare the last. Arabella stood up afterwards and went towards the door.
'May we call tomorrow afternoon? Will that be convenient?'
'Yes. Goodbye.' Arabella was almost through the door, but then turned back. 'No, make it next Tuesday afternoon. All my new clothes will have been delivered by then, and you can match the colours.'
'Of course. Thank you for your custom. Until next Tuesday then,' the proprietor replied bowing, but Arabella left the shop, without acknowledging him further.
Marks jumped out to help Arabella into the automobile. Eventually they got home and Arabella decided to have a rest before the evening meal. 'Shopping is just so exhausting!' she complained to no one in particular and went to her bedroom.
Lizzie hurried up to her own bedroom once Arabella was settled and showed all her purchases to the scullery maid, Ginny, who was in the next bedroom.
'You're so lucky getting all them new things, Lizzie. And going on the ship. I bet I never get to go on a ship, ever. Perhaps if I get to be a lady's maid like you, I might, but I feel as if I'll spend all my life in that kitchen,' moped Ginny.
'I used to feel like that, too. It was only when Miss Arabella came to live here that I got promoted to lady's maid. They wanted someone who was Miss Arabella's age, after all her troubles.'
'Was she only nine when she lost her parents and brothers?'
'Yes, she was very sad for a long time. She didn't speak for over three months. That's when they decided to give me a job. The governess was useless; couldn't get a word out of her.'
'Was it you that helped her?'
'Not really. Mr Montague bought her a puppy. She never looked back after that. It was as if she had someone to love again. That little

dog followed her everywhere. Called Mitch it was. A black cocker spaniel.'

'Where is it now? I've never seen it since I came here.'

'It got killed. Went out with the hunt and got in the way of one of the horses.'

'What was she like when it died?'

'Terrible. Stopped speaking again for months. She was never the same. She eats, sleeps and talks now, but she has become hard. Won't help herself at all and treats everyone like dirt.'

'And has she never had another dog?'

'No, her uncle bought her one, but she wouldn't look at it. It's like her heart is frozen. She can't seem to give love anymore, or receive it. She doesn't seem to be interested in getting married at all. Not like most of the young girls.'

'It's a sad story,' replied Ginny. 'I suppose we're lucky, even though we have nothing, because at least we have the love of our families.' Lizzie nodded morosely.

Chapter 3

The time of the journey was getting near. After much discussion about going to Ireland for the launch, Robert Montague changed his mind and decided to catch the Titanic at Southampton.

'Don't like the Irish,' he muttered to Arabella. 'Not an easy time in that country. Too much rebellion around. We'll board at Southampton and I can look up an old friend from my navy days at the same time.'

'How long were you in the Navy uncle?'

'Fifteen years. I loved it too.'

'Why did you give it up then?'

'When your Father died, my dear. He was the heir and I was the spare. Had to become Lord of the Manor so to speak.'

'But I didn't come to live at Montague Hall until I was nine. How come we didn't live there before if my father was the heir?'

'You lived with your mother's parents in their house. They were elderly and infirm and it was easier for you all to live there.' Arabella remained silent for a few minutes, pondering on what he had said. Suddenly she spoke again.

'Will we stay at your friend's house, Uncle?' asked Arabella, her mind as usual working on whether she would need extra clothes just in case.

'No, we'll stay at the Grand. I'll just invite him to dinner at the Hotel. That will suffice. His is a bachelor establishment, so I won't put him out by expecting him to provide a formal dinner. He lives quite frugally, with just a housekeeper to look after him. Spends all his money going on voyages. You'd think he'd had enough of ships for a lifetime, but he loves the big ships. He'll be quite envious that we're going on the Titanic. Now have you got your final list ready for the voyage? Is this the hundredth attempt at making your list? You seem to have been doing nothing else for weeks now,' he teased gently.

'Uncle, I have to make sure I have got everything. I can't send out to a shop in the middle of the Pacific, can I?'

'Atlantic.'

'Atlantic what?'

'Ocean. We'll be on the Atlantic Ocean.'

'Oh yes, that's what I meant. But I can't, can I?'
'I suppose not. I'm not sure all that expensive schooling has done you any good. Didn't they teach you about oceans?'
'Oh course they did,' replied Arabella airily, 'but that was ages ago when I was a child.'
'And now you're an old lady of eighteen, I suppose?'
'Yes, uncle, I left those sort of things in the classroom. There are far more important matters to occupy a young lady's mind.'
'Such as?'
'Oh well, what one should be wearing for a particular occasion; what accessories should go with what outfit; how to greet a new acquaintance; oh, so many things.'
'All froth and nonsense by the sound of things. What about politics, the state of the world and poverty?'
'Oh I think all that sort of politics stuff can be left to the men. They don't like women interfering in them anyway. Look at the poor suffragettes. Mind you, can't see why they need to do all that disrupting and demonstrating stuff. Can't see what they get worked up about. And the poor? Well, I blame them to be honest. If they worked hard, they wouldn't be poor.'
'Oh Arabella. Some poor people do work hard but are still poor.'
'Then they should limit their families, then they wouldn't have as many mouths to feed.'
'But some employers are very cruel and don't pay their workers a fair wage.'
'Nonsense. They probably spend it all on drink,' snorted Arabella.
'You have some very cruel opinions, Arabella. It grieves me to hear you. One day I will take you in to the poorer areas. Perhaps whilst we are in Southampton, then you will see what real poverty is.'
'I'd rather not. Can't think of anything worse.'
'I'm sure the poor would rather not, but they have no option.'
'Uncle, you are making me feel quite queasy. Please change the subject. I won't want my tea if you carry on so.'
'We'll leave it for now then. I'll write to the Grand and to my friend and make the arrangements to pick the ship up at Southampton. Now I'll have to go and do some making of lists myself.'
'Of your clothes, Uncle?'

'Certainly not, girl. Lists of jobs that Horrocks, the estate manager, will need to attend to in my absence. A place like this doesn't run itself, you know.'

Arabella smiled at her uncle's retreating back. He was all bluster really. She could twist him round her little finger and get her own way in anything. Well, almost anything, she remembered with a frown, I didn't get to go to Paris for my new clothes, but never mind, I'm quite happy with what Miss Juliana had.

The days flew by and soon the morning arrived when they were setting off for Southampton. Robert Montague had decided to take both automobiles to accommodate all the people and luggage. Robert had two trunks, Lizzie and Vickers had one between them and Arabella had twelve. Her uncle had tried remonstrating with her about the excessive amount of luggage, to no avail. He only got more lectures from his precocious ward. On the journey down, Robert drove one automobile, whilst Marks drove the other. One automobile was to be left at the Grand during the voyage and Marks was to drive the other one home. He would then return in time for their arrival back at Southampton.

After much fussing, Arabella and Robert set off in one automobile whilst Lizzie, Vickers and the luggage were cramped into the other one. They had a leisurely journey down, stopping outside Lincoln the first night and Cambridge the second night. A third night was spent south of London, and they finally arrived at Southampton, weary from their journey. Lizzie was awestruck. She had never been beyond York before and was amazed how big the country was.

'Wait until you see America then, if you think this is big.' laughed Arabella. 'England is tiny compared with America.' But Lizzie was still full of the journey as they settled into the hotel bedrooms.

After a boring dinner with uncle's old friend, Arabella excused herself and had an early night. Although she didn't say so to Lizzie, she was also excited about the trip and couldn't wait to see America again. She had only been a small child when she went before and it had seemed huge then. And before they got to America, there was a gorgeous voyage on a magnificent ship. Arabella was asleep almost as soon as her head touched the pillow.

Next morning, after much fussing, the trunks and their owners were transported to the docks and boarded the Titanic. Lizzie ran a constant commentary on everything they were seeing.

'Look at the size of the ship! What a lot of decks. I never dreamt it would be so big.' Arabella smiled indulgently at Lizzie and tried to hide her own excitement, but this ship was bigger than anything she had seen either, and she'd been on a few voyages in her lifetime. They were taken to Arabella's suite of rooms first. Her ample luggage had all been deposited in the bedroom. It was hard to believe that they were on a ship. The bedroom was sheer opulence. As well as the large bed, there were several wardrobes and chests of drawers, with occasional tables dotted around.

'Look at the funny rims all round the tables. I wonder what they are for, Miss Arabella?'

'So that things don't slide when the boat is moving, especially in a gale.'

'Ooh,' said Lizzie looking pale, 'I wish I hadn't asked. You don't think there will be a storm do you?'

'There could well be, but it's such a safe ship, we'll be all right. Stop worrying Lizzie. What a baby you are.'

'Yes, Miss,' replied Lizzie dutifully, and then started putting the clothes away in the wardrobes and drawers. There was a knock at the door.

'Come in,' called Arabella. It was her uncle Robert.

'Have you settled in, my dear?'

'Almost. I'm so excited. Shall we have a stroll round the deck? I can't wait to set off.'

Robert laughed. 'Come on, then. We'll leave Lizzie to sort things out. Give her a bit of peace, shall we? That's why I've come out. Vickers prefers to be alone when he's sorting my things out.' The pair set off arm in arm and strolled round the first class deck. They stopped at a little café and ordered tea. The café was already half full with other couples, trying out the facilities.

'Do you know anyone, Uncle Robert?'

'Fraid not, m'dear. All Americans by the sound of their voices. I'm sure we'll get to know some people. We'll be seated with about eight others at table, so we'll get to know them quite quickly.'

'Won't we be on the Captain's table tonight? We usually are on the first night.'
'No. Don't forget this is an American ship. I have no sway here.'
'But you are Robert Montague of Montague Hall. Does that not count for anything?'
'Not here. All these people will have earned their wealth by hard graft, not merely inherited it by a chance of fate. They may think it's a poor show that I don't work.'
'But you do uncle, you work hard around the estate.'
'Not really, Horrocks and his men work hard and I just say yes or no. And pay the bills,' he laughed.
'Perhaps we will get on the Captain's table another night.'
'Perhaps. But I wouldn't count on it. Now shall we see what this gymnasium looks like? I don't think we've been on a ship with one before.' The pair strolled amicably towards the gymnasium and marvelled at the equipment that was available. Robert booked himself on a session to learn about the equipment straight away, but Arabella was more hesitant, deciding to wait for a day or two before she did anything too strenuous.
Arabella wanted to have a look at her uncle's suite of rooms next. She found them similar to hers, but not identical, which was another example of the care that had been taken when planning the suites.
'On the last ship we went on, the suites all looked identical. You couldn't tell if you were in your own rooms or someone else's,' Arabella laughed. Vickers hovered silently, awaiting his master's pleasure.
'Was there something you wanted, Vickers?'
'No Sir, except may I have leave to go to my own room now?'
'Of course. Is Lizzie settled in satisfactorily?'
'She is still putting Miss Arabella's clothes away.'
Laughing, Robert replied, 'Well go and rescue her then. She will spend most of the voyage attending to Miss Arabella's clothes, I suspect.' At that moment, there was a gentle knock on the door. Vickers opened it. A steward entered and spoke to Robert.
'The ship will leave in five minutes, Sir. Just checking there are no visitors still on board.'
'Thank you, no. We are all sailing.'

'Very good, Sir. May I recommend that you watch the departure from the deck? It will be quite splendid.'
'Good idea. Come Arabella. Let's go. Vickers, go and get Lizzie. It'll give her a break from looking at the wardrobe! After all, it's quite an historic moment. You'll both be able to tell your grandchildren about it.'
'Thank you Sir. I'll go and get Lizzie now.' Robert and Arabella went on to the First Class deck to watch the boat set off. Vickers hurried out and went to Miss Arabella's suite. Grasping Lizzie by the hand, they ran downstairs on to 'G' Deck where their quarters were, and hung over the side, like everyone else.
There were many small vessels in the harbour, waiting to watch the Titanic begin its maiden voyage. Suddenly, a small ship was pulled towards the Titanic, by the suction from the big ship. There was a lot of panic from the ladies, but eventually, the smaller vessel pulled away.
'That's a bad omen,' said a female Irish servant on 'G' Deck. 'Not good to have the ship hitting another one. Begorra, it's a bad omen.'
'Oh be quiet,' snapped Vickers. 'Can't you see that you're frightening everyone? Keep your thoughts to yourself, woman.'
Lizzie was visibly trembling. 'I can't swim, Mr Vickers. Will we be all right?'
'Course we will, girl. Don't be silly. This is the safest ship in Christendom. Don't listen to that ignorant peasant. The Good Lord won't let this ship sink, so stop worrying.'
Vickers led Lizzie away from the woman, but an uneasy silence had settled over the crowd of servants and lower steerage passengers. As they walked away, the boat set off amidst lots of cheering and hooters blaring, but on the lower decks, there was not much excitement. It was as if the day had a cloud cast over it.
Lizzie didn't have long to think about her worries as Arabella was waiting for her in the suite of rooms.
'I want to start getting ready for tonight, Lizzie. So get my new ball gown out.'
'Which one do you want tonight, Miss Arabella?'
'The one with the very low décolletage and the lace overdress. That should make people look.'
'Yes, Miss, and which accessories?'

'Hardly anything. The dress is so fussy; I don't need much else to startle people. Just my lace shoes and reticule and the white feather for my hair. And fasten the feather in with the white lace which I got from Miss Juliana for just such a purpose. Now I want a bath. Let me know when you have run it.' Arabella promptly sat down on the chaise longue in the sitting room and opened a novel, whilst Lizzie ran round collecting items for the bathroom.

Whilst all this was happening, the boat docked at Cherbourg and took on some more passengers, but Arabella was oblivious to it all. Her toilette was far more important.

Over the next two hours, Lizzie helped Arabella get ready for dinner. When Robert arrived, he stared at Arabella for a moment.

'Do I look all right Uncle?' she asked nervously.

'Yes, dear. You look just like your mother.'

'Do I? You've never said that before.'

'I think it's the way you've done your hair. I've always thought you favoured the Montague side of the family, but I can definitely see your mother tonight. Come, you make an old man proud to be taking you into dinner. Take my arm.' They linked together and set off to the dining room. Robert and Arabella swept slowly down the magnificent staircase towards the dining area. It was as sumptuous as any staircase in a country mansion. The rooms on the top decks were of the same opulent standard. There were sitting rooms, music rooms, smoking rooms, ladies rooms and many cafés.

The orchestra was playing light music and there was a swirl of gaily-coloured ball gowns throughout the room, in contrast with the men's black and white dinner outfits. Animated faces showed that many people already knew each other and were chatting together. A steward enquired their names and led them to a table in the centre of the room.

'Good,' said Arabella, 'this is a prime position. I can see everything that is going on from here.'

'Trust you. I suppose you will know who everyone is by tomorrow?'

'Hopefully. Oh, look at that elegant woman over there. And her husband. So charming.'

'They are Ida and Isador Straus. They own Macy's, a large department store in New York. And the people with them are Carrie and Herbert Chaffee. He's a multi-millionaire. Probably two of the richest families in America.'

'My! They are elegant. Any sons?' asked Arabella hopefully.

'I don't know,' chuckled Robert, 'but things are looking up. It's the first time you've mentioned young men for a long time. Perhaps I will get you off my hands on this voyage. It'll have been worth every penny then. Although I wouldn't want you to settle in America. That's a little too far away for my liking.'

'Oh Uncle, I couldn't settle too far from you either. Oh, is that the Captain?' Arabella was looking at an elderly man dressed in full uniform, sporting a neat white beard.

'Yes. Captain Edward J Smith. A very experienced captain.'

'He looks very smart. Is he looking over here?'

'No dear, he isn't, so stop preening yourself.'

'I wasn't at all,' retorted Arabella. Her uncle then turned to greet the other diners that were sharing their table. To his right were a honeymoon couple, the Jarvises. They were very enamoured of each other and had just travelled all round Europe. The trip on the Titanic was to be the climax to their honeymoon. They were both very chatty and told the Montagues all about themselves very quickly.

Mr Jarvis was tall and dark haired, with a curling moustache. Mrs Jarvis was tiny and blond. They were originally from the southern states of America and spoke with the drawl common to that area. His family dealt in real estate in New York and it was back to work for him next week, whilst Mrs Jarvis would take up voluntary work within the city, with her mother.

'And are you from America?' drawled Mrs Jarvis to Robert.

'No, England. My niece and I live near York, in the North of England.'

'Oh York. We've been there, haven't we honey? It's so beautiful. That big church was amazing.'

'Church? Oh, you mean the Minster. Cathedral actually,' replied Robert politely, whilst inwardly cringing about the Minster being called a big church. Mrs Jarvis turned to Arabella.

'So is this your first time on a ship, dear?'

'No. I've been on several voyages,' replied Arabella rather stiffly.

'But I bet none of them were as grand as this ship?'

'No, they weren't. It is indeed a magnificent ship,' conceded Arabella.

'The Americans know how to build ships. Bigger and better. That's what is happening to ship building nowadays.'
Arabella smiled and was grateful when her other neighbour asked her a question.
'Is your home near Leeds?'
'Not very far. Just a day's journey probably. Do you know Leeds?' asked Arabella looking at her rescuer. She was a tiny elderly lady, with a large nose and receding jaw line. It made her look like a little bird. She was dressed all in black so Arabella assumed that she was in mourning.
'My grandfather was born in Leeds, but I've never been there myself. The family emigrated in 1840. I had hoped to visit it one day but I haven't managed to this trip. By the way, I'm Mrs Johnson.'
'How do you do, Mrs Johnson? I'm Arabella Montague and this is my uncle, Robert Montague.'
'Charmed, madam. Pleased to meet you,' Robert leaned over to say. He introduced the Jarvises to Mrs Johnson. The final three people had by now arrived and they announced themselves to the table.
'Richard Tomkins, and my daughters Isabella and Henrietta.' The rest of the table welcomed them and names were exchanged. Isabella looked up sharply when Arabella's name was announced.
'My, your name is almost like mine, Miss Arabella,' she gushed.
Mmm, but thank goodness I'm not almost like you, thought Arabella snootily, but smiled stiffly all the same.
'We shall have to be special friends,' Isabella continued to simper. Arabella merely smiled and talked to the father instead.
'Where are you from, Sir?' she asked politely.
'Baltimore. I'm taking my girls on a trip round the world. They deserve it. We've had a bad three years. We lost my wife to a wasting disease. It was slow agony.' The girls looked on the brink of tears and Arabella wished she hadn't asked. It was just so embarrassing when people poured their heart out in public. Why couldn't they wait 'til they got home and mourn in private?

Mrs Johnson retrieved the situation. 'I'm sure this trip will do the girls a lot of good, especially meeting lots of other young people. Have you seen the itinerary for activities each day? Have you seen the gymnasium? There is even a swimming pool!'

'Yes, Uncle Robert has already booked for the gymnasium tomorrow, but I thought I would wait a day or two,' replied Arabella brightly, glad of a turn in the conversation.

'Oh, let's go together,' bubbled Isabella, 'you, Henrietta and me.'

'Perhaps,' replied Arabella not committing herself. At that point, the food arrived and the diners spent most of the rest of the evening discussing the food and wines.

During the meal and the dancing afterwards, Arabella kept having surreptitious glances at the other dresses and decided that her gown was by far the most attractive in the room. She must remember to tell Miss Juliana that when she returned home.

Although she danced with her uncle twice, he was keen to go and have a game of chess with a gentleman he'd met earlier. Mrs Jarvis offered to chaperone Arabella and she was grateful for that. She wasn't short of partners that evening, but she also enjoyed sitting out, so that she could get a better look at all her fellow voyagers and their clothes. Mrs Jarvis didn't dance; she confided to Arabella that she had just found out that she was expecting a baby, but Arabella danced with Mr Jarvis.

It had been a long and exciting day and Arabella wasn't late in going to bed. The gentle hum of the ship's engines soon lulled her to sleep.

Chapter 4

Next morning, Arabella woke early for once. Lizzie was already in the room, preparing the day's clothes. She brought a tray of tea over for Arabella.

'Good morning Miss Arabella and Happy Birthday,' said a beaming Lizzie.

'Thank you Lizzie. I'd forgotten it was my birthday – so much happened yesterday.'

'Begging your pardon, Miss Arabella, but would you accept this small token from me.' Lizzie shyly passed a small parcel wrapped in coarse tissue paper to Arabella. She opened the parcel and found a small handkerchief which Lizzie had laboriously embroidered with the initial 'A'. Arabella put it down without comment and asked Lizzie what time breakfast was being served. Lizzie's face fell at the lack of reference to her gift, but replied civilly.

'It's being served now, and until eleven am, Miss Arabella. Will you go down to breakfast now?'

'Yes, I think I will.'

'What do you think your uncle will give you as a birthday present?' Lizzie said graciously.

'Absolutely nothing! He told me that the voyage and the new clothes were all that I was getting as my birthday treat. I'll just get dressed and then go to the dining room. What clothes have you got me out today?'

'The grey suit with black trim.'

'Oh no, I don't want that one on; I'll have the lilac wool one. It might be cold on deck.' Lizzie went off to change the outfit and then helped Arabella to dress and complete her toilet. As she was leaving the room, Arabella asked 'And what have you prepared me to wear for tonight's dinner?'

'The ivory dress with burgundy trim, like you said you wanted yesterday, Miss Arabella.'

'So I did, that will be fine,' and promptly walked out of the room without another word. As she walked into the dining room, her uncle was just coming out. He re-entered the dining room with her and they ordered coffee, sitting at a small table for two.

'My goodness, you're up early. I didn't expect you for another few hours, after all the dancing last night.'

'I can't lie in bed all day; there is too much going on. I want to have a good walk round the deck and have a look at the swimming pool.'

'Oh, Happy Birthday, I nearly forgot.' He rummaged in his pocket and brought out a card and a small package.

'Thank you uncle,' she said with a big smile on her face, 'I thought that you weren't buying me anything?' she teased.

'I haven't bought you anything, but I thought that as we were away from home, you may not get any presents, so I brought one with me, but I haven't actually paid any money for it.'

'Lizzie must have thought the same. She gave me a handkerchief with my initial embroidered on,' said Arabella laughing.

'That was kind of her,' replied her uncle without getting a response.

By now, Arabella had ripped the package open to reveal an old leather jewellery case. She opened the box and found an exquisite sapphire necklace, in the form of a collar, with drop earrings to match.

'Oh uncle, they are so beautiful, thank you so much. They'll match my sapphire bracelet perfectly.'

'They were your aunt Grace's. You'll get them eventually when I die, so you might as well have them now.'

'Don't be silly, you've many years left yet, uncle, but I do appreciate that they were your wife's. I shall treasure them all the more because of that. I'm only sorry that I can't remember her very well.'

'No, you were only young when she died and she spent many years in bed, losing one child after another. Now enough of this morbid talk on your birthday. What are you planning?'

'I'm going to walk round the deck and have a look at the swimming pool this morning. Oh, the boat has stopped. Is anything wrong?'

'No, this is one of the scheduled stops. It's the last stop before New York. This is Queenstown, Ireland, where we were originally going to board.'

'But you didn't like the Irish, as I remember. I think that was just an excuse to see your old navy friend.'

Robert was about to reply when they were interrupted by the Jarvises.

'Good morning Miss Arabella, Mr Montague,' said Mrs Jarvis. They made their polite replies.
'Shall we sit together again tonight do you think?' persisted Mrs Jarvis.
'Oh, I forgot, Arabella, we've been invited to the Captain's table tonight, in honour of your birthday.'
'Captain's table? Birthday? My, you are fortunate,' said Mr Jarvis, getting a word in for once.
'And many happy returns of the day too,' said Mrs Jarvis. 'Have you had some nice presents?'
'Yes, my uncle has just given me this lovely sapphire set.'
'Oh what a lovely surprise! You are lucky.'
'It was a surprise. He told me I was getting nothing – the voyage and new clothes was my present. I didn't get any other presents obviously, with being on holiday.'
'Yes, Arabella,' interjected Robert, 'Lizzie gave you a present.'
'Lizzie?' asked Mrs Jarvis.
'Oh just my maid. She embroidered a handkerchief for me,' replied Arabella dismissively. Further comments were avoided by the appearance of the Tomkins girls.
'Hello Miss Arabella, Mr Montague, Mr and Mrs Jarvis,' burst in Isabella. 'Isn't it a lovely day? Shall we go to the gymnasium Miss Arabella? You said you wanted to go.'
'I rather think it was you who wanted to go,' replied Arabella archly.
'I'll walk down there with you both,' suggested Robert. It's almost time for my appointment anyway.' Despite a glare from Arabella, Robert took hold of both Arabella and Isabella's arms, and led them down to the gymnasium. Robert had an appointment with the chirpy gymnasium instructor, Mr McCawley and he wouldn't like to be kept waiting.
Isabella chattered for most of the way whilst Arabella politely nodded. After duly looking round the gymnasium, the girls made appointments for later in the day, and left Robert to his instruction with Mr McCawley and went back on deck.
'It will be so nice to have you as a friend on board, Miss Arabella. Our life has been sad so it's a relief to be amongst other young people who have happy lives and can't know what we have been

through. It's very kind of your uncle to take you on a voyage. Is he your Godfather?'

'No, he's my uncle. Actually I've been through worse than you. I lost both my parents and brothers at the same time, and I was only nine. So what you went through is trivial compared to my loss.'

Isabella's face crumpled and she burst into tears. Arabella turned away so she didn't have to watch the obvious emotion that Isabella was struggling with. Why did she say that? Arabella asked herself. She rarely mentioned that she had lost all her family to anyone, so why had she told this girl in such an unkind manner? Perhaps she ought to apologise for the unkindness, she decided, but when she turned round, Isabella had gone. Shrugging her shoulders, Arabella went back to the lounge and ordered coffee.

After luncheon, Arabella changed into her sports wear and plimsolls and made her way down to the gymnasium. Isabella didn't turn up for the appointment so Arabella learnt about the equipment on her own.

Afterwards, she went for a drink in one of the cafés, where her uncle found her.

'Did you enjoy the gymnasium? Where is your friend Isabella?'

'She didn't turn up,' replied Arabella vaguely.

'That's a surprise, she seemed to be so attached to you.'

'Perhaps she changed her mind.'

'Oh well, you can find out later. No, you can find out now. She's coming into the café.'

'I think I'll go back to my room,' said Arabella jumping up hurriedly.

'What's the rush, Arabella?' asked Robert, and then stared as Isabella walked straight past them both without speaking, averting her head as she drew near to them.

When she was out of earshot, Robert told Arabella to sit down. 'What has happened between you two? Come on Arabella, I can tell by the look on your face that you're guilty. You never could hide your guilt, even as a small girl.'

Arabella remained silent.

'Well, I shall just have to ask her myself. I don't want to cause upset on this voyage, those poor girls need a good experience after losing their mother.'

'Lost their mother, so what?' replied Arabella angrily. 'You'd think they were the only ones who ever lost anyone.'

'And I bet you told Isabella that?'

Again Arabella was silent.

'You did, didn't you? That's just the sort of selfish thing you'd do. Don't you ever think before you speak? Really, sometimes, I could get very cross with you. You can be very thoughtless when you want to. I'm going back to my room now. I'll see you later.'

'Uncle,' Arabella said in a quiet voice, 'please don't be angry with me. I'm sorry, really really sorry.'

'You had better apologise before the day is out, then.'

Arabella nodded miserably, but when her uncle had walked away, her face changed. She wouldn't apologise if she could help it. She didn't even like the girl. And she had been whining and feeling sorry for herself.

Arabella stayed slumped in her chair in the café for quite some time and then had a walk around the deck, trying to calm herself. She was glad the Tomkins were not on their table tonight. Probably she could get away with not speaking to them. Horrible family. And he was probably a tradesman too. She wouldn't expect to have to mix with their sort of class at home. No, she would avoid them for the rest of the voyage if she could.

A breeze was getting up and Arabella felt cold, so went back down to her suite of rooms. She went into the bedroom and decided to have a rest and read a book until it was time for dinner. She fell asleep straight away.

Lizzie came quietly into the room later on and gently woke Arabella up.

'Good evening Miss Arabella. I've come to get you ready for your dinner. Your ivory dress with burgundy flowers is all ready.'

'But I don't want that dress on. I want the white one with dark blue trimmings. I need something to show off my new necklace from my uncle. Really Lizzie, I thought you'd have realised that.'

Lizzie looked stunned, but just said 'Certainly Miss Arabella, I am sorry.' She went to the wardrobes and got out the required outfit and accessories in silence. Lizzie could do nothing right that evening. Arabella complained about everything. Her hair didn't look right; she was hurting her when she hooked her dress up; she wasn't being quick enough; and Lizzie stood on the hem of Arabella's dress as she was walking away. Fortunately the dress wasn't ripped, so Lizzie only got a severe telling off. Lizzie gave a big sigh of relief when Robert Montague called for Arabella – glad that she would have a few hours of peace before she was needed again to undress Arabella and deal with her clothes.

Lizzie decided she would have a bath in Arabella's bathroom, as there were no private bathrooms on the servant's deck. She would never be found out. Lizzie hurried down to her room to get her bathing things and wallowed in the bath for quite some time, luxuriating in the lovely scented water.

Fortunately, Arabella had had a bath just before getting dressed, so she would think that the scent of bath oils that Lizzie had used were from her own bath. Afterwards, she got Arabella's night attire out and ready on the bed. Lizzie debated with herself whether to get the next day's outfit ready, but decided against it. Whatever she got out, Arabella would change her mind tomorrow morning. I'm sure she does it for sheer spite, thought Lizzie wearily to herself. But then she chided herself. Poor Ginny would have given her eye teeth to come on this trip and I certainly wouldn't have got a chance otherwise, so thank your blessings, girl, she said. I shall buy Ginny a nice present from America, she decided. That will cheer her up.

Lizzie couldn't believe how calm the ship felt. If it weren't for the hum of the engines, she would hardly think she was out at sea. It was reassuring, as she'd been worried about whether she would be seasick or not, but she had had no problem at all.

In the restaurant, Arabella was oblivious to what was going on in her room in her absence. She was thoroughly enjoying her time at the Captain's table. She was dining with some of the foremost families of America. They had a lovely meal and then the head chef brought her a large birthday cake, complete with candles. The entire table wished her a Happy Birthday and there was a posy of roses by her table, with her name on. A special present from the Captain.

Again, Arabella danced several dances with some of the other guests, whilst Robert disappeared to the Smoking lounge. He only stayed a short while and then returned to Arabella.

'The men are all laying bets on how fast we'll get to America. Apparently, we've gone faster today than yesterday. There is every chance that we will be in New York earlier on Wednesday,' said Robert to Arabella.

'Taking bets? And have you placed a bet?'

'No,' laughed Robert, 'I'll save my money. I need it to keep you in the extravagant lifestyle which you seem to expect.'

'Oh uncle. I'm not that extravagant really.'

'You're not? Oh, well if you say you're not, that's all right then. I must have been mistaken.'

'Uncle, are you teasing me?'

'Not really,' he said with a twinkle in his eye, 'I'll just make sure that I see the bank balance of any potential suitor – to see if he can afford you!' At this point, Robert burst into laughter, but sobered up quickly when a young man approached him to ask for Arabella's hand to dance.

'Do you work in a bank?' asked Robert, whilst Arabella nipped his arm.

'No Sir,' replied the young man looking puzzled, 'is that a requirement to dance with your daughter?'

'Not at all, young man, I just wondered.'

'I don't work as such; my family have a lot of real estate. I just help out there sometimes, sort of learn the ropes from my father and grandfather. When I finish university I will eventually work there. May I have your daughter's hand for this dance?'

'No,' replied Robert.

'I'm sorry for asking Sir. I do apologise.' The young man started to back away, looking uncomfortable.

'Uncle Robert, what has got into you?' asked Arabella. 'Of course I'll dance with you,' she said to the young man.

'Yes, of course young man. I'm sorry; I don't know your name. As you heard, I'm her uncle, not her father. That's why I said that you couldn't dance with my daughter' he started laughing again.

Arabella grabbed the young man's hand and set off towards the dance floor. 'I do apologise for my uncle. He has these strange ideas sometimes. My name is Arabella Montague and that is my uncle Robert. I live with him in Yorkshire.'

'Not with your parents, then?'

'No, they both died in an accident when I was small.'

'I am so sorry for asking. My name is Harry, by the way, Harry Brooks. I live in Dallas, Texas.'

They carried on dancing whilst Arabella looked at him surreptitiously. He was much taller than her, but had a similar shade of blond hair to hers. She couldn't catch the colour of his eyes without staring, but they looked quite dark, maybe brown; unusual with fair hair, she thought. He had a neat moustache which was curly at the edges.

Harry was a good dancer and she felt very light in his arms, sort of comfortable. As if she was meant to be there. It felt very nice. Also, he wasn't talking very much; he seemed to be looking at her thoroughly, too.

Suddenly, they both spoke at once, then laughed.

'You first,' said Harry.

'No you first, it was only trivial.'

'Ladies first, I insist.'

'I was just wondering if you were here on your own, or with your family?'

'On my own. I've been doing some research in England for my dissertation for my degree at university. I've been to your Bodleian Library. It was very impressive.'

'Oh,' replied Arabella vaguely, not knowing where or what the Bodleian Library was. 'What were you going to ask me?' she said to change the subject.

'I was going to ask if this was your first voyage? Also trivial,' he laughed, a loud laugh that echoed round the dance floor.

'No, I've been on several voyages before, but this is the biggest ship I've been on. It's amazing, isn't it?'

'Certainly is. Where are you going when you get to America?'

'We're having a few days in New York, before returning to England.'

'That's where I'm at university. Perhaps I could call on you at your hotel?'

'That would be nice, but you'll have to ask my uncle.'

'I wouldn't dream of not asking him. I wouldn't want to compromise your reputation.'

It was Arabella's turn to laugh. 'No, I mean you'll have to ask my uncle where we're staying. I don't know the name of the hotel.'

Then Harry laughed. He has such a lovely laugh thought Arabella. He laughs so loud and naturally and she ended up laughing with him.

Robert came over to greet them and it was only then that they realised that they had danced more than one dance together. The time has seemed to flown past, thought Arabella.

'Sir, I wonder if I might call upon you in New York?'

'Indeed you may,' replied Robert, looking surprised. 'You will be very welcome. We're staying in the Waldorf Astoria.'

'I know it. Perhaps I can call on Thursday evening?'

'Yes, and I will order dinner for you at the hotel. Will that be satisfactory?'

'Excellent, Sir. I will look forward to that. Miss Arabella, Sir.' Harry bowed and left.

'Well well, Arabella! Have you made a conquest?'

Arabella blushed. 'A conquest? Don't be dramatic, uncle. This is the twentieth century.'

'Then why are you blushing?' he teased.

'I'm not,' retorted Arabella, blushing more furiously. 'He is a very pleasant young man. That is all.'

'You weren't averse to him coming to the hotel, I notice.'

'No, we won't know anyone in New York, so it'll be nice to have some company.'

'Mmm, we'll see,' replied Robert, unconvinced. The dance was coming to an end, so Robert offered to escort Arabella back to her rooms.

'Not a bad birthday, then, little miss?'

'A wonderful birthday, uncle. The best ever. Thank you so much.'

'Goodnight, then.'

'Goodnight, Uncle Robert.' Arabella almost skipped into her room and caught Lizzie drowsing in one of her armchairs.

'Ooh, sorry Miss Arabella. I must have fallen asleep,' mumbled Lizzie, jumping to her feet.

'That's all right Lizzie. You must be tired looking after me all the time,' reassured a smiling Arabella. Lizzie couldn't believe how friendly Arabella was, but hurried to help her out of her dress.

'You seem to have had a lovely time tonight, Miss Arabella?'

'Perfect. I sat at the Captain's table, had a lovely meal and danced with the most divine young man.'

'A young man? Ooh, tell me about him.'

'He lives in Dallas, his family have real estate, he goes to the university in New York, and he's coming to see me in New York.'

'Well I never. That has all happened fast!'

'What do you mean? Happened fast? Nothing has happened. I've just danced with him, that's all.'

'Yes, Miss Arabella,' replied Lizzie, just a trifle knowingly. Further talk was difficult as Lizzie got Arabella ready for bed and the two young women parted company for the night; Lizzie to fall asleep instantly after her busy day, Arabella to daydream for a while about Harry and what might happen in the future. Yes, she thought sleepily, a very nice day. Her best birthday yet.

Chapter 5

On Friday morning, Arabella got up reasonably early and attended breakfast at the same time as her uncle, a fact which amazed him.

'What are you planning today, my dear?' he asked her.

'I'm going to the gymnasium again. I really enjoyed riding the bicycle. Mr McCawley is going to introduce me to Mr Wright, the tennis professional and he will help me to improve my tennis.'

'Improve your tennis? He must be good. I don't think you've played for years.'

'I do play occasionally, when the mood takes me,' replied Arabella huffily.

'But the mood doesn't take you very often does it? Is there some other attraction down there?'

'I don't know what you mean, uncle.'

'Well, I saw Harry going for a game of tennis this morning. Were you planning a game?'

'I may, but I didn't know he played. I learnt about Mr Wright before I met Harry anyway.'

'Well enjoy your day. I'll see you for luncheon, shall I?'

'Yes, shall we have luncheon in the Café Parisian?'

'Good idea. I'll see you there about one o'clock then?'

'Until one, then uncle,' said Arabella as she tripped off back to her suite. Changing into her sports wear, Arabella was soon in the gymnasium. She spent some time on the bicycle again, and then was introduced to Mr Wright, the tennis coach. Climbing off the bicycle to speak to Mr Wright, Arabella caught her foot in the chain and fell to the floor.

Both Mr Wright and Mr McCawley rushed to her aid.

'Are you hurt Miss Montague? Here let me help you up,' said Mr Wright as he extended his hand to her.

'Thank you,' said Arabella shakily, but as she tried to stand, she got a searing pain in her ankle and cried out. A chair was brought for her and they managed to sit her down without hurting her further. One of the other staff ran for the ship's doctor, and then went to find Arabella's uncle.

By the time he had arrived, the doctor had pronounced that there were no bones broken, strapped up her ankle, and prescribed a period of bed rest. A light canvas chair was found and Arabella was lifted back to her rooms on it. Vickers had sent for Lizzie, when Robert got the message about the accident, so she arrived shortly after Arabella.

The doctor followed everyone into the room and gave instructions to Lizzie that Arabella must not put her foot to the floor again that day, and he would call to see her again tomorrow morning. He left some pain relieving tablets with Lizzie, giving her instructions on how and when to use them. Eventually, after a lot of fussing, the girls were left alone.

Arabella exploded.

'It's not fair. I'll miss the dinner tonight. How will I get to know anyone if I'm laid up in bed all day? Oh, it's not fair.' Lizzie gave her the tablets with a drink of water and tried to encourage her.

'Perhaps by tomorrow you'll be all right, Miss Arabella. That's what the doctor said, if you rest.'

'What do doctors know. I could be laid up here for days. Oh, it's not fair.' She slammed the glass down on to the bedside cabinet.

Lizzie sighed. She knew that the next day or two were going to be even more difficult than usual. She would have no pockets of peace when Miss Arabella was busy and would be constantly at her beck and call. She was not wrong. Lizzie was run ragged by Arabella, who wasn't a good patient. Indeed, patient was definitely the wrong word.

Arabella picked fault with all the meals that were brought up from the kitchens, demanding alternatives to what she had ordered and generally making a nuisance of herself. Robert called in several times during the day to see how she was, but didn't stay long; her petulance making him weary of her.

All the next day Arabella continued to be confined to her rooms, but by bedtime, she declared that she was going up on deck on the Sunday, as she couldn't stand another day being cooped up. What made her worse, was that Robert casually commented that Harry and Isabella had danced together several times. Arabella fumed all day Saturday and tended to pace up and down the room, which hadn't helped the healing process much.

On Sunday morning, Arabella was up and dressed far more quickly than usual. When Robert called to see how she was, she was ready to go out with him.

'I was just on my way to the church service, my dear,' Robert said to Arabella.

'Fine, I'll come with you, I feel much better, and the doctor has strapped my foot and said that I might walk a little today' replied Arabella, only wincing slightly when she set off down the corridors. They walked slowly into the lounge and took their places in the middle of the rows of chairs.

Arabella looked casually around, but could not see Harry. Perhaps he didn't go to church, she decided. Then she saw the Tomkin family and looked the other way, so that she wouldn't have to acknowledge them. After that, she studiously appeared to be looking at her hymnal, until the service commenced.

It concluded with singing the lovely maritime hymn, 'For those in Peril on the Sea,' and people returned to the decks, or their rooms, to await luncheon.

Arabella wouldn't go to her rooms. She made Robert walk around the deck with her, until they found a secluded corner with free deck seats. Her foot was beginning to pain her, but for once she kept quiet about it. She didn't want to waste another minute of this voyage in a sick bed. Life was too short and she had to be at the dinner tonight, if only to see what was going on between Harry and that Isabella.

Robert persuaded Arabella to have a short rest in the afternoon, on the grounds that she wouldn't be able to dance that evening if she didn't. She was soon persuaded. Despite declaring that she could never sleep, she actually did sleep for two hours and woke fully refreshed and ready for the dinner.

Arabella chose a dress that was the palest of blue gossamer, with ruffles around her neck and shoulders. She again wore the sapphire necklace that was her birthday present. For once, Arabella was quite animated with Lizzie and even told her about Harry.

'He's very handsome and rich and funny. A perfect man all round, for an American,' she laughed.

'Oh Miss, could you marry an American? Wouldn't you have to go and live there?'

'Oh Lizzie, don't be so dramatic. I'm not marrying him. I only said that I liked him. Besides, he danced with that Isabella last night, so I'm not sure that I'll speak to him tonight,' she ended haughtily.

‘But would you Miss,’ Lizzie persisted, ‘would you go and live in America if you married an American?’
‘I would probably have to. Girls don’t get the choice, do they? They have to go and live with their husbands at their house. It’s not fair really. There is plenty of room in Montague Hall for any husband of mine. And plenty of work to do on the estate to keep him busy.’
‘But isn’t Mr Harry a businessman? Wouldn't he have to stay in America?’
‘Yes, I suppose he would. I suppose if I loved a man enough I would go and live in America. There, I’ve said it. How would you feel, Lizzie?’
‘Me Miss Arabella? I’d be very pleased for you if you got married.’
‘No, I mean about going to live in America.’
‘I’m not likely to meet a boy from America, Miss, so I’ll not likely be going to get married there.’
‘Not you getting married, Lizzie. I meant if I got married. Would you like living in America?’
‘With you, Miss?’
‘Yes, with me, you goose. What’s the matter with you tonight? I couldn't go and live in America without my maid, could I?’
‘Oh Miss Arabella,’ said Lizzie with awe, ‘that would be marvellous,’ then her face clouded over. ‘But what about my family? I’d never see them again.’
‘Nonsense, they could come and visit you. I’d allow that. So there, it’s settled. If I marry an American, you’ll come and live with me in America.’
‘Yes, Miss Arabella,’ replied Lizzie dutifully, wondering how on earth her family could ever raise the fare to visit her in America.
There was a knock at the door and Lizzie rushed to open it. Robert entered and after complimenting Arabella on her appearance, led her to the dining room. They were on a different table that night, with new people except for Mrs Johnson. Arabella sat next to the old lady gladly and was pleased when she enquired after her health.
‘Your Uncle tells me you had a fall in the gymnasium, Miss Arabella?’
‘I did indeed, and very painful it was, but I’m much better now, thank you Mrs Johnson.’

'I'm glad to hear it. It's no fun sitting alone in your room at your age, is it?'
'No, it isn't. I thought I would go mad if I had to sit there another night. No point coming on a voyage and missing all the social activities,' Arabella laughed.
'You'll have to be careful when the dancing starts, though. It would be a shame if you made your ankle worse again.'
'Oh, I'll be careful, I promise you. Just to make sure that I don't have to stay in my room again.'
'There is only a short time for dancing anyway tonight, with it being the Sabbath.'
'Of course,' said Arabella, thinking what a waste that would be. She felt like she could dance all night tonight. Indeed, the night passed far too quickly and Harry paid far too much attention to Isabella. Granted, he danced several dances with Arabella, but not enough, she thought to herself. I shall have to watch that Isabella for the rest of the voyage, I can see.
On return to her rooms, Lizzie was all attention, asking how her ankle was and had she had a good night?
'My ankle is fine, Lizzie, thank you. It obviously paid off resting all day yesterday. I think that I'll read for a while before I go to sleep.'
'Did you dance with Mr Harry, then?' urged Lizzie.
'Of course, he seems very fond of me. Perhaps it was good that I was ill as he was very solicitous of my welfare tonight.'
'I'll just get your clothes out for tomorrow then Miss. What will you wear?'
'Oh I can't be bothered to think Lizzie. You chose for me.'
'Yes, Miss Arabella. I'll get two or three outfits ready then you can decide in the morning.'
Arabella lay in bed, reading her novel whilst Lizzie hurried around in the dressing room. Eventually, she said goodnight and left Arabella reading.

Chapter 6

Lizzie was wakened by a knock at her door. It felt like she had only just got to sleep. Feeling disgruntled that her early night was being interrupted; Lizzie went to the door and opened it with force. A steward was standing there.

'Sorry to disturb you Miss, but Captain's orders are that all passengers are to get on the deck and prepare to go into the lifeboats.'

'Why, what has happened? Is there a problem?' asked Lizzie hurriedly.

'Just a precaution Miss. We've bumped into an iceberg and they want to do some repairs. It'll be easier to do them on an emptier ship.'

'Thank you. I'd better get up to my Mistress. She will be worried.'

'Right-ho Miss. Sooner the better,' he said as he moved on to the next cabin.

Trying not to panic, Lizzie collected some things together and ran up to Arabella's rooms. Arabella had already been notified, but didn't seem in any great urgency. She was more bothered about what she would wear.

'Miss Arabella, hardly any of your things will be any good. They are too fine and fancy. You can't wear this fur wrap or your mink coat either. That'll be no good on an open boat. Here, I've brought some of my things up for you. Take this flannelette nighty and my best coat. They will keep you much warmer than your own clothes.'

Arabella hurriedly put the clothes on, whilst Lizzie chivvied her along, adding a woollen scarf, hat and gloves to her attire, and pushing the newly embroidered handkerchief in her pocket.

Lizzie too wore a flannelette nighty but a shorter less warm coat. When dressed, Lizzie hurried Arabella towards the door.

'Stop rushing me, Lizzie. It's not as if the ship is going to sink, is it?' she laughed.

'No Miss, but they said we'd to be quick. Sooner we're off the ship, quicker they can mend it.'

'And then we'll be allowed back on?'

'Yes, it shouldn't delay the journey by more than a few hours.'

'Good. It really is inconsiderate that we have to get off the ship in the middle of the night. I'm sure if they tried they could manage the repairs without all this upheaval. I shall have a word with the Captain when I see him,' replied Arabella haughtily.

As they set off for the deck, they met up with Robert, who was on his way down to Arabella's rooms.

'They you are, my dear. You've had the message have you?'

'Yes uncle, and mightily inconvenient it is too,' Arabella continued to complain. 'Anyone would think the ship was about to sink. What a fuss about a bit of damage.'

'Well, I suppose the Captain has to be cautious. Apparently, the ship is not in danger because it was built in compartments which can be sealed off if there is a leak, so we are completely safe. Here we are, let's get some seats on the deck whilst we wait for further instructions.'

A loud voice was issuing instructions. 'Women and children on board the lifeboats first please.'

'Oh Uncle, I'd rather go with you. Surely they'll let you come on board with us?'

'Sounds as though they won't. I think I'll go and get a drink from the bar. I presume that'll still be open.'

'Lizzie and I will go and wait our turn then.'

'Yes, goodbye my dear, I'll see you later when we get back on the ship. Bye Lizzie. You'll look after Arabella for me, won't you?'

'Bye Mr Montague, of course I will,' replied Lizzie quietly.

'Bye Uncle,' called Arabella cheerily, as if she was setting off on a picnic.

Robert went towards the smoking room, leaving the two girls waiting in the queue.

'What's going on over there, Lizzie?' asked Arabella.

'It's Mr and Mrs Straus. She's refusing to get on board without her husband.'

'Are they letting him on board?'

'No. She's moved aside to let the other women get on.'

'I can't see what all the fuss is about, can you? Surely there will be room for all of us, so why does it matter if women and children go first? It'd be far more sensible to keep families together, wouldn't it?'

'I suppose so,' replied Lizzie. They watched as the Jarvises made the same decision as the Mr and Mrs Straus. Mrs Jarvis would not board the lifeboat without him and stayed behind.

The two girls waited a while longer, not speaking but watching the lifeboats being filled up and then lowered into the sea. Suddenly, one of the boats stuck when it was being winched down to the sea and everyone gasped. But slowly it righted itself and no one fell out.

'Lizzie, I've forgotten my jewellery,' said Arabella, 'can you go back and get it for me?'

'Your jewellery Miss? Will you need it?'

'No, but you can't be too careful. Some of those steerage passengers might take advantage of the empty rooms. So I'd rather take it with me.' There was a moment's uncomfortable silence.

'Yes, Miss. I'll go straight away. I'll get on a later lifeboat.'

'I'll see you later on the other ship that's waiting for us. Bye Lizzie,' replied Arabella, without a backward glance. Lizzie stared at the waiting lifeboat for a few seconds and then went back towards the rooms.

Arabella moved up to the front of the queue and was handed down in to the lifeboat. She pulled Lizzie's coat round her closely against the damp and sat in the farthest corner of the lifeboat. The senior crewman was urging the rest of the passengers to hurry up, as he wanted to set off.

'What's the hurry?' asked a strident female voice.

'Once I've got you on to the other ship, I'll need to come back and collect some more passengers,' he replied.

'Why?' asked the same voice.

'Not enough lifeboats for all the passengers,' he muttered.

'What did you say, man? I couldn't hear you.'

The crewman repeated himself.

'That's ridiculous,' continued the voice, 'an expensive ship like this and there aren't enough lifeboats. I've never heard anything so disgusting in my life. Well get on man. Get going then we can let you come back for the others.'

'Thanks, Missus.'

The boat was lowered quietly into the water from the side of the ship, this time without mishap. The four-crew members started to row as quickly as possible, to prevent the boat being sucked under by the larger ship. The passengers remained calm as the boat gently pulled away. Desultory talk started between the occupants of the boat, mainly women and children. They had been reassured that as soon as the repairs had been done to the ship, they would be going back on board. It would only be a matter of time.

Arabella sat in the corner of the lifeboat. She didn't join in the conversation, even though her neighbour tried to initiate some small talk.

Another lady started to question the senior crewman. 'Did you say there aren't enough lifeboats or there aren't any more?'

'Both Missus,' he replied with respect. 'There aren't enough, and yours was the last lifeboat. There are no more.'

'But my husband is still on deck. How will he get off? And what about the others? There are still hundreds of people on board.'

'There may be no need to. The engineer said that once most of the people are off the ship, they can repair it and we'll all be going back on again.'

'And there are absolutely no more lifeboats on the ship?' asked another lady.

'None. Except for some life rafts. They were preparing to launch them as we left.'

'And how many will they hold?'

'About twenty each probably. There's two of them.'

Oh well, thought Arabella, I'm glad that I asked Lizzie to go for my jewels. Especially when so many people are staying on the ship.

* * * * *

At that moment, Lizzie was walking into the first class lounge. Nobody seemed to stop her or think it unusual that a maid was where she shouldn't be. In fact, thought Lizzie, the whole ship felt eerie. There were groups of people – mainly men – talking quietly together. The orchestra was playing stirring music; trying to entertain the remaining passengers, as if nothing was happening.

Lizzie looked round the room, trying to keep herself under control. She spotted Robert Montague, chatting to another man, sat at ease in the lounge; a glass of brandy in both their hands. The other man turned out to be Vickers.

'Sir, Sir, I've got Miss Arabella's jewellery. But the last lifeboat has just left. What am I to do?' she shouted across to him, forgetting all social niceties.

'Lizzie? What are you doing here? I thought you had got on the lifeboat with my niece?'

'I was just about to get on board when Miss Arabella remembered that she'd left her jewellery, so I went back for it. And now there are no more lifeboats.'

Typical, thought Robert. Selfish as usual. Fancy sending Lizzie back just for some trinkets. Where had he gone wrong in her upbringing? When did she become so selfish? He was roused from his thoughts by the sound of tears. Lizzie was utterly distraught.

'Come here, Lizzie. Sit by Vickers and me. Don't despair, you can stay with us. Then when they repair the ship, we can be first back to our cabins, can't we? Here, have a drink of this.' He passed her his brandy and encouraged her to drink it at one gulp. The spirit caught in her throat and she coughed and spluttered.

'Oh Sir, I've never had spirits before. It took my breath away.'

'Here, have another one,' said Robert as he turned to the decanter on the small wine table. 'It'll make you feel better.'

'Oh yes,' she said after taking the second large drink, 'that's much better the second time. I think I could get a liking for this,' she giggled.

'Good. Glad you feel better. Now come and sit beside me and listen to the band. They're very good.'

'I'm frightened. I don't want to die. I can't swim. What if they can't repair the ship?'

'Hush Lizzie. This is the greatest ship afloat. Of course they will be able to repair it. We'll laugh about this in the morning.'

'If you say so, Sir,' replied Lizzie, very dubiously, but she accepted another large brandy from Robert all the same. Slowly, she began to relax and even started tapping her feet to the music. It must be nice to be rich, she thought to herself. For some reason, her eyelids started to feel heavy and she closed her eyes. Robert looked at her and smiled.

'Good,' he whispered to Vickers, 'she's asleep. She'll never know what happened to her.' But Vickers was staring at the floor and Robert turned his head to see what he was looking at.

Robert's face changed as he saw water coming on to the deck and was glad that Lizzie didn't see that. He poured Vickers and himself another large brandy. They looked at each other with admiration.
'Thanks for everything, Vickers. You've been a loyal servant.'
'Nay, Sir, thanks to you. I've enjoyed working with you. I think I'll go over nearer to the band, if you don't mind.'
'Not at all, whatever you wish.' They looked at each other one more time, then both turned away: Robert to pick up his brandy and Vickers to walk towards the band.
Robert glanced at Lizzie. She was still asleep. Turning back to sip his brandy, Robert concentrated on the music and thought about his wife. I'll be coming soon, my dear, he said to himself.

* * * * *

Suddenly, those on the lifeboat heard a sound from the large ship. All talk on the lifeboat ceased and eyes were riveted towards the Titanic. The lights flickered off, and then briefly came back on again, before finally going out completely. There were a few more ominous creaking sounds and then the ship slowly but inexorably upended. It stayed in that upright position for several minutes, then slowly slid deeper into the water. Within a few more minutes, the ship had completely disappeared. This brand new vessel, that was supposed to be unsinkable, had disappeared under the water.
After a few seconds of silence and disbelief, one or two women started to quietly cry or moan. They were crying for their husbands. Children began to sob, unnerved by their upset mothers. For a while, they could hear the cries of people in the water.
'Turn back, we need to pick up the survivors,' screamed one woman.
'We can't,' replied the crewman, 'we're already full. The other lifeboats that weren't as full will go back.' There was silence again, whilst the occupants listened to the cries, getting weaker and weaker. Eventually, they stopped altogether.
'They must all have been picked up now,' said another woman quietly. The others nodded, but the crewmen merely looked at each other and looked away.
Arabella sat staring at where the Titanic had been. She thought not of a husband or lover, but of her guardian, her maid and her jewels.

Her guardian was the only member of her family left and now he was probably gone. But it was the loss of her maid that was troubling her. Not from a closeness of relationship, although she had served her for eight years. No, it was the fact that she'd sent the maid back to their suite of rooms just as they were boarding the lifeboat, to get her jewellery box. As it turned out, it was the last available lifeboat. And now the maid would probably be drowned along with many others for whom there was no way of escape. In effect, she had sent the maid to her death; all to satisfy her own greed and desire for possessions.

The girl pulled her coat round herself, trying to keep the cold out, but it only reminded her afresh that her maid had given her this warm coat just as they went to the lifeboats; her own coats too flimsy and impractical for a journey like this. Arabella felt even guiltier, that she had taken the maid's warmest coat, as well as sending her back for the jewels. How would she ever live with herself?

An elderly woman sat next to the girl and asked her questions. Arabella stared at the woman but found that she couldn't speak. It wasn't that she was too emotional to speak, but she seemed to have lost the ability to speak at all. The girl turned quickly away from the woman, wondering whether she would ever be able to speak again, or ever want to. Her brain seemed to have gone all foggy and she couldn't concentrate on anything. She knew that she would never assuage her guilt: not even if she lived to be a very old lady.

Chapter 7

Arabella felt the strong arms lift her on to the Carpathia from the sling. She lay inert in the crewman's arms and didn't respond when he carefully laid her on the floor.

'Will you have a drink, Miss?' a lady asked, but Arabella ignored her. 'Must be in shock, this one. Can't speak.'

'Just give her a stimulant, that should help,' replied the first officer. 'It usually brings them round.' The lady administered some brandy, but it only succeeded in making Arabella choke. No speech resulted, so after wrapping her in a warm blanket, Arabella was escorted downstairs to the makeshift hospital.

All the other people in the hospital bay were talking quietly, but Arabella remained silent. The orderlies were making their way round all the people. Eventually someone arrived at Arabella.

'What's your name, Miss?' he asked, but there was no reply. He gently shook Arabella and repeated his question, just a little louder, with the same result. 'We need to know for the lists. Need to know who has survived for the relatives, you know.'

Eventually he gave up. He informed his superior who suggested trying to get Arabella to write her name down on a piece of paper. But he still got no response. Having many other people on board, he left her and went to someone else's aid.

The first officer tried again to find out who she was, but to no avail. 'Does anyone know who this young lady is? Judging by her clothes, we think she is someone's servant,' he asked the other survivors, but they all shook their heads. Arabella saw Isabella in the crowd that was being asked about her. Isabella stared at her and then shook her head along with the others. So be it, thought Arabella. No one knows who I am now and I don't care.

For three days and nights, Arabella lay in a sort of trance, not speaking or reacting to anything around her. But in the depth of the nights, Arabella sobbed long and loud. Sobbed as she remembered her uncle, and how she had sent Lizzie back for the jewellery. If only she could turn back time. She hadn't known at the time that hers was the last lifeboat. There were so many people still on board, she was sure there would have been many more lifeboats on the other side of the ship.

But she could still hear the cries of the people who were left on the boat as they plunged into the water. Their cries were echoing in her brain; they wouldn't go away. At least the cries didn't last for long. First they got weaker and then stopped altogether.

Arabella had thought that the cries getting weaker meant that they would have been picked up. Although she wasn't speaking to anyone on board the Carpathia, she was listening to the other people talking. She had heard that several people were saved through climbing on to two collapsible boats, one of which had overturned, but those people had transferred to another boat and were all accounted for. Most of those left on the Titanic when it sunk, had gone down with her or drowned in attempting to get off the boat.

The thoughts of what happened to her uncle and Lizzie and Vickers went round and round in her brain, giving her no peace. How could I have done that to Lizzie, she asked herself for the umpteenth time. Did Lizzie know it was the last lifeboat, she asked herself? Would she still have gone back for the jewellery if she knew? Lizzie couldn't even swim and was frightened of water. How terrible to drown when you had such a fear. The guilt overwhelmed Lizzie again but then she heard an orderly coming near her. She instantly stopped crying and pretended to be asleep.

And Harry, she thought when the orderly had gone. What had happened to Harry? she asked herself. Even though she had been cross at him on the last night for dancing with Isabella, she didn't wish him any harm. And now he would probably be dead like everyone else that she cared for. The days were torment enough, but the nights were far worse when she started to blame herself for all that had happened. How could she have been so selfish? Her sleep was fitful and she soon looked weary and bedraggled.

Eventually, the Carpathia arrived at New York, where many relatives were waiting on the quay to meet their loved ones. Slowly, all the occupants of the boat were retrieved by family or transferred to waiting vehicles. Arabella remained alone, sat on the side of the deck.

'Come along Miss, is someone coming to pick you up?' asked a porter.

Arabella stared back at him with a blank expression, her mind unable to decipher what he was saying through the fog.

'Think this one has lost her mind, Captain,' he shouted.
'Yes, this is the mystery person. Nobody seems to know who she is. We're calling her Miss 'A' as she has a handkerchief in her pocket with the initial 'A' on it. Take her into the ambulance and we'll get her checked over at the hospital.'
'Righto, Sir, will do.' He led Arabella into a waiting ambulance carriage and eventually she was taken to the hospital. After a long wait, a nurse entered the foyer and took her down a long corridor.
'Put these clothes on, Miss A, then we can get the doctor to examine you.' Arabella looked at the rough gown but said nothing. Turning her back on the nurse, she undressed and pulled the gown over her head.
'Right, I'll go and get the doctor,' said the nurse and left the room. Arabella remained stationary, without looking round. The doctor and nurse soon returned and the nurse let out an irritable sound.
'Tsk, what are you doing stood there like that? Get on the bed. Have you no sense? How can the doctor examine you if you stand there gawping?' Arabella got slowly on to the bed, whilst the nurse told the doctor in no uncertain terms that she thought Arabella was a lunatic or imbecile.
'Now, nurse, let me make judgements like that,' he said with a look that quelled further comments from the nurse.
'Now Miss A, what is your name?' There was silence. He tried again. 'Can you hear me?' He tried a few more questions, speaking much louder, as if she was indeed an imbecile. Still there was silence. Then he had an idea. 'Can you write it down? Can you write your name?' He gave her a pen and a piece of paper but she held the pen and paper in her hand, just staring at them.
'See, told you she was an imbecile,' said the nurse.
'She obviously can't speak or communicate at this moment, but I don't think that she is an imbecile. Have no family come forward?'
'No, doctor. They think she's a servant and comes from the North of England, as her clothes were bought in Yorkshire, England.'
'Well I will recommend that she is sent back to England and they can sort her out. Physically, she doesn't seem to be ill, but she is not fit to help herself or make any decisions. Yes, that will be best; we'll send her back to England. Right, who's next Nurse?'

'It's a gentleman from Baltimore in the next room. Will you see him next?'

'Yes, thank you nurse.' As he left the room, the doctor turned and looked at Arabella. She was sat on the bed, staring at nothing, her face expressionless. He shook his head sadly, and left.

As soon as Arabella was on her own, she curled up in a ball on the bed, with her back to the door. She felt exhausted. Why could she not speak? She certainly didn't want to speak at the moment, but words would not come anyway. So why didn't I write my name down, she thought to herself? Why didn't I tell them who I was? I'm quite capable of writing but I didn't. Because I don't want to admit who I am. I don't want people to know who I am and what I've done to Lizzie.

And then the tears came again. She sobbed and sobbed until she had no tears left, and eventually fell asleep. On waking, her body ached and she had a splitting headache. How long she had been left in the room she had no idea, but it was now dark. She gingerly sat up, then slowly got off the bed. Her mouth was dry and she looked around for a drink, but there was nothing in the room except the bed, a locker and a wardrobe. She sat back down on the bed, a little apathetically. Still she waited until eventually a new nurse brought her in a tray of food.

'Here's your supper, Miss A. Can you manage it yourself?' Arabella made no comment and the nurse shrugged and left. Moving slowly over to the tray on the bedside locker, Arabella drank the lukewarm tea but left the food. She had lost all interest in food. Getting back into bed, Arabella was soon asleep and didn't hear the nurse return to collect the tray.

Next day, the doctor returned to talk to Arabella. 'We have decided to send you back to England. We will be in contact with the White Star Line medical representative and he will arrange your return to England. Is that all right Miss A?' Arabella remained silent. 'That's what we'll do then,' he said, and then left the room.

Alone again, Arabella was relieved that she was returning to England. She had no desire to stay in this country and yet she no longer wanted to go home to Montague Hall. No longer wanted to be part of the life that she had before. And yet she didn't know what she wanted to do or where she wanted to go. She wondered where they would put her when she got home, but decided she would have to wait and see what happened.

A few days later, a nurse bundled up her few possessions in a bag and told her to get ready for a journey. The nurse took her downstairs and left her sitting in the foyer for a long time. Arabella watched the people come and go, but made no eye contact with any of them. Eventually, a new nurse and a porter came and stood in front of her.

'Are you Miss A for England?' said the porter.

Arabella simply stared at both of them.

'This is her,' said the nurse. 'They said she'd be here. Said she's lost her mind, 'cos of being on the Titanic.'

'Cor, you don't say!' Mind you, at least she's alive. Not like the other poor sods.'

'Charming, watch your language.'

'Sorry nurse, but it's been terrible hasn't it? About 1500 lost. Has this Miss A lost anyone?' asked the porter, as if Arabella wasn't there.

'They don't know. She's never spoken since they picked her up out of the sea. So they don't know who she is or if she has lost anyone. But I bet someone out there is looking for her.'

No, no one is looking for me, thought Arabella to herself. I have no one left now. The tears started to form at the corner of her eyes and she tried to sniff them away, but they started coursing down her cheeks.

'Eh, look at her. She's crying. She's not that daft, then?' remarked the porter. 'Come on Miss A. We'll look after you. We're taking you to the ship and nurse is going all the way back to England with you.' He spoke slowly and carefully, as to a child.

Arabella was led towards an ambulance carriage and the slow journey to the docks began. The carriage was uncomfortable and occasionally Arabella still sniffed her tears back. The nurse pushed a grimy handkerchief into her hand, but Arabella didn't respond: merely wiped her tears away and let the handkerchief drop on the seat beside her.

Her cabin on the ship that she shared with the nurse, who was called Rosie, was small and bare: a far cry from her sumptuous rooms on the Titanic. The journey passed uneventfully. At times Rosie tried to make conversation or get Miss A talking about herself to no avail. Most of the time, Arabella lay on her bunk and only left it at mealtimes or when Rosie insisted on a walk around the deck. However, on these occasions, Arabella tended to stand at the ship's railings, looking down in to the sea, so Rosie got a little worried that Miss A would try and jump in.

On arrival at Portsmouth, Rosie accompanied Arabella to a local hospital. Again Arabella was examined but didn't communicate at all. Rosie reported that Miss A had not spoken at all in her charge and had seemed to spend too much time looking down at the water over the ship's railings. The doctors looked at each other and shook their heads, but didn't say anything to Arabella. The doctors left, followed by Rosie.

Some time later, Rosie came in to say goodbye.

'I've just come to tell you that I have to go back to the ship now, Miss A. Sorry I couldn't be any more help to you and I wish you well. Bye.'

Arabella stared at Rosie, then nodded.

'Cor,' said Rosie, 'that's the first time you've acknowledged me. Perhaps you're not as daft as you seem. Well, that's for you to show them. I'm going now,' and walked out of the room. Arabella was once again alone, with no friend to look after her. A doctor came in to tell her that they were taking her to a hospital in the North of England.

'It's a nice place. They specialise in cases like yours,' he said, then patting her on her shoulder, he left the room without a backward glance.

'That's for you to show them' and 'Cases like yours': the words of the doctor and nurse rolled round Arabella's head. She was just a case to them and a nameless case at that.

Her brain was tired and she couldn't cope with the constant questions that were being asked of her. It was hard to beat back the fog that was encompassing her brain now; it seemed to be deepening with each day. Better to let the fog take over as she had done previously as a child. Yes, that's what she would do. Just let the fog take over and she would not need to think clearly any more. And that would be better because it wouldn't hurt. Arabella gave in to the fog and lapsed into a deep pit of darkness.

Chapter 8

It was soon time for Miss A to be transferred nearer her home. The staff at Portsmouth Hospital still talked to her, but they got no response at all. Miss A allowed them to dress her and feed her, but she made no effort to help herself. If she was taken to the toilet, she would perform for them, but if the nurses were too busy, she didn't help herself and was often incontinent.

Early one morning, a nurse packed Miss A's meagre possessions into a bag and taking her hand, led her downstairs into the sitting room. An ambulance carriage arrived shortly afterwards and the accompanying nurse led Miss A to the carriage.

After checking that she was seated comfortably, the groom set off. This time there was no response from Miss A; she merely sat staring out of the window of the carriage. The journey was long and slow, the carriage making many stops along the way and staying overnight several times. The nurse soon gave up trying to get any conversation from Miss A and left her to herself.

Eventually they arrived at the hospital on the outskirts of a village called Langho, near Blackburn, in the north of England. It was a large place, purposely built for the feeble minded and imbeciles. It was also a reformatory for inebriate women. There was nowhere else for Miss A to go, as the authorities had still not determined who she was. Rather than a large hospital, it was grouped into houses and smaller buildings and the inmates were placed according to their needs.

The hospital was completely self-sufficient, having its own farm and kitchen gardens. It was seen as a model of modernity and innovation. Some of the more able inmates were allowed to help in the garden and farm work; others helped in the kitchens and laundry. Some of them had to be locked away for their own safety, as they were a danger to themselves and anyone else.

Miss A was taken to a mentally defective ward and placed in a room with three other ladies. She was assigned to the care of a young girl called Laura Woods, who had only just arrived herself.

The sister brought her up to the ward and told Laura about the patients.

'This is Miss A. She hasn't spoken since she was rescued from the Titanic. Nobody knows who she is. They found an handkerchief in her pocket with the letter A on it, and that's why she's so named. She needs full care; can't even take herself to the toilet. These three other ladies are going to be your responsibility, Woods, all right?'

'Yes, Sister. What is wrong with the other ones?'

'The one by the door is Agnes. She can't move herself and has fits. Her dad couldn't cope with her after his wife died, so he sent her here. There weren't any sisters at home to help – they'd all died or were married and moved away.'

'Can she talk or anything, Sister?'

'No Woods. She can't do anything. She just lies there. You'll have to do everything for her.'

'What if she has a fit, Sister? What do I do?'

'Try and stop her choking. We keep a padded spoon by the bedside and shove it in her mouth to stop her biting her tongue, but that's about all you can do. If it goes on for a long time, we can give her some paraldehyde.'

'Paral – what Sister?'

'Paraldehyde, Woods. It's an injection to stop fits. I'll show you how to give it when you've been here a bit longer. Now the woman opposite is a moral defective. She had a child out of wedlock and her family put her in here.'

'Is she an imbecile or anything, Sister?'

'No. Just immoral.'

'Oh, what happened to her child?'

'It died. Best thing that could have happened. It would only have had a slur on it all its life. The woman's called Martha and works in the main kitchen during the day.'

'Well, if she hasn't got a baby, why can't she go home now?'

'They don't want her, so she's stuck here. You ask a lot of questions, Woods. I hope I'm not going to be here all day answering your questions, I have work to do.'

'Sorry Sister. What about the other inmate then?'

'That's Annie. She's an imbecile. Like a five year old she is, but harmless enough. If you tell her to do something simply, she'll do it for you, but you need to watch her. She'll be down on the farm most of the day. The other sixteen patients in the house are your responsibility as well, but their care will be shared with the other staff. That's all the time I have for now. I'm going to my office if you need anything urgently, but I don't want pestering with your trivial questions. Understand?'

Laura Woods opened her mouth to ask another question but thought better of it, after seeing the look on Sister's face. She merely nodded and Sister left the room.

'Well,' said Laura to Miss A. 'this is a fine to do. Haven't a clue what I'm doing and it's only my second week. I was on another ward last week, but I'm glad they moved me here. The other ward was men. Didn't like looking after the men. Did all sorts of nasty things if you weren't careful.'

Miss A didn't respond.

'It's a shame you can't talk Miss A. We could have some grand times together. Never mind, I suppose I'd better take you to the toilet if you can't fend for yourself. Don't want to be mopping up after you, do I?' Laura laughed at her own joke and led Miss A to the toilet.

'And I can't go on calling you Miss A either. I wonder if Sister'll let me give you a name? I'll ask her next time I see her. Now let's see. They say you are probably called something beginning with A. Let me see. Anne, that's a nice name. Shall I call you Anne? No perhaps not, you'll get confused with Annie. And we've already got an Agnes in here as well. Alice? That might be nice. Or Agatha? No, I don't like Agatha. It reminds me of an old aunt that I had. Wouldn't wish her name on anyone. No, I must think up a really nice name for you. Angela? No, Sister would probably say it was too fanciful. Same with Amanda, far too posh for the likes of us. Have you done Miss A? Oh good girl. Let's go back to the dining room.' The two of them ambled along the corridor from the toilets.

'I know, I'll try and say all the names and see which you react to.' Laura made a valiant attempt, but it was all in vain as Miss A didn't react to any name or anything else that Laura had said.

'Well, I'll give it some thought and see what Sister says tomorrow. Now I'm going to help set the tables for tea. Do you want to help me?' but there was no response, so Laura shrugged and got on with the job herself, leaving Miss A stood by the window, staring sightlessly out.

Laura busied herself with setting the tables and serving the food when it arrived. With the evening meal came Martha, returning from her kitchen duties to eat her meal. Martha was quiet and sullen and did little to respond to Laura, beyond asking who Miss A was.

Whilst feeding Agnes, Laura watched Miss A but she didn't make any attempt to eat her food. 'Martha, could you help Miss A with her food, please. She doesn't seem to know how to feed herself.'

'S'pose so,' muttered Martha ungraciously and fed Miss A, who docilely opened her mouth for each mouthful of food.

'How long've you been in here then Martha?' asked Laura.

'Long time,' was the short reply.

'Wouldn't you like to go home?'

'No. They don't want me anymore.'

'I'm sorry,' said Laura. 'Can we be friends then? I need to be able to talk to someone in here. I've been talking to Miss A all day, but I got nowhere. Please, can we be friends?'

'S'pose so,' replied Martha. 'They don't talk to me down in the kitchen.'

'Why not?'

'Say I'm a loose woman.'

'Oh,' replied Laura, not sure how to respond.

'But I'm not. Not a loose woman. Never went near the lads at the mill. It were him that got me at work. I didn't let him. He tricked me into staying late. Said I'd not finished my work right. Then when everyone else had gone, he got me on the sacks in the back room. Forced himself on me. It was awful. He really hurt me, and he wouldn't stop.' At this, Martha began to sob. Laura ran to put her arms round her and calmed her.

'I'm glad it died, the baby. Didn't want none of his spawn. Although I'd have loved it and looked after it. It wasn't the bairn's fault. It didn't ask to be born.'

'Did you tell anyone?'

'Oh yes,' she replied bitterly, 'I told everyone, but with him being a tackler, they believed him and said I'd led him on. They sacked me at the mill. As soon as I was showing, my dad threw me out. I had to come here. No one else would take me in.'

'I'm so sorry. You've had a hard life,' replied Laura with feeling.

'Life is hard, isn't it?'

'I suppose so,' replied Laura.
'Well yours must be hard or you wouldn't be working here.'
'Yes, I lost all my family in an influenza epidemic. I'm the only one who survived. So I needed a job where I could live in. They took the cottage off me as it was tied to the farm where we worked. Dad was a farm labourer and we all helped on the farm.'
'Do you like it here?'
'I'm not sure yet. I've only been here two weeks, but I like caring for other people. Mum always used to say I was a proper little helper.'
'Perhaps we can help each other?' asked Martha. 'It's the longest conversation I've had with anyone since I came here four years ago. Most folk shun me, 'cos of what I did. Huh! What I did. I didn't do anything, but I get all the blame and he got away scot-free. I hate men.'
Wanting to change the conversation, Laura told Martha about Miss A having no name.
'Perhaps you can help me think of a nice name beginning with A?'
'Yes, I'll try and think, but I have to go to the house kitchen now and wash up our tea things.'
'Shall I help you?' asked Laura, trying to befriend this unfortunate girl.
'No, best not. You need to be putting Agnes to bed, and Miss A, I suppose. Then you'll have to help the other nurses to get their patients to bed, especially the heavy or difficult ones.'
'Right. Sister didn't really tell me what the routine was. I'd better take Miss A to the toilet again. She seems to know what to do if I take her there, but doesn't seem capable of taking herself. Then I'll do Agnes afterwards, Martha.'
Martha looked nonplussed.
'What's the matter Martha? Have I upset you?' asked Laura.
'No. It's the first time anyone has used my first name in ages. They just call me Barnes in the kitchen.'
'I know. Sister calls me Woods. I'm Laura by the way. Please call me by my first name, too.'
Martha looked cautiously over her shoulder, then grinned and said 'All right, Laura. Just when we're on our own. Now I'd better get

these pots into the kitchen. Where's Annie, by the way? Hasn't she been in for tea?'

'No, not yet. Should I go and get her?'

'No, go and get one of the orderlies to get her. She'll be mooning over the new calf that's just been born. Proper soppy she is.'

Just at that point, Annie ran breathlessly into the room.

'Have I missed my tea? Is there any left? I'm hungry.' She ran over to the table.

'Yes, you're late,' scolded Martha. 'Now get this tea eaten quickly. I'm waiting to wash up.'

'Who are these two?' Annie asked pointing to Laura and Miss A. Martha explained who each person was and Annie nodded seriously, her large tongue lolling between mouthfuls of food.

As soon as the duties were finished with her own patients, Laura went off to help the other nurses, but complained that they were unfriendly when she got back to Martha.

Laura soon learned the ropes and was quite happy in her work. Martha helped her a lot, explaining the routine and showing her things. When Laura had plucked up courage to ask Sister about a name for Miss A, she gave permission for Laura to name her.

'Have you thought of anything?' Martha asked.

'Yes, when I was younger, my mum bought me a book for Christmas called Little Women by Louisa May Alcott. It was about four sisters in America, during the Civil War. One of them was called Amy. What do you think about Amy as a name?'

'That sounds nice, was she a nice girl?' asked Martha.

'Not really. She was a bit selfish at first, but she learned to be gracious when she was older and became really nice,' replied Laura.

'Amy it is then, but have you thought about a surname?'

'No. Have you any ideas, Martha?'

'My granny was called Wilson. She was my mum's mum. She was always good to me. She believed me about the man at the mill and would have taken me in, but my dad said no.'

'Wilson? Amy Wilson. Yes, that sounds good together. One name from me and one from you. That's a good way to share. I'll let Sister know what her name is tomorrow, then.'

She turned to Miss A. 'Now Miss A, you've got a new name. It's Amy Wilson. Understand? Amy Wilson,' she repeated a little louder. Amy Wilson made no response as usual, but stared out of the window.

The weeks passed by slowly. Martha and Laura got no further with Amy; she remained as unresponsive as she had been since her admission. But she was no trouble. They just had to think for her. She ate when she was told, would perform on the toilet when she was taken there, but made little effort to do anything else for herself.

Laura continued to talk to Amy, even though she got no response, but was always glad when Martha came back from the kitchens, so that they could have a good chat. The unlikely friendship between nurse and patient grew deeper as the weeks went by.

Very quickly, Laura learnt to care for the other sixteen patients in the house, and to manage her time between the five rooms. It was a hard way of life for a young girl, but Laura never complained. It was better than living in the workhouse up in Blackburn. Some day perhaps, she would be able to get more training and get a better job, but for now she was happy.

Chapter 9

Amy stood at her usual position by the window, but today the black fog didn't seem as dense. There seemed to be space in her brain that was allowing her to think. She wasn't sure where she was, but it seemed to be some kind of hospital or home. The same people were here each day; some of them all the time and the others just for part of the time.

The people kept calling her Amy, so that must be her name now. It was unfamiliar, but when she tried to remember her real name, it was painful, so she didn't try very hard. Amy was warm and comfortable; her clothes weren't very pleasant but they were clean and changed regularly. Were smart clothes important to her once? she wondered, but didn't pursue the thought.

Slowly, Amy started to take more initiative, by starting to eat her food without being told to, but still she didn't speak or try to communicate with anyone.

Day by day, the fog in her brain lifted and Amy took in more of her surroundings and was able to watch the goings on in the living room and bedroom. But still she didn't want to think about how she got there or what had happened to her.

Amy was alone in the bedroom one day with Agnes when she started to have a fit. It wasn't one of the short-lived fits, but one of the longer types. Amy watched as her whole body convulsed. She appeared to be choking, but no one appeared to be coming to help Agnes.

She rushed out into the corridor and stood at the top of the stairs.

'Ag . .Ag . .' Amy called and then could speak no more. Laura came running up to Amy, who pointed into the bedroom. Laura ran in and started turning Agnes over on her side, and pushing the spoon in her mouth.

'Florrie, Florrie,' called Laura loudly, and one of the other nurses came running in, urged by the panic in Laura's voice.

'I'll go and get Sister,' said Florrie. 'She needs paraldehyde. Will you be all right with her?' Laura nodded and kept holding Agnes to prevent her from hurting herself as she thrashed around the bed.

Sister soon arrived with a silver syringe and needle and injected the solution in to Agnes' buttocks. Slowly, the fit resolved itself and Agnes slept.

'It's a good job you were around, Woods,' said Sister. 'That was a bad one.'

'I wasn't around, Sister, I was in the living room, clearing up the table.'

'How did you know then?'

'It was Amy. She made a grunting noise that sounded like Ag. She was pointing to the bedroom, weren't you Amy?'

There was no response from Amy, who was too frightened to speak.

'Amy spoke, you say?' asked an incredulous Sister.

'She did, too,' replied Laura. 'I wouldn't have known otherwise. Come on Amy, talk to me again.' There was only silence as Amy looked at the floor.

'Perhaps it was seeing someone else in distress that jarred her brain for a while. Watch her Woods, and report anything untoward to me instantly.'

'Yes, Sister.' Laura watched the Sister leave and then turned to Amy. 'You did speak, didn't you?' But Amy merely looked at her with frightened eyes. It was too soon. She didn't want to speak yet.

'Don't be frightened Amy. I won't harm you. I want to help you. When you're ready to speak, you just speak to me. And thank you for helping me today with Agnes. That was good. You looked after her for me.' Amy turned away and went to look out of the window. It was comfortable here, she didn't have to speak or think by the window.

Slowly, the fog lightened each day until Amy could remain silent no longer.

'Where am I?' she said to a startled Laura.

'In Brockhall Asylum, near Blackburn.'

'Asylum,' repeated Amy.

'That's right. You were brought here after the ship sunk. Can you remember that?' Amy nodded.

'Can you remember who you are?'

Yes, thought Amy, but I don't want to remember who I am yet. It's too painful, so she just shook her head.

‘I’ll have to tell Sister,’ said Laura, ‘you’ll talk to her when she comes, won’t you? I think she thought I was making it up when I said you’d warned me about Agnes.’ Amy nodded again.

‘Right, I’ll go and get Sister,’ said Laura, looking dubiously at Amy, in case she made a fool of her again.

Sister soon returned with Laura, and Sister asked Amy a question. ‘Woods tells me you can talk. What is your name?’

‘Amy,’ she replied quietly.

‘See, told you she could talk,’ interrupted Laura.

‘That’s enough Woods.’ Sister turned to Amy again. ‘Now dear, Amy is the name we have given you. What is your real name?’

‘Can’t remember,’ replied Amy.

‘And do you remember going on the ship?’

‘Yes.’

‘And what else?’

‘Nothing. Mind all mushy.’

‘Well, you go and sit with Agnes for a while. I’ll speak to you later.’

When she had gone, Sister told Laura that whatever had started her talking again might never be known, but she was still sure that it was seeing Agnes in distress that started the healing process.

‘Don’ t push her too much, Woods. Let her talk to you as little or as much as she wants to, so that it doesn’t tax her brain. Too much stimulus might send her back again. Understand?’

Laura nodded.

‘I’ll let Matron know what has happened. She still has to send a report periodically to the White Line shipping people. She may want to see you.’

‘Matron to see me?’

‘Don’t worry Woods, it’s only routine, as you were the one to notice that she was different. I’m pleased with your work, Woods. I think you have a future working here and I shall tell Matron so.’ Laura glowed in Sister’s praise and found herself almost longing to go to see Matron instead of the dread she felt when Sister first mentioned it.

As the days went by, Amy started to ask questions.

‘What is the date?’ she asked one day.

‘It’s the second of September,’ replied Laura.

'In the same year?' asked Amy.
'Same year as what?' asked Laura, not sure what Amy meant.
'Same year as the ship.'
'Oh yes, it's still 1912. You've been here about five months.'
Amy went quiet again, thinking her own thoughts that she couldn't share with Laura.

Soon, Amy started to talk more and more until Laura and Martha could have a full conversation with her, as long as it wasn't about her former life. Amy was able to a take on a caring role with the other inmates and she was often found in the other rooms in the house.

Eventually, Matron came to see Amy.
'I'm hearing good things about you Amy. I believe you have recovered your power of speech.'
'Yes, thank you.'
'We need to talk about your future. You were only placed here because nobody knew who you were. Although you are talking, I believe you still cannot say who you are?'
'No, I can't remember.'
'What do you want to do with your life?'
'I like it here. I'd like to stay. Can I help with the work?'
'Wouldn't you prefer to go out and have a life again?'
'Nowhere to go. I feel safe here.'
'Well, I think I can find you work for a short time, but I don't think it's an answer for the long term. You can help in this house where you have been living. They are short staffed now since Whittaker left. We'll talk again in two months.'

So started the hardest days of Amy's life. She was only employed to do the menial tasks at first. She spent long days scrubbing the house, making beds and helping with the inmates. Her hands became roughened and sore; her knees hardened to the floor surfaces; her back aching constantly.

At nights, she fell into bed and slept immediately, but for all this Amy was happy. She was doing good and helping other people. She even began to sing as she worked, although she didn't know where the tunes had come from.

In November, Matron sent for Amy.
'How are you doing? Are you happy at your work?'

'Yes Matron,' replied Amy politely.
'Have you thought any more about your future?'
'Not really, I'm happy here now.'
'Wouldn't you like to pursue a career in caring for other people?'
'Yes, I would. That's what I'm doing now.'
'But I think that you are an educated woman. I think that you could train as a nurse.'
'Me? A nurse? I don't think so.'
'Why not? You have some good qualities that are wanted in modern day nursing. Think about it and let me know.'
'Thank you Matron, I will.'
Amy went back to her house and pondered the idea of nursing for the next few days. Laura encouraged her to go ahead. She only wished Matron had asked her to go as well.
Eventually, Amy plucked up courage and asked to see Matron.
'I am interested in nursing. What would I have to do?'
'If you wanted to train in one of the big hospitals in London, you would have to pay for the training course, but other hospitals are now starting training courses. My friend is a Matron at Burnley Victoria Hospital, about ten miles away. She is looking for intelligent young women like you to fill her training schools. I could arrange for you to get a place on a three year nursing course, if you wish.'
'Yes, I'd like that.'
'Good. I'll write to her today, I'll tell her of your work here and also explain your circumstances. That will by-pass the usual application questions that might be difficult for you to answer.'
'Thank you again. I feel that this is the way forward for me now. At least if I'm a trained nurse, I can support myself and eventually find a home.'
'It's probably the best you can do, in the circumstances. I'll let you know when I hear from her.'
It was after Christmas before Amy heard from Matron again, but when she did, it was good news. There was a place for Amy on the nursing course in a few months time. Amy could hardly wait. As a nurse, she could help people and if she helped people, it would start to cancel out the awful thing that she did to Lizzie. But she would never be free of guilt. No, not ever.

Chapter 10

Amy walked up to the hospital with some trepidation. Was she doing the right thing? Would she be happy working in a new environment with strangers? Would they continually question her about her past? Her mind was in a whirl with the thoughts of the new venture.

Feeling in her pocket, Amy checked that the letter from Matron was still there. Suddenly she wished she was back in the familiar house, but she knew that there was no point. If she wanted to progress in her work, she would need to have some kind of training. Besides, she felt inadequate in many situations and didn't know what to do. The training would help her and give an opportunity to work for her living.

It was a strange looking hospital from the outside. There was a main block with four floors, but then the rest of the hospital was on two floors with three circular wards stuck out from a main corridor, almost like children's lollipops, on the ground floor.

Amy approached the porter's lodge and knocked on the window. A large grumpy looking man opened the window.

'Yes?' he growled.

'Miss Amy Wilson, coming to start nurse training.'

'You'd better come in then. The others are already here. Given up on you.'

'Sorry. My train was late and I've had to walk from Bank Top station as I'd just missed the tram,' Amy stuttered in reply. But the porter didn't speak; he merely opened the gate and let her in. 'Nurses home is on third and fourth floors. Your room is on fourth floor. Stairs to left of door as you go in.'

'Thank you,' replied Amy, as she walked towards the door. After walking up four flights of stairs, Amy was a little breathless and was glad to have a rest at the top and look round her. The walls on the corridor were bare and painted light grey; the curtains a darker shade of grey with white stripes. A lot of doors led off the corridor and appeared to have names on them. Amy went closer and looked at the names on the first door. Katie Rennolds and Emily Windle. She looked at the next door. Frances Thresh and Olivia Galloway.

Rebecca Shutt and Laura Stockburn were on the next door and Hannah Heaton and Victoria Baldocke after them. Amy was wondering whether she would ever find her name as the next door said Eleanor May and Sophia Wilby. Finally on the last door, she found her own name, along with Molly Smith.

Cautiously, after knocking and hearing no reply, Amy opened the door. The room was empty. She went into the room and looked around. There were two narrow looking beds with a small chest of drawers between them. A small wardrobe stood on the side and a bookcase. A sink completed the room's furniture. There was no sign of occupation. Amy's heart sank. Was she going to be alone for her time here?

She put her bag on to the bed nearest the window and sat down, staring at the pile of uniforms awaiting her. They were grey, like the walls of the corridors. Fortunately, the walls in the room were cream and it made a change from all the grey she had seen so far. Amy wondered whether she should start putting her belongings into the drawer when somebody could be heard coming along the corridor.

Her door burst open and a tall severe looking lady wearing formal uniform entered.

'Ah, you're here at last. Which are you? Smith or Wilson?'

'Wilson,' replied Amy quickly, standing to attention.

'Any idea where Smith is?'

'No, I've only just arrived myself and I've not seen anyone else. Not until you, that is,' Amy babbled.

'And why were you late, Wilson?'

'The train was late and I missed the tram. Sorry, Sister.'

'Home,' she barked in reply, 'I'm Home Sister. Look after the home, do you see?'

'Yes, Home Sister.'

'You'd better come downstairs to the common room and meet the other entrants.' With that, Home Sister marched out of the door and Amy ran after her. They went quickly down one flight of stairs and almost collided with a young dark haired girl running up the stairs.

'Oops, sorry,' she giggled. Home Sister glared at her.

'Are you Smith?'

'Yes, Molly Smith. Sorry I'm late.'

'Come with me. Too late to show you your room. I can see you're going to be trouble, Smith. I can tell straight away. I'll be watching you two. Couldn't even get here on time on your first day.'

Molly's giggles had disappeared by now and she was looking worried. As Home Sister set off down the stairs, Molly looked at Amy and pulled a face. Amy giggled but turned it into a cough when Home Sister turned round and glared. They were taken into a large room, where the ten other girls were waiting. All talking stopped as they entered.

'Right, now everybody is here we can get started. Here are the rules and regulations of the home. Sister Tutor will inform you about rules and regulations for the wards, but off duty, you are under my jurisdiction. You are not allowed to leave the home without my permission. I am responsible for you and need to know where you are at all times. You should write your off-duty on the pad outside your door so that I know if you are working. Got it?' she asked without stopping for a reply.

'On your time off, you must tell me where you intend to spend your afternoon or day off, and I will decide whether that is a suitable occupation for a nurse. Remember, you are always at the beck and call of the public and your behaviour must be above reproach at all times. No one is allowed in your room except your room mate of course, and any other student in your group, that is you twelve. You should not take any of your family up to your room at any time. Or any other nurse from the other groups. Is that clear?'

'Yes Home Sister,' they all dutifully replied, their spirits sinking fast.

'Tomorrow morning you will start at eight am, so be on the ground floor, at the bottom of the stairs, with your uniform. Not wearing it, just carrying it. And some paper, pen and ink. That is all, you may now go to the dining room for your evening meal and then I suggest you all get an early night. Any questions?' Twelve heads shook their answer.

'I'll be off then. Your room inspections will take place once a week at my convenience and nurses will be penalised if there rooms are untidy or even worse, unclean.' Home Sister marched off out of the room, leaving the girls in silence for a few seconds. It didn't last long. As if on cue, they all started talking at once.

Molly turned to Amy. 'Well Amy, looks like I've upset old Home Sister already.'

'Don't worry, she's already watching me 'cos I was late as well.'

'Not as late as me, though,' said Molly mournfully. 'It was my mum's fault. She would just make me feed our Billy before I came out and he was in a right grizzly mood, then I missed the tram, and then everything fell out of my case in the road outside.'

'Well, my train was late and I missed the tram as well. What a pair we are! I'm glad we're sharing a room though. Especially if Home Sister has her eye on us!' The two girls laughed together.

'What are your names?' asked a dark haired petite girl. She had a blond haired tall girl with her.

'I'm Amy Wilson and this is Molly Smith,' replied Amy.

'I'm Laura Stockburn,' said the girl who had spoken 'and this is Rebecca Shutt. Where are you from, Amy?'

Amy hesitated before replying. 'I've just come from the asylum at Langho. I was working there.'

'Yes, but I mean where do you come from originally?'

Amy took a deep breath.

'I don't know. I was on the Titanic and lost everything. Then I couldn't remember who I was or where I came from. I stopped talking altogether and it was as if my brain wasn't working.' Amy stopped speaking. She realised that the whole room was quiet and the other girls were all listening to her, with looks of horror on their faces.

Laura recovered first. 'How awful for you. I'm sorry I asked. So you have no family left?'

'No.'

'Well, we'll be your family now,' replied Laura. 'I'm from Blackburn and I live with my dad and I'm the youngest of five brothers and sisters. Rebecca, you tell next. In fact, girls, why don't we go round the room and tell a little about ourselves, if we're going to spend so much time together for the next three years?'

'Weren't we supposed to be going to the dining room?' asked Rebecca.

'Oh yes,' said Molly, 'let's go there first and then we can talk.'

The twelve girls hurried off to the dining room and ate a good tea. There was no one else in the dining room so they assumed that they were later than everyone else as the staff were tidying up behind them. They returned to the common room.

'Shall I start, as I was just going to speak?' asked Rebecca. The others nodded. 'I'm Rebecca Shutt and I live here in Burnley with my mum and brother and three sisters. I'm glad to come here 'cos I only have to share with one person instead of three others, and I'll get a bed to myself.' The others all laughed and some agreed. The others all gave their names and where they came from and soon there was a lively discussion group going. Eventually, Amy and Molly went to their room.

'Amy, I'm sorry about what happened to you. If ever you want a family, come to my house. Mum wouldn't notice another person – the house is so full to start with.'

'Molly, that's so kind of you. I'd nowhere to go when I was at the asylum. I often just sat reading on my days off. It will be a lovely change.'

'That's if Home Sister deems it a suitable place for you to go,' replied Molly, imitating Home Sister perfectly.

'Oh Molly, you sounded just like her then. You are clever.'

'My teachers never thought so. Always telling me off for imitating them!'

'How many are there in your house, then? You said your mum wouldn't notice another.'

'Ten of us. Mum and dad and eight kids. Well, there were eleven but two died of whooping cough and one of fits a few years ago.'

'Your poor mum. How does she get over loosing babies?'

'It's not easy. Folks think 'cos you've got other children that it doesn't matter if you lose one, but it does. My mum has never got over each and every baby that she's lost. You can always tell when it's an anniversary or birthday of one of the lost ones. She goes all quiet and thoughtful and sometimes I catch her with tears in her eyes.'

'I know how she feels,' replied Amy.

'Why? Have you lost a baby?' said Molly viciously.

'No, not a baby.'

'Then you don't know how she feels, so don't say so.'

'I just meant that I didn't have anybody, that I'd lost all I had,' replied a mournful Amy.

'How do you know if you can't remember anything?' said Molly gruffly.
'I don't know, I just know I have nobody. It's sort of a feeling inside of me. Don't be angry Molly. I want us to be friends.'
'I'm not angry. Just sad for mum. And for you as well. Come on, let's change the subject. Have you got a boyfriend?'
'No,' said Amy quite surprised, 'why have you?'
'Now that'd be telling,' replied Molly mysteriously. 'Besides, I won't be able to see much of him now. Home Sister would never approve of him, would she?'
'Probably not,' laughed Amy. 'But if you have a boyfriend, why are you doing training? Surely you know that nurses can't work if they are married?'
'Who said anything about marriage?' laughed Molly, but then became more serious. 'No, I've always vowed I would train to be a nurse since we lost the babies. I want to help people who are ill. Especially poor people who can't afford doctors. If we'd had a doctor for the babies, they wouldn't have died.'
'I'm pleased that you're going to be a nurse then. I hope you get what you want.'
'And you Amy, why do you want to be a nurse?'
'Partly the same as you. I want to help others.'
'Well, shall we set up our own hospital and cure the world?' asked Molly.
'Yes, why not,' responded Amy in like vein. 'But first, I think we need to get to sleep early or else we won't be ready for Sister Tutor tomorrow.'
The two girls settled into bed, quickly said their prayers, and were soon fast asleep.

Chapter 11

Molly woke before Amy next morning and had already been to the bathroom and had her wash.

'Come on lazybones. If Sister Tutor is anything like Home Sister we'd better not be late. The other girls are all up and getting washed.'

Amy yawned but got out of bed and gathered her clothes and wash things about her. By half past seven they were in the dining room, eating large bowls of glutinous porridge, and at a minute to eight, they were at the foot of the stairs.

Home Sister was standing at the bottom of the stairs, waiting for them. Next to her was another woman looking equally officious. Home Sister ticked them all off on her list and then turned to the new lady.

'Sister Tutor, here is your new group of trainees. Already two have come to my notice by arriving late yesterday, so I would watch them like a hawk.'

'Thank you Home Sister. I'll make my own assessments of the girls.' Molly and Amy looked down at their toes and hoped that Home Sister wouldn't single them out. But they were reprieved, as Sister Tutor said 'Follow me,' and set off at great speed down the corridor.

The twelve followed as quickly as possible, nearly losing Sister Tutor at times. She took them down the long corridor, right to the opposite end of the hospital and then took them into a small room.

There were twelve hardback chairs and tables in rows of threes. The girls walked towards the tables with their room mates but Sister Tutor called out.

'Alphabetical order please,' so Amy moved to the front and sat down. Molly sat in the middle.

'That's Baldocke, May and Galloway on the front row,' shouted Sister Tutor, consulting her list. The other girls stared when she used their surnames, but Amy was used to being called by her surname now, and quietly moved nearer to the back.

Once they had got themselves in order, Sister Tutor started to read out a long list of rules and regulations. Amy was glad that she had worked at the asylum as many of the rules were the same and governed every aspect of their working life.

'No speaking to any senior nurses, you can only talk to your own group and the group immediately above you,' snapped Sister Tutor. 'If you need to inform a senior nurse of anything, you must tell the next senior nurse to you and she will pass the message upwards. When Matron passes you on the corridor you must press yourself against the wall and avert your eyes. Don't speak until you are spoken to. No running in the corridor, except in case of haemorrhage or fire.'

Sister Tutor droned on and on detailing every possible eventuality. Amy's heart sank. There had been no mention about the patient and the care that they would be given. Many of the rules were petty and unnecessary but Amy wouldn't have dreamed of saying so.

Next they learned about personal hygiene and cleanliness and how to keep the ward scrupulously clean. During lunch, they were lectured about rules in the dining room, such as not sitting on a table with more senior nurses, and always standing to attention when Matron and the senior nurses arrived or departed. Then they returned to the classroom and learnt about the hospital itself.

It had been built from subscriptions by the people of Burnley and had been opened by Prince Albert. It was named Victoria Hospital after his wife, the Queen. Those who could afford to pay were treated in this hospital, the rest of them had to go to Primrose Bank, the workhouse higher up the road, on the outskirts of town.

The last part of the day was spent in learning how to wear their uniforms: the making of their caps causing a lot of hilarity. The caps seemed to have a life of their own, even though they were heavily starched. At five o'clock they were dismissed and told to report at seven am next morning to the same classroom. The next day would start with a short test of the hygiene rules. The class groaned, but was soon silenced by Sister Tutor.

'Today was a concession as it was your first day, but you need to get used to starting work at seven o'clock, as this is what you will be working in future,' she warned grimly.

That night, Amy and Molly feverishly read their notes and tested each other on the hygiene rules. Eventually, worn down by facts and figures, they settled down to sleep.

The second day was spent much like the first, with some basic lectures about nursing care being given, plus a practical lecture on bed making. At the end of the second day, the change list was introduced. Sister Tutor explained that this would show them which wards they were working on throughout their training. A new change list would be written every three months.

After saying that, Sister Tutor told them that they could now look at the change list and then go and find the ward that they would be on the next day. She wished them well and told them that lectures would be every Monday morning and Thursday afternoon and if they were off duty or on night duty, they were still expected to attend. Once Sister Tutor had gone, the girls all made a dive for the list but Rebecca got there first.

'I'm on Female Medical ward,' she shrieked 'and you're on with me Amy.'

'Let's look,' said Olivia, grabbing the list. 'Oh, I'm on the eye ward with Emily. You're on Male Medical with Frances, Molly.'

'I'm on Male Orthopaedics,' shouted Victoria, 'whatever that is. Sounds terrible. Hannah, you're on with me.' Laura and Sophia were on Female Orthopaedics and Katie and Eleanor were on the accident ward.

Next morning, Rebecca and Amy set off together to Female Medical ward. It was in the four-storey section of the building, on the ground floor. It was a long Nightingale type ward, with beds arrayed on both sides and three cubicles on the corridor outside the main ward doors. An open fire was on one wall opposite the windows and at the end of the ward was a circular extension with extra beds in.

Amy and Rebecca walked up to the office and knocked on the door.

'Come in,' said a stern voice.

Rebecca opened the door and they both crept in. A Sister sat behind the large desk but she ignored them when they walked in. Amy and Rebecca looked at each other, wondering what to do next when a voice boomed out.

'Palmer? Come here now.'

After a few seconds, a frightened looking girl arrived in the office.

'Yes Sister?' she asked nervously.

'Take these two and get them working.'

'Yes Sister, thank you Sister,' replied Palmer, looking absolutely terrified. She herded Amy and Rebecca out of the office and led them down the ward to the sluice without speaking. On arrival at the sluice, she shut the door and turned to the two girls.

'I'm Jean Palmer, what's your names?'

'I'm Rebecca Shutt and she's Amy Wilson.'

'Well you can forget your first names for the next three years. No one ever refers to you by your first name here. So you'll be Shutt and Wilson, so if anyone asks your name, that's what you must answer. Got it?' The two girls nodded.

'Those in black are sisters and those in dark grey are staff nurses. Those in light grey are students like you. The brown dresses are orderlies. Never go to the dining room with your pinny on and see that you have clean cuffs on every morning. Oh and take your cuffs off to go to the dining room, too. Now this is the sluice. This is where you'll be spending most of your days for the first few weeks. Your job is to take bedpans to the patients and bring them back here. Once you have noted what the patient has performed, you have to record it on the chart, and then dispose of it in this sluice toilet. Then you have to keep the bedpans clean and warmed ready for the next round. You'll only go out on the ward at bedpan times or if you are asked to do something else. Is that clear?'

'Yes, Jean.'

'Palmer. You have to call me Palmer, I've already told you that. Now, I've been promoted from the sluice so I'll be doing temperatures. You may watch me if you like, but you won't be allowed to do them yet,' said Palmer condescendingly.

Another grey dressed student interrupted them in the instructions.

'Palmer, lady in bed eight needs a bedpan. Quick.'

'Yes, Cocks. I'll take these two with me and show them.'

'Good idea,' replied Cocks and then scurried away.

'Cocks is a third year, not long to go now. She's doing dressings and giving out medicines now,' remarked Palmer proudly, obviously in thrall to this senior student.

Palmer got a silver coloured bedpan and a cloth to cover it, and telling Amy and Rebecca to follow her; she set off into the ward. Here they were shown the easiest way to insert a bedpan and screen the bed whilst the patient performed, using movable screens that were situated at the bottom of the ward. Then they scurried back to the sluice.

The bedpan rounds continued all day. The girls were in and out of the sluice, washing, scrubbing and cleaning. In the brief moments when they had nothing to do in the sluice, they were expected to scrub the floors in the ward and keep the fire burning brightly. But woe betide them if they were on the ward when Matron or the doctors arrived. They had to hide in the sluice.

Later in the afternoon, Palmer showed them the intricate way of testing urine and let them help with setting up some of the urine tests. During the day they were allowed short breaks and eventually at seven fifteen, they were allowed off duty and told to report the next day at seven am.

Molly had arrived back at their room just before Amy. She was already undressed ready for bed and looked up wearily when Amy came in.

'Hi Amy, I'm exhausted, how about you?"

'Same here, straight to bed I think, don't you?'

'Too tired to talk, see you tomorrow, night night Amy.'

'Night Molly.'

Amy turned out the light then quickly fell asleep and slept until the maid knocked on the door to waken them for breakfast. Over breakfast, Molly and Amy compared notes about their first day on the wards. Molly's day had been very similar to Amy's – mainly spent in the sluice with bedpans. It was quite confusing, Molly said, as many of their patients had their eyes bandaged and they couldn't see them. The girls hurried their breakfast down, then separated to their different wards.

On arrival at the ward, Amy was told by Cocks that she would be off duty from twelve noon until four pm.

'Oh but I have lectures this afternoon,' blurted Amy.

'Well, you'll know what to do with your time off then,' replied Cocks icily, 'and tell Palmer that she is off from nine this morning until 2pm,' and she started to walk away.

'But wouldn't it be better if I was off from nine until two?' asked Amy. Cocks spun round on her heels and glared at Amy.

'Are you trying to tell Sister her job, girl? If I was you, I'd keep such thoughts to yourself.' Cocks turned again and walked out of the sluice. Amy was cross at herself. Why had she said anything? She'd been told that she had to go to lectures in her own time, why had she argued? I must keep my mouth shut tight, she decided, or else I will be in trouble.

It was soon twelve noon and Amy hurried off to the dining room before going to the classroom for her lecture. The other girls were already there and the room was buzzing with noise. Amy was soon drawn in to the conversation and nobody noticed Sister Tutor enter the room, until they heard her voice.

'In all my born days, I have never, I repeat never, had a group of unruly hooligans like you twelve. We have struggled for years to get nursing to be seen as a respectable profession and listen to you. You sound like farmer's wives on market day. Now silence.'

The twelve all looked sheepishly downwards and avoided each other's eyes. Sister Tutor rambled on a bit about standards and etiquette and then suddenly asked a question. It took them all by surprise.

'Come on, I'm waiting for an answer. What three things have you learnt so far whilst on the wards? Wilson?'

Amy thought rapidly. What had she learnt? Not to use her first name; not to speak to anyone and not to think for herself. Not much else, but she knew that she wouldn't dare give that as an answer.

'Hurry up girl, I'm waiting.'

'I've learnt how to give a bedpan and care for it afterwards, Sister Tutor.'

'It? It? What do you mean it? Care for it afterwards? What sort of statement is that Wilson?'

'I mean, er,' Amy stumbled, 'I learnt how to measure urine and observe faeces, and put the results on charts, and then wash the bedpan afterwards.'

'That's better. Say what you mean girl and don't mumble. May, you next. What did you learn?'

Eleanor struggled to give an answer and then Sister Tutor went round the class until they had all given an answer. Next she lectured on the correct storage and care of bedpans and bottles and taught about urine testing. She had just finished talking about faeces then told them to go for tea, then back to the wards.

'Cor, said Olivia, 'fancy eating tea after all that talk of faeces. I don't think I'll eat again.'

'Me neither,' replied Sophia, looking a bit green around the gills.

'Course you will,' said Amy. 'You get used to it. I was like you at first when I was working at the asylum. And you should have seen what some of those patients did with their urine and faeces.'
'Don't,' said Sophia, covering her mouth. 'I think I'll give tea a miss and go straight back to the ward.'
'I'll come with you,' replied Olivia and Rebecca.
Amy tucked into her tea and then hurried back to the ward, only to be met by the staff nurse.
'Wilson, where have you been? You were supposed to be back by four pm.'
'But I've been to my lecture, I did tell Cocks that I had to go.'
'What time did your lecture finish?'
'Four pm, but Sister Tutor told us to go to tea.'
'She would have meant only if you were off duty. You had no right to go straight to tea. You should have thought about your colleagues on the ward. They need their tea too. What gave you the right to put your needs before the senior nurses?'
'But Staff Nurse, I . . '
'And don't interrupt me Wilson. How dare you speak to a staff nurse? Just answer questions, not answer back. I'll be watching you from now on. And for this, you will forego your off duty time tomorrow'
Amy's heart sank. Not again. She always seemed to be upsetting people. Well, she would keep quiet now. At the end of the shift, Staff Nurse kept her late, even after the night staff had arrived. Amy was sure that she'd done it on purpose.
Eventually, she got off duty but there was no sign of Molly. Amy got ready for bed and was in bed reading before Molly returned.
'Where have you been?'
'Hi Amy, I went in Katie and Emily's room. I finished at five pm, and so did Emily, so we had a good chat. You look fed up. Has anything happened?'
'Not really, just the usual petty hierarchy. I got told off for going for my tea with you lot. Should have gone back to the ward first. Staff Nurse told me off in no uncertain terms. Said she's watching me. I'm going to be the most watched nurse in training.'
'Oh no you're not,' replied Molly, 'that's me. I've upset Sister already. She knows my name and it's only our second day. Frances

seems to be the blue-eyed girl on Male Medical. Sister had her making her tea today. Apparently that's a great honour usually reserved for more senior nurses.'

'Lucky Frances,' replied Amy mournfully. 'Anyway, I'm tired and I can't have any time off tomorrow, so it'll be a long day. I'm going to bed.'

'Night night, God Bless, then.'

'Same to you, night.'

The weeks passed quickly and soon the twelve were moving on to new wards. Amy changed to male orthopaedics and Molly to the eye ward. They got used to the long days of work and poor working conditions, although they always got decent food. Often, they were too tired to go anywhere on their day off and spent most of it in bed.

After their next move, a new group of nurses started and they were no longer the newest recruits. Suddenly, they were promoted to doing temperatures and had to initiate the new girls into the rules of the sluice.

'Were we really so green?' asked Sophia. 'That new nurse I had to look after today was hopeless. I had to keep going over it again and again.

'I suppose so,' replied Rebecca, 'probably worse. But it's their fault, you're so frightened of putting a foot wrong that you lose your common sense.'

'That's if we had any,' quipped Olivia. 'We can't have had much common sense or we'd have stayed at home with our mothers, or got married or something.'

'That's a bit drastic, getting married,' said Amy.

'There's nothing wrong with getting married. I might just do it myself shortly,' replied Molly. At that, all the girls laughed.

'Some chance of us getting married for the foreseeable future. Sister Tutor wouldn't allow it. Home Sister neither,' said a mournful Laura.

'What man would look at us anyway with our red raw hands? Hardly tempted to take our tiny hand in his and quote sonnets to us, are they?' Eleanor commented.

'And when could we do our courting?' asked Frances, ever the practical one. 'We only get one day off a week, and it's usually in the middle of the week, so no suitor would be so accommodating with our off-duty rota.'

'Never mind, we could do worse,' quipped Hannah, 'we could be like Sister Norton or marry doctors instead.' The girls laughed. Yes, better to be single than be like some of the horrid ward sisters that they had met. Or married to some of the haughty doctors that had swept past, totally oblivious to them at the hospital. Chuckling to themselves, the girls retired to their own rooms and were quickly asleep.

Chapter 12

The twelve girls had all become very close friends over the last few months and knew that they would stay in touch with each other for life. Although Molly and Amy were closest to each other, still they had a close friendship with the others. On the rare occasion that their day off coincided, Molly would take Amy to her home, not far from the hospital.

It was a chaotic household which Amy loved. They welcomed her like one of the family and made a fuss of her. Not the least was Molly's oldest brother, Jimmy. Molly would tease her when they got back to hospital and say that their Jimmy was keen on her, but Amy was having none of it.

'I haven't time for all that. All I want is to get my training finished. There'll be plenty of time for romance afterwards,' insisted Amy.

'Just you wait 'til you meet someone special. You'll soon change your tune,' teased Molly.

'No I won't,' replied Amy hotly.

'Well, I just hope I'm around when it happens. I can't wait to say I told you so.'

'We're getting a weeks holiday soon, before our second year,' said Amy changing the subject. 'What are you doing with yours?'

'Nothing probably. Just go home and get roped in for helping with the babies.'

'Why don't we have a holiday together? That would be good fun.'

'A holiday? Where to?' asked Molly.

'I don't know, what about Blackpool?'

'Mmm, that sounds like a good idea. Just the two of us?'

'Yes. Although, why not ask all the twelve? We're all on holiday at the same time,' suggested Amy.

'They might not all want to come.' replied Molly. But they did. All twelve of them booked into a boarding house near the Promenade and had the time of their lives, with no work and lots of fun and laughter. It made them relax and enjoy life to the full: a thing that was difficult when they were working such long hours.

It was whilst they were at Blackpool that news came of the assassination of Arch-Duke Ferdinand and his wife in Sarajevo. The event completely passed them by. What relevance was it to them what happened in other countries they asked?

The holiday came to a close far too quickly and the girls returned to the Victoria Hospital and back to the hard grinding routine of their lives.

They were welcomed back with a test. They all groaned, but passed it nevertheless. Although Sister Tutor was still saying they were the worst group she had ever had, the twelve had now found out that she said that to every group, so it didn't upset them anymore. It was a proud moment when they received their second year stripes to fasten on to their sleeves.

Now as second year students, they were allowed to undertake more direct care of the patients and bed bathing became the new task to learn. Soon they were expected to observe dressings in readiness for learning how to do this skilled procedure themselves. Most of the ward cleaning was no longer part of their duties but left to the first year students.

Amy really felt that she was learning a lot, although keeping out of trouble was hard, too. There were so many unwritten rules to be broken. In their lectures, they were learning much more about how the human body worked and how to care for specific diseases.

Their innocence in political affairs was soon demonstrated when following on from that assassination in Sarajevo, England declared war on Germany. The twelve talked at great length about the events and worried about brothers who were going to have to fight.

Molly was especially worried as, at the first announcement of war, her four brothers had all signed up and were in France even now. Molly's mum was beside herself with worry, but reassured that it would be all over by Christmas. Then she would have her Jimmy, Harold, Tommy and John home again. Thank goodness Peter and Billy were only babies yet.

'Our Jimmy wants to know if you'll write to him?' asked Molly one day. 'Says it'd help him put up with the hardships.'

'I suppose so,' replied Amy. It was the least she could do for the poor brave soldiers. Although she had no great feelings for Jimmy, she suspected that he had feelings for her. But if it kept him happy in the trenches, why not? It wouldn't do any harm.

All too soon, news of casualties arrived in Burnley and many families were in mourning. Molly's family seemed to have charmed lives as, though they were in the midst of battle, they survived; the others were not so lucky. One of Olivia's brothers died and also Rebecca's father. He had formerly been in the Boer War, and had been recalled very early in the war.

The other girls tried to help Rebecca and Olivia as much as they could but they worked with heavy hearts. Eventually Rebecca left training as her mother couldn't cope with the loss of her husband and wanted her daughter at home. The other eleven felt Rebecca's loss keenly, but kept in touch with her.

At the end of their second year, the girls didn't have a joint holiday. It didn't feel right with a war going on, and Rebecca no longer being with them. Molly went home to be with her mother and Amy just went for days out to surrounding places of interest. One place she visited was Towneley Hall. It had been the home of the Towneley family but it had been sold to the local council and opened as a museum. The grounds were beautiful and suddenly reminded Amy of Montague Hall. As she remembered her childhood, she wept for the past and the losses that she had experienced in her young life. And now, many more young men were losing their lives. Life was hard and no mistake, she reflected.

Amy could have gone back to Montague Hall at any time, but she still didn't feel like she could face going there yet. Perhaps some day, but she doubted it. That was her old life. This was her new life and she felt better in herself living her new life. She pulled herself together and, seeing someone coming in the distance, wiped her tears and walked away with a determined step.

Molly looked very self-satisfied on her return from her holiday. When they were on their own, Molly pulled a necklace out from under her uniform. It had a plain gold band dangling from it.

'Look,' she said proudly, 'I'm married.'

'Married? said Amy aghast. 'When? Where?'

'Whilst we were on holiday. Edwin volunteered for the army.'

'But I thought that he was in a reserved occupation, being a miner?'

'He is, but he wanted to do his bit. Felt he was missing out on something,' said Molly sadly. 'Yes, missing out on being shot at and maimed in the trenches.'

Amy didn't know what to say, so she just hugged her.

'I'm sorry I didn't tell you,' said Molly. 'I just didn't tell anyone in case Matron found out. I know I'd lose my place if she found out I was married. But I didn't want to let Edwin go until we were married. I may lose him, so I had to do it. I'd have liked you to be there, really. My mum wasn't too pleased either, I can tell you. Never mind Edwin's parents. But it's too late now. We just sneaked away and got married.'

'I'd always imagined that we would be bridesmaids for each other when we got married,' said Amy sadly.

'I know, I'm sorry, but you can be Godmother to my first born, there, will that do instead?'

'You're not. . . '

'No, of course not. I only got married last week, silly. I'm just saying that to cheer you up. But it's me that will need cheering up. Edwin left for the trenches yesterday. Just five days honeymoon. It's not fair. Oh I hate this war. Don't you?'

'Yes. And I forgive you. How can I be angry with my best friend? Are you telling the others that you're married?'

'No. Not at the moment. I'm not going to change my name whilst I am training.'

'It's perhaps as well. That would make it obvious if you changed your name. What is Edwin's surname anyway?' Amy asked.

Molly laughed. 'I was hoping you weren't going to ask me that. It's Jolley. Isn't it awful? I'll be Molly Jolley!' They both laughed at that and Amy suggested that they both would be better changing to her name. Molly Smith sounded much better and Edwin Smith sounded all right, too. Molly said she didn't think that Edwin would change his name; it just wasn't done. But that was all in the future. For now, the men had to fight and the women had to weep, or as in the case of the eleven friends, finish their nurse training.

The beginning of the third year of training brought changes to the Victoria Hospital. They were advised to prepare for receiving soldiers from the battlefields. It was the only topic of conversation between the staff as, although they all wanted to do their bit, they were worried about the different types of nursing that would be required.

Major overhauls took place in the wards. The two orthopaedic wards were changed into male military wards and the accident ward was extended to provide more beds. Only emergency operations were carried out, so that the beds could be reserved for the soldiers.

News filtered through of a big push that was taking place in France. It was rumoured that this could end the war. All that war did was make many more young men dead and families in mourning, with no end of the war in sight. As the soldiers gained a foot or two of land, the enemy grabbed it back, and so the battle went on, slowly. It also made a lot more work for nurses and doctors as they attempted to heal the so-called lucky ones who survived, but were left maimed in some way.

During the third year of their training, 1915, groups of wounded soldiers started to arrive at the Victoria Hospital. Many of the nurses were moved on to these wards so that the soldiers could have the best nursing care. Some of the nurses didn't like caring for the soldiers, as they were complex cases and some of them had lost limbs or their faces were damaged.

Amy and Molly didn't feel like that. They liked helping the soldiers. Sister Tutor said that they could stay on the ward for the rest of their training as they were learning more on that ward than they would on the other wards. The only drawback was Sister Brown. She was a downright tyrant and the two girls both hated her. Whatever they did, it was wrong and even though they tried their level best, it still seemed to fall below Sister Brown's standards.

The other nurses on the ward didn't seem to get the same reaction from Sister Brown, although she wasn't particularly pleasant with any of the staff. At one stage, the staff nurse stood up to Sister about her treatment of Molly and Amy but it made no difference. In fact, it was even worse afterwards.

But Molly and Amy just kept their heads down and worked hard at their studies. Some days Molly was ecstatic when she had a letter from Edwin and she waited eagerly for his leave, which never happened. Soon, it was time for their State Final Examinations. If they passed them, they would be allowed to write SRN after their name, to show that they were State Registered Nurses, and take up a post as a staff nurse. The exams were hard, but a question on wound care was easy for Molly and Amy: they had spent hours caring for wounds on the soldiers. The practical exams were also easier since they had made great progress in bandaging and setting up trolleys since being on the soldiers' ward.

At long last, the girls were summoned by Matron to receive their results, before they were posted on the dining room wall. Victoria went in first, being the first alphabetically. She came out with a glowing face. It was agony for Amy as she and Sophia were at the end. Eventually, they all went in and received the same news. They had passed and were State Registered Nurses. Matron even smiled, for the first time in their career, they all commented.

Once they had all been in individually, Matron called them back in together. She explained that as there was a war on, the girls could do no better than stay here, looking after the soldiers. Besides, she said, they ought to stay at their training hospital as a thank you to the hospital for having trained them.

'Matron, if you please, I would like to go and do midwifery training,' said Laura.

'Why is that, Stockburn?'

'My mother died in childbirth. I'd like to help other mothers.'

'Very commendable, Stockburn. Would you like me to put a word in with Matron Dawson down at Bank Hall Maternity Hospital?'

'If you please Matron, I come from Blackburn. I would prefer to go back to train at Blackburn.'

'Very well, I shall write to Matron Bell at Blackburn. Now, Windle and May, Sister Stockdale on Eye ward says she would like you to stay on her ward.'

'Thank you Matron,' replied Emily for both of them. The Eye ward had been Emily's first ward and she had always loved it best. Thank goodness I didn't get the Eye ward, thought Amy. She had hated the Eye ward; couldn't stand some of the treatments they had to do on there. Give me blood and guts anytime rather than eyes, she thought.

The other girls were all given posts until there was only Molly and Amy left. 'Probably no one wants us,' whispered Molly to Amy.

'Now, Smith and Wilson, Sister Brown has specifically asked that you are given posts on her ward. What's the matter, you look surprised? I'll have you know that this is a great honour. Sister Brown is very choosy whom she picks.'

'Thank you Matron. We're surprised because of the honour she has given us,' squawked Amy, whilst Molly was too stunned to speak.

'Right, that's all of you settled. You may go.'

'Thank you Matron,' they all chorused and got out of her office as quick as they could.

'Fancy old Brown asking for you two,' remarked Olivia. 'I thought she made your lives miserable?'

'She does. Picks on us all the time. She must be some kind of sadist, then.'

'Perhaps she'll be nicer to you, now that you're qualified,' said Victoria and they all laughed at the unlikeliness of that. They had all been at the mercy of Sister Brown at some stage during their training.

But strangely as it seemed, Victoria's prophecy was almost right. Sister Brown was different with them. Yes, she still shouted at them and made their lives a misery at times, but she was more respectful of them; more understanding. That's the only way they could explain it; it was a very subtle difference. But they weren't necessarily unhappy. They were still learning a lot from Sister Brown, for all she liked the sound of her own voice.

The war dragged on, with heavy losses on both sides. It felt as if they had always been at war and there would never be an end to it. Molly continued to get letters from Edwin and spent a lot of time writing back to him. He had only managed to get a short leave from the hostilities but Molly was able to get some holiday so that she could spend time with him.

One day, whilst they were doing dressings, Molly said that she wanted to talk to Amy tonight.

'Why not now?' asked Amy.

'No, it's better tonight. Too many ears around on the ward.' Amy was mystified but Molly wouldn't be drawn any further.

After their shift finished, Amy dived on Molly and demanded to know what she had to say that she couldn't tell on the ward.

'I've decided to apply for another job.'

'Where? On Female medical? I know that you liked it on there,' asked Amy.

'No. Further afield than here.'

'Blackburn?' asked Amy.

'No. France. I've decided to join the Queen Alexandria's nursing corps. Or the Queen Alexandria's Imperial Military Nursing Service, to give it the full title. QAIMNS they're calling it for short.' Amy was silent. Eventually she spoke.

'What's made you decide that?' she asked quietly.

'I want to be near Edwin. And besides, I want to do my bit for the war. Why should it just be the men who have to go to war? I know we can't fight as women, but at least we can be there, helping our men.'

'But you won't be near Edwin. You could be miles away and never see him. And anyway, you're doing your bit by working on the ward here in Burnley,' replied Amy.

'I know, but I can't explain it, I just want to be nearer him.'

'I suppose you're right. They were asking for more volunteers in the Nursing Times recently, weren't they?' The two girls were silent for a moment, then Amy spoke suddenly.

'All right. When do we go?'

'We?' asked a bemused Molly.

'Well, you don't think you're going without me, do you?

'Honestly? You'll come with me? Oh Amy, that's great. I must admit I was worried how I would cope without the friendship that I've had here. I'm so happy. Here are the application forms, we could send them off together.'

'I hope we'll be allowed to stay together,' said Amy.

'Perhaps if we apply together, we'll get sorted out at the same time and so stay together.'

'Well, we can but try. Now give me those application details before I change my mind.'

'Bags I tell Sister Brown that we're leaving,' shouted Molly.

'I want to tell her,' replied Amy.

'It was my idea first.'

'All right then, you tell her, and then I'll tell her I'm going too straight after.' The two girls fell about laughing, their joy in anticipating telling Sister Brown what was happening, overshadowing any anxieties they might have about going to France.

The next few weeks flew by, as their applications were accepted and approved and they found themselves in another training school, learning about working under battle conditions and other essential information necessary during wartime. The news came that the whole of the group would be travelling together to France. Amy and Molly were delighted. Also, they had made good friends with

Jocelyn, Madeleine, and Celia and were glad they were going to be together.

Chapter 13

The charabanc ground to a bone shaking halt as the driver yanked the brake on. The girls shuddered in their seats, trying to protect their sore arms, where they had received their typhoid and enteric fever injections. Eventually they started to gather their belongings together. The driver stood up and shouted to all the occupants.

'Don't move yet, I need to report to this office and find out where we are going. You wait here and don't move off the charabanc,' he barked. He stomped down the steps and disappeared into the office. The door was left open and Amy could smell the sea. It was the first time that she had been near the sea since being rescued from the lifeboat, except for their time at Blackpool and then she had only looked at the sea, not gone near it or sailed on it.

Her heart began to pound and she became agitated. What would she feel like as she got into the boat? Would she be able to stand a journey across the sea again? Why had she not considered this before? She knew that going to France involved a sea journey, so why was she not prepared? Her wild thoughts were interrupted by the return of the driver.

'Right then. I'm going to drive the charabanc down to the embarkation point where you'll be setting off from.' He quickly started up the crank and eventually the engine fired. He drove down nearer to the sea and then ordered the girls off.

'That's where you have to wait,' he shouted. 'You'll be leaving within the hour.' Fortunately it was fine, but it was a cold night and the girls were soon feeling the effect of the chill. They talked quietly between themselves, and eventually some light-hearted banter commenced. Amy ignored the chatter and stared transfixed at the boat that was in front of them. It was a mere toy one compared with the last ship she had sailed in. The waves were lapping into shore and breaking against the boat's side. The noise was making Amy feel nauseous, even though she had always been a good traveller before that fateful trip.

'You all right?' murmured Molly. Amy simply nodded, without looking away from the boat and the sea. The voices of the other girls were getting louder and snippets of the conversation penetrated Amy's brain.

'Looks a right old tub, does this one,' joked Celia.
'Yes, hope it doesn't sink,' replied Jocelyn.
'Is its name Titanic? laughed Celia. Amy's heart began to pound harder; sweat pouring on her brow. There was a rushing sound in her ears. She was aware of Molly holding her hand and speaking to her, but she couldn't make out what she was saying.
'Perhaps we should write to our nearest and dearest in case we don't make it,' roared Jocelyn.
Blackness seemed to be swirling in Amy's brain, like the colour of the sea. Quietly, she sank to the floor and lost consciousness.
Molly dropped down to Amy and cradled her head on her lap. 'You fools,' she shouted harshly, 'what did you say that for? Didn't you know that Amy was on the Titanic? That this is the first time she has been near the sea or a boat since then?' The group had gone suddenly silent at Molly's outburst. Madeleine was the first to recover her wits.
'Can I help you, Molly? Shall I get a blanket from somewhere?' Molly shot her a grateful glance.
'No, I think she's coming round now. Amy, can you hear me? Are you all right?' Amy stirred and tried to sit up. 'Stay there a minute Amy. Let's make sure that you haven't hurt yourself. Do you feel all right?'
'Er, yes, I think I'm all right. What happened? Did I faint?'
'It was our fault Amy,' said a contrite Celia. 'Jocelyn and I were joking about the boat. We didn't know about . . .er . . y'know, what happened. We didn't mean any harm, just a joke really,' she finished lamely. Amy gave a wan smile and sat up.
'Don't worry, no bones broken,' replied Amy getting up. The girls chatted quietly to each other after this, whilst Amy and Molly stood apart from the crowd.
'It does feel strange to be going on a boat,' said Amy to Molly quietly. 'I never really thought about it before. But as soon as I smelt the sea and then saw the boat and the waves lashing, it brought it all back.'
'Don't think about it anymore, Amy. That's all in the past. Let's look to our future. It can't be worse. At least we'll have no more Sister Brown to worry about in France.'
'We might even have a worse Sister,' giggled Amy.

'Never,' roared Molly, 'I can't imagine anyone worse than Sister Brown. Besides, we'll be Sisters now.' The two girls laughed together, recalling stories of Sister Brown and Molly was able to divert Amy from her worries. Before long, they were climbing on the boat and too busy vying to get the best bunks to be worried about the sea.

Amy bagged the top bunk and Molly the lower one. 'I've no head for heights, Amy. I'm glad you wanted the top one. Just don't fall out and land on top of me in the middle of the night.'

'Don't worry, I won't. We won't be on the boat for that long anyway, we can have a rest and then we'll be there. There was no chance of sleeping on that charabanc. No wonder people call them boneshakers,' replied Amy.

'True, after years of nursing and longing to sit down, I never thought I'd yearn to stand for a long time. Oh my poor posterior.'

'At least we're used to standing. Especially during Matron's rounds. Oh weren't they agony? All having to stand to attention throughout the whole performance. I'm sure she took her time just to make us miserable.'

'I bet they don't have Matron's rounds in France. They won't have time,' replied Molly.

'Good. I'm sure that Florence Nightingale used to do rounds, but battles today are more powerful.'

'You mean that men are getting better at killing themselves?' said Molly cynically.

'Yes. Those stories about the soldiers and the mustard gas are awful. There is so little that we can do for them. It must be hard to nurse them,' said a mournful Amy.

'Not much worse than those moaning old biddies we had to care for sometimes, Amy.'

'Oh Molly, don't be nasty. They couldn't help it. I don't mind helping people who can't help themselves.'

'That's rather philosophical for a Saturday evening.'

'Hmm, I was thinking about the people who were in the same asylum as me, when I was a patient. The staff had helped me there, and I wanted to help other people. That's why I came to Burnley to do my nursing training.'

'Well, I'm glad you did. Otherwise we would have never met. And anyway, you'll certainly get the chance to do that in France.'
'What?' said a bemused Amy.
'Help people. And meet lots of eligible young men into the bargain,' chuckled Molly.
'Honestly Molly. Is that all you can think of?'
'No, I'm also thinking that I'm going to visit France. Nobody in my family has ever been further than Blackpool before. Apart from my brothers of course. Mind you, they haven't been too impressed with France up to now. Mud, mud and more mud, is all they say when we ask. And Edwin says the same too.'
'Perhaps we'll meet up with them when we are in France.'
'I hope not.'
'Why not? I thought you were all very close. And you've spent so little time with Edwin.'
'We are close, and I'd love to see Edwin, but the only way I'd get chance to see them is if they were in a hospital bed.'
'Oh, I never thought about that, sorry Molly.'
'Our Jimmy would be made up if he met you, though. Sweet on you, he is.'
'Don't be silly,' said a blushing Amy.
'Well why else would he ask me to send a picture photograph of us both? Not of me on my own, you understand, but us two together.'
'I'm sure I don't know. I'm quite looking forward to going to France. I think I've been before, but I can't really remember.'
'It must be awful to have lost your memory.'
'Mmm, it is. Hey, listen Molly.'
'What?'
'We're moving.'
'Yes. So what?'
'I hadn't noticed.'
'Oh good, it worked then.'
'What worked?'
'Keeping you talking, whilst we set off.'
'Yes, it did, Molly. Thanks. I feel much better now. In fact, I think I could go to sleep now. Night night.'
'Night.'

After an uneventful crossing, the boat landed in France and they were transferred over to a hospital near the battle front in of all things, a London bus. Molly and Amy stayed together but the other three friends were sent to another hospital.

But nothing in their brief military training prepared them for what they saw in the first few hours. The building was already a hospital in civilian times so there were little changes made to it apart from a much larger accident ward.

Molly was assigned to the casualty receiving room and Amy to a ward. They fondly imagined that they would start the next day after travelling, but they were both wrong. Before they had even put their things away in the cupboard, they received a call to go to the casualty receiving room.

'But I'm assigned to a ward,' protested Amy.

'Look girl, when I say casualty receiving room, that's where I mean. We've just had notification that a fleet of ambulances and buses are on their way here, so move!' barked an older Sister who looked very tired.

Amy and Molly needed no further orders. They got into their uniform and hurried off to the casualty receiving room. It was mayhem. There were people all over the room, nurses and doctors rushing around, trolleys being laid up in waiting and earlier casualties being transferred up to the ward, to make space for the newcomers.

And then the first ambulance arrived. The patients were taken into the casualty receiving room and sorted out into priority. Sadly, some had died on the way, and they were put into a building outside, fondly called Ward Thirteen by the orderlies. Some men were designated for immediate surgery and others for the waiting ward, but they would have a long wait for their restorative surgery.

Molly and Amy realised that the men they had nursed in the Victoria Hospital were a long way towards recovery compared with these men. The men here were coming straight from the battlefields and still had the remnants of uniform on; most if it covered in blood and in some cases blown away.

The men were all in different stages of pain, from stoically bearing it, to screaming in agony as treatment was instigated. There was often no time for anaesthetic to deaden the pain, but emergency surgery was done as fast as possible, partly to save the soldier's life, but also to get on to the next patient, waiting in line. Molly and Amy were involved in cleaning the initial wounds to assess what priority was needed. They had never had to do anything like this before. At home, patients were clean and orderly compared with these patients.

These soldiers were none too clean either and Amy was horrified to see lice crawling about their bodies and hair. But she didn't let it stop her caring for the men to the best of her ability.

The doctors were amazing. Gone was the snooty attitude of the doctors at home. These doctors were working round the clock and looked as if they hadn't had a wash in years. In fact, some of them looked as bad as the soldiers. And even more amazingly, they spoke to the nurses and knew their names.

Amy was working with a doctor for a few minutes when he spoke to her.

'You're new, aren't you? What's your name?'

'Wilson, Sir,' replied Amy, used to years of hospital etiquette.

'No, first name,' he said. 'Don't bother with surnames here. Haven't time to learn them,' he laughed; never stopping sewing up the soldier that he was dealing with.

'Amy,' she replied.

'Amy? Right. I'm Jack. Now could you hold this arm up a bit higher? Great. Is it your first trip, Amy?'

'Yes, only arrived today, not even unpacked my bag,' laughed Amy back. He was easy to chat to was this doctor. She looked closer at him. He must have been about sixty years old; surely he should have been thinking about retiring not working in a battlefield. He had bright blue twinkly eyes and a shock of white hair and Amy knew that she was going to like working with him. As if he could hear what she was thinking, Jack suddenly said, 'I've just retired from the army. Decorated in the Boer War. Thought I'd finished with all this nonsense. But you have to do your bit.'

'But surely you could have done your bit by staying at home caring for the sick, without putting yourself through all this?

'No, not as much fun. Besides, I know the ropes in battle hospitals,' he said. 'Now, let's move on to the next boy. Mmm, that leg'll have to come off. It's blighty for you, young man. Just hold it there, Amy. Good, now steady.' Whilst Jack was working on the leg, Amy tried to talk to the young man. There had been no anaesthetic, only a morphine injection. Eventually he fainted, holding Amy's hand. Amy had never seen a surgeon work so quickly. The boy was bound up and ready for the recovery ward before she knew it. Jack washed his hands under the tap and then shouted 'Come on Amy, next one.'

Amy gave the soldier over to the orderly who was taking him to the recovery ward and after washing her hands, followed Jack to the next soldier.

This boy was unconscious already so Jack got on with sewing him up as quickly as possible.

'You're very quick, Jack. I've never seen a surgeon work so quickly.'

'Years of practice. Don't forget, when I trained as a doctor, there were no anaesthetics, so you had to be quick. And working in the Boer War didn't give you chance to slow down. You never knew when those Boers were going to attack, so you had to operate quickly, with one eye over your shoulder,' he laughed.

The two of them worked solidly together, never stopping for several hours. Amy was amazed at his stamina. Suddenly he shouted to her to stop.

'Come on Amy, it's our break time. Leave them to the others. Come with me.' Other staff came across and took over what they were doing and Jack led Amy away from the casualty receiving room into a room further down the corridor.

A jug of coffee was standing on a heated tray and Amy gratefully received a cup from Jack. He also gave her a large sandwich. There were one or two other doctors in the room, but no nurses, Amy noted.

'And who have we here, Jack? Got your self another little friend?' a man asked him.

Jack laughed. 'Well, Arthur, I had to replace Annie. I've missed her so much. I think Amy'll do fine as Annie's replacement, so hands off, find your own nurse.'

'But I'm due to go on a ward,' bleated Amy. All the men laughed.

'Not now you won't,' laughed another doctor, a very tall man. 'Old Jack is the senior doctor in this outfit and what he says goes. He gets the pick of all the staff and leaves us with the bones.'

'Besides,' said Arthur, 'he hasn't had a battle with Matron for a day or two, so this'll be his latest crusade. The battle for Amy.'

Amy stood amazed at the way the conversation was going.

'Who was Annie?' asked Amy eventually.
'A fine nurse. Able to put up with all Jack's foibles. Sadly she had to go back to England to nurse her husband. He was injured in the trenches. I hope you have a strong constitution, Amy?'
'I think so,' replied Amy cautiously.
'Good,' said Jack 'and now I suppose we'd better get back to work.' Just as they were about to go, the door opened and Matron entered the room.
'Nurse? What are you doing here, in the doctors' mess?'
'I didn't know. .' Amy started to say, when Jack interrupted.
'I brought her here, Matron, any objection?' Matron's lips pursed, but she said nothing. Jack continued, 'we'd been working all afternoon without a break. It's easier to bring her with me, then as soon as I'm ready to get back to work, she is ready too. Makes sense doesn't it Matron? The girl's only just arrived this afternoon and doesn't know the rules yet. Silly rule anyway if you ask me.'
'I wasn't asking you, Major Bowes.'
'No, I suppose not. Oh by the way, Matron. I want Amy on my team in casualty receiving room. See to it will you?'

Matron pursed her lips even further, then said 'If you say so Major. I will reorganise the other new arrivals,' then she left the room, her head held high.

Amy worried that she had made an enemy of Matron on her first day. Oh well, she thought to herself, after Sister Brown, I can cope with anything, and scurried off after Jack.

Chapter 14

It was nightfall before Amy was allowed to leave. In all that time, she hadn't seen Molly once. They met up in the dining room and compared notes; Molly looking in horror when Amy described being in the doctors' mess with Jack, and Matron walking in. They soon went to bed and fell asleep as soon as their heads hit the pillows.

Next day, there was a message that Amy had indeed to go to the casualty receiving room instead of the ward, and Molly was to take her place on the ward.

'The old doctor has won, then,' laughed Molly, 'he must have power here, if Matron does as she is told.'

'Do you mind, Molly? I feel that you've been pushed out.'

'Not at all. No doubt I'll be going there at some other time. After yesterday, I don't mind at all. I've never been so busy in all my life.'

'So you would like to go back to Male Orthopaedics for a rest, with Sister Brown then?'

'No, I'm not that desperate!' replied Molly laughing.

The next day was much like the first and all the days afterwards. Time had never gone so quickly for Amy and Molly and they barely had time to speak to each other.

Amy was glad that she was working with Jack. He was so easy to work with and soon she was anticipating what he was going to need or use. Each day, she went to the doctors' mess with Jack and was pleased to hear him tell another doctor that she was even better than the famous Annie.

Occasionally there were lulls in the ambulances arriving, but on the whole, there was a relentless queue of traffic. During one lull, Jack sent Amy out for some fresh air.

'It's important for you to keep going out; the air gets too stale in here. Go on, have five minutes. I'll come with you. Need a fag anyway.' Jack and Amy went outside and he lit a cigarette.

'Do you smoke?' he asked.

'Me, no of course not,' said Amy.

'Some women do. Was going to offer you one, but I won't bother. Waste of money anyway. And they're in short supply over here.

'Looks like the break may be over, I can see an ambulance coming,' said Amy.

'We'll stay here a bit longer. We can weigh the casualties up from here as it passes.'

The ambulance drew nearer and stopped outside the casualty receiving ward. The ambulance driver jumped out of the cab and ran round to the back of the vehicle. Amy watched him working and liked what she saw. His movements were quick and lithe; he was a tall thin man with a mop of dark brown hair, flopping under his cap. He was wearing his hair longer than was usual in the army, and it curled round his ears and into the nape of his neck.

His face looked sensitive and caring as he lifted the patients out of his ambulance and yet he had a strong jaw line. His eyebrows were thick and well defined and . . .

'Amy, Amy, what's the matter with you girl?

Amy pulled her gaze away from the young man and turned to Jack.

'What's the matter?' she stammered.

'I've been speaking to you for ages. Were you in a trance?' He shook his head and turned towards the young man. 'Hello Geoffrey. How are you? Not seen you for a bit. What've you brought us today?'

'Hi Jack. Just a couple of minor injuries. Poor lads couldn't get an ambulance yesterday, so they've only had first aid in the trenches.'

Amy stood transfixed whilst Jack was talking to Geoffrey. Geoffrey, she tried the name on her lips without speaking out loud. She hadn't known a Geoffrey before, but it was a name she approved of. She liked his voice as well. Strong and comforting. Suddenly, she realised that they were both looking at her, as if they were waiting for an answer.

She smiled and hoped that Jack would repeat what he or Geoffrey had said to her. She hadn't a clue. She had been too busy admiring Geoffrey. What was the matter with her, she wondered. She'd never been like that before.

'I was introducing you to Geoffrey, Amy. Are you back from your trance now?'

Geoffrey laughed. A deep laugh that shook his whole body. 'I wish I could go in a trance now and then. Make my job a lot easier. Now what were you going in a trance about, Amy? I can't wait to hear,' asked Geoffrey.

Amy blushed and couldn't think what to say. She'd been in a trance because of him, but she couldn't say that. Jack was looking at her closely but didn't say anything to help her.

'I, er, I was . .'

'Yes, I'm all ears,' asked Geoffrey, his eyes twinkling at Amy.

'I was thinking what a hard job you have,' answered Amy lamely.

'No harder than you, I shouldn't think. Beats being in the trenches and getting shot at. Although some of the Hun have had a try at shooting me. Obviously don't understand the meaning of a Red Cross on my ambulance.'

'Amy is one of our new nurses.'

'Pleased to meet you. Where are you from?' asked Geoffrey. Amy's heart sank. Why this continual obsession with where you came from.

'I'm not sure. I was on the Titanic and I sort of lost my memory afterwards.'

'Why that's awful! You could be a rich heiress and missed out on claiming your inheritance. You wouldn't need to be working anymore, then.'

Amy gasped. He was so near the truth that she was speechless. Geoffrey immediately apologised after he saw the dreadful look on her face, and touched her arm. His hand felt warm and strong and made her tingle.

'It's all right. I should get used to people asking me about my past,' said Amy miserably.

'Hey, stop upsetting my best nurse,' Jack interrupted.

'Wouldn't dream of it. Wish she was my best nurse,' replied Geoffrey, smiling at Amy. 'But for now, I'd like her to be best nurse to my patients. They've had a long wait. By the way, I'd take some leave if you can. Apparently there's going to be another big push.'

Jack groaned. 'Thanks for nothing, Geoffrey. As if we haven't been busy enough. Now let's see what you've got here.'

Amy and Jack looked at the patients and took them in to the treatment area. Neither had life threatening injuries, so they were patched up and sent up to the ward to recuperate. They would soon be returned to the trenches to carry on the fight.

Geoffrey had returned to the battlefield to collect more patients, leaving Amy thinking about him all day. Even Jack noticed her mind wasn't on her work.

'What's the matter girl? You've gone all thoughtful on me. Sorry if Geoffrey upset you.'

'No, he didn't upset me.'

'Didn't know myself about your past, or lack of past, should I say. I'd have fended the question off for you. You should have said earlier. Don't get much chance to talk much, do we?'

'No,' said Amy ruefully. 'I don't even know anything about you, and where you come from.'

'Not much to know about me. Born in Cannock in Staffordshire. Got two sisters, Margaret and Angela. Got three nieces and nephews. That's about it.'

'Have you never been married Jack?' asked Amy, but regretted it as soon as she watched his face crumble. But as fast as it did, he wiped the look from his face and gently smiled back.

'Yes, I was married once. To Marjorie. She died in childbirth, our son with her. I've been married to the army ever since. Doesn't break your heart, doesn't the army.'

'I'm sorry Jack. I didn't know.'

'And I didn't know about your past, so let's leave it at that. We have work to do.'

Amy carried on with her work, but couldn't stop thinking about Geoffrey. In the end she asked Jack about him.

'Why's Geoffrey not in the army? He's seems a fit young man,' asked Amy. 'Is he a conscientious objector? A Quaker or something? Most of them are ambulance drivers, I've heard.'

'Dear me no, you couldn't be farther from the truth. Geoffrey would've been in the army at the first bullet being fired, but they wouldn't have him. Nor the Navy. Nor the new Flying Corps. He tried his hardest, but he has a fast heartbeat – tachycardia of unknown origin they call it, so they wouldn't let him serve. He wasn't pleased and so volunteered for ambulance service. Apparently his mother was not happy about that. She was quite glad that her precious son wouldn't be fighting. He's the heir, you see. And they haven't got a spare. All girls apart from him.'

'You seem to know a lot about him,' said Amy.

'Yes, we spend an evening together now and then. He's a good chap. I've been trying to persuade him to train as a doctor. He's very good with the patients and seems to have a natural instinct for helping them to survive, above and beyond the training that they're given. But he won't hear of it. Says he has to go and run the estate; it's his rightful duty. Shame really. Could do with more good chaps in the medical profession. You'd make a good doctor, Amy. Perhaps I should pin my hopes on you.'

'Me? A doctor? I don't think so. Women doctors aren't very popular. Hardly any of them are being taken seriously yet.'

'But that will all change after this war. Women have taken on jobs that they've never done before. No, this war will have done more for the Suffragette movement than all their window smashing and chaining themselves to railings ever did. The government couldn't have managed without them. One of the other ambulance drivers was a big noise in the Suffragettes. Maisie, she's called. She's certainly achieved equality now. Works as hard as any man and doesn't expect any allowances for being of the fairer sex.'

'I think I've seen her. Tall girl with red hair?'

'Yes, that's her. Temper to match as well,' Jack giggled. 'She could put a navvy to shame when she's riled.'

'It seems to have quietened down here. Do you think what Geoffrey said was right? About the big push?'

'Probably. The ambulance men and women seem to know what's going on most of the time. I suggest you get some rest. Just in case.'

The next few days were quiet. Too quiet, said Jack. He reckoned it was the quiet before the storm. How right he was. Suddenly in mid July, all hell broke loose. There was a steady stream of ambulances coming one after another. The only time Amy saw Molly was in the receiving room, as Molly came down to help assess the wounded soldiers.

Everyone worked for hours on end, getting no breaks, and collapsing in exhaustion at the end of the day. Sometimes, they didn't even get a full night in bed, as calls were made for help when a new batch of ambulances arrived.

Despite working hard, Amy was never too busy to look out for Geoffrey, and snatch a few words of conversation with him when she could. Although she hardly knew him, he was beginning to be important to her, but she chided herself for being silly. He hadn't shown any interest in her, so why let her thoughts wander, she rationalised. But her thoughts refused to be rational and his face came into her mind unbidden.

After a hundred days of onslaught, the chaos stopped as quickly as it had started and things returned to their less chaotic ways. Soldiers being brought into the hospital said that just a few yards of ground had been gained during these hundred days, and yet thousands of men had been slaughtered, lost or maimed.

One young boy that arrived wept continually for his friend who had been sucked down into the mud and couldn't be found. Whole battalions had been wiped out in a day. Bodies buried where they fell. It was so senseless, just for a few yards. Amy wept that night when she got off duty. When would this carnage end? There was just no sense to it all.

As the work calmed down for a while, Jack was sent off on holiday for a week. Matron immediately transferred Amy to the ward, and put Molly in the receiving room.

The girls laughed about that. They knew Matron was having her moment of power without Jack thwarting her at every turn. Amy quite welcomed the change, all except for one thing. She would not see Geoffrey on the ward and she fretted about this. She had looked forward to his almost daily visits with a sense of anticipation.

But she need not have worried. A few nights later, Molly brought her a letter and was full of mystery when she gave it to Amy.

Amy took it and shoved it in her pocket, as if it was of no import, but Molly wasn't having any of that and pestered her to open the letter. Amy did and her heart leapt when she saw that it was from Geoffrey. It said that he'd missed her in the receiving room and he wondered if she would go out for a walk with him. Amy sat down with the sheer emotion that surged through her. He wanted to go a walk with her. He must like her as well. She couldn't hide the joy on her face and turned to look at Molly.

'Now what's been going on that you haven't told Molly about' she asked. 'Having me carry letters from young men? You never mentioned him, Amy. Keeping secrets from your best friend are you?'

'There's nothing to tell. We've just talked a few times. And anyway, who are you to criticise me about secrets? You went and got MARRIED without telling me.'

It was Molly's turn to look embarrassed. 'True, but it was quite sudden with Edwin signing up, especially since we were in training. I'd have been thrown out if Sister Tutor had found out. Anyway, what does the letter say?'

'He's asked me to go a walk.'

'So shall I tell him that you are not that sort of girl and you haven't been properly introduced, and you can't possibly go for a walk without a chaperone?'

'Stop it Molly. Of course I can go a walk with him if I want to. I have nobody to answer to.'

'I could come with you as a chaperone, me being a respectable married woman . . .' but suddenly a pillow landing on her head and knocking her over interrupted her. 'Hey, be careful. I nearly fell off the bed then.'

'Well next time, I'll make sure my aim is better,' laughed Amy. 'Now leave me alone. I have a letter to write.'

'Are you going to go for a walk with him?'

'Yes I am.'

'Mmm. Could my little friend be smitten at long last? Will I need to be getting a bridesmaid frock at long last?' teased Molly.

'Don't get carried away, Molly. He's only asked me for a walk, not to elope.'

'Hey, no talk of eloping. You missed my wedding but I'm definitely not going to miss yours.'

'Don't worry; I'll let you know well in advance. I hardly think he's going to propose on a first date now is he?'

'You never know. Some men work fast these days,' warned Molly.

'Oh be quiet Molly. I won't have time to write this letter if you don't shut up and then I won't be going a walk, never mind getting married.' Amy turned her back on Molly and wrote a note to Geoffrey saying she'd be delighted to take a walk with him.

Via Molly as a messenger, they managed to arrange a time and date for their walk. Amy could hardly wait. She looked at her meagre number of dresses and despaired. She picked out her best brown one, but even so, it was very mundane. After spending five years in uniform, there had been no need for lots of clothes and they hadn't been encouraged to bring many clothes with them, because of storage space. They were hardly going to many balls, the training sister dryly reminded them.

Chapter 15

On the evening of the walk, Amy washed her hair and brushed it until it shone. She caught the brush in her birthmark and was suddenly swept back to the old life and remembered telling Lizzie off for not being careful. Poor Lizzie. She hadn't thought about her for weeks now. At least helping all these poor soldiers was trying to repay her debt to Lizzie and the life she had led before. But she mustn't let her guilt surface tonight. She must concentrate on Geoffrey and the future.

With her heart pounding as if it would burst, Amy went to the end of the hospital drive, where she had arranged to meet Geoffrey. Thank goodness rules were much more relaxed here. Her usual hat and gloves had even been discarded for this evening appointment; a thing she would never do in England. She would never have been allowed to go out with a young man if Home Sister had been around. Amy laughed as she walked down the drive. She was twenty-four and this was the first time that she had been going out to meet a man.

If she had not been on the Titanic, she would probably have been married for three or four years and had children by now. What was the matter with her tonight? All these thoughts of her former life, when usually, she could keep them well below the surface.

Then she saw Geoffrey, walking towards her and her heart surged with joy. He hurried towards her and thrust a posy of wild flowers in her hands, keeping hold of her hands for quite a while as he did.

'I'm sorry they're only wild flowers, they're the best available in this neck of the woods.'

'No, they are lovely, thank you.'

'You look lovely without your nurse's hat. Your hair is like a golden halo round your head. It suits you so short.'

'It's just a lot easier to look after out here. I've had it so short for about five years and didn't want to grow it back.'

'Good, it suits you. If we were in England I would have taken you to the theatre and brought chocolates and an orchid nosegay.'

'Stop worrying Geoffrey. I'm just happy to spend some time alone with you.'

'Really? You're really happy just to walk with me.'

'Yes, so come on, let's walk,' said Amy and held out her arm to him. He quickly took hold of her proffered arm and led her away down the road towards the village. At first they didn't talk, just happy to be together, but slowly they talked about everything under the sun. He talked about his mother and how jealous she was of him, and hated him being a volunteer ambulance driver.

'A manipulative woman is my mother, even though I love her dearly, I don't always like her. If she could have found a reason for me not to get accepted as an ambulance volunteer, I'm sure she would have done. My dad just agrees with her most of the time. Anything for a quiet life is his policy. As long as he can have his dogs, go hunting and smoke his pipe, he is happy. You've told me that you lost your memory since the Titanic. Do you remember your parents at all?'

Amy hesitated. She wanted to tell Geoffrey the whole truth from the beginning; to have no secrets from him, but she didn't think she could tell him everything yet. The pain would be too much.

'I don't think I have anyone left since the Titanic. Nobody came to claim me. But I can tell you about my life since then,' said Amy; pleased that she had said enough but not told any lies. Perhaps one day she would tell him more.

'What's your first memory after the Titanic then?'

'You mean after the black fog lifted?'

'Black fog? What do you mean?'

'I sort of had a black fog inside my head that stopped me thinking or speaking or reacting to anything. Then the fog started to lift and I started being aware of things again. I noticed the room I was in and the people around me.'

'Where was this room?' Geoffrey asked.

Amy blushed. 'It was an asylum. They'd put me in there because I couldn't speak and say who I was. Apparently I was dressed in maids clothing purchased in the North of England. So they put me in an asylum in the North of England. When I came round properly, I got a job at the asylum. I couldn't go on living there really, once I had recovered. The Matron then got me a place to train as a nurse in Burnley, in Lancashire. That's where I met Molly. We've been close friends ever since.'

Amy stopped speaking. She'd probably spoilt this lovely friendship now, telling him she was from the asylum. But it didn't matter. Geoffrey stopped walking and drew her into the circle of his arms. Amy felt safe, comfortable, at home in his arms and relaxed against him.

'I'm so sorry Amy,' he whispered in her hair. 'You've had an awful life, haven't you?' To Amy's consternation, she burst into tears. This was the first time that anyone had ever offered her physical comfort for what she had been through, apart from Molly.

'Please don't cry, you'll end up making me cry,' said Geoffrey with a catch in his voice. But it made Amy laugh instead.

'You? Cry? I don't think you will,' she laughed, but without drawing away from his arms.

'No, I won't cry now, because you've stopped crying. Oh look, there is a teardrop still on your lashes.' He leaned forward and gently kissed it away, then moved ever so slowly to the tip of her nose, and then to her lips. At first, he kissed her gently, but then with more force, always watching her, to make sure that it was what she wanted; ready to withdraw if he was offending her or trying to make her do what she didn't want to. But it was what Amy wanted. Most definitely. She felt as if she was sinking into his arms and she would fall if she didn't hold him tightly.

Eventually he drew away from her lips, but continued to gaze into her eyes.

'I think I'm falling in love with you, Amy. I can't think about anything else. You're in my thoughts all the time.'

Amy felt that her heart would burst with happiness.

'Me too,' she managed to whisper back before his lips swept down on her lips again, taking her breath away.

Suddenly, Geoffrey pulled away for her, his voice ragged, his eyes deep pools of brown.

'Amy, you're doing terrible things to me. Let's start walking again or I might not be responsible for my actions.'

He set off down the path, pulling Amy behind him until they reached the village. They strolled round for a while and then had a drink at the village inn, before turning back home again. They talked incessantly about everything and nothing. But mostly about what they were feeling for each other, in this wondrous state of emerging love. Temporarily the war was forgotten.

The evening came to an end far too quickly and they both pledged to meet again as soon as possible. Amy went home on a cloud of happiness; a smile on her face that looked as if it was fixed. It was this that Molly noticed first.

'I take it you've had a nice time then? Judging by the silly smile on your face!' teased Molly.

'Oh Molly, it was wonderful. He is wonderful. I've had a marvellous time.'

'My goodness Amy, you have got it bad. I knew it'd happen to you some day. You laughed at me when I told you how I felt about Edwin, but now I can say "I told you so," can't I?'

'Now I understand why you wanted to get married to Edwin in such a rush.'

'Cor, he hasn't asked you to marry him, has he?'

'No, of course not. Don't be silly.'

'Well I suppose we'd better get off to sleep now. We've an early start tomorrow, love or no love.'

But Amy couldn't sleep. Her mind going over and over again what they had said and done; the strange feelings that had happened to her body when he kissed her; the desire for him to kiss her again and do more than just that, but she wasn't quite sure what. Her mind was in turmoil.

Eventually, she fell in to a fitful sleep and woke unrefreshed next day. There was a batch of new arrivals and Amy found it difficult to concentrate on the information she was being given; her mind kept drifting back to the previous night. But once the shift began, she had no option but to concentrate as the needs of the sick young men took over.

When Molly went on her break from the casualty receiving room, she dropped into the ward with a letter for Amy.

'Some chap asked me to give this letter to any lovesick nurse that I could find,' she said dryly.

Amy snatched the letter off Molly. 'No he did not,' she answered vehemently.

'No, you're right, he didn't say anything like that. He just gave me the letter and grinned at me with the same silly love struck expression on his face that you had last night.'

'Molly, how could you!'
'Perhaps it's not for you, then? He didn't actually say it was for you,' said Molly, reaching to take the letter back. 'Perhaps I should check.' Amy plunged the letter into her pocket, away from Molly and told her that she was wasting valuable eating time. Reminded of her stomach, Molly made a hasty retreat to the dining room and left Amy in peace.
Until her own break, Amy fingered the letter in her pocket, wondering what he would say. Would he be feeling the same way as she was? Or would he think it was all a mistake and didn't want to see her again. Getting herself into a panic, Amy told the other nurses that she was going to the toilet, and there, unceremoniously sat on the toilet, she read her first love letter.

My dearest Amy

Thank you for such a wonderful evening. I have never enjoyed myself so much. I hope you will come out with me again as soon as possible. I can't wait. I keep remembering kissing you and holding you and wanting to go on holding you for the rest of my life. I only hope you feel the same way as I do. Please say you'll come out with me again. I await your reply on tenterhooks.
Until I kiss you again

Your Loving Geoffrey
xxx

Amy shivered with delight then realised that she had better be getting back to work before she was missed. She carefully folded the letter, giving it a little kiss, then put it in her pocket. She would answer him tonight when she finished her shift.
But the next evening they met, there was little time for romantic talking, as Geoffrey had taken delivery of a new Ford ambulance and he was eager to talk about it.
'It's a Model T Ford chassis, converted to hold the crew and either two stretcher cases or four sitting cases. It'll be great. Henry Ford is a pacifist, y'know, but he donates the Model T chassis to be made into ambulances. It has a four-cylinder engine and gives twenty

horsepower. It's a really comfortable ride for the patients as well. Much better than my old one.'

'Really,' said Amy, bemused by the technical talk. Instead she concentrated on looking at his lips and eventually Geoffrey took the hint and Amy was rewarded for her patience.

They only managed to meet about one evening a week, and sometimes went for a week or two without even seeing each other, but after three months, he said that he needed to talk seriously to her. Amy was worried. Had he changed his mind? Was he being transferred to another area? She couldn't wait to see him that evening.

He was quiet and thoughtful when they met, which further compounded Amy's fears. What was he going to tell her? When they met, he took her down by the riverside and they sat on the bank; a favourite spot with them both. He sat facing her on the bank and took her hands in his. Amy waited nervously.

'I need to tell you more about myself Amy. I've told you of my jealous mother and father who likes a quiet life, but there is more I need to tell you. I am heir to an hereditary title and an estate, which I inherit on my father's death, although I hope that is a long time off. I am the only son, so it's important that I marry well, to quote my mother.'

Amy's heart contracted. Here it comes, she thought. He loves me but can't marry me. And in that second, Amy knew that whether he married her or not, she wanted to be with him in any form that he suggested, even if it was only as a mistress. She was shocked to the core by her own thoughts, but he had become so precious that she wanted him at any price, even if it meant betraying all the principles that she held dear about marriage.

'My mother will not like me marrying a person with an unknown history, but I don't care. Amy, will you marry me?' For a second, Amy thought she had misheard him and just stared at him. Had he just asked her to marry him, not be his mistress?'

'Well, Amy, please don't leave me in suspense, will you?'

'Marry you? Oh yes, I will, oh Geoffrey.' She pulled him towards her and kissed him soundly on the mouth.

'When?' he asked breathlessly after she released him from the kiss.

'Today?' she replied, so great was her need to be with him.

He laughed and rolled back against the bank. 'Think it might take some arranging Amy. Don't think we can manage it today.'
'Tomorrow then,' she replied.
'Do you mind getting married in France? That way it would be quicker. And then we could tell my mother afterwards. It would be too late for her to interfere then. She's been trying to get me married off ever since I left Cambridge. You won't believe the number of eligible debutantes that have been paraded before me. It was a relief to come to the war just to stop that.'
'I'd love to get married in France. I wouldn't have anyone on my side of the church anyway, seeing as I have no family.'
'At least I don't have to go and prove myself to your father and ask him formally for your hand.'
'Yes, being on my own does have advantages. But shouldn't you be getting married in some enormous Abbey or somewhere if you are heir to a title?'
'I suppose so, but I'd have hated all that pomp and ceremony. But the service will be in French. Will that be all right?'
'Yes, I speak French. That'll be no problem.'
'Do you? I wonder when you learnt it?'
'I don't know, I just knew it when I came here.'
Geoffrey was quiet for a while then said he would arrange the marriage in the village, with the priest, after a civil ceremony.
'Is a Catholic ceremony all right? We can have a blessing in my own church when the war is over. That will please my mother. She won't like to miss an opportunity to get dressed up. Were you Catholic?'
'I don't know, but as long as it is before God I don't mind.'
'Good. Start preparing your trousseau, Mademoiselle.'
'Trousseau?' Amy looked aghast. 'What on earth can I get to wear here?'
'I'm sure you will find something. You look beautiful in anything to me.'
'But to get a wedding outfit will be hopeless in a village. I never envisaged that I'd be getting married without proper wedding attire.'
'Don't you want to get married yet then?' he asked while pulling her closer for a kiss.

After the kiss, she managed to reply in the affirmative. He said that was good because if she kept kissing him like that he would forget himself and do things that they shouldn't do before they were married. She replied that she would like that, even though she was shocked at her own behaviour. With a great strength of character, Geoffrey pulled away and took her back to the hospital.

Chapter 16

When she got back to her room, Molly was crying. Dreading the worst, Amy held her and asked her what the matter was.

'I've just nursed a young man of twenty who has had his genitals blown off. He just had a silver tube coming out from where they should be. The rest of him was unmarked. How cruel is that? He'll probably survive too. What a situation to be in. He was married on his last leave as well. His poor wife. This war is so cruel. I wish it would end. So many young men dead, so many others wounded beyond endurance. If only there was a way to help them.'

'I'm sure you helped all you could, Molly. You're tired. Why don't you ask for some leave? Isn't Edwin due any? We've both been here over a year now and Edwin over two. You've only managed a weekend with Edwin up to now, since you came to France.'

'I wish we could. You're right, I do need a rest. But what about you? You looked very happy when you came in. What's been happening in your life? Been out with Geoffrey again?'

'Oh yes, Molly. We're getting married. How on earth will I get a dress fit for a wedding out here?'

'Congratulations! We could ask around and see if anyone has any ideas. How long have we got? When's the big day?'

'As soon as Geoffrey can arrange it with the priest. At least you'll be here when I get married, not like at yours.'

'Yes, so that's two frocks we need, as I'll need a bridesmaid's outfit as well. Or will I be a dame of honour, seeing as I'm already married? Actually Amy, I brought a dress with me, just in case I ever met Edwin. You could wear it if you like. It's blue silk. It's fairly plain, with just a few frills around the neck and the bottom of the skirt and cuffs. I'm sure it would fit you. But we'll keep trying for new ones for you.'

The next week, Geoffrey came and told her that the wedding was fixed for two weeks hence. She told him about Molly's offer of a frock and he seemed pleased about that, as he said that he didn't want her feeling that her wedding was going to be a low key affair.

'Marrying you will never be low key; it will be the best thing I've done in my life,' she replied, for which she was rewarded with a hug.

One week later, Molly and Amy's lives were turned upside down. She got back from her shift to find that Molly had gone. Packed up and gone back to England. She had had a phone call to tell her that two of her brothers had been killed on the same day and she was given compassionate leave to go and stay with her mother. It was all in a letter waiting for Amy on her bed. Underneath the letter was the blue silk frock. Amy wept. Despite having the worst possible news, Molly had got out the frock for Amy's wedding. 'Sorry I'm going to miss your wedding, perhaps I can be Godmother to yours as well?' was at the end of the letter.

Amy wept, for Molly, for Harold and Tommy who had died, and for herself, for she would have no one at her wedding now. Because of their close friendship and their long hours of work, Molly and Amy had made few friends in the hospital, not feeling the need for other close friends, when they had each other.

And then she had an idea. She wondered if Jack would come and be at her wedding? Did French brides have anyone to give them away she wondered? She asked Jack and he was delighted to attend, almost claiming responsibility for getting the two of them together. At least Amy would have someone there and Geoffrey was pleased he was coming as well.

Geoffrey was only allowed three days off for the wedding, but he had arranged for them to stay at the little village inn where they had gone on their first walk. His landlady at the farm where he was billeted had offered them a room, but he preferred to use the inn.

The morning of the wedding arrived and Amy got washed and put on the blue silk dress and brushed her hair until it shone. The other girls had arranged some wild flowers into a bouquet for her, and a little coronet of flowers for her hair. She looked radiant, even though her attire was more suited to a rustic peasant wedding than a member of the landed gentry, but she didn't care. She was sure that Geoffrey's mother would come round when she met her.

Amy suddenly remembered the sapphire necklace that Uncle Robert had given her for her nineteenth birthday on the Titanic and her eyes filled with tears. How nice it would have looked today. It would have exactly matched her blue dress. She pulled herself together when she heard a knock on the door. It was Jack.

Jack had managed to borrow an automobile and took her to the Mayor's office for the civil ceremony and then to the village church. Geoffrey's landlady was also present along with some of her friends from the village who always loved a wedding. One nurse and two ambulance drivers were also present. Nobody else had been able to get time off.

Amy didn't care as long as she and Geoffrey were there, although she would have loved Molly to be with her on this important occasion.

Jack walked her into the church and Amy only had eyes for Geoffrey from then on. She went through the service making the right responses and eventually Geoffrey slipped the thin gold band on the ring finger of her left hand. Afterwards, they all went to the village inn where the landlord had made a small meal for them. The others soon slipped away back to the hospital and Amy and Geoffrey were left alone.

'Well Mrs Storm. Shall we retire to the bedroom?'

Amy blushed. 'Yes please husband,' she said coyly but with pride in her voice. Once the bedroom door was closed, Geoffrey took her in his arms and hugged her, before kissing her. As she responded to him, he gently undid the buttons on the back of her frock and before she knew what had happened, the frock slid to the floor. He gently lifted her and placed her on the bed and carefully but passionately made love to her. And again later in the evening. Amy was asleep in a trice afterwards.

Waking next morning, Amy turned slowly to look at Geoffrey who was still asleep. She looked down at her wedding ring and wondered again at the bliss she had felt yesterday afternoon and again last night, all made legal by this thin band of gold.

Geoffrey stirred in his sleep, so Amy leaned over and kissed him.

'Mmm, good morning Amy, and how do you like being married?'

'I like it very much,' replied Amy, and this time, she took the initiative as they made love again before breakfast.

After a large breakfast, Geoffrey suggested a walk but after an hours stroll, they rushed back to their bedroom; so besotted with each other to bother about anything or anyone else. After three days and nights of loving, Geoffrey said that he was sorry but he would have to go back to work. He would write to his mother tomorrow as soon as he got chance to tell her about the wedding, he promised.

Amy had managed to have all week off, so she decided to stay at the inn. She knew full well that she would be called back into work if a big convoy arrived. No, she would just stay at the inn and luxuriate in being married and resting. Nobody warned her how tiring being married was. She was exhausted. Mind you, they had worked hard at being married. Besides, if Geoffrey got any time off, he could come back to the inn and stay with her.

It was a forlorn hope as he only managed one brief afternoon with her. All too soon, the honeymoon was over. She packed her few belongings together into her suitcase and checking she hadn't left anything in the room, she shut the door and went downstairs.

As she got downstairs, Jack was waiting for her in the entrance hall of the inn. Her face lit up and she rushed over to speak to him. His face did not light up in response. He took hold of her hands and sat her down on the settee.

'Amy, I have some terrible news for you. You have to be brave. Geoffrey's ambulance took a direct hit from an aeroplane. He was killed instantly, he wouldn't have suffered.

'No,' screamed Amy, 'it can't have happened, we've just got married. I need him. Are you sure? They may have made a mistake. It might be someone else's ambulance,' said Amy wildly.

'There is no mistake. It was your Geoffrey. I'm sorry. Do you want me to arrange some leave for you?'

'No, just leave me here at the inn for another day or two whilst I mourn him in private. Is there a funeral to arrange?' she suddenly asked.

Jack winced. 'No funeral.' And then Amy realised what he meant. Geoffrey had been blown apart, there was nothing to bury. 'They found his identification tag. Here, I rescued it for you. Otherwise it will go to his parents as next of kin. I don't suppose he notified his bosses about his change of circumstances?'

'Probably not, he was just about going to write to his mother when he went back to work. Thank you, I will treasure that. It's all I have of him, besides my wedding band. Please leave me now.'

'I'll speak to Matron for you. Wouldn't you be better going home?'

'Home? I have no home. Geoffrey was my home,' she said sadly as she walked back upstairs into her bridal suite. She threw herself on the bed and gathering the sheets in her hands, sobbed and sobbed until her throat was sore. She kept smelling the sheets, trying to capture the essence of him that still lingered on the bedding. He had left a handkerchief behind and she had washed it in the tiny sink in the bathroom. How she wished she hadn't washed it now, but she would keep it with her forever.

The landlady kept knocking on the door, leaving drinks and snacks but Amy left them untouched. She sobbed on and off for two days and then she felt the familiar black fog beginning to descend into her mind. It pulled her up sharp. She must not let the black fog descend this time. There was too much to do. She jumped out of the bed and opened the window as if fresh air would wipe away the fog.

Before, when the fog had descended, she had been too upset or too young to fight it, but now she knew that she had to fight it. That she still had to work at serving people, to be forgiven for all the wrong she had done to Lizzie. This time, she was going to be strong. She hurriedly got dressed and went down into the bar area of the inn.

'Mon Dieu, elle vit!' burst the landlady when she saw her and scurried off for her husband who could speak a little English. Heavens, thought Amy, did they think she was dead? The landlord came rushing in, offering her food and drink and any other help he could offer.

'Merci, je veux Jack, le docteur? Oui?'

'Oui Madame, I get him for you. A drink, n'est ce pas?'

'Oui.' Amy sat down, exhausted by her conversation, however short it had been. The landlady brought a tray of coffee in with some small tempting sandwiches. Without thinking, Amy tucked into the sandwiches and drank three cups of the strong rich coffee. She realised she hadn't eaten for days and felt better for it.

The landlady was jibbering away to her husband in very rapid French and Amy was struggling to keep up with her. In the end, he told Amy that his wife was very sorry for what had happened and she could stay there for a long time if she wanted to.

Amy thanked her, but said that she needed to get back to her work. The landlady listened to the translation, then shook her head slowly, and went back to the kitchen. She had to get back to work; it was the only way to keep the black fog away. To keep working until she dropped each night and she had no time to think.

Later in the evening Jack arrived and told her that he had been several times in the last day or two but not been able to see her.
'No, I was fighting the black fog,' she replied.
'Black fog?'
'Three times in my life I've stopped talking and reacting to anything for about three months. The first time was when I lost all my family in an accident. Then the second time was when my dog died and . .'
'The third was when you survived the Titanic,' completed Jack.
'You know? How do you know?'
'How else would you have landed up in an asylum? You are obviously well born and educated, so your story didn't ring true. And was the black fog descending again?'
'Yes, soon after you told me about Geoffrey. But I fought it this time. I have too much to do in this world.'
'Why?'
'To make up for sending my maid to her death.'
'What?'
'I sent my maid back to the suite to get my jewellery box and then got on the last lifeboat off the Titanic, so I sent her to her death. I've got to serve people to make up for that. That's why I can't let the black fog win.'
'Did you know it was the last lifeboat?'
'No, not when I got on it. We were told that it was only temporary whilst they repaired the boat anyway. Then we would all be getting back on. The crewman told me it was the last lifeboat, but we still thought it was only a minor event. It was terrible when the ship just suddenly upended and disappeared into the water. Such a large ship. Gone.'
'And you've been blaming yourself all these years for your maid's death?'
Amy nodded. Jack took hold of her. 'Amy, listen, you were not to blame; you didn't know it was going to happen. Even the engineers didn't know and they built it.'
'But God will never forgive me. Look, he's even taken my husband, that shows he hasn't forgiven me?'
'Amy, this has nothing to do with God not forgiving you. Didn't you know that God is a forgiving God?'
'But I've committed such a big sin, sending someone to her death.'

'No Amy, that wasn't a sin. That was just unfortunate circumstances. And anyway, even if it was a sin, Jesus died because of all our sins, so God will forgive you anyway, because he sent His Son to die on the cross for our sins.'

'Are you sure?'

'Perfectly sure. Don't you remember your Sunday School lessons? Now, dry your tears and let's get you back to the hospital. Do you feel ready?'

'Yes,' Amy sniffed, 'I do. Work will help keep the black fog at bay.'

'I know. It helped keep my black fog away after my wife died.'

'Did it? Do you know what I mean then?'

'Sort of. I didn't stop speaking altogether, but it was similar to what happened to you. Come on, we should just be in time for morning coffee. And perhaps you can tell me what else you now remember about your past.'

It was then that Amy realised that she'd had spoken freely about her past and was able to tell someone else. Perhaps healing could come from talking about all that happened. It was making her feel vulnerable and raw, but if it eventually allowed her to come to terms with what happened, then it could only be good. She would think about things when she got to her own room in the hospital. Yes, she would think long and hard about these things that Jack had said.

Chapter 17

At first, Amy was silent on the way back from the inn, but then she started talking. She told Jack about her upbringing and about her families death and her uncle taking care of her. And then about the Titanic and about her awful guilt feelings that Lizzie had died. Then she told him how when nobody claimed her, she was sent to an asylum, where she stayed until she entered nurse training.

'And is Amy your real name?'

'No. But I like it now and I'm going to keep it.'

'What is your real name?'

Amy took a deep breath. 'Arabella Charlotte Sophie Montague,' Amy replied to Jack. 'Quite a mouthful, isn't it? Now you see why I prefer to stick with Amy Wilson.'

'Who gave you that name, Amy?'

'A young nurse in the asylum. I had a handkerchief in my pocket when they were trying to trace who I was and it had the letter 'A' embroidered on it. Actually, Lizzie had embroidered it for me for my birthday, just before the Titanic sunk. So when I was rescued but couldn't speak, everyone called me Miss A. Young Laura at the asylum asked if she could give me a name and chose Amy because she liked the book Little Women. I can't remember where Wilson came from.'

'Where did you come from?'

'Montague Hall near York. A lovely old house that had been in the family for years. I was the heiress. There was no one else to inherit.'

'What happened to it?'

'I've no idea. I've never acknowledged my past until today. And I don't want to acknowledge it yet, Jack. Perhaps some day I may, but not for a long time yet.'

'So you are still Amy?'

'Yes, and I'll thank you not to tell anyone what I've told you.'

'Don't worry, your secret's safe with me, Amy. But if ever you want to talk about it, or want to claim your inheritance, I will help you all I can.'

'Thanks Jack. I appreciate all that you have done for me. I'll go straight to my room now. Thanks for the lift, and everything.'

'My pleasure.'

Amy walked into the hospital and put her things away, carefully putting her marriage certificate in the drawer with her state registration certificate and other valuable possessions. She added the envelope that Jack had given them as a wedding present, but she didn't open it. She would save it for later when she felt calmer. Then she went to see Matron. Matron tried to persuade her to take some more leave and perhaps go home for a while. Amy merely shook her head, reflecting that she had no home to go to anyway.

'Thank you Matron, I would rather work. It'll take my mind off things.'

'Well if you change your mind, I will arrange for you to have some leave.'

'Thank you. Where do you want me to work?'

'Could you go on night duty on B ward? The senior nurse on there has just gone home and of course, Jolley hasn't come back yet, so we're short staffed there.'

'Yes, Matron, I'll go on Ward B. Shall I start tonight?'

'Do you feel able to?'

'Yes, the sooner I get back to work, the better I'll feel.'

'Tonight then. Thank you. It'll probably be easier on night duty as you won't meet as many people at first, until you feel a little stronger.'

'I suppose so, I'll go and try and get some sleep now, Matron.'

'Thank you, Wilson, and I was very sad to hear your news, we all were. Oh, I'm sorry, should I use your new name now?'

For one wild moment, Amy thought that Jack had told Matron her secret, but then realised Matron was referring to her married name.

'No, you can still use my maiden name,' replied Amy and left the room quickly.

She shut the curtains in the bedroom and laid down, desperately trying to sleep before she went on duty, but it eluded her. In the end, she got up and went down by the river for a walk, and lay resting on the river bank, remembering the happy times she had spent there with Geoffrey.

Eventually she returned to the hospital and got ready for night duty. The ward was full and it took her all her time to remember the names and conditions of all the patients. That was the advantage of working in the casualty receiving room as you were concentrating on one patient at a time, even though you were sometimes having to break off to assess other arrivals.

Amy carried out the urgent dressings and medicine rounds and then prioritised the rest of the night's work. Amy was on duty with a Voluntary Aid Detachments nurse, or VAD as they were called for short. She was very experienced, so it was a lot easier than if Amy had had a new recruit. The VAD nurses varied a great deal. Most of them were volunteers and had little, if any, nurse training. Many of them were from the upper echelons of society and had probably never got their hands dirty before coming to France. A bit like I would have been, she reflected ruefully. But they were keeping the hospitals going with their tireless service.

When they had a lull, the VAD who was called Edith, said how sorry she was to hear about Geoffrey. Amy was touched; she'd never worked with this girl before, but it seemed that the whole hospital had heard about her tragedy.

'Thank you Edith. It's kind of you to say so, and I suppose I'm not the first war widow and I won't be the last.'

'No, that's very true. It's a cruel war, isn't it? Although the troops are saying that we are winning now. They reckon it will all be over this year.'

'I certainly hope so. I'm weary of it all.'

A little later, Amy was bandaging a new soldier that had come in when Edith asked her to have a look at her own patient, higher up the ward.

'I don't think he's going to do, Amy,' said Edith quietly.

'Could you just finish this bandage off and I'll have a look at him, please?'

Edith nodded and took over the bandaging.

Amy approached the young boy. Edith was right; he didn't look like he was going to make it. His breathing was ragged and his colour very pale. She bent down to examine his stomach wound that was bleeding profusely. As she applied some more pads on the dressing, the boy opened his eyes and stared at Amy.

'Miss Arabella. I thought you were dead?'

Amy froze, looking at the boy in her care. Oh no, it was young George Grimscar, son of the head gardener from Montague Hall. Why, he couldn't be more than twelve years old she thought, but then she remembered that she had been away from Montague Hall for at least five years, so he would be much older by now. What could she do? What if anybody heard him? Instead of acknowledging him, Amy hushed him gently and asked him to wait a while whilst she treated his wound. The boy looked puzzled but stayed quiet. Suddenly he spoke again but very quietly.

'I know, you've come for me, haven't you? I've heard of that before. Someone who's died earlier, comes to take the dying ones to Heaven, someone they know, then they won't be frightened. That's it, isn't it? You've come to take me to Heaven, haven't you?' Edith came and joined Amy.

Suddenly, he started coughing and as he coughed, blood began to spout from his mouth, covering the bedclothes and Amy's pinny. He quickly became unconscious and then slowly his life ebbed away.

Amy closed his eyes and they both stood looking at him for a while. Amy was glad that he had died, as her identity would remain a secret until she was ready to tell everyone, if ever she was ready. And then she recoiled in horror at her own thoughts. Why, she had almost wished this boy's death on him, just to keep her own life a secret. In that moment, Amy hated herself and felt that those thoughts were more like the old Arabella, not the new kind caring Amy that she had invented and worked hard at. Edith's quiet voice disturbed her from her thoughts.

'What did he call you, Amy? Was it Miss Arabella?' asked Edith.

'Oh, it was nothing. He mistook me for someone he used to know, who apparently had died. He thought I'd come to take him to Heaven. Poor boy. Not very old, was he?' asked Amy, trying to deflect the conversation away from her.

'No, none of them are. It's their parents I feel sorry for,' replied Edith. 'Shall I perform last offices for him?'

'No,' said Amy. 'I'll do that; you carry on with the other dressings that you were doing. No, better still, here's Sheila to relieve us for breaks. You go and take a supper break now. I'll go later.'

'See you later,' said Edith to Amy, as she explained to Sheila where she was up to with the dressings.

After the obligatory hour, Amy performed the age-old ritual of last offices: the nurse's final gift to her patient. She thought about this young man and what Edith had said about feeling sorry for the parents.

Amy thought about his parents. They had only the one boy and six daughters; all older than young George. The sixth daughter was a pretty girl called Jean. The parents jokingly called her 'the last disappointment', before they got their precious boy. Much good it had done them, thought Amy as she washed him carefully.

Remembering the boy's parents, Amy thought again about the strong tall gardener and his little round wife, with a chubby face. She was always smiling. She wouldn't be smiling once she gets this news, reflected Amy sadly. She wondered if the family was still at Montague Hall, but then Edith returned from her break and it was Amy's turn to go.

Fortunately, during her break, the conversation in the dining room was lively, so Amy didn't get chance to think her sad thoughts about young George. On return to the ward, Edith reported all that had happened during her break, one of the things being that George had gone to the mortuary. Amy nodded sadly.

The two of them then got on with their duties and had little time for conversation again that night. After a twelve-hour shift, Amy was exhausted and fell asleep straightaway. That evening she felt much better and ate a decent meal for the first time in days.

Amy stayed on night duty for another two weeks. Soon, she hoped that Molly would be coming back as she was really missing her. It was the longest they had been separated for five years and she felt like Molly was the nearest thing to a sister that she had.

Getting ready for night duty that night, she decided to ask Matron if she could go back to the receiving room. She felt ready for it now. She could cope with the ambulance men and women coming through the door without looking for Geoffrey.

Two weeks later, she got her wish and Jack cheered as she walked in the door.

'It's great to have you back, Amy. I've missed you. What was Matron doing banishing you to night duty?'

'I didn't mind, it eased me back in to the work.'

'Well, come on, we've just heard there is going to be another convoy.'

Amy groaned. 'I wish I'd ten shillings for every time I've heard that phrase. I could retire and live a life of luxury.'

The convoys of ambulances soon arrived and Amy spent the whole day sorting them out. She soon got into the routine again and enjoyed working closely with Jack. He was true to his word and never mentioned her secret again and she felt confident working with him.

One week later, the ambulance brought a young man in who was covered in the usual blood and gore. As she started to clean him, she got the shock of her life. It was Edwin Jolley, Molly's husband, and he looked poorly.

'Jack, Jack, it's Edwin, Molly's husband. Come and look,' she said urgently.

'Edwin, Molly's husband? Who do you mean?'

'My friend Molly, who I trained with and came here with.'

'You'd better go and get her then. Where's she working at the moment?'

'She's not here. She's gone home to England. Her two brothers were killed on the same day and she went home to be with her mother.'

Edwin started groaning and then opened his eyes, recognising Amy.

'Amy, where's Molly?' he croaked.

'She's gone to England on leave.'

Edwin just closed his eyes, as if the knowledge of Molly not being there was too much for him.

'I'll look after you,' said Amy, 'don't worry, Jack will patch you up.' A brief smile came over his face, then he lapsed into unconsciousness.

'What's his chances, Jack?' Amy asked even before Jack could finish his examination.

'I think that gash to his head looks worse than it is. It just needs stitching up, but I think he's got internal bleeding somewhere. His pulse is weak and thready and his abdomen is tense. I'm going to have to go in and operate, see what I find. Will you get him ready, or do you want someone else to take over?'

'No, I'll be fine. I want to help him.'

Together the two worked hard. Jack opened the abdomen and found a ruptured spleen, which he removed quickly and stopped the bleeding.

'Another hour and he'd have gone. Good job they got him here when they did. I just hope that he hasn't lost too much blood. Now, I'll stitch that head wound up and then look at his hand and foot. They're not looking too healthy, either.'

Amy carried on working with Jack, constantly praying silently whilst he worked. Jack had to remove three fingers on his right hand that were beyond repair. He also had to splint two breaks in his leg bone.

'Was he right handed? He asked Amy.

'I think so. I'm not sure.'

'What was his job?'

'A miner.'

'Mmm. He may not be able to go back to that job anymore. We'll have to wait and see. For now, he needs to get over the splenectomy. That's his first priority. Let's get him to the ward to recover.'

With a twist of irony, Edwin was placed on Molly's ward. The other nurses were understandably upset when they heard who Edwin was and promised to take special care of him. Not that they didn't take great care of all their charges anyway.

After the shift finished, Amy went to see Matron.

'Matron, you kindly said that if I needed time off, I could have some leave.'

'Yes, Wilson. Do you want some now?'

'Yes, Sister Jolley's husband has just come in as a patient. He's had a splenectomy and is critical, plus he's got other injuries. He will need transferring to England when he is well. I would like to accompany him on the journey and take him home and then have a short leave.

'That is very unusual, to accompany a soldier home, Wilson.'

'I haven't asked for much since I came here and have only had one weeks leave in over a year. I would like to go home now, along with Edwin.' Matron thought for a moment and then nodded.

'Very well, Wilson. It will probably do you good to get back to England for a while, especially after your tragedy. Will you be all right for money?'

'Thank you Matron. May I stay in England for about three weeks? And I have enough money, thank you. Not much to spend it on here, is there?'

'No that's true. And yes, you can stay three weeks. But I would appreciate it if you came back then.'
'I will. This means a lot to me Matron. Thank you.'
Amy indeed had enough money. When she had looked in the envelope containing Jack's wedding present, she found one hundred pounds. She had argued with him, saying it was too much, but he insisted that she needed it all the more now. Along with her pay, Amy had a veritable horde of money and would bank it as soon as she possibly could in England. It would perhaps buy a house when the war finished.
Edwin's life hung in the balance for the next forty-eight hours, but then he started to rally. Within a week, he was much improved and ready to be stretchered to a convoy ship and back to England.
He protested that Amy didn't need to accompany him, but she told him that she wanted to see Molly anyway and was due some leave.

Chapter 18

The journey home was long and hard; Edwin crying out in pain many times, but there was inadequate pain relief for the soldiers being transferred back home. Most of the pain relief was saved for the front line hospitals, and even they didn't have enough most of the time.

Edwin was admitted to a military hospital in Portsmouth and, once he was settled, Amy made the long weary journey home to Burnley. Getting a tram from the train station, she was soon at Molly's house. She knocked on the door and young Peter opened it.

'Lo, Amy. Didn't know you were coming. Come in.' He opened the door wider to let Amy in. She went up the passage into the back kitchen where everybody always congregated. The front parlour was never used. There was Molly and her mother, sat by the black leaded stove, having a cup of tea.

'Amy, how lovely to see you. Did Matron let you have some leave at last? How did the wedding go? Let's have a look at your ring? How did you manage to get a ring like that in France? Geoffrey must have known someone to be able to buy such a lovely ring.'

'Hello Molly, Mrs Smith. Yes, I got leave, but I've also got some sad news. Edwin has been injured, Molly. Don't worry, he's going to be all right, but he's in hospital. I brought him home with me.'

All Molly's joyous expression drained from her face and her many questions changed in nature from Amy's wedding to her own husband.

'Edwin hurt? When? How do you know? What are his injuries? Where is he? Can I go and see him?'

'He had a splenectomy and has lost three fingers on his right hand, and a head wound. And his leg was broken in two places. But he seems as if he'll be all right. He's in Portsmouth hospital, and yes, you can go and see him. Matron knows about him, so doesn't expect you back. He came into our casualty receiving station.'

'Did Geoffrey bring him in? Did you and Jack sort him out?'

'Yes, Jack and I sorted him out, but Geoffrey didn't bring him in.' At this point, Amy burst into tears.

'Amy what's the matter? Are you overtired from the journey?'

'That's my other sad news. Geoffrey was killed a week after the wedding.'

'No,' cried Molly in horror, running over to hold Amy, 'and here am I nattering on about Edwin. I'm so sorry. What happened?'

'His ambulance got hit by an aeroplane. It was instantaneous.'

'And did Matron not allow you to go home straightway?' Amy shook her head. 'She did offer, but I said I preferred to work. Besides I've no home to go to have I? I was frightened I would stop speaking again like I did after the Titanic. So I kept working, but when Edwin came in, I told her that I wanted to go home with him.'

'That is so kind of you, thank you,' said Molly, hugging her again.

'What do you mean, you've no home girl?' said Mrs Smith. 'You've always known that you've a home here with us. It might be a put-you-up bed in the kitchen but we'd never turn you away from here. I'm so sorry lass, for what you've had to go through. Why didn't you come here?'

'You had your own troubles. I didn't want to intrude on your grief.'

'You wouldn't have been intruding. Never mind, you're here now. How long can you stop? You'll be some company for me when our Molly goes down to Portsmouth.'

'Yes, I must get down town and find out how to get to Portsmouth,' said Molly.

'I've got all the information for you, I've just come from Portsmouth myself, after I delivered Edwin safely. Here are the train times.' She handed a piece of paper over to Molly, who carefully read its contents.

'Oh of course, thank you Amy. What would I do without you? I could get a train tonight if I rush. Mum? Amy? Do you mind if I go and get ready now? ' Both mum and Amy encouraged her to go and Amy sat down with a sigh of relief. She had done what she had to do and now she was exhausted. Mrs Smith made a cup of tea and some sandwiches for her, and also some for Molly to take with her on the train.

Once Molly was off to the railway station, Amy and Mrs Smith sat companionably by the fire.

'Now lass, you tell me all about your Geoffrey. Molly said you'd met a nice young man but didn't say much else. Now you tell me all about him,' said Mrs Smith.

Amy found that she could tell Mrs Smith everything without getting upset, even when she told her about his death, so soon after the wedding. And then she cried. Long gasping sobs that shook her whole body. Mrs Smith held her in her arms and rocked and comforted her as if she was one of her little children. Amy was much cheered by the older woman who was the nearest thing she had to a mother.

After an hour, Amy calmed down sufficiently for Mrs Smith to get organised for bedtime.

'You might as well have our Molly's bed whilst she's not here. No doubt we can think again when she gets back. Her and Edwin don't have a place yet, what with the war, and usually stay here, or at her granny's.'

'Thank you. That's so kind of you. I'd like to go to bed now if you don't mind.'

'Aye lass. You go on up. You know where the girl's bedroom is.'

Amy went upstairs and found the empty bed, creeping round the other two girls who were already in bed fast asleep. She also was soon asleep and slept like a log; probably due to the healing tears that she had wept that evening.

The next two weeks flew by and Amy felt better than she had for months. Being cosseted by Mrs Smith and eating properly, and with no work to do, Amy improved rapidly. They heard regularly from Molly who said that she wasn't going to go back to France but would try and get some work locally so that she could visit Edwin and look after him when he came out.

Soon, it was time for Amy to go back to France. She went in to town and bought Mrs Smith lots of food and a bunch of flowers. Mrs Smith protested that she shouldn't, but Amy could see that she was really pleased with the flowers.

'I've never had a bunch of flowers before, Amy. I feel like a posh person, now. Only posh folk have money for flowers in Burnley.'

'You deserve it, Mrs Smith. I'm so grateful that you took me in.'

'Well take care of yourself, and let us know when you get back safely to France.'

'I will. Thanks again, bye,' Amy replied as she walked down the street. Earlier in the week, she had contacted the local army recruiting office and asked for passage back to France, which they were glad to help with. Yes, Amy was glad to be going back to France, to do her bit for the war. It was all she had left now.

Chapter 19

The journey back to France seemed to take no time at all and Amy was relieved at getting back safely. She didn't forget her promise to Mrs Smith, and wrote a postcard immediately, and also one to Molly at her digs in Portsmouth.

Amy reported to Matron and was told that she was a welcome sight and she was glad that Amy was back. She even asked about Edwin, which surprised Amy. She told Matron that Molly would not be returning to France, but was going to stay in Portsmouth until Edwin was ready for home. She gave Matron the letter from Molly explaining all that Amy had just told her.

Matron said that she would write to Molly, releasing her from her duties and giving her a reference so that she could seek employment in Portsmouth. Suddenly, the rule about married nurses was being ignored because of the war.

To start with, Amy was allowed to go back to casualty receiving room, but Matron said that she would have to go on the wards at some time. Amy thanked her and went to her room to prepare for work.

Within several hours of returning to work, Amy felt like she had never been away. The onslaught of patients continued relentlessly. It became almost automatic, assess, treat, refer to doctor, or assist the doctor to treat: round and round with different patients. Always trying to treat each soldier as special, whilst he came to terms with his injuries and the pain, and also his worries about his future.

Jack was a good help to her in those first weeks and months but eventually Matron moved her back to a ward – ward A this time, to cover for another girl who was taking leave. Amy didn't mind, especially being on night duty, as it tended to be slightly less chaotic at nights. She found the quietness at nights more relaxing. But there was still a lot of work to do and sometimes, the nights were as bad as casualty receiving room.

One evening, the ward was quieter than usual and Amy was taking a tray back to the treatment room, when she heard the noise of quiet sobbing.

Amy walked back down the tightly packed wards, trying to locate the sound of sobbing. As she got nearer to the sound, it stopped suddenly. Amy realised that it was coming from the bed of the youngest admission. Trying to remember the handover on each patient, Amy recalled that this young man wasn't expected to survive. Both his legs had been amputated shortly after he arrived and the doctor said that he had lost too much blood to survive. He did indeed have a deathly pallor, thought Amy. His eyes were closed and Amy had a chance to observe him closely. His was a very young face, showing signs of recent tears.

Amy gently touched his arm.

'Are you in pain, private?'

The young man turned to look at Amy and shook his head. He looked at Amy and although she had seen it before, she shuddered at the old look in his eyes. His face was that of a young boy and yet his eyes were as old as time.

'Can I get you anything? A drink perhaps?'

The boy shook his head again.

'Well, just call me if you need anything,' she replied, as she started to walk away.

'Nurse,' a little voice whispered. Amy turned back.

'Yes?'

'Could yer sit wi' me a while? If yer not too busy.' Amy thought of all the jobs that needed doing, but her heart went out to this young man, who didn't have much longer to live; the smell of gangrene pervaded the whole area around his bed.

'Just for a while.' She crouched by his bedside. 'Where do you come from?'

'Accrington, i' Lancashire,' he whispered.

'Well, that's a coincidence, I come from Burnley.'

'Were yer born an' bred?'

'Pardon?'

'Born an' bred i' Burnley?'

'No. Just did my nurse training there. What's your name?'

'Private Smithies, nurse.'

'No, your first name.'

'Tommy, Miss.'

'How old are you?'

'Four . .er . . eighteen, Miss.'

'So you're fourteen really, Tommy. Don't worry, I'm not going to tell anybody.' Tommy nodded bashfully.

'How did you get away with it at the recruitment centre?'
'Well, wi' being' tall, I looked older, but I took mi' brother's birth certificate wi' me. He's eighteen.'
'Won't he need it someday?'
'Nah, he's simple, like. He won't be able ter fight, lucky sod. Oh, beg yer pardon Miss, for swearing.'
'That's all right Tommy. I've heard worse than that in this job.'
'Bet yer 'ave,' he chuckled, before a wince of pain crossed his face.
'Can I get you something for the pain?'
'Nah, I'm all right. I know anyway.'
'Know what Tommy?'
'That I'm not gonna mek it.'
'We're doing our best for you,' Amy trotted out in her best reassuring manner.
'Aye, but yer best's not good enough, is it? Go on, tell us. I can tek it.'
'I can't guarantee that any of you will survive.'
'Well, I've bin around a bit and I know when someone's copped it. I just wish I'd bin able ter see me mam agin. I miss her dreadful. Wilta write to 'er, nurse? Tell 'er I were brave and that? She'll like that.'
Amy stroked his forehead gently. 'Yes, I will Tommy. I'll write and tell your mum how brave you were. Now try and rest. The pain will be easier if you sleep.'
'Thanks, nurse. I feel better now. Can I just hold yer 'and for a bit?'
'Of course,' replied Amy, reaching out to his hands and kissing him on the forehead. He seemed to settle down and Amy cursed herself for not getting a stool to sit on, as her legs were beginning to get cramp. No matter, she would just have to stay and suffer. She shuffled her position so that her legs felt easier.
After some time, Amy carefully looked down at her fob watch, wondering how long she could afford to stay with Tommy. He was sleeping peacefully now, but whenever she tried to move her hands from his, they tightened round hers. His pallor was deepening and a tell-tale seepage of blood was showing beneath his bandages.
Suddenly he cried out 'Mam,' and then breathed his last, as if the effort of crying for his mother had taken his last vestige of breath

away from him. Amy covered his face with the rough blanket, then left him whilst she went to find an orderly to assist with last offices.

It was with a heavy heart that Amy finished her night duty. So many boys and young men had died before in her arms, but this young boy seemed to upset her more than the others. I'm too tired, she thought to herself. Absolutely bone-weary. I can't keep this pace of life up. After handing over to the day nurses, Amy dragged herself to her bedroom.

After a quick wash and teeth clean, Amy was getting into bed when she remembered her promise. She slowly climbed out and got her notepaper out.

Dear Mrs Smithies, she wrote wearily. Once she had finished the letter, she got in to bed, but despite her tiredness, sleep was a long time coming.

That evening, feeling completely unrefreshed, Amy wondered again how long she could continue working in this job. She had been here two years and yet she seemed to have less stamina than she did before. Perhaps it's because of Geoffrey, she thought to herself. As she was about to drag her self to work, the alarm rang to say that there was a convoy coming. Amy was asked to attend casualty receiving room and the day staff would stay on duty on the wards for now, until they were relieved.

Amy was working with the doctor called Arthur as Jack had gone for a night off. She quickly got used to working with him and was surprised how quickly the time went. About three in the morning, Arthur said that the next soldier needed both legs amputating. Amy got the necessary equipment ready and was just about to assist Arthur when her head started to go dizzy. Must need some food, she thought to herself. Perhaps someone could bring us something before we start.

Arthur looked at Amy. 'Are you feeling all right, Amy?' he asked.

'No, I feel a bit dizzy to be honest,' replied Amy, 'I was just thinking that . .' but what Amy was thinking was never heard, as she slid to the ground in a faint. Arthur and one of the nurses carried her into the operating alcove and Arthur checked her over. Amy started to come round, and wondered what had happened to her. She stared at Arthur and the nurse.

'Well, young lady, you gave us a fright,' laughed Arthur. 'Were you trying to get out of work, or what?'

'No, but I did feel hungry. Perhaps I didn't have enough to eat before I came on duty.'

'Perhaps not,' replied Arthur, 'but that's not all that's the matter with you.'

'The matter with me?' repeated Amy. 'Is there something the matter with me? I haven't been feeling ill at all.'

'Oh, you're not ill, Amy, just about to be a mother in a few months.' Amy was stunned into silence. 'Yes, I think the baby will appear in about three or four months time.'

'But, I'm a widow,' gasped Amy eventually.

'I know, but you were married, weren't you?' asked Arthur gently.

'A baby. Geoffrey's baby,' said Amy quietly and then burst into tears. At this point, night sister came bustling into the alcove.

'What's going on here? Someone said that one of my nurses had fainted. What's happened Doctor Marsden?'

'Amy has fainted and it's all due to her being enceinte, sister.'

'Since when? Nobody told me,' night sister replied.

'Nobody knew, least of all the mother-to-be. I suggest we get her to her bedroom and let her rest.'

'Yes, certainly Doctor Marsden,' said night sister, bustling around. 'And first thing in the morning, I'll tell Matron and arrange your discharge.'

'My discharge?' asked Amy.

'Of course, Wilson, we can't have girls in your condition working here. Far too dangerous.'

'Right,' replied Amy, thinking what on earth she was going to do if she was discharged. Well, never mind, she must worry about that tomorrow. She was bundled up to her room and encouraged to rest.

Once she was on her own, Amy lay in bed and felt her stomach. There was definitely a large mound there, under her belt. She had noticed that all her dresses were getting tight but had put that down to eating more.

A baby of Geoffrey's! She hugged herself and gently explored her abdomen. Why had she never thought that she might be expecting a baby? Probably because she had been too busy trying to fight the black fog and keep her mind on her work, she reflected to herself. And Arthur said that the baby would be due in about three to four months. Where would she live? How would she manage? But even though she was excited, Amy fell asleep and slept for twelve hours.

A knock on the door woke her the next evening. It was a maid asking if Amy was able to go and see Matron. Amy said that she could be there in ten minutes and quickly got dressed.

Amy knocked on Matron's door and was ushered in.

'Come and sit down, Wilson. What a surprise you've given us?'

Amy laughed. 'I've given myself a surprise, too. I'd no idea.'

'Didn't you miss your monthly courses?'

'Not altogether. I've had some small ones, but I've never had them regularly anyway, and with all the upset, I just thought they would sort themselves out again later. I did notice that my dresses were getting tight, though,' Amy said sheepishly.'

'Never mind, you can get the rest and help you need now. Your discharge will come through immediately in the circumstances. You're owed a considerable amount in wages as you have hardly taken anything whilst you have been here. I can arrange a bank draft for the amount due. Also, I'll arrange some transport home. What address is that?'

Amy looked forlorn. 'I'm not sure. I don't have a permanent address,' and then she remembered Molly's mum telling her she could have a home there anytime. 'I'll be staying temporarily at Sister Jolley's house at Burnley, in Lancashire.'

'I'll arrange transport for you then. Until then, please could you refrain from working? It shouldn't be more than a day or two, but I won't be responsible for any harm coming to your unborn child. It horrifies me to think that you've been putting yourself at risk these last few months. But we didn't know, so there was nothing we could do, was there?' Amy merely nodded at this long speech, and thanked Matron and returned to her room. Finding herself restless, she went out for a walk, but the evening sky was darkening so she returned fairly soon.

Next morning, she walked down to the river bank and sat watching the river flow by. She sat and told Geoffrey all about the baby and then cried tears of sadness and joy. Sadness, that he would never hold his child. Joy, that she would have something of Geoffrey forever more.

The transport was soon arranged and Amy was back in Burnley two weeks from first finding out about the baby. Arriving at Molly's without warning was a big shock to the family, but nothing to the shock when they heard the reason for her return so soon. Mrs Smith assured Amy of help and that she could stay until the baby was born.

The following day, Mrs Smith reorganised the front parlour and let Amy live in that room. As the days passed, Amy got used to the new shape of her body and felt the baby making lots of movement. It was a time of peace and relaxation.

During this time, Amy made a very frivolous purchase. She bought a small Ford automobile and had lessons in how to drive it. She decided that it would be useful to her when she had the baby. Mrs Smith was aghast. No one she knew had an automobile. Only the rich people in Burnley had them, she said. At first, she was reluctant to go in the automobile, but young Peter had no such qualms, or little Judith and Heather, either. The young Smiths loved being taken out in the automobile, although Amy could only just get behind the steering wheel.

Although Amy was very happy for the first few weeks, she felt that perhaps she ought to try and find Geoffrey's family and let them know about the baby. It would be something of Geoffrey that they could hold on to and help assuage their grief.

'Mrs Smith,' said Amy the next evening, 'I'm very happy here, but I think I owe it to Geoffrey's family to tell them about the baby.'

'Good idea, Amy. I'm surprised you haven't contacted them before,' replied Mrs Smith.

'I don't even know if Geoffrey told them we'd got married. He was going to do it after our honeymoon.' Amy's eyes filled up with tears as she remembered the abrupt end to her honeymoon and Mrs Smith tried to divert her thoughts.

'Cuppa tea time, girl,' she said jovially. 'You start thinking about the letter you are going to write.' Amy sat quietly whilst Mrs Smith pottered about the kitchen.

'I think I want to go and see them. Really, I should let them have some say in where their grandchild is brought up. As far as I remember, Geoffrey was the heir, so that means this child, if it's a boy, will become the next heir.'

'But don't they live down south?'

'Yes,' replied Amy, 'near Bury St Edmunds in Suffolk.'

'That's a long way to go in your condition, Amy.'

'I know, but I feel like I want to go, even so.'

'That's up to you, but I'd think very carefully about it if it was me.'
'I have thought carefully, but I know it's what Geoffrey would want, so I'm going to go. I'll have to work out a map for myself, and find out where I can stay along the way. I'll ask for advice at the garage in town, the one under the culvert.'
'Good idea. And I'll pack you some food to take with you, in case you don't find nice eating places.'
'Bless you, Mrs Smith. What would I have done without you? Thank you for everything you've done for me. I can never repay you.'
'No need, girl,' replied Mrs Smith gruffly, 'you've paid your way more than enough whilst you've lived here, so no need for thanks.'

A few days later, Amy set off with the car packed up with her belongings and sandwiches. Mrs Smith waved a tearful goodbye, but was considerably cheered up when the postman arrived with a letter from Jimmy, saying that he was coming home on leave. It was a much happier Mrs Smith that waved Amy off that bright morning. Amy wondered what the future would bring, but knew she must do it for Geoffrey's sake and for their baby.

Chapter 20

Amy pulled the car on to the side of the road and checked the name of the house. Fornham House proclaimed the sign. She turned the wheel, her heart pounding, and released the clutch slowly, allowing the car to roll forward into the drive. Amy drove cautiously up the tree-lined drive: the path being made darker by overhanging trees. After about half a mile, the trees became less dense and she could see the side of the house. She drove round the side of the house and stopped at the front door.

It was just as Geoffrey had described it. A house obviously built in Elizabethan times, with the traditional 'E' shape to it. Nobody came out to welcome her, so Amy slowly heaved herself out of the car, stretching her aching back as she did so. She reached for her handbag, walked over to the front door and rang the bell.

Eventually, an elderly butler, who looked Amy up and down with distaste, opened the door.

'Yes, Miss?' he said in a haughty manner.

'I wonder if I could see Lord or Lady Storm?'

'Do you have an appointment?'

'Er, no.'

'His Lordship doesn't usually see people without an appointment. The family is in mourning, you know.'

'Yes, I know, I knew Geoffrey,' replied Amy, her heart contracting inside her as she thought about Geoffrey.

'What name is it then Miss?'

'Amy. Amy Wilson. Well, Storm really.'

'Stand here,' ordered the butler, pointing to the porch. 'I will ask His Lordship if he is available.'

Amy was left standing in the porch for several minutes. She could just see into the large entrance hall, which had been the main hall of the house in its early history. Its walls were adorned with shields and helmets and other weaponry.

The butler returned.

'What do you wish to see His Lordship about, Miss?' he sniffed.

Amy was getting just a little fed up of this man's attitude. Besides, she was tired and her back was aching. 'That's my business. I will only speak to His Lordship about why I want to see him,' she snapped back. With a decided humph, the butler walked back down the corridor without speaking. He soon returned and told Amy to follow him.

Amy was escorted through the large entrance hall and into a small room at the side. Amy noticed the circular rent table in the middle of the room. They had shown her into the room where the tenants were interviewed. There were only formal stand chairs and an uncomfortable looking sofa, and yet the room had an elegance all its own, despite its austerity. There was no one in the room so it gave Amy chance to look round. She was longing to sit down, but no one had told her to and she knew her manners.

It was a pleasant room, she decided. It could be made very comfortable, as it overlooked the side of the house and a small rose garden. She went over to the side of the room to get a better look at the roses. These would be Geoffrey's mother's roses. They were her pride and joy, Geoffrey had told Amy.

Standing sideways, looking out of the window was how Lord Storm found her: her pregnancy very evident from her side profile.

'I believe you want to see me about some private business, Miss?'

'Yes, are you Lord Storm?' asked Amy, with a quiet reminder that he hadn't introduced himself.

'I am. And who are you and what business could you possibly have with me?'

'I am Amy Wilson, well, actually Storm. May I sit down? I feel a trifle faint.'

'Yes, of course. Sit there,' he directed, pointing to the uncomfortable sofa. 'Would you like a glass of water?'

'Yes please,' whispered Amy, her head beginning to swim. She started walking towards the sofa but didn't make it and fell to the floor in a faint. Lord Storm hurried over to the bell push and summoned help.

A chubby maid entered and was politely asking what His Lordship wanted when she saw Amy's body curled up on the floor.

'Goodness, whatever's happened here?' she exclaimed and ran over to Amy and helped her on to the sofa. Lord Storm stood by the fireplace doing nothing; a disdainful expression on his face.

'I'll just get Mrs Bird, the housekeeper,' said the maid and made to leave the room.

'No, don't leave. I'll ring for Mrs Bird to come.' He rang the bell once more. A tall thin maid answered the summons this time.
'You rang Sir?'
'Yes, could you get Mrs Bird to help this woman and ask Her Ladyship to come here as well?' The tall maid ran out of the room and returned shortly accompanied by Mrs Bird. She assessed the situation straight away, but by this time, Amy was beginning to come round.
'I'm so sorry. I don't know what came over me,' she stammered.
'Don't worry Miss,' whispered Mrs Bird. 'Has your time come?'
'No, I'm not due for another three weeks.'
'Have you had any pains?'
'I've had backache all week, but I must admit, it has got worse today.'
At this point, Her Ladyship entered.
'What is all the commotion about?' she asked. 'Smith says that a young woman has fainted. Who is she?'
'I don't know,' replied her husband. 'I asked her the self same question and she just went and fainted.'
'Well, she seems to have recovered now. Who are you, girl.'
'My name is Amy Wilson, or should I say Storm now. I was married to your son Geoffrey.' At this, Lady Storm started shrieking. 'Get her out, the brazen hussy. Get her out. How dare she come here and say she was married to my son. My poor dear Geoffrey.' The maid and housekeeper were all agog at this news and Lord Storm saw the looks on their faces.'
'Right, you can all leave the room. Now,' he thundered and the maid and Mrs Bird left quickly. 'You too my dear,' Lord Storm said to his wife. 'I shall deal with this . . this person . . better without you present.'
'Indeed I will not leave,' she replied. 'No one insults my beloved son and gets away with it. I will stay and deal with this hussy. Now what do you really want? Is it money?'
'I don't want anything,' whispered Amy. 'I really was married to your son in France. We got married by special licence.'
'Nonsense. Our son would have told us if he was getting married. And anyway, he died eight months ago,' she said supremely.

'Yes,' said Amy sadly, 'he died before we could finish our honeymoon.'
'Looks like you already had a long enough honeymoon by the condition of you,' said Lady Storm spitefully. 'But I don't believe there was a marriage.'
'I assure you there was. We were married by special licence in France. We had the civil ceremony and a church service and intended coming home to have a blessing in church and have a reception here after the war. Then we would have had a proper honeymoon afterwards.'
'And you expect me to believe you?' spat Lady Storm. 'You're just trying to sully my son's reputation.'
'I have a marriage certificate with me. It's in my bag,' Amy replied, looking round for her bag. It had fallen to the floor. As she stood up to retrieve it, a sharp pain went from her back round to her front. She gasped but said nothing. Getting her bag and looking inside, she produced her wedding certificate and passed it to Lady Storm, who carefully perused it.
'But it's in French!' she exclaimed.
'Yes, Lady Storm, we were married in France, as I said,' replied Amy politely, trying to ignore the pain in her stomach.
'How do we know you really got married? You could have forged this to try and get something out of us.'
'We were married and Geoffrey said that he had written to tell you. He said that you wouldn't be pleased as you had wanted him to marry your neighbours' daughter,' gasped Amy.
'They were practically engaged. He had no right to dally with you.'
'But he didn't want to marry Lavinia,' Amy replied. 'He told me so. And she didn't want to marry him either. Geoffrey said it was just in your minds.' Lady Storm ignored this comment but soon started bawling again.
'And anyway, how did you meet him, if he was in France?'
'I was a nurse in France.'
'A nurse? My son married a common or garden nurse? Nurses are little better than whores!' screamed Lady Storm.
'Really my dear,' Lord Storm intervened. 'I don't think there is call for such language. Just sit down and talk about this calmly.'

'Calmly? Calmly? You ask me to be calm when this women is making all these false allegations about our beloved son.'
'But think dear, if she is right, then she is carrying Geoffrey's baby. At least we will have something of Geoffrey left to us,' suggested Lord Storm sadly.
'Never! I will never accept her as Geoffrey's wife. How would we know it was Geoffrey's baby anyway? She could have been with any amount of men out there and decided to foist it on Geoffrey. Knowing he was dead, he couldn't speak up for himself. And anyway, why has she only arrived now? Why hasn't she been before?'
The pains were getting more intense and Amy fidgeted around in the seat. She decided she was getting nowhere and wished she hadn't come. But she would have to answer that last question. They deserved to know why she had taken so long.
'I didn't realise I was with child for some months. I thought that it was grief after Geoffrey's death. And then I fainted at work and the doctor was brought to me. He told me what had caused the faint. I was instantly relieved of my duties and sent back to England. But I was very weary and have only just recovered sufficiently to come and find you. I can see you don't want to know me and don't believe my story so I will go now and never bother you again. Goodbye.'
Amy stood up and started walking towards the door when she was suddenly aware of wetness running down her legs: a pool appearing on the floor beneath her.
'Oh dear, I am so sorry,' she said. With an expression of disgust on her face, Lady Storm hurried to the bell pull. Mrs Bird answered it.
'Yes, My Lady?'
'Get Doctor Thistlethwaite. Immediately. And take this woman up to the servants' quarters. She appears to be in childbirth.'
'The servants' quarters?' Mrs Bird looked at Amy. 'I don't think that she could climb all those stairs, your Ladyship, if you'll pardon me saying so. Perhaps we could put her in a room on a lower level?'
'Very well. Put her where you think, Bird.'
'Thank you your Ladyship. Come dear; let's get you upstairs,' she said gently to Amy. Amy smiled in return; the first kind words she had received in this awful house.

On leaving the room, Mrs Bird shouted instructions to the other servants, whilst guiding Amy towards the staircase.
'Just take your time, dear. Stop and rest when you have a pain, if you like.'
Amy rested gratefully on Mrs Bird's arm and slowly took each step at a time, heaving her bulk onto the step. Mrs Bird steered her into a large bedroom situated at the front of the house. Between pains, Amy reflected that probably this wasn't where Lady Storm would want her to go but she didn't really care anymore. All she wanted to do was lie down or even better, for the pains to go away.
Mrs Bird led Amy to a large bed and helped her onto it. One of the maids arrived in the room, bringing hot water and old towels.
'There you are my dear. Let's get you out of those wet things,' said Mrs Bird.
'Thank you for helping me. I'd no idea the baby would be born so soon. I would never have come otherwise.'
'So you are Mrs Geoffrey?'
'Yes, I am, not that they believe me.'
'Oh never mind them. Let's concentrate on you. I'm pleased you're going to have Mr Geoffrey's baby, I really am. He was a special lad to me. Oh, is that another pain?' she asked as Amy gasped out loud. Amy merely nodded, unable to speak until the wave of pain subsided.
'How long will this go on Mrs Bird? I don't think that I can stand it much longer,' asked Amy.
'You asking me, when you're a nurse?' laughed Mrs Bird.
'I never did midwifery. The war was on and I wanted to do my bit. Oh, here it comes again.' Mrs Bird stroked her back whilst the pain passed.
'Have a sip of water, that will make you feel better,' said Mrs Bird.
'Thank you. You're right. I needed that water. My mouth is all dry. Oh no, I think that I want to go to the toilet urgently. Have you a chamber nearby? I don't think I could walk to the bathroom.'
'Let me look at you first.'
'Why look at me, I tell you, I need the toilet.'
'Do you mean you want to bear down?'
'Yes,' gasped Amy irritably.

'I think that means your baby is coming soon. Next time you get a pain, start pushing down into your bottom. Southam, go and see if that doctor has arrived.' The maid scurried off on her errand and soon returned with the doctor in tow. He was just in time to see Mrs Bird deliver the head of the baby.

'Now then young woman,' said Doctor Thistlethwaite. 'You seem to be doing all right, you and Mrs Bird between you.' Amy grimaced, feeling as though her insides were going to split irrevocably, but then another pain erupted and she had no choice but to bear down.

With this next pain, the baby's body slid out. Amy fell back against the pillows exhausted, not even caring what she had given birth to; just relieved that the pain had stopped.

It was only when a faint mewling cry was heard that she lifted her head up and looked at the baby. It was covered in a white creamy substance and a lot of blood.

'What is that white stuff? Is it all right?' Amy asked in alarm.

'Was your baby due, child?' asked the kindly doctor.

'No. Not for about three weeks.'

'That's why it is covered in the white stuff. Because it's a little early. It's called lanugo. It will soon disappear with the first bath. Now, don't you want to know what sort of baby you've had?'

Amy nodded, still too weary to care very much.

'You have a boy and to say he is early, he seems to be all right. I will check him over thoroughly when I have finished with you. Now let's get rid of the afterbirth. Just one more push, if you please. And again. Try and push harder, like you did with your baby. There that's it. I'll just have a look to see if there is any damage down below.' The doctor started to prod around but seemed satisfied with what he found.

'Not a tear at all. You're born for childbirth. I assume this is your first?'

'Yes, my first,' replied Amy with her eyes shut, 'and probably my last.'

'Come come, my dear, don't say that. All new mothers feel like that when they have given birth, but by this time next year, I'm sure you will be eager to have another one. Now where is the proud father? I don't think I know you. I had no idea anyone who was with child was visiting Lady Storm. I wish I'd been informed.'

'She came unexpected Doctor,' replied Mrs Bird, 'and then her time came upon her. It caught us all by surprise, I can tell you. Oh Miss, whatever is the matter?'

'I'll never have another baby. Geoffrey is dead,' wailed Amy.

'Geoffrey?' said Doctor Thistlethwaite.

'This is Mr Geoffrey's widow,' said Mrs Bird proudly, 'and this is his son born in his own bed.'

Amy stared at Mrs Bird. 'What do you mean? Born in his own bed?'

'I brought you into Mr Geoffrey's bedroom. Her Ladyship won't like it, but it's too late now. It was the nearest bedroom anyway. Yes, you've just given birth on your husband's bed.'

Amy dissolved into even greater tears. Doctor Thistlethwaite left the room hurriedly

'Now, now, Mrs Geoffrey,' said Mrs Bird, 'here's your little boy. You give him a cuddle.' She placed a bundle of towels into Amy's arms. Peeping out was a little face, with Geoffrey's defined black eyebrows and his turned up nose: two bright blue eyes staring out at her. Amy was overwhelmed with a fierce love that she could never have imagined. Her baby. Hers and Geoffrey's baby. If only he had lived to see him, she thought to herself. Or even if he had known that she was going to have a child.

'Whatever happens, my son, I will always look after you, even though your father's family don't want to know,' she vowed out loud to the baby.

'I'm sure that the family will come round, Mrs Geoffrey, as soon as they see the baby. He's just like Mr Geoffrey was as a baby. They can't deny that.'

'I doubt it,' replied Amy, 'not from the look of disgust on Her Ladyship's face.' But further discussion was brought to an end as the maid came into the room, bearing cups of tea for both Amy and Mrs Bird. Mrs Bird carefully removed the baby from Amy.

'Best cup of tea I've ever had,' enthused Amy to the maid. 'After years of hospital tea, I've forgotten what real tea tastes like.' She started to yawn. 'I feel like I could sleep for a week,' she said, but her son, who started to wail, interrupted her.

'I think junior is jealous of us all having a cup of tea,' laughed Mrs Bird. 'I think he wants a feed, too.'

'Oh, what shall I do? I don't know how to feed babies,' said Amy aghast.

'I'm sure between you you'll find out what to do. Here, let me put him to the breast.' Mrs Bird helped the baby to latch on to Amy's breast and after a few seconds, he seemed to get the gist of it and started sucking vigorously.

'Oh,' said Amy, 'he feels like he has got teeth already.'

'You wait 'til he has, then you'll know about it,' laughed Mrs Bird.

'Have you had a baby, Mrs Bird?' asked Amy. Her laughing face closed instantly. 'Yes, I had a baby, two in fact,' Mrs Bird replied dully.

'I'm sorry, have I said the wrong thing?'

'No, it's all right. I lost both my babies to diphtheria. The big one was two and the baby was six months.' Amy hugged her son more tightly: fearful of unknown diseases that might attack him in the future. Mrs Bird continued, 'I nearly went mad. And then my husband died in an accident at work, so I'd no home and no babies. I came here as a wet nurse, for Mr Geoffrey. Her Ladyship wouldn't feed him. That's why he was so special to me.'

'And you stayed on?' asked Amy quietly.

'Yes, I never wanted to leave after that. I felt like God had given Mr Geoffrey to me to heal my heart. He certainly did, although I was very careful not to talk like that to his mother. Very jealous woman she is. Here, let me take him off you and put him to bed in this old drawer. It'll have to do until I can get someone to retrieve the family cot from the attics.' Amy reluctantly relinquished her hold on her son and watched Mrs Bird tenderly handling the baby.

'I am so sorry for you. You must have been heartbroken when Geoffrey died.'

'Yes, I was, but then I was so thrilled when you said who you were. I knew how Her Ladyship would react, but I don't care. I shall always love this little boy, as much as I loved Mr Geoffrey. Now what are you going to call him? You'd better give him a name.'

'I'll call him Geoffrey Arthur. Arthur was my dad.'

'Geoffrey Arthur Storm, yes, I like that,' reflected Mrs Bird.

'Oh no,' laughed Amy. 'Not Geoffrey Arthur Storm. That'll mean he's G A S, you know, gas.' The two women laughed.

'Well perhaps I can call him Geoffrey Arthur Robert instead. That will be GARS. That sounds better, doesn't it?'

'Yes, it does. Who is Robert?'

'My guardian, after my father died. He was actually lost on the Titanic.' Amy stopped dead in the middle of the sentence. What had happened to her? She had just talked naturally about her past. Is this what childbirth did to you?

'What's the matter? Are you all right?' urged Mrs Bird.

Amy pondered for a while then replied in the affirmative. 'Yes, yes, I am all right. That's only the second time I've ever been able to talk about my past. I've kept it very closely hidden until now.'

They were disturbed from further confidences by the arrival of Lady Storm.

'Oh, the brat's been born I see. What are you going to do now, madam?' she asked Amy. Amy merely stared at her.

'Oh Lady Storm, do you want to see your grandchild? He looks just like your son, Mr Geoffrey when he was a baby.'

Lady Storm glanced casually at the baby. 'Nonsense, Bird. I see no such likeness. Now what are you going to do, I ask again. When can you go to your people as I don't want you staying here.'

'But she's just given birth!' spluttered Mrs Bird.

'That's not my fault. She shouldn't have come out in public, showing herself in that condition. It just shows she is ill-bred.'

'I am certainly not ill-bred as you so delicately put it, Lady Storm,' Amy coolly replied. 'Indeed I lived in a far grander house than this, although my family were not aristocrats. I most certainly will leave here as soon as possible, as I find it claustrophobic. I'm sure Mrs Bird will assist me to find some lodgings.'

'Why can't you go to your family then? And your grand house that you brag about.'

'Because I have no family. They were all lost on the Titanic. And it is only lately that I have remembered who I was and where I came from. Be assured, Lady Storm, I will leave here at the earliest opportunity. In my own grief, I thought that knowing your son had a wife and a grandchild on the way would be a comfort to you. I now see the error of my ways. I will trouble you no longer than I need to.'

'Good, I'm glad we understand each other.' She turned her back on Amy. 'And now Bird, will you explain why you let this creature give birth in my son's bed?'
'It was the nearest bedroom, Your Ladyship. I thought she was going to give birth on the stairs.'
'A likely story, I suppose you believed all that talk about my beloved son. How dare she sully his name!'
'Yes, I did believe her. Especially when I saw the youngster. Just like Mr Geoffrey. At least he's got his father's name,' she said defiantly.
'Father's name, what do you mean?' shrieked Lady Storm.
'She's calling him Geoffrey Arthur Robert Storm.'
'Oh no she is not. Over my dead body, I'll sue her.'
'I don't think you could. Anyway, why tell the whole world your business?' Mrs Bird retorted.
'Bird, you have overstepped your mark. You are dismissed. And when you go, make sure you take this baggage with you.' With that, Lady Storm marched out of the room.
Silence reigned in the room for several seconds and then both Amy and Mrs Bird started talking together.
'You go first, Mrs Geoffrey.'
'I am so sorry, Mrs Bird. I have just lost you your job.'
'Don't worry. It's the best day's work ever. I've been fed up here for a long time. Her Ladyship never liked me. She knew that Mr Geoffrey preferred me to her. Since he was killed she has been evil. She has almost blamed me for his death.'
'How can she do that? It was an aeroplane that killed him.'
'She was so pleased when he got refused to go in the army. He tried the navy and the new flying corps as well, but they wouldn't take him. When he came home to tell us that he had volunteered to drive the ambulance carriages, I thought she would have a heart attack. I made the mistake of sticking up for him in the ensuing battle. She never forgave me. She wanted to keep him at home.'
'But what will you do now, Mrs Bird?'
'I've got a nice nest egg hidden away. I won't starve.'
'But where will you get a job? She won't give you a reference. Well, not a fair one anyway.'

'That's a point. But I won't worry for a while. I have enough to buy a little cottage and can look around for work. I've been here thirty years and never been on holiday or spent very much on myself. I'll be all right, don't you worry. But what about yourself and the little one? What will you do?'

'I've no idea. I never dreamed that they'd throw me out like this. I'll have to think as well.'

'You could come and live with me in my cottage until you sort yourself out, if you like?'

'Why Mrs Bird, that's ever so kind of you. But I'm not without money either. I had nowhere to go and nothing to spend my wages on whilst I was in France. I too, have a reasonable nest egg, and intend buying a cottage myself. Look, why don't we go to my hotel rooms for a while until we decide what to do? Perhaps I can employ you until I get stronger and the baby is older. At least then I could give you a reference.'

'That would be useful. If you're sure, I think that would be the best solution for both of us. Let me go and make some plans. I need to find out how soon you can be moved.'

'I'll leave it with you. I just need to sleep, for about a week!' laughed Amy.

Chapter 21

Amy woke up next morning and for a moment wondered where she was. She had slept in so many strange beds over the years and she had often felt like this on waking. Then she felt her almost flat tummy and remembered. Her son, where was he? She looked anxiously round the room but he wasn't there. What if Lady Storm had taken him in the night to harm him? She would never forgive herself. Fancy falling asleep and not caring about her son. She sat up in bed, and felt blood draining away from her.

Not daring to get up from the bed in case she fainted again, Amy sat fretting. Fortunately, it wasn't long before Southam, the maid, came in.

'Where is my baby?

'He's quite safe, Miss. Mrs Bird took him to her room last night. I'll bring him down for you now you're awake. He's ready for a feed.'

'Thank you.' She rearranged the old nightdress that someone had put on her and got ready to feed. Southam brought the baby in and helped her start to suckle.'

'He's a bonny baby, Miss, if I may say so.'

'You're right, he is, and yes, you may say so,' beamed Amy.

'Just like the photographs of Mr Geoffrey when he was a baby. Especially the one in the lounge.'

'Really? I'd love to see it. Do you think you could bring it in to me, when no one's looking?'

'Oh, I don't know Miss. What if Her Ladyship should catch me?'

Amy's face fell. 'It doesn't matter then. It's just that I never saw any pictures of Mr Geoffrey when he was small, with meeting him in France.'

'I'll see what I can do Miss. Leave it with me. I can always tell her that the frame broke when we were dusting, if she misses it.'

'Thank you, I would really appreciate it.' Southam left, looking rather worried. Amy hoped that she didn't get into trouble or she would be the cause of more staff getting dismissed. On her own with the baby, Amy considered him minutely. She examined every part of him, trying to see images of Geoffrey or her own family imprinted in that little face and body. He definitely had Geoffrey's eyebrows and eyes, and the turned up tip of his nose, but his jaw wasn't the same. It was more like Uncle Robert's jaw, Amy reflected. His hair looked as if it would be dark too, unlike her own family who were all fair-haired.

Amy examined his tiny fingers and toes and exclaimed in delight when Geoffrey curled his fingers round hers. She explored the little soft spot on top of his head and worried that she might damage it. Then with bated breath, she turned him to sit forward to see if there was the ugly birthmark on the back of his head that she carried herself. One of the other nurses said that birthmarks often continued down the family line. She let out a sigh of relief. No birthmark on his head, or anywhere else she was delighted to note.

Some time later, Southam returned with a duster in her hands. Closing the door firmly, she took the duster off and brought the silver photo frame over to Amy. Taking the baby away, she placed him carefully in the drawer.

Amy looked down at the picture of a small baby, lying on a rug. Mrs Bird was right. The picture was just like her own son. Mrs Bird coming into the room interrupted them. Southam looked worried, but Mrs Bird soon reassured her.

'You go now Southam. I'll take the brunt if Her Ladyship sees this picture.' With a grateful smile, Southam hurriedly left the room.

'How are you this morning?'

'Sore!'

'Mmm, and your milk hasn't even come in properly yet. Wait until tomorrow or the day after,' warned Mrs Bird ominously.

'I can't wait,' said Amy laughing.

'I've spoken to the doctor. He says that you can be moved if you go by ambulance, but only to a hospital.'

'That's no good. I don't really want to go in to hospital now. Is he here?'

'No. I caught him at his house this morning. He's coming in to see you later today though.'

'I'll have a word with him then.'

'Is there anything else that you want me to do?'

'Yes, can you inform the hotel what has happened to me and ask them to keep my room vacant? Oh and also could you ask them to reserve a room for you, near to me?'

'I can do both of those things. Anything else?'

'I don't suppose you can drive an automobile can you?'
'Afraid not.'
'My automobile is here. I won't be able to drive for a while, so could you arrange for it to be collected and taken to the hotel?'
'I could ask Rowlands to take it for you. He's the Lordship's chauffeur. I'm sure he would oblige when I tell him the circumstances. It was Mr Geoffrey who taught him to drive when Lord Storm first got an automobile.'
'That would be a great help. And also, could you buy some clothes for the poor little baby? He can't stay in towels all his life.'
'I'm sure there are plenty of old clothes up in the attics but I wouldn't dare suggest it to Her Ladyship. I'm avoiding her at all costs at the moment. She wants me out of here by tonight.'
'Leave her to me. She'll be so glad I'm going that she won't care. As soon as you leave here, go and take up residence in my hotel. I'll join you as soon as I possibly can.'
'Right. I'd better get on with all those instructions. Goodness, it's going to be hard working for you, if you give instructions at this rate!' joked Mrs Bird.
'Yes, you might be sorry you agreed to come and work for me, Mrs Bird. I'm used to bossing young nurses around on the wards.'
'Please, don't call me Mrs Bird. My first name is Jane. Nobody ever calls me by my first name anymore.'
'And I'm Amy.'
'But you will be my employer. I can't call you by your first name.'
'Then I can't employ you,' laughed Amy. They both laughed but were disturbed by Doctor Thistlethwaite entering the room.
'And how are mother and child this bright morning?' he asked heartily.
'Coping very well with motherhood,' Mrs Bird answered for her.
'Well you should know, Mrs Bird. You did a grand job of bringing young Mr Geoffrey and his sisters up.'
'Doctor Thistlethwaite, can I go home please?' asked Amy.
'Where's home?'
'At present it's a hotel room until I decide where to live. Mrs Bird is coming with me as my nurse.'
'Mrs Bird?' started the doctor, but was too well bred to ask for explanations.

'Yes, she's decided to have a change of employment. Please, it's really important that I get away from here. I'm not welcome.'
'So I gather,' he said mysteriously. 'Well, if Mrs Bird is going to look after you, I suppose in the circumstances, you could go to the hotel. Which one is it?'
'It's the Angel in Bury St Edmonds.'
'Yes, I know it well. Certainly, you can go there and I will visit you in due course.'
'Today, can I go today?'
'Yes, but I will send an ambulance for you. I'll go and arrange it now.'
'Thank you so much. And I will pay you later for all my care that you have given here. I don't have sufficient funds with me here. It's in the hotel safe.'
'Surely Lord Storm will be paying for your confinement?'
'No. I don't wish him to. I insist that I meet all your bills.' Doctor Thistlethwaite looked puzzled, but agreed nevertheless and took his leave of the ladies.
Jane Bird told Amy that she would go and carry out all her instructions and await her arrival at the hotel. As she was going out of the room, Amy called her back.
'Can you return this photograph, please?' she asked reluctantly.
'Of course, I'll return it immediately before I leave, but I need to finish my packing now,' replied Jane and took the photograph frame away.
Amy had another sleep and then was informed by Southam that the ambulance was coming at three o'clock in the afternoon. She had brought a brown paper bag in with her which she shyly gave to Amy.
'These are from Mrs Bird. She said you'd need them.'
'Thanks. Oh look. They are beautiful baby clothes. Here's a vest, some nappies, a liberty bodice, a dress, a cardigan and woollen leggings. Oh and look at this beautiful shawl. He will be well dressed. Better than these old towels.'
'They are all very pretty. Shall I dress him, Miss?'
'Yes please, we haven't much time to spare. Could I also have a wash as well if you have time?'

'Yes, I'll get you a bowl now and then you can get washed whilst I dress the baby.'

Amy gave herself a wash all over and put her own clothes back on, but they were far too big now that she had had the baby. She would be glad to get back into clean clothes, but she would wait until she got to her hotel room. By a quarter to three, both mother and baby were ready. The ambulance carriage arrived promptly and they carried Amy out, whilst Southam carried the baby. Lord and Lady Storm were conspicuous by their absence, Amy noted sadly. How different this homecoming should have been for her son, their grandchild, so she turned away from the house and cuddled her little boy to her breast.

As she waited for the horses to move off, she heard Lady Storm's strident voice in the foyer.

'Get my son's room fumigated. Remove all traces of that woman's presence. And then strip and clean Bird's room. Good riddance to bad rubbish, is all I say.' Lord Storm said not a word, although Amy could see him looking out through the window when she got in the ambulance carriage.

Tears welled up in Amy's eyes. 'That's your grandmother shouting, little Geoffrey. May you never see her again.' Amy wiped her eyes on her sleeve and held on tight to her little boy as the horses pulled away.

The journey was not comfortable. The carriage hit many ruts on the highway and each jolt was painful to Amy. After what seemed like a long time, Amy was delivered to the hotel. She couldn't wait to get to bed. Jane was fussing about her like a mother hen and Amy was glad to give her the care of Geoffrey.

Soon, Amy was tucked up in bed and after feeding Geoffrey again to settle him after the journey, she too slept. When she awoke it was dark. Her sleep had been disturbed by a knock on the door. Jane was quick to answer it. It was the hotel manager.

'Is Mrs Storm there?' he asked.

'Yes, but she is not available to visitors. She is recently confined don't forget.'

'I'm aware of that, but I have a police constable downstairs. He insists that he sees Mrs Storm.'

'Let him come in, then,' said Amy wearily.

The young constable soon returned, looking very embarrassed at being in the room of a lady so recently confined.

'I have come at the instruction of Lady Storm. She believes that you have er, well er, taken something that belongs to her.'

'What? Have I heard you right? What could I have possible taken from Lady Storm?'

'She says that a silver photograph frame has disappeared and you were the last one to be seen with it.'

'I certainly haven't got the frame. How does she know I looked at the frame?'

'I'm only repeating what she said, Miss. Now may I look through your things?'

'Look through my things? How dare you. Are you taking me for a common thief?'

'No Miss, just doing my job. Lady Storm insisted you would have it.'

'Well, you're welcome to look through my things, only be quick about it. I don't want my baby to be disturbed, Lady Storm or no Lady Storm.'

The young constable went even redder in the face but made a cursory glance through Amy's belongings in the room.

'Thank you Miss, that all seems in order. Sorry to have troubled you.'

'Good night constable,' Amy said very gravely and he hurried out of the room.

'I can't believe the cheek of her. Fancy sending a constable after me,' raved Amy. 'I asked you to put it back Jane. What happened?'

'I don't know, I put it back where it belonged. I don't know what happened,' said Jane sharply.

'I wonder how she knew that I had been looking at it?'

'Probably bullied it out of Southam. Lady Storm could make you confess to things that weren't even your fault, just by her looks.'

'Yes I can believe it. Why did you stay?'

'I was waiting for Mr Geoffrey to come home. I was hoping that I would be there when his children were being brought up in the house. I was distraught when he died. But never mind, I've got his son now, and so help me God, I'll try and bring him up as well as I can.'

‘Thanks Jane. I am so grateful to you. I don't know what I would have done without you.’ Both women were near to tears and so Jane tried to make a joke about how soppy they both were. Anyone would think I’m getting the ‘third day blues’ like a newly confined mother.’

‘What’s third day blues?’ asked Amy.

‘Most newly delivered mothers get a bit weepy around the third day. They don’t know why. Just a reaction to birth I suppose.’

‘So I’ve that to look forward to tomorrow? They don’t tell you all these things when you are having a baby.’

‘You are quite naive about birth, aren’t you?’

‘Yes, I don't really know much about it. Not had any dealings with it.’ It was then that Amy remembered Martha in the asylum. A cloud passed over her face.

‘What’s the matter? Did I say something to upset you? Your mother didn’t die in childbirth or something?’ asked a concerned Jane.

‘It was in the asylum where I lived. There was a girl in there who had been made with child against her will and her parents sent her to the asylum. Even though the baby died, they wouldn’t take her back because of the shame, and so she was forced to stay in there with all the others.’

‘You lived in an asylum?’ gasped Jane.

‘Yes. You don’t really know anything about me and yet you have lost your job through me and decided to look after me.’

‘Any woman who married my Mr Geoffrey can’t be all bad. I can tell that you loved him dearly.’

‘Yes, I certainly did. So I’ll tell you a little about myself. I survived the Titanic but I lost the power of speech. That had happened to me on two previous occasions when I was a child. Because I couldn’t talk and I had no identifying names, they put me in an asylum, as they didn’t know what to do with me.

‘But why in an asylum? You are obviously well born.’ Jane butted in.

‘I was wearing my maid’s clothes when they found me so assumed I was of that class and as no one come forward to claim me, they put me in the asylum.’

‘That’s terrible. And when did you learn to speak again?’

‘About four or five months later. It was like a fog lifting in my brain; that’s the only way I can describe it. I got myself a job working in the asylum and then went to train as a nurse – the matron at the asylum helped me to get a place. Then virtually as soon as I qualified, I went out to France.'

'And there met Mr Geoffrey?'

'Yes, and you know the rest.'

'And do you know who you are really?'

'I suppose so, but look, little Geoffrey is stirring. I'll need to feed him. Can you pass him to me Jane.' Amy concentrated on feeding Geoffrey and avoided all talk about her past for the rest of the night.

Chapter 22

Waking early next morning, Amy felt as though she had rocks in her breasts. She could barely put her arms down by her side. Hearing Geoffrey stir, she cautiously got out of bed and went over to the crib that the hotel manager had managed to find.

With difficulty, she picked him up out of the crib and tried to suckle him. It was excruciatingly painful. She tried to reposition him, but every way still hurt her. She didn't know what to do for the best. Geoffrey was getting hungry and fretful and the more she struggled, the more he cried. Eventually, Amy burst into tears.

Jane arrived shortly afterwards to find both Amy and Geoffrey howling their heads off.

'Oh dear, are you all right Amy?'

'No, I'm not. I can't stop crying. My breasts are like rocks and I can't get Geoffrey to feed. What am I going to do? Am I going to need a wet nurse, like you were for Geoffrey?'

'Deary me, not at all. It's just that your milk has come through. It'll be like this for a day, or two at the most and then they'll go back to normal.'

'Are you sure?' asked a nervous Amy.

'Quite sure. Now, let me express a little milk to get your ducts flowing. We don't want you getting engorged. Once the milk flows, it will be easier for Geoffrey to suckle, you'll see.' Whilst talking, Jane had been massaging Amy's breasts and milk started to trickle from them. She put Geoffrey back to the breast, and once he had tasted the dribbling milk, he latched on eagerly. Amy cried out in pain, but as he continued to suckle, the milk flowed more easily and it became a little less sore. Jane put warm flannels on Amy's breasts to further ease the discomfort.

'I can't believe I just cried because he wouldn't feed. I'm not going to be a very good mother am I?'

'Of course you are, it's the third day blues I warned you about. You'll feel much brighter tomorrow.'

'Well I couldn't feel any worse, that's for sure,' Amy replied miserably. Once the feed was finished, Jane asked Amy about where she thought of getting a cottage.

'Not round here anyway,' replied Amy. 'As far away from the Storms as I can get. Why, have you any ideas?'
'No. Just wondered where you fancied living.'
'I've not thought about it really. I was waiting to see what happened when I met Geoffrey's parents. Much good that did me.'
'Where did you come from originally?'
'Yorkshire, but I don't want to go to my old home. I'm not ready for that yet. Where did you come from?'
'Ipswich, but I have no ties there now.'
'I wouldn't mind going to Lancashire. That's where I trained as a nurse. The town of Burnley was mainly full of cotton mills and coal pits, but the people were friendly enough. And houses were cheap too.'
'Shall I enquire if we can buy a house there, then?'
'Yes, but not in the centre. I wouldn't want Geoffrey to grow up in Pickup Croft. A little further out from the centre, perhaps.'
'I'll go and enquire in the town today as to how to go about finding property in Burnley. I'm sure the land agent will have contacts in other counties.'
'Probably. That's a good place to start anyway.'
'If you don't need me anymore, I'll go now. I'll just change Geoffrey first and settle him down for his nap.'
'And I'll go and have a sleep whilst you are out. Exhausting, this motherhood, isn't it?' Amy yawned. Jane laughed and before she had finished settling Geoffrey, Amy was sound asleep.
When Jane arrived back in the hotel room, Amy was starting to stir.
'Come on lazybones. You'll sleep your life away,' teased Jane. Amy stirred luxuriantly in bed and grinned.
'I've never spent so much time in bed. There was a distinct lack of sleep in France. Just as we were allowed to go to bed, there would be a fresh arrival of patients from the front. So it was back to the wards to receive them. Mind you, there was always a chance of seeing Geoffrey, so most of the time I didn't mind,' she chuckled.
There was a gentle knock at the door and Amy worried that it might be the constable again. Jane opened the door and they were both relieved to see Rowlands.
'Begging your pardon, Mrs Bird, I've just delivered the automobile for the lady.'

'Do come in,' shouted Amy, 'Rowlands, isn't it?'
'Yes, ma'am,' he said removing his hat and shuffling a little way into the room. At his feet behind him Jane noticed a large parcel as she went to shut the door.
'Is this parcel yours, Rowlands?'
'Oh yes, it's for the baby. All the staff have collected together and bought some things for the baby, if you'll accept them of course ma'am.'
'Why, how kind of them. They don't know me at all. Let me look at them.' Amy opened the package and out fell lots of baby garments and necessities, in all different sizes and suitable for different kinds of weather. Amy was overwhelmed. This set of clothes would last her many months.
'How can I thank you all? I only met three or four of you but you said that these were from all the staff?'
'They all loved Mr Geoffrey and felt that they dealt with you shabbily. So it's good luck to you ma'am.'
Rowlands was obviously embarrassed and appeared keen to depart so Amy didn't delay him.
'Please thank all the staff for their kind gifts. I can never repay them all, but I am very grateful.'
'Thanks ma'am, we just wanted to do our bit.' Rowlands nodded and backed out of the room. As soon as he had gone, Amy burst into tears at the wonderful kindness she had received from strangers, in direct contrast to her baby's own flesh and blood.
'These clothes will last the baby for ages,' said Jane on a practical note. 'It's just the mother who might need some new clothes!'
'I agree. I didn't have many anyway. I've gone almost from nurses uniform to loose clothes. With wearing uniform for so many years, I didn't buy many clothes. I had a few serviceable outfits, mainly skirts and blouses. Why, I even borrowed my wedding dress! I had just one nice frock that I bought when I was in France, but I can't get into that at the moment. I'll have to regain my figure first,' she said sadly.
'Where are all your clothes at the moment?'
'In the wardrobe. That's all I possess.'
Jane crossed the room to have a look inside and shook her head. 'I have more clothes than you, Amy. Look, we're about the same size

at the moment. I could lend you some of my day dresses. They are rather drab but serviceable, and I don't think you are ready for going out to balls yet,' Jane joked.

'No not this week, perhaps next week,' Amy replied in the same vein. 'I'd be very grateful for the loan of some of your dresses. At least I could wash the clothes I had on when I arrived at Fornham House.'

'I'll do that for you and I could alter them to fit your new figure.'

'Could you? That would be good. I wouldn't need to buy any new clothes until I regained my figure.'

'I could start on your other clothes now if you like? All the clothes you have been wearing whilst you were with child can be taken in.'

'And also Jane, I would like you to ask a photographer to come and take a picture of little Geoffrey lying on a rug, just like the one that I'm supposed to have stolen. It will be a reminder of my Geoffrey if little Geoffrey is lying in the same pose.'

'Yes, I'm sure I can find a photographer in Bury St Edmunds.'

Once the baby and Amy were both fed and resting, Jane took the opportunity to slip into town. She found a land agent on the square near the Corn Market and asked his advice.

'I don't know of any land agents in Lancashire, it being so far away. I suggest you go and stay in an hotel in the area and you can ask the local land agent.'

'Thank you. I'll inform my employer. You've been most helpful.'

'Good day and I wish you success,' he replied.

Jane bought a few necessary purchases and returned to find Amy up and about in the bedroom, wearing one of Jane's dresses.

'Should you be up and about so early Amy?'

'If I worked in a mill in Burnley I'd be back to work by now. It doesn't seem to do them any harm. Did you find a land agent?'

'Yes, but he didn't know any names and addresses. He suggested that we go to Burnley and stay at an hotel and look for a local land agent there.'

'Sounds like a good idea. But how soon will they let me go? We'll have to ask the doctor when he comes to see me.'

'Also, the photographer is coming tomorrow morning to take his photograph.'

'Oh good. Now let's look at what he is going to wear for his photograph.' The two of them happily sorted the new clothes out and decided what Geoffrey would wear for his first photograph.

At his next visit, Amy asked Doctor Thistlethwaite how soon she could go, but he said that it was far too early to be even thinking about such a journey as far away as Lancashire.

'Well, I'm going when Geoffrey is three weeks old whether or not,' Amy said to Jane when he'd gone. 'We just won't tell him. Perhaps the hotel manager can find out from the stagecoach driver the name of a suitable hostelry in Burnley.'

'Yes, but I'm not going by stagecoach. It's silly when I've got an automobile at my disposal.'

'You can't start motoring so soon,' said Jane aghast.

'I don't intend doing, but I must get some person to do it. Do you want to learn, Jane?'

'Goodness me! I couldn't learn to drive. But perhaps Rowlands would do it for us if he can take some time off for holidays. Then he could get the stagecoach back again. Shall I ask him?'

'Please, that would help us a great deal. I would rather not give up my automobile just yet. I may have to one day but I love it so much. It's the one thing I miss from my former days – the ability to go where I want, when I want.'

'Did you have an automobile before then?'

'Yes, or rather my uncle did. It was a lovely Rolls Royce Silver Cloud. Mine is a very poor relation by comparison.' Amy realised that she was on dangerous ground and was perhaps revealing more to Jane than she intended doing just yet, so she changed the subject quickly. 'Will you ask Rowlands then?'

'Yes, I'll ask him tomorrow. He brings His Lordship into town on Wednesdays when the market is on and waits for him, so I'll easily be able to find Rowlands in one of the hostelries.'

The days began to take on a pattern of eating, sleeping, and changing young Geoffrey and Amy gained in confidence in handling him herself, rather than relying on Jane all the time. Amy began to get her energy back, even though the night feeds still tired her and she was inclined to rest in the afternoons with Geoffrey.

Jane returned from market and had a surprise for Amy. She gave her a parcel and inside was a photograph frame with little Geoffrey's

picture inside. The frame was almost like the missing one from Fornham House.
'Oh Jane, This is beautiful. How much do I owe you?'
'Nothing. It's my gift to you for all that you are doing for me. I'm sorry I couldn't afford a real silver one like the original, but this is best quality silver plate. It's looks very similar to the real one of his father though, doesn't it? I was pleased at how similar it looked.'
'It's nicer than the one at Fornham House, because you bought it for me. I can't wait to have my own house now, so that I can put the picture on a shelf somewhere.' Jane looked pleased with herself and then suddenly started speaking again.
'Oh, I almost forgot. Rowlands will able to accommodate your wishes. Lord and Lady Storm are going to town for two weeks to stay with their married daughter and would not require Rowlands as Lord Storm wanted to motor down himself. They are going in two weeks time.
'Perfect timing then,' commented Amy. 'Things are going to get better for us. I'm sure of that.'
'I do hope so. You've not had an easy time up to now.'
'Neither have you, living at the beck and call of Lady Storm.' They both laughed together.
'Well at least we can plan now. I've also got an address for a coaching house near Burnley. It's on the moors above Burnley and can accommodate us. Shall I write and let them know when to expect us?'
'Yes, what is it called?'
'The Waggoners, apparently it is a very reasonable and clean establishment. The coach driver personally recommended it.'
'Sounds satisfactory. Ask for a room for Rowlands as well, as he will need a rest before he returns home again.'
'I will,' said Jane. 'And he has also given us some names of coaching houses on the way up there. There are several on the Great North Road, which we will spend quite a bit of time on.'
'I don't think we need to book them, as we don't know when we will get there or how far we will motor each day.'
'True, we'll just take our chance with the other travellers.'
'Well,' said Amy, 'everything seems to be coming together for our trip. Now I need to inform the hotel manager of our intentions and also Doctor Thistlethwaite. I need to settle his account.'

Two days prior to their trip, Doctor Thistlethwaite attended for the last time. Amy tried to pay the bill for her care, but he hummed and hahed and said that there was no bill to pay.
'Why not? I expressly said that I would settle your account.'
'The estate manager from Fornham House came in and settled it in full, on Lord Storms' instructions. Said he was sorry for any inconvenience.' Amy sat and stared. Had they relented after all? Were they sorry for the way they had treated her? She thought that it was probably only Lord Storm who had changed his mind. Lady Storm would never move.
'Please could you convey my thanks to Lord Storm. I think it would be impolitic of me to write.'
'I think so, madam. I will pass your wishes on through the estate manager and I wish you well.'
The doctor left, leaving Amy sitting alone with her thoughts. Was there some interest in little Geoffrey after all? As the only son, Geoffrey had been due to inherit Fornham House and the title, so technically the estate and title should come to her son, but she locked these thoughts away for the future. Perhaps some day, when he was much older, she would investigate this further. For now, it was more important to let little Geoffrey know that he was loved and cared for. Between her and Jane, there was no danger of this not happening. Amy looked forward to the future with joy.

Chapter 23

Amy felt that they had been travelling for months, but they had arrived in Lancashire in a relatively short time. Rowlands was a safe and competent driver and seemed to instinctively know when it was time for a rest or overnight stay. Despite much stopping and starting, so that Rowlands could 'add water to the inside of the automobile engine somewhere' he explained, they made good progress. They completed the journey north in only four days and were settled into their rooms at the Waggoners Inn by nightfall of the fourth day, which was a Saturday.

The inn was in a wild location, and even though it was on a main coaching route there were no houses nearby, as it was situated on the edge of moorland. It was on top of a hill and the views into the surrounding valleys were spectacular.

The rooms were clean, if a little basic, but were adequate for a short stay and the women were glad to put their belongings away. Jane looked down out of the window towards the valley. 'You can see for miles, Amy. Is that Burnley down there?'

'Yes,' replied Amy, 'but you won't see it like that on Monday.'

'Why not?'

The mills are idle on Saturday nights and Sundays. On Monday, all those mill chimneys you can see will be firing and a thick fog will descend over the town. As you can see, Burnley is built in a valley. On clear days, that's good, as in every direction that you look, you can see hills. But when the chimneys are working, it's like living in permanent fog.'

'Now I know why you wanted to live on the outskirts of town. Well we can start looking tomorrow, or rather Monday, with tomorrow being Sunday.'

On the next day, it was decided that Rowlands was to stay an extra night so that he didn't travel on the Sabbath. Jane wished to go to church so she and Rowlands went off into Burnley to the Parish church on Church Street. Amy wasn't allowed to attend, as she had not yet been 'churched' since childbirth. Amy grumbled about this, but they knew that she would have to attend the service before she would be welcome in any church.

Instead, Jane and Amy took little Geoffrey for a short walk along the road so that they could have some fresh air after being cooped up in the automobile for so many days. The air was bracing but it had the desired effect of making them feel the benefit.

Geoffrey seemed to enjoy this environment, as he appeared to listen and look at every noise or passing vehicle. Amy commented on this to Jane, but she laughed and said that he couldn't really see anything yet. Amy was unrepentant and like all new mothers, felt that her son was extra special and knew that she was right.

On Monday morning, Rowlands took Jane, Amy and Geoffrey into town in the automobile and found a land agent on Bank Parade at the far side of town, near the Parish church that Rowlands and Jane had attended the previous day.

He apprised them of many building projects that were ongoing in the town and gave them some leaflets to read about properties that were available to buy. Armed with much reading matter, and several keys, Rowlands took them back to the Waggoner's Inn. He then decided he would set off back home that night and try and get part way home. Now that he had delivered them safely, he was hoping to visit his sister in Nottingham on the way.

Thanking him again for his services, Amy gave him some money, which he tried to refuse, but she insisted.

'I couldn't have managed this trip without you. It has made such a difference to have my automobile with me. I look forward to motoring again soon. Goodbye and safe journey.

Rowlands went out and cranked up the engine several times before it spluttered into life. With a final cheery wave, he left them and swung out on to the main road back into town. He had arranged to leave the automobile in a garage in town for safety and catch the stagecoach from there.

Jane appeared a little despondent as he left. Amy wondered perhaps if there was some interest from Jane in this worthy man.

'Will you miss Rowlands?' asked Amy casually.

'Not particularly Rowlands, but it's a severing of all my friends that I've worked with for many years.'

'Are you regretting coming with me then, Jane?'

'No, not when I can see that dear little baby over there, just a bit wistful that's all. Come on, let's look at these leaflets.'

The two women perused the literature and made a shortlist of potential properties in the town. Next morning they asked the landlord to order them a hansom cab and set off to town. They explained to the driver that they wanted to view some properties, so they would need his services for most of the day. The driver grinned his agreement, probably thinking of the nice fee he would get for a full and easy day.

'Where's your first property then Missus?' he asked.

'There are some on this side of town, just off Manchester Road. Perhaps we could view these first? There is one on Scott Park Road, one on Lansdowne Street and one on Manchester Road itself. The others are all further away.'

'Shall us start with the Manchester Road one first?'

'Yes, is that the nearest?'

'Yes, it's only a little way down here. Whoa there girl,' he called to the horse, who was having difficulty trying not to let the carriage run away down the steep hill.

Shortly afterwards they pulled up at a large house on the main steep road going into the town centre. It had a flight of stairs up to the house, with a little garden in front, and was the middle house of a long terrace. They alighted from the cab and climbed the stairs. Taking the key, they opened the door, whilst the driver sat talking to his horse.

The rooms were spacious and well appointed, and Jane enthused as they walked around the house. There were two reception rooms and a large kitchen, which led in to a backyard. Upstairs there were three large bedrooms, with a further two attic rooms on the top floor.

Amy was silent whilst viewing the house. It was a lovely house but she couldn't see herself living there. The road outside was too steep for the automobile and she worried about the future if little Geoffrey got out of the house and under a passing horse, or even worse, an automobile.

'Let's go to the next one,' suggested Amy. 'I can't see myself living here.'

'Righto,' said the driver, 'what about Scott Park Road then? It's just round the next bend. This here wall is the outside of Scott Park, so's it'd be 'andy fer the little lad ter play in when he gets older.'

'Scott Park, that sounds nice,' replied Jane. 'Is it a public park?'

'Yes,' replied the driver, 'we've got lots of 'em in Burnley. This one was opened just afore the turn of the century.'

They arrived at the house and started looking round. It was similar in size to the one on Manchester Road, but with only one attic bedroom. It was also in a terraced row. This house had lovely views over the park, especially from the bedroom windows, but there was little outside space for Geoffrey to play when older.

'There's one wi' a lovely big garden on yer list, if it's a garden yer after,' commented the driver. 'That one on Padiham Road. Lovely big gardens they have. Big houses too. Plenty of room for the three of yer.'

'Let's go to that one next then. Is it far?'

'Not too far, just down here and past the Army Barracks, then along a bit. Shouldn't tek us more than 'alf an hour at most.'

'I'll need to see to the baby soon. Is there somewhere I could stop?'

'There's a 'otel near to the next house, Tim Bobbin it's called. Shall I stop there for yer?'

'Yes please, before we go to the house, I think.'

On arrival at the Tim Bobbin, Jane was first to alight and asked to go in the private lounge so that Amy could feed the baby. They ordered meals for themselves and the driver as well. He had disappeared round the back of the hotel to tend to his horse.

A pleasant meal was brought to them; cheese and bread and a piece of pork pie, before they started their searching again. The driver thanked Jane for the meal; he obviously wasn't used to being provided with a meal during his working day. He got back on the front of the carriage and started a tuneless but happy whistle as he drove away.

After a short drive, he pulled up outside a large house with a small garden at the front. It was the middle one of three houses. This house was much larger than the others and the garden was larger at the back of the house, but it was still on a main road and there were a lot of passing carriages and an occasional automobile.

'I think that all these houses are situated on roads that are too busy or too steep,' remarked Amy. 'What is this Lansdowne Street like?'

'A nice quiet street, just off Manchester Road. A bit below Scott Park Road, on t' other side of the road.'

'We'll go there next then.'

The driver set off again and they were soon back near Manchester Road. He crossed Manchester Road and turned into a steep side road, with a large house at the top.

'Goodness, that's too big for us,' exclaimed Amy.

'No, that's just the big house. The other houses are round the corner.'

As the horse struggled up the hill, Amy saw the row of neat terraced houses, curving round and then flattening out into a straight, flat street. The street was then interrupted by another side road, and then continued. The house that was for sale was the very last one on the row.

It had a small garden in front and faced a large private house in its own grounds, owned by the local doctor. There was a large open space to the side of the house, where there was plenty of room for the automobile, or even a garage to be built.

Inside the house were two reception rooms and a large kitchen. Upstairs had three bedrooms and even a bathroom. This house was new and had been constructed for the builder himself to live in, but he had moved on to another development. The house was bigger than all the others in the row. It even had gas and electricity supplied to the house. Amy and Jane went into the back garden and saw that it was enclosed and safe for playing in. It was quite high up over the town and they would be able to see for miles on a clear day.

'I like this house best of all,' said Amy. 'It's not the biggest but I think that I can be happy here. And it's got room for the automobile as well, that isn't on a steep hill. And it's not far from my friend Molly's family. She lives on Healeywood Road nearby. Yes, I think this is the one, what about you, Jane? Could you be happy here.'

'Yes, I could. It's peaceful, isn't it?'

'Would you take us back into town to Bank Parade please? Then when we've seen the agent, I think it's time to go back to the Waggoner's Inn. It's been a long day,' Amy said, but she was much pleased with the days work.

Chapter 24

Amy was excited. It was the first time that she had owned her own home; always having lived in someone else's house or in nurses' accommodation. She got the keys to 44 Lansdowne Street and moved in within two weeks of first seeing it. The builder had never moved in, so there was no delay. It just needed some decorating, now the plaster was dry.

A local painter and decorator Joe Sprason, decorated the downstairs of the house prior to them moving in. His wife had made new curtains for the house and Amy and Jane had scoured the second hand shops looking for furniture, although she insisted on having a brand new cot for Geoffrey and new mattresses for themselves.

Everything was in place and Amy and Jane went to their new home, leaving Geoffrey with the landlady whilst they got organised. The first thing that Amy did was place the picture of Geoffrey, taken in Bury St Edmunds, on the mantelpiece. Next, she took the box of Geoffrey's clothes upstairs and decided to make up his cot first, so that he could have a sleep when he arrived. Whilst there, she also made up hers and Jane's beds.

Amy had the middle bedroom, and Jane's was the larger front bedroom. She had argued against this and said that Amy should have the front bedroom as it was her house, but she explained that it was next to Geoffrey's in case he woke in the night. At this, Jane gave in. She knew it was important for Amy to be near her son at all times.

When Amy came downstairs, she found Jane unpacking some food supplies that they had bought in town the day before.

'Shall I make a cup of tea for us?' asked Amy.

'That would be very welcome,' replied Jane. 'Shall I do it?'

'No, you carry on. I'll make it.' The two women busied themselves in the kitchen together: Amy being well pleased with her modern kitchen stove as she put the kettle on to boil. Soon the drinks were ready and Amy encouraged Jane to go into the lounge for a rest whilst they had their drinks.

Amy sat down in the armchair and looked up at the photograph frame of her son. There besides it, was another photograph frame, virtually identical to hers.

‘What’s that?’ exclaimed Amy jumping up and going to the mantelpiece. When she got nearer, she realised that the other photograph frame was much older and of a far greater quality than hers.
‘Where’s this from?’ she asked Jane, a trifle suspiciously.
‘That picture?’ said Jane far too innocently, ‘it’s something I picked up earlier. I thought you’d like it.’ Amy took a closer look.
‘Why,’ she exclaimed, ‘it’s the picture of my Geoffrey that I saw in Fornham House. Jane, is this the one that the police constable was looking for?’ Jane’s look of innocence turned to sheepishness.
‘Yes, I admit it. I took it from Fornham House.’
‘But the police constable came and searched the room at the Angel. Where was it? Why didn’t he find it?’
‘Because it was in the hotel manager’s safe, along with your other personal possessions.’
‘But you promised me that you would put it back in its rightful place. Oh Jane, how could you?’
‘Quite easily, you told me to put it back where it belonged. So I did. I reckoned it belonged with you more than it did with them.’ There was a long silence, Amy staring at the picture and Jane looking down at the floor.
‘I’ll have to send it back.
‘Nonsense, they won’t miss one picture. They have lots of them. Why, they even have a large oil painting which was done when he came of age. Doesn’t little Geoffrey have a right to have a picture of his father? Do you have any pictures of him?’
‘No, I don't,’ said Amy sadly. ‘We never got time to take photographs. Neither of us had a camera in France. We were going to take lots of photographs on our proper honeymoon, when we came back to England.’
‘Well then, why not keep this one? It’s all you have of your husband.’
‘I suppose you are right. But if ever they get in touch with me, I will confess that I have the photograph.’
‘So you still think that they’ll get in touch with you Amy?’
‘No, I suppose not. You’re right,’ she said smiling, ‘I don't think they’ll get in touch, so I’ll keep the photograph until they do. Thank

you Jane, it was a lovely thought. The two photographs do look well together.' Jane smiled, and took a drink of her tea.

They soon settled into their new home and got used to the area. Amy enjoyed introducing Jane to Mrs Smith and her family, and they got on famously. They spent some happy times together.

Besides Scott Park, they found a wild open area even nearer to the house called Healey Heights. There were long walks across land that was like moorland, and yet it was near the houses. From the top of Healey Heights, they could see for miles around, all over the valley of Burnley and beyond. Well, on the days when the mills weren't working that was!

Amy took herself and Geoffrey to the nearest church, St Matthew's, just off Manchester Road for her churching ceremony and then they had a private christening for baby Geoffrey. Molly was still in Portsmouth, so was unable to attend. Jane and Mrs Smith were the only godparents. The vicar wasn't happy about that, but Amy simply said that she had no other relatives or friends available, so he had to concede.

It was a welcome relief when the war was declared over in November and Jane and Amy took little Geoffrey down to the Town Hall where all the people of Burnley were celebrating and organising street parties. Geoffrey was bewildered by it all, but Amy was glad that she had taken him, because it was an historic moment, she told Jane.

'Besides, they're now calling it the Great War, and they say it was the war to end all wars. Thank goodness for that,' said Amy. 'I hate war, it's so futile. Just think, if there was to be another war, my Geoffrey would have to go and fight. I couldn't bear that.'

'It looks as though there won't be another war, so stop worrying in advance, Amy. And the politicians say it really was the war to end all wars, and they should know.' Jane replied.

'Yes, I suppose I'm being a bit silly, aren't I? No more war, it's a lovely prospect, isn't it?' and Jane agreed.

At first, when the two of them lived together, Jane had railed against Amy not taking any money off her to help with household expenses. Amy argued back that she should be having wages as her employee. They came to a compromise. Jane would not receive any wages, but would live entirely freely with Amy, in return for caring for Geoffrey. Thus she could save her little nest egg for the future.

'Anyway,' said Amy, 'it's only a temporary arrangement. Eventually, my money will run out and then we'll have to think again.'
'If you need any money, you have only to ask,' replied Jane sincerely. But in the meantime, she put her life savings in the Burnley Building Society for safe-keeping.
At times, besides going to the park and Healey Heights, they took Geoffrey out in the automobile. Geoffrey especially liked being by water and they would take him to the riverside at Edisford Bridge in nearby Clitheroe. A little hut served tea in the summer and it was good to get away from the mill chimneys once in a while. Or they took him to the seaside at St Annes on the west coast. Amy become popular in the street as no one else had an automobile, so she often took all the children out for rides in it, too. Geoffrey was never short of little friends, as he got older.
During 1919 a terrible influenza epidemic spread throughout the country and many people died. Because of the war and the influenza outbreak, nearly every family in Burnley was affected by loss. After all the killing that occurred in the Great War, it was a further blow to many families. Many of the soldiers whose lungs had been damaged by the gas in the trenches, succumbed to the epidemic. Fortunately, no one known to Amy and Jane suffered. Indeed, 1919 was a good year, as Jimmy Smith announced he was getting married. The only cloud on the horizon was that Molly and Edwin were unable to come to the wedding, as Edwin was unwell.
A few months later, a letter came from Molly and Edwin to say that they were now the parents of an adorable little girl, named Emma. Edwin had managed to get some temporary work, but his health wasn't very good at times. Amy reflected sadly that she had missed this event in her friend's life, but hoped that one day soon they would be able to see them.
Geoffrey's second birthday came and went. He was developing his own little character and had them amused many times over with the comical things that he said and did.
When it was nearing Geoffrey's third birthday, Amy said that she needed to have a talk with Jane.
'My funds are running low now and . .'
'Let me help,' interrupted Jane.

'No, that wasn't what I had in mind. When I was out in town yesterday, I motored up to the Victoria Hospital where I trained and saw Matron. I've got myself a position, two nights a week. That is, if you'll look after Geoffrey for me.'

'Gladly. But wouldn't it be better if I went back to work somewhere instead of you?'

'With all due respect, I can earn more than you. This way, I can work but Geoffrey will hardly miss me as he will be in bed whilst I am working.'

'That does sound a good solution, but I thought that married women weren't allowed to work as nurses?'

'They're not really, but when I told them I was a war widow, struggling to bring up my child on my own, Matron made an exception. I can start next week, if that is all right with you. Besides, they lost a lot of staff in that influenza epidemic. Nearly as many people died from that as died in the war.'

'That's true. But yes, that's fine by me. I just feel guilty that you are having to go out to work when I'll be staying at home, and I still have money in the Building Society.'

'That's for your future and that money can stay there.'

So it was that Amy became a nurse again. Secretly she was relieved to be back in uniform. Much as she loved being a mother, there were times when she wanted to be a nurse again. And there was no denying that the money was a great help. They could have managed without it, but Amy would have had to sell her automobile and she didn't want to do that. It gave them such a lot of pleasure.

Amy very quickly slipped back into the hospital routine again. Matron had put her on a surgical ward and was impressed at all the things relating to wound care that Amy had learned whilst in France. Many times, she asked Amy to take a full-time Sister's post on day duty, but Amy refused. Her son was more precious than a career; for all that she enjoyed the money that she earned.

Besides the money and actually nursing, Amy also enjoyed the company of the other people on the wards; both the nurses that she worked with and the patients that she cared for. Although she always had adult company from Jane, their conversation was sometimes a trifle limited, to Geoffrey, the neighbours, the Smiths and the events in the town. Jane was an avid reader of the Burnley Express and would read snippets out to Amy at breakfast time.

Amy preferred to read her nursing journals. She only bought one, but sometimes swapped for a different one with a colleague at work. It was reading the Nursing Times one day that an advertisement for a position caught her eye.

Wanted
Highly Qualified nurse to work as Assistant Matron. Living-in position with generous salary. The successful applicant will stand in for the Matron during her holidays and days off.
The patients are ex-soldiers suffering nervous problems due to the war and incapable of living independently. Knowledge of wartime nursing would be an advantage.

But it was not the description of the work that gripped Amy's attention; it was the name and address of the hospital that had her transfixed.

Apply in the first instance to Matron Newton.
Montague Hall
Upper Poppleton
Near York
Yorkshire

Amy's heart began to beat rapidly. Montague Hall. Her own home was now a hospital. She had heard of many large houses being taken over by the government and used as hospitals during the war, but she never dreamt that her own beloved Montague Hall would have suffered that fate.

Her mind went back to her youth, and all the happy times she had spent at Montague Hall. Why had she turned her back on her inheritance? Since her Uncle was lost on the Titanic, she could have owned it all now. Why had she not told anyone who she was? Why had she ignored the memories that came flooding back, once she had got rid of the fog in her mind? She couldn't answer herself. She just didn't know. Perhaps I was trying to protect myself, she thought, too frightened to go back and have to relive memories without her uncle being there. Whatever the reason, her mind had not allowed her to dwell on Montague Hall or what might have happened to it since 1912.

She tried to think what might be the ruling when there were no apparent heirs to the estate. Did it revert to the government? Or was that when there was no will? Amy shook her head. She wasn't sure. Perhaps the government were trying to find some distant cousin that could inherit? She supposed that it was convenient to the government that no heir could be found as they could use it as a hospital. The remoteness of the Hall would lend itself to caring for soldiers who were unable to live normal lives anymore.

Suddenly, a longing to go and see Montague Hall overwhelmed Amy. Even more than just seeing it, she wanted to go and live there again; wanted Geoffrey to grow up there and know and love it. It was the only inheritance that he would ever have, as none would be forthcoming from his father's family.

But it was too late. No one would believe her if she tried to claim who she was. It was 1921, nine years since the fateful events on the Titanic. It had never seemed important to claim her inheritance before, but suddenly it became the most desirable thing she could wish for.

Jane had been watching Amy reading and had seen the sudden change that had come over her. 'Is everything all right Amy? You look as if you have just seen a ghost.'

'I think I have. How do you fancy living in Yorkshire, Jane?'

'In Yorkshire? What has given you that idea?' Amy pondered before she gave a reply and decided that she would only tell Jane what she needed to know. She wouldn't mention that it was her old home.

'It's a job here in the nursing magazine. It's in a hospital near York, helping care for soldiers who are damaged by the war.'

'Would you like that kind of work?'

'Yes, I'd feel like I was helping them. They gave their all to help win the war and now no one wants to know them because they have problems. Why, some of the less fortunate ones were even shot for desertion, just because they couldn't take any more killing.'

'And would you seriously leave here and go to this hospital to work?'

'Only if you would come with me. I couldn't take the job on my own.'
'What about this house?'
'We'd keep it in case it didn't work out. We could rent it I suppose. Or if you didn't like it, you could come home and live here. I'd have to get someone else to mind Geoffrey when I was working.'
'Over my dead body,' threatened Jane. 'Yes, I'll come with you. Are you serious about applying for the position?'
'Yes I am. Thank you for offering to come with me, Jane. I'll send for an application form now.'
Amy busied herself with pen and ink whilst Jane pondered this sudden change of career that Amy envisaged. She hoped she knew what she was doing.
Before long, the application form was filled in and in due course, an offer of interview came through. Amy smiled a secret smile to herself when she got the letter. Perhaps this was a way back to her past? Time would only tell.

Chapter 25

The journey to Montague Hall would take about two days, Amy reckoned, so they decided to stay overnight at Harrogate. They booked into the Majestic Hotel and spent a pleasant stay there. Jane was worried about the expense; the hotel seemed so grand, but Amy reassured her.

'I've stayed here before. It's an excellent hotel. Besides, I'm going to be earning more money soon, so we can afford a little luxury.'

'You're very sure you are going to get the position, aren't you?'

'Yes. I've been checking in back issues of the journal and the position had been advertised for several months, so it's obvious that they haven't been able to get anyone to work there.'

'Doesn't that worry you, Amy? What if the men are awful? What if the Matron is an ogre?'

Amy laughed. 'Most Matrons are ogres,' she replied. 'And if the men are awful, that isn't their fault, is it?'

'I suppose not. But it's not a work I could do.'

'Well, I'd like to try. If we don't like it, we still have our house to come back to, don't we?'

'I suppose so,' replied Jane, still obviously unsure about the wisdom of this opportunity.

Next day, they set off early to reach Montague Hall for 2pm. Geoffrey was ecstatic and kept saying 'holiday, holiday,' as they motored along. Jane tried to keep him occupied by singing to him and pointing out animals in the fields, then eventually, he fell asleep.

As she arrived in Upper Poppleton, Amy told Jane that she would leave them here in the hotel. She didn't want the Matron to see Geoffrey, because she thought she wouldn't get the job. Once they were comfortably settled, Amy set off on her own.

Soon, she was approaching the road to Montague Hall. Her heart was beginning to beat faster, as she swung the automobile into the drive. She drove through the long park and tree lined approach and then parked outside the front door. She stayed in the automobile for some time, drinking in the lovely view of the old Hall. It was nine years since she had been here, and so much had happened in those years.

Amy sat a while longer with her memories and then became aware of people walking round the grounds. There were people being pushed in wheelchairs; blind men being led by others; and some just sitting staring into space. Her heart went out to the poor unfortunates. But at least they can live in this lovely home, she told herself, then reflected that they would probably far rather live at home with their own families, and in their right minds.

Pulling herself together, Amy took her mirror out and tucked her hair under her hat. Taking a deep breath, she walked towards the front door and rang the bell. It felt so strange to be standing there ringing the bell, but she must pretend to be a stranger for now.

As she waited for the door to be answered, she wondered if there were any of the old staff still here. Would they recognise her? Or would they think they were seeing a ghost, like young George Grimscar in France. Mind you, with my short hair, they probably wouldn't recognise me, she thought.

An old man answered the door and asked her business.

'I've an appointment with Matron Newton at 2pm,' Amy replied crisply.

'This way, Miss,' the man said and set off into the hall. 'Wait there,' he said, pointing to a stand chair at the bottom of the large staircase.

Whilst she waited, Amy took the opportunity of looking round her old home. Nothing much had changed really, except some of the old paintings had gone, and the walls looked shabby.

'Storm?' a deep voice boomed. Amy turned round and stood up. There in front of her was a large overbearing lady; her hair scraped back off her face in an unbecoming way; a ridiculously small hat perched on her large head. It was all Amy could do not to laugh. 'Come this way,' she boomed. Amy followed her quickly. She was taken into her uncle's study and Amy instantly felt the deep pain of her last visit here. It was the night before they had set off to the Titanic and she and her uncle had spent an hour together chatting inconsequentially about life. Then he'd packed her off to bed, saying that she needed to be up early next morning.

'What's the matter, girl?' boomed the voice bringing Amy instantly back to the present day. 'Are you deaf?'

'Er, no matron, sorry, I was miles away.' Shaking her head in disgust, Matron resumed talking.
'We have forty residents here. Most of them should be in asylums but the government felt guilty after the war I suppose. Made them a nice place here instead. We have a staff of forty on the nursing side. Ten State Registered Nurses and the rest orderlies. Hours are very generous. You only work sixty per week, with two days off. Nursing's going soft, that's all I can say. Three weeks paid holiday per year as well. There are ten bedrooms, four to a room generally, but some have to be kept in single rooms. Any questions?' Matron had rapidly fired these statements out leaving Amy bewildered.
'No Matron, not at the moment,' Amy gasped.
'Good I'll ask you some questions then show you round.'
Matron proceeded to fire pertinent questions to Amy about her nursing training, her experiences in the war and her current position. She seemed very satisfied with her answers and almost, but not quite smiled.
'I think you'll do well here. You seem to have the experience I need. Come, I'll show you round.' She walked rapidly and Amy struggled to keep up with her. 'This is the dining room, rather grandiose I know, but they kept the old hall to its original use as much as they could. This is the lounge area, then through here is the corridor down to the kitchens, but you don't need to see those today.' She backtracked the way they had come to the main hall and led Amy up the staircase.
'All the main bedrooms are in use as patients' rooms. Here is bedroom one.' She opened the door of one of the old guest rooms. Amy nodded, then was taken to another room and another. Eventually they worked down the corridor until they came to Amy's old room.
'And here's another bedroom.' Amy froze as she looked at her old bedroom. Although stripped of her own personal furniture and dressing table, it still looked very much like her old room.
'And here's another bedroom,' boomed Matron, then realised that Amy hadn't followed her. She came back to find her.
'What's the matter girl? Can't you keep up?'
'I was just thinking what a pretty room this was.'

'Yes, it's a lovely house. Been empty for years before the war. All went down on the Titanic, you know. Mind you, it's disgusting that just one family lived here and had about thirty servants to run it just for them, isn't it? Only a man and his niece, so the story goes. They left a retainer looking after it, but he left when the government took over. All the families personal things are locked away in the attics in the west wing.'

Amy nodded, unable to speak at all.

'Well, come on, there are some more bedrooms to look at yet.' Matron hurried on, throwing doors open to right and left. Next she turned to the upper staircase where the servants had slept.

'The nurses rooms are all up here. You would have one of these. Now what do you think? Do you want to see the laundry and the other service rooms?'

'No, I don't think so.'

'Good, well, I like what I've seen of you and your Matron has given you a very good reference. As you have come a long way, I will tell you the result of the interview now, rather than sending a letter. I am pleased to offer you the position, Miss Storm. Will you accept it?'

'Mrs.'

'Pardon?'

'Mrs. I'm Mrs Storm.'

The Matron started to bluster. 'You never said you were Mrs on your application form. I wouldn't have interviewed you if I had known. How come you are working if you are married? What sort of husband have you that allows you to work?'

Amy was getting angry at the Matron's attitude by now. 'A dead husband, that's what sort of husband I've got Matron, a dead one,' Amy shouted. 'I'm a war widow.'

Matron had the grace to look abashed. 'I'm sorry Mrs Storm. I had no idea. Did he not leave you well provided for?'

'Unfortunately not. He died one week after we were married in France. Killed by a shell when collecting patients in his ambulance.'

'At least you didn't have children then.'

'Oh but I did. I have a son Geoffrey aged nearly four.'

'How can you apply for a position when you have a son to care for?'

'I have a lady living with me who cares for him when I'm working.'

'And what about your husband's family? Didn't they help you?'
Amy smiled. 'No, they didn't believe we were married.'
'Well, I'm amazed. Must admire your spirit though. Are you still interested in the position?'
'Yes, but I'm wondering if you could let me work part time hours and bring my son to live here with his nurse?'
'That is highly irregular. I'll have to think for a moment.' She stood staring out of the window for a few minutes. 'Yes, I suppose I could bend the rules for once. If it means you'll accept the position. It's so hard to get staff to work here, so I suppose beggars can't be choosers. But if the other staff complain about your little boy, I may have to ask you to make new arrangements.'
'Then I accept the position.'
'Good, when can you start?'
'In one month from now?
'Excellent. I'll send you a contract through the post.'
'Thank you. I'll see you in a month then. Goodbye.' Amy reached her hand out to shake Matron's and felt a limp, weak handshake that made her cringe. What a surprise, she had expected the Matron to nearly wring her hand off.
Amy walked slowly away from the house without looking back. She would be returning to her old home and surprisingly, after all these years of avoiding it, she couldn't wait.
On arrival back at the hotel, she told an amazed Jane about her interview and the fact that she had not only got the position, but she had arranged for Geoffrey and Jane to live there with her.
'How on earth did you manage that?' asked Jane.
'She was desperate. I could tell. She said that she had trouble getting anyone to work there. Mind you, it's probably her rather than the patients. She's a bit of a battle-axe,' laughed Amy.
'But can you stand to work with her?'
'Oh yes. I've worked with people like her before. Besides, I've got plans.'
'What plans?'
'When I know more about them, I'll tell you,' replied Amy, leaving Jane beginning to wonder about her sanity. If she had known the full extent of Amy's plans, Jane would definitely have doubted Amy's sanity.

Chapter 26

The next month flew by and soon the trio were making the journey to Montague Hall again, having managed to rent Lansdowne Street. When they arrived, Matron told them that they would be living in the small cottage at the back of the house.

'It was the keeper's cottage,' she informed them. Amy was delighted. She remembered it as a cosy cottage. The keeper had always had a lot of time for her, especially when she had the dog, and his wife had always made special biscuits for her. She wondered what had happened to him and his wife. She supposed that he would have been called up to fight, as he was only about thirty or forty.

It made her wonder about all the other staff that had lived there. Apart from young George who had recognised her in France, she had never met anyone from her former life, and George had died anyway.

They were soon settled into the cottage. Amy had insisted on having two days with Geoffrey to settle him in before starting work and she was glad she had done. The day after they arrived, she told Jane that she had to go into York, but didn't give her any explanation as to her business.

The next day, Jane was busy sorting the cottage out, so Amy took the opportunity of taking Geoffrey round the grounds. He loved very minute of the walk and came back full of enthusiasm, telling Jane all about it.

'We've seen lots of trees, peacocks, rabbits, birds and cows and all sorts of things,' he enthused. 'I love it here. I want to live here forever. Can we Mummy?' Amy laughed. 'I'll do my best, Geoffrey,' she replied.

The following day, Amy reported for duty. The uniforms were quite pleasant. A long light grey dress with the usual white pinafore. Amy had a small fluted cap like Matrons and white cuffs to wear. Amy fastened her silver buckle to her belt and her state registration badge to the left hand corner of her pinafore. Taking a quick look at herself in the mirror, she walked briskly towards the main house.

On arrival at the house, Matron was waiting for her.

'I'll introduce you to some of the staff today. They are all in my office waiting for report.' Matron briskly walked off towards her uncle's old study. In the study were five nurses dressed in dark grey dresses and small hats and four in black dresses and large mob caps. All of them wore white pinafores. There were also two men who wore white tunics and black trousers. They all stood to attention and didn't look round. They looked frightened, Amy thought. Certainly not happy at their work.

'This is Assistant Matron Storm,' Matron started in her rapid-fire manner of speaking. 'This is Loughlin, Payne, Lord, Higgins and Birtle, all SRN's,' she said pointing to the nurses in dark grey. 'And these are Barnes, Cronshaw, Riley, Laycock, all orderlies,' pointing to the nurses in black. 'The men are both orderlies, Gore and Black. Now for report, night staff have reported a mainly quiet night.' She then proceeded to give a report on each patient – names that meant nothing to Amy, but which she would have to learn. The staff were then dismissed and Amy waited to see what Matron would have to say to her.

'The staff are a difficult lot. They don't like authority and argue with every decision I make. I rule them with a rod of iron or else I don't get anywhere. You must do the same and carry out all my instructions to the letter. I'm going on holiday in two weeks. I'll be away for three weeks, so I expect to have the place running in exactly the same way when I get back. Understood?' she barked.

'Yes, Matron, perfectly,' replied Amy. Huh, she thought to herself, no wonder she was keen to give me the position, she wanted to make sure that she got away on her holiday. She'll probably sack me after she comes back.

'I'll take you to meet the kitchen and laundry staff. They will be your special responsibility from now on. It's your job to plan all the menus and ensure that all the wards have sufficient clean linen; and supervise all the nurses and orderlies, and do all the ordering. You will also do a round every two hours to make sure that the nurses are working hard.'

'Yes, Matron,' replied Amy. And I wonder what that leaves you to do, thought Amy rebelliously. I seem to have all the running of things. Well, we'll wait and see.

By now they had arrived at the kitchen. Nothing had changed since she had lived in the house but she was soon introduced to the staff, who were all different. From there, they went to the laundry and again, Amy met all new staff. Walking back past the kitchen, Matron shouted 'We'll have our coffee now, Cook,' and marched Amy to her office, the old study. Coffee and biscuits were soon delivered on a silver tray. Amy recognised the coffee cups and also the coffee pot, milk jug and sugar bowl. She was sure that they had belonged to her uncle.

'This is a lovely set.' she remarked innocently to Matron.

'Yes, I like nice things, don't you?'

'Yes, I do.' And I bet they are my uncle's things and that you aren't supposed to be using them either, Amy thought to herself, but said nothing.

'Shall I go round the wards and check the nurses now then?' she asked Matron.

'Yes, will you find your way round?'

'Oh yes. I'm sure I can ask if I get lost,' replied Amy sweetly. She set off upstairs to meet the staff and patients. At this hour of the morning, she would expect all the patients to be up and out doing some kind of activity. Funny, she reflected, Matron never mentioned activities. She would have to ask about that later.

She went into the first bedroom. The nurse jumped to attention and curtsied and said 'Good morning Assistant Matron Storm.'

'Good morning,' replied Amy smiling. 'What is your name?'

'Birtle,' the woman replied looking terrified.

'And your first name?'

'Ellen,' she replied, looking totally shocked.

'Right, I'll try and remember that. Ellen Birtle,' she repeated to herself. The nurse nodded. 'What are you doing at present, Nurse Birtle?'

'I'm dressing Carter's wound. He had a fall last week and got a nasty cut.'

'What is his first name?'

'Er, let me see, Johnny I think. Matron doesn't allow us to use first name terms, not for patients or each other.'

'I see,' said Amy, not at all surprised. 'Can I look at the wound?'

'Of course.' Nurse Birtle took the dressing away and Amy had a good look. 'Do you think it is getting better then Nurse Birtle?'

'No, it was getting better when we were using a new solution but Matron says it is too expensive.'

'Have you told her that the other solution was better?'

'Indeed no, it would be more than my job was worth.'

'But surely it would be better for Johnny?'
'Well, yes, but I can only do what Matron says.'
'But wouldn't it better for you as well?' Amy argued, 'you wouldn't have to keep on doing the dressing if it got better quicker, so surely that would save money and your time?'
'I suppose so,' Nurse Birtle replied somewhat reluctantly. It was obvious that she had never been encouraged to think for herself or have an opinion.
'I will order the other solution. Was it Eusol?'
'Yes, Assistant Matron Storm.'
'Mmm, I thought as much, it's very popular at the moment and it certainly keeps wounds clean. Very well, Nurse Birtle, you may carry on.' Amy left the room and went into another room. Here she met another member of staff who again, was fearful of her. During the morning, Amy met all of the staff and found them to be nervous, frightened and blindly following orders, without thinking about what they were doing.
The patients were little better. They were dull and unresponsive and often flinched when Amy came into the room, as if they feared violence. Amy knew that this was part of their illness for some of the men, because the slightest noise or upset was enough for them to have an attack of nerves. In all, Amy's first day was unsatisfactory. She felt as if there was a lot she could do with the patients but the staff were too frightened to disobey Matron.
At the end of the day, Amy went to report to Matron, before going off duty.
'How have you found your first day, Assistant Matron Storm?'
'Interesting,' replied Amy diplomatically. 'I've met many of the patients and staff but it will take me a while to get used to everything. Johnny Carter's leg is not healing so I'm going to order some Eusol; that'll sort it out quickly.'
'But I expressly ordered that Eusol should not be used. It is far too expensive.'
'But it was healing the wound up quicker,'
'Are you criticising my orders, Assistant Matron Storm? Don't forget I'm in charge around here, and I have made a special case to take you on with a child, so you had better follow my orders to the

full, or you will be leaving again. Besides, how do you know it got better with Eusol?'
'The nurse told me,' replied Amy.
'Did she, indeed, then I shall have her in my office tomorrow. She deserves to lose her position. Which nurse was that?'
Amy's heart sank. She had hoped to improve things but had probably made things worse and on her first day too.
'I'm not sure which nurse it was. I haven't got all their names off by heart yet,' faltered Amy.
'No matter,' said Matron, pulling a clip board towards her and looking at the staff rota, 'I can find out. Ah yes, Birtle, right, I'll see her tomorrow after report. I can see you're going to be as much trouble as the other staff, Assistant Matron Storm. I shall have to watch you as well,' glared Matron giving a dismissive wave of her hand. Amy slunk out of the office and hurried back to her cottage.
A small whirlwind rushed towards her as she opened the door.
'Mummy, mummy, I've missed you,' said Geoffrey, hugging her closely.
'And I've missed you as well son. What have you been doing with Jane today?'
'We've walked in the woods and seen a pheasant and a rabbit and a deer, didn't we Birdy?' he turned to Jane for confirmation. 'And here, I've picked you these,' Geoffrey replied, thrusting a small bunch of wild flowers in to her hands. Amy took them with great delight, but then remembered the first bunch of flowers that his father had given her in France had also been wild flowers and burst into tears.
'What's the matter, mummy? Don't you like them?'
'I love them, sweetheart,' Amy replied. 'I was just remembering when your daddy brought me a bunch like this and it made me sad that he wasn't here anymore.'
'Will he come back from Heaven, mummy?'
'No Geoffrey, nobody comes back from Heaven. But we'll go and be with him there one day.'
'Can we go tomorrow?'
'No son, mummy's working.'
'Can Jane take me then?'

'No, you can't just go when you want to, besides, what would I do when I came home from work and my boy wasn't there, waiting for me? I'd be very, very sad.'
'All right then, I'll wait until you can come,' replied Geoffrey and trotted off in to the garden. Jane and Amy looked at each other and smiled.
'How has he been really, Jane? Have you both coped with your new life?'
'We've had a lovely time. I thought I'd take him into the village tomorrow and let him see the schoolchildren playing in the schoolyard; get him used to the idea of going to school.'
'Good idea. At least I have to be grateful that Lord and Lady Storm threw me out, as they would be getting him enrolled for Eton by now, like they did with Geoffrey. I couldn't stand him going away to school. I'd miss him too much.'
'I'm glad you're sending him to the local school. I hated it when Mr Geoffrey was sent away. It'll be good for him to have little friends as well. He's missed all the Lansdowne Street children since he came here.'
'Jane, perhaps you could go out in to the village and try and make friends, so that he'll feel more at home when he goes to school. Have you seen any children yet?''
'No, but I haven't been into the village yet. I'll try tomorrow.'
'Yes, bit of a come down from going to Heaven,' quipped Amy, 'but I think he'll enjoy the village.'
'What about your day? How was Matron?'
'Awful, the patients are cowed and the staff are frightened of her. She's a real bully. I've already upset her today.'
'Oh dear, that doesn't bode well for your working relationship.'
'No it doesn't. And she calls me Assistant Matron Storm all the time. It's such a mouthful. The sooner she goes on holiday the better, then I can change a few things.'
'But won't she change them back when she returns?'
'Not if I can help it.'
'Amy, you'll probably get the sack.'
'Don't worry Jane. I've got a few things up my sleeve. But what about you? Do you like it here so far?'

'I love the peace and quiet and anyway, you know that anywhere little Geoffrey is, I'm happy.'
'Thanks Jane, I'm so glad you came with me. I couldn't have taken this job without you. And now what's for supper? Are you going to let me bath Geoffrey tonight? I'm sure it must be past his bedtime.'
'You go and bath Geoffrey, whilst I finish the tea. It's cottage pie and carrots tonight.'
'Great, I'll go and work up an appetite in the bathroom.'
The bath completed, the three of them had a lovely teatime and Geoffrey went straight to bed.
'I think that most nights you'll have to feed Geoffrey before I come home. He's too tired tonight, but with it being my first night, I wanted to keep him up. Perhaps he can have his tea and then sit up to table in his nightshirt with us whilst I have my tea. What do you think, Jane?'
'Yes that's probably better. We can play it by ear each day. I wouldn't like him to think he can't come to the table with you, Amy.'

Chapter 27

Next morning, Amy was determined to keep her mouth shut and not upset Matron but it was very difficult. Nurse Birtle was kept back after report and given a strict telling off and told that a day's wages would be deducted from her salary. Amy gasped at the harshness of this punishment but said nothing. When Nurse Birtle had gone, she said to Matron that it seemed steep, but Matron again lashed out at Amy and said that it was just another sign of the insubordination of the staff and you had to keep them under. And if she argued anymore, she would lose a day's wages as well.

Amy stalked out of the office, merely telling Matron that she would go on her rounds. She sought out Nurse Birtle first.

'I am sorry if you got into trouble because of me, Ellen. I didn't give her your name, but she knew.'

'I don't care, I'm leaving this place as soon as I can,' Ellen replied viciously. 'She doesn't care about the men. Only about her accounting. It makes me sick.'

'Please don't leave Ellen. It will get better, I promise you.'

'No, she'll grind you down, like the rest. All the Assistant Matrons have been like you. They are appalled at what goes on and argue with Matron, but they get nowhere. Then they leave.'

'And why haven't you left, Ellen?'

'It's the men. They have such a rotten life. They've been put in here because they need peace and an easy life after suffering and being damaged by that awful war. But I can't take much more.'

'Please try a bit longer. I will make changes, you'll see.'

'It won't stop me looking in the nursing papers, but I won't go yet. I'll see what happens and I hope you can make a difference, Assistant Matron Storm.'

'Call me Amy.'

'I couldn't,' said Ellen aghast.

'Why not? Just when we're on our own, if you like.'

'I'll try. Did you order any Eusol?' Amy nodded, to which Ellen giggled. 'I think perhaps you are going to make a difference,' she shyly replied, as Amy left the room.

The days went from bad to worse. Amy managed to offend Matron nearly every day either about the treatment of the staff or patients.

When she got home each night, she let rip at poor long suffering Jane. Jane was very concerned that Amy would be sacked, but Amy always smiled a secret smile and told her not to worry.

At long last, the day came for Matron to go on holiday. Amy gave a great sigh of relief. Next morning, she called a meeting of all the staff.

'There are going to be changes round here now. I want you to tell me all your ideas that would make life easier for these men. I already know about the Eusol for the dressings. What else would you like to see?'

There was silence for a few minutes and Amy had to prompt them.

'Come on, if you were Matron, how would you run this hospital?'

Eventually Nurse Loughlin spoke. 'No more punishments,' she said simply, and everyone nodded their heads.

'What do you mean? Do you mean when you are told off by Matron and she docks your wages?'

'Well, yes, but we mean the patients. No more locking them up in the cellar when they have screaming attacks.'

'What?' asked Amy not believing her ears.

The staff all looked at each other sheepishly, not wanting to be the one to spill the beans.

'Nurse Harling, I believe you're just back from holiday and we haven't met before. What do you mean? You were nodding your head fairly vigorously.'

'If a man has a screaming attack,' she started slowly, 'we have to lock him in the cellar in the dark.' There was silence in the room.

'Any patient or one in particular?'

'It could be anyone,' replied Nurse Harling, 'but it's mainly Isaac Spencer.'

'Isaac Spencer? Is that the boy who has nightmares about being buried alive in the trenches?'

They all nodded.

'So the treatment for a boy, who is frightened of the trench falling in on him, is to be put in a dark room with limited roof space?'

They all nodded again, looking down at their feet.

'This treatment will stop instantly. It's barbaric. I will not have this sort of treatment going on here. The whole point of this hospital is to give them rest from the awful things they saw in the trenches which made them unable to live a normal life.' Amy was quiet for a moment, then looked at her staff sternly.

'Are any of you prepared to sign an affidavit about what you have just told me?'

'What's one of those?' asked Nurse Payne.

'An official letter written and signed in the presence of a lawyer. I would require statements about these bad things that Matron has been doing.'

The staff all looked worried.

'We value our jobs, even though we are unhappy here,' said Nurse Lord. 'When Matron comes back, she'd send us all away.'

'But what if Matron didn't come back? What then?'

'I'd gladly sign,' said Nurse Higgins quietly, 'as long as I knew she wasn't coming back.' One by one, they all agreed.

'And how would you treat the men instead?'

'Give them their dignity back,' said Nurse Payne.

'Call them by their first names,' suggested Nurse Loughlin.

'Give them something to do,' said orderly Cronshaw.

'Stop calling it a hospital,' said Nurse Lord.

'Look,' said Amy, 'let's write all these ideas down. They sound great. The easiest one will be to remove the name 'hospital' from the board outside. I'll get a workman in today. Shall we just call it Montague Hall and leave it like that?' The staff all nodded in agreement.

'But,' said orderly Gore, 'won't Matron be furious when she comes back?'

'From what I've seen and heard here, I'll make sure that Matron doesn't come back,' said Amy. 'Now, who will stay and work with me if I become Matron?' She was pleased at the show of hands and smiles of agreement.

'Right, who wants to go and tell the men that we are going to call them by their first names, and that all punishments will stop? And you can call each other by your first names too. It'll make it more homely.'

'Can the men call us by our first names too, Assistant Matron Storm?' asked orderly Black.

'Only on one condition,' Amy said severely. The staff looked cowed again. 'That you call me Amy, not Assistant Matron Storm. I hate it. I feel about ninety years old when you call me that.' The

relief of tension was palpable in the room, as Amy beamed at all the staff.
'Who is senior here amongst the staff nurses?' Amy asked.
'I am,' replied Nurse Payne.
'Then I'm leaving you in charge for the day as I need to make some telephone calls and go into York. Will you be all right?'
'Of course, Assistant . .'
'What's my name?' thundered Amy.
'Sorry,' giggled Nurse Payne, 'I mean Amy. Yes, I'll be fine. You go and do what needs doing. Are there any special orders? Like ordering Eusol?' The staff all giggled at that, because they knew how Amy had stood up to Matron about the Eusol.
'Certainly not,' replied Amy, 'that's a job I'm saving for Ellen Birtle. Now off you all go, or I might have to start thinking up some punishments.'
Amy watched the staff go out of the office with fondness. They were completely different. The whole atmosphere of the room had changed during their conversation. They were a good bunch of staff and Amy knew that she could make something of this home for the soldiers, who deserved better than they were getting.
First of all, she made some telephone calls to the Board of Trustees that were in charge of the home. Then she went back to the cottage.
'Goodness, Amy, don't say you've been dismissed from your position. What are you doing home so soon?'
'I've been talking to the staff. There are going to be sweeping changes made. I need to go in to York to the lawyers, but first I need to talk to you. Where's Geoffrey?'
'He's gone down the lane to play with a little boy on the outskirts of the village. He told me to go home again, as he was a big boy now,' Jane added proudly.
'Good,' said Amy. 'I need to talk to you and I can do without Geoffrey butting in at every turn. Let's have a cup of tea, and then I'll tell you my plans.'
Intrigued, Jane made a cup of tea, whilst Amy got a pen and paper out and started making notes for herself.
'Now, where do I start?' Amy asked, almost to herself. 'I need to tell you a lot about myself, Jane, things that I should have told you years ago. You asked me when we first met if I could remember who I was and I said I couldn't. I'm sorry but that wasn't strictly true. I

did know who I was, but didn't want to acknowledge it, if you know what I mean.'

Jane was looking bewildered. 'Not really Amy, you're talking in riddles.'

'Well, my real name is Arabella Charlotte Sophie Montague.'

'Montague? What a coincidence that you've come to work in Montague Hall,' Jane interrupted.

'Yes, but it's no coincidence. This is my home, Jane. I am the heiress to this estate.'

'But I thought you were a servant?'

'No, I borrowed my servant's clothes to go on the lifeboat. That's just typical of the person I was. Not a care for anybody but myself. I was very selfish, proud and cruel.'

'Oh surely not Amy?'

'Fraid so. I didn't like myself really and treated everyone abysmally. I sent my maid Lizzie back to get my jewellery box, then got on the last lifeboat, leaving her to die, along with my uncle and our butler.'

'Did you know it was the last lifeboat?'

'Not until we had rowed a long way away. I felt terribly guilty and hated myself. I was so upset that I sort of lost my mind for a while. A black fog descended in my brain. By the time I came round, I was in an asylum and called Amy Wilson. So I decided to keep the name and start living for other people instead of being so selfish. I went to do my nurse training so that I could be a better person. Most of the time I think I manage, but just sometimes, I get angry and haughty and feel like the old person again. I still don't like the old person, so I keep the new name, just to keep me humble. Besides, if I'd used my real name, I'd have had to admit I was the heiress to this place, and I wasn't ready to come back and face people.'

'Until you saw the advertisement for this job.'

'Yes.'

'Oh Amy. It must have been awful for you.'

'Yes.'

'Have you never told anyone else?'

'Only Jack. I never even told Geoffrey. I was going to tell him that night, but he never came home.'

'Who's Jack?'

'An old doctor who I worked with in France.' They were silent for a while.
'But how are you going to prove who you are?' asked Jane.
'I'm going to go in to our family lawyers in York. They will remember me. I'll go today. I've also made a telephone call to the Trustee Board who manage this hospital, asking them to visit urgently.'
'Goodness, this is all a lot to take in, Amy. Are you going into York now?'
'Yes, the sooner the better. Once Matron has been removed, I will assume the position of Matron.'
'Are you still going to work, if you're an heiress?'
'Oh yes. It's so important that I keep working in some capacity, but now I can use my wealth to make life better for the unfortunate men who were damaged by the war.'
'Do you want me to come in to the lawyers with you?'
'No, I'll be fine. You stay and look after Geoffrey. Now is there anything special that you'd like me to bring back for tea?'
'I can't think of anything. You've filled my mind completely, with all that you've told me. I think I'd like to sit down and have another cup of tea and absorb everything.'
'Sorry, I should've told you earlier, but I was denying it all myself and didn't want to talk about it. Well, I'd best get going in to York or it will be teatime before I go. Bye.'
'Bye,' Jane echoed faintly, shaking her head as she went to the kettle to replace it on the stove. She needed another cup of tea to calm her nerves.

Chapter 28

Amy parked the automobile in Piccadilly and walked through to Goodramgate. It felt good to be back in York, and she looked in amazement at all the different shops that had opened since she had last been here shopping. Why, it must have been when she was shopping for her new clothes for the Titanic and she wondered if Miss Juliana's shop was still trading. If only she had known what was going to happen, she reflected sadly, but then wondered if she would have acted any differently, or even believed it.

Crossing Goodramgate, she entered the offices of Waddington and Sons, lawyers and asked for an appointment with Mr Waddington senior. The clerk looked at her strangely and then went in to the inner office.

A tall elderly gentleman came out with the clerk and asked if he could be of any help.

'I'd like to see Mr Waddington senior, if I may,' Amy repeated.

'I'm sorry, Mr Waddington senior has passed away, seven years ago.'

'Oh dear, I didn't know, I'm sorry. What about Mr Waddington junior?'

'Have you been away for a while, madam? Mr Waddington junior died in the war, at Paschendale.

'I'd no idea.' Amy stared at the floor, unable to think what to say next. Both men dead. She hadn't thought about that eventuality.

'Could I get you a drink? Let me take you into my office. Giles, get the lady a cup of tea and bring it through.' The clerk sprang up and went into another room.

'I'm John Coates, by the way. How may I help you?'

'How long have you worked here?' asked Amy.

'Since 1918, when I came home from the war.'

'Oh.'

'Does when I came here matter?'

'Yes, I've come to claim an estate and I never dreamt that both Mr Waddington's would be gone. I just thought I could walk in here and they'd know me and everything would be all right.'

'I'm sorry. Ah, here's Giles with the tea. Now, which estate are you referring to?'
'Robert Montague's estate, Montague Hall.'
'Ah, the hospital for war veterans. Just a moment, I'll get the file.' He rummaged in a filing cabinet and brought out a large file.
'Yes, let me see, the owner and his niece who was heiress went down on the Titanic. Did you say you have a claim to this estate? Are you a distant cousin.'
'No. I'm the niece. I didn't go down on the Titanic.'
'But it's 1921. Surely you don't expect me to believe that you forgot to claim your inheritance for nine years? That sounds a bit far fetched, you must admit. So what's your name?'
'Arabella Charlotte Sophie Montague. I've been living under the name of Amy Wilson and since I got married I am now Mrs Storm.'
'Why did you change your name to Wilson?' Amy then outlined all that happened to her since leaving the Titanic. Mr Coates sat in silence for a while. 'And you expect me just to hand over the estate, because you say you're the heiress? It's not as simple as that. I'll need proof.'
Amy burst in to tears. 'I have no proof. I thought that when I saw the Messrs Waddington, they would recognise me and it would all be all right. I don't know how I can get proof.'
'Where are you living at present?'
'In Montague Hall.'
'In Montague Hall? How did you manage that?'
'I'm a nurse and I applied for a position there. I have reported the Matron to the Trustees for gross incompetence, and I would like to run the hospital myself.'
'I see, so you just happened to get a position there, didn't like the Matron, heard the story about how the niece disappeared on the Titanic, and decided to try your luck, is that it?'
'No, it isn't. I assure you. I am the heiress,' replied Amy, sniffing her tears back. 'My uncle Robert was my only relative after my family died.'
'Didn't any of the staff recognise you when you came back?' he asked.
'No, all the staff have changed. If you could find someone who worked there before the Titanic, I'm sure they would recognise me.'

'I'm not sure that I can find them. Perhaps you had better find someone yourself. Then I might be more interested in your claim.' I'll bid you good morning, Mrs . . er . . Storm, did you say?'

Amy was dismayed. What had she done? She had reported Matron on the strength of her being the rightful owner of Montague Hall. But now she would have to prove it. Where would she start? Holding her head high, Amy nodded to Mr Coates and left the office as quickly as possible.

Outside, she took several deep gulps of breath, then straightened her shoulders and walked towards the automobile. Driving very carefully because of her heightened emotions, Amy was glad to get home safely and hurried in to the keeper's cottage to tell Jane of the unexpected events that had occurred.

'What am I going to do, Jane? I've gone and reported Matron, fully expecting that when I went to see the lawyers, it would all be straightforward.'

'There must be someone who would recognise you? Can't we find some of the staff who worked here before?'

'I suppose we could try in the village. Could you ask around tomorrow?'

'Yes, I'll try, but I don't hold out any hope. Oh dear, Amy. What will we do if we can't find anyone?'

'I'm not even going to think about it. For now, let's not worry about it or Geoffrey will pick up on our distress. Let me know how you get on tomorrow night.'

Next day, Amy made sweeping changes in the running of the hospital. She gathered all the men together and told them that things would change from now on. She also asked them what sort of activities they would like to do, if they could.

Amy was surprised at some of the men's comments. One man, Charlie, asked if he could help in the gardens as he had been a gardener on a large similar estate before the war. Amy looked at this nervous twitchy man and knew that being in the garden would heal him and help him feel useful again.

'Yes, Charlie, I'll have a chat with the head gardener today; anyone else?'

Len, a blind man, asked if he could have some wood to whittle. Amy asked him to explain what he meant.

'If I had a bit of wood and a sharp knife, I could make figures for children to play with.'

'Wouldn't it be dangerous for you to use a knife?' Amy asked.

'No, I could do it carefully. They used to give me some in the other hospital I was in before I came here. It kept me going really. I feel so useless here; no point to living really.'

Amy's heart went out to him. 'Of course we'll find you some wood and a knife. Anyone else got ideas?'

'I could help Charlie. I was a joiner before I lost my arms, so I could be his eyes.'

'Good idea, Fred. That would be really useful. Arnold, what about you?'

'Can't think of anything, Miss. But I'm sure something'll come to mind. Must say, I quite fancy learning gardening. I was in a mill before, and I hated being inside all the time. Could I learn, do you think?'

'There's no harm in trying. We could give you all your own plot of land and have competitions, couldn't we? See who could grow the best flowers or vegetables. Perhaps we could even have some prizes. Anyway, the rest of you, if you think about anything, come and see me. I'm available to all of you at any time.'

'Thanks Miss, we appreciate what you're doing,' said Len, and all the other men nodded, glad that Len could put into words what they were thinking.

Amy went to the old study and wrote some notes about the men, then she went in search of the head gardener. She hadn't really taken any notice of the gardeners since she came back, so asked the cook if he could come and see her when he next came in for a drink.

The house bush telegraph soon worked and only half an hour later, a timid knock on the door revealed the gardener.

'Hullo Matron, you wanted to see me?' The man was uneasy and looked uncomfortable.

'Yes, come on in. I'm Amy, what is your name?'

'I'm Hodges, Miss,' he replied, not quite liking to call this superior person by her first name.

'And your first name?'

'Matthew, Miss.'

'And how many staff do you have?'

'Just three of us, Miss. There's young John Simpson and George Shapcott.'
'How long have you all been here?'
'I came here just after the war. The lads have been here a bit longer, but I'm not sure how long.'
'Do you know what happened to the previous gardeners that were here before the war?'
'When I came, old Grimscar was the head gardener, but he wasn't well. His only son died in the war and he never got over it. He died himself in 1919.'
'What about his wife?'
'Gone, Miss. Went back to her sister's family.'
'Do you know where?'
'No Miss,' replied Matthew Hodges, wondering why she was asking all these questions.
'Are there any staff here who worked here when there was a family?'
'Only young Sarah. She's in the kitchen.'
'Thank you Matthew. That's great. You've been really helpful.'
'Was that all Miss?' Matthew asked.
'Oh no, sorry, I got sidetracked. Have you enough staff to work in the gardens?'
'We could always do with more hands, Miss, but the other Matron said we'd have to manage.'
'I've got a bit of a funny question for you,' asked Amy.
'Yes, Miss?' said Matthew, thinking that all this young woman's questions had been a bit funny really.
'We have two men here who would like to do some gardening work. Could you accommodate them?'
'Is one of them Charlie?'
'Yes, so you already know him?'
'Not really, he used to sit and watch me working, but once Matron caught him and tore a strip off him. He's kept away since then.'
'Well, Charlie has worked on an estate garden before but the other man, Arnold, has never done any gardening, but would like to try. What do you think?'

'That's grand, Miss. If it helps them, it's worth it. It would help me as well. I could always do with another pair of hands. Can't get people to work on these estates nowadays.'
'Good, you make contact with the men and sort out a small plan of work for them, and keep me informed as to their progress.'
'Right Miss, I'll do that,' replied Matthew as he left the room.
Amy hurried down to the kitchen and asked for Sarah.
'Here Miss,' replied Sarah.
'Do you remember me, Sarah?'
Sarah gave her a strange look. 'Course I remember you, you're standing in for Matron.'
'But don't you remember me from before?'
'No Miss, should I?'
'How long have you lived here?'
'Since March 1912.'
'And did you meet the family?'
'No Miss, I was only a kitchen maid then. Never left the kitchen. I met Mrs Seeney and Mr Vickers when I got the job. But after that I only saw cook and the other kitchen staff.'
'Did you meet Lizzie?'
'Her that went down on the Titanic? Yes, I met her once or twice.'
'What happened to Mrs Seeney?'
'Went to another job, she didn't like it when the family went.'
'Where was the job?'
'In York, I think, but I'm not sure.'
'Are there any other staff still living in the village or near here?'
'Don't think so, Miss. A lot of staff left when the family died. Didn't need them anymore.'
'Thank you Sarah. If you think of anyone else, please tell me. I want to get in touch with people who lived here when the family did.'
'I will Miss.'
Amy went back to her office and sat down heavily in the chair. Where could she find someone who could help? Was she never going to prove who she was?
Jane had not had much better luck in the village. Most people had moved away after the family left. It was most frustrating.
The next day however, Amy had no time to ponder on proving her inheritance. The Board of Trustees arrived and wanted to know what

all the fuss was about. Amy explained all that had been happening with Matron and told of how she kept the staff and patients living under a rule of fear. All that Amy was telling them, especially about men being locked in the cellars as punishment, appalled them. Amy offered to bring Nurse Payne and they gladly accepted.

The faces of the men looked glum all the time that Nurse Payne was talking. They asked her many questions and then asked her why she hadn't done anything about it before. Nurse Payne told them that Matron ruled with such a rod of iron, nobody dared to contradict her or even suggest anything; so reporting her would have been out of the question. The Trustees asked Nurse Payne to write everything down so that they could make sure that Matron didn't come back to work there again.

After Nurse Payne had gone, Amy told them a little about herself and explained that she was the rightful heiress to the estate, but was having difficulties in proving it. They asked her what she intended doing if and when she did inherit.

Amy told them that she intended keeping it as a hospital, so they didn't need to worry that they would lose the building. If they carried on paying the wages to the staff and paid for the upkeep of the place, Amy would be happy to run it for them, as long as she could introduce more humane treatment of the men.

After Nurse Payne and Amy wrote their statements, the Trustees left, promising that Matron would lose her position and thanking Amy for having the courage to inform them. They also agreed to her suggestions that they would still be paying for everything. They even agreed to pay Amy rent for use of the building, which pleased her greatly.

It was not long before Matron would be back and Amy was dreading the showdown that would occur. In the meantime, Amy put an advertisement in the Yorkshire Post, asking for anyone who worked at Montague Hall prior to 1912. She asked people to get in touch with herself or Waddington's lawyers.

A week later, Mr Coates rang her, asking her to call in the office. He wouldn't give any details over the telephone, so Amy had to be patient. When she eventually met him the next day, he told her that there had been a response to the advertisement, from a girl called Ginny Alderson, who was a scullery maid in 1912.

'Did she remember me?' burst out Amy.

'Yes, I've brought her in to check. If you'll wait a moment.' Mr Coates left the room and returned with a young woman, who Amy vaguely remembered.

'Miss Alderson, this lady tells me that she is Miss Arabella Montague, who was supposed to have drowned on the Titanic. Do you recognise her?'

The girl stared. 'Can't say I do really,' she replied. Amy's heart sank. What was she going to do?

'Wait a minute,' said the girl, a flash of inspiration crossing her face, 'the birthmark, she had a horrible birthmark. A big red one, behind her ear.'

'Which ear?' asked Mr Coates.

'Now let me see, I think it was the left one. Yes, it was, the left one, I remember now,' beamed the girl.

'May I ask you to remove your hat, Mrs Storm?'

'Certainly,' replied Amy with a smile, never before had she been glad that she had this awful disfigurement. Mr Coates looked under her hair, behind her left ear, whilst Miss Alderson looked too.

'Yes, that's it, that's the birthmark. You'd never forget that, would you? Horrible isn't it? Oh, I beg your pardon Miss, or are you called Mrs now?' the maid started blushing in embarrassment.

'Don't worry Ginny, I never thought I'd be glad to tell anyone I had this birthmark.'

'I know where Mrs Seeney is as well. She got me my place after they all drowned. Or we thought you had anyway. Did anyone else survive?'

'No, only me. I stopped talking for a while and couldn't say who I was.'

'Oh yes,' remembered Ginny, 'Lizzie told me that you'd done that before when your parents and your dog died. Shock, she said it was.'

'Thank you Miss Alderson. I think we can safely assume that this is Miss Montague.'

'Are you going to live in the Hall now?' Ginny Alderson persisted.

'I already do. I trained as a nurse and then got a position there about three months ago. It's a hospital now.'

'I've always missed working there. Are there any positions going? Can I come and work for you?'

'Really Miss Alderson, I think . .' interjected Mr Coates.

'No, it's all right, Mr Coates. There will be a position for you any time, Ginny. Come on, I'll take you home if you like. We can talk in the automobile. Perhaps you can sort out the details of my estate please, Mr Coates?'

'Certainly Mrs Storm.'

'By the way, I'll still use my new name of Amy. It's much simpler than all the rest.' Mr Coates nodded. Amy and Ginny were about to leave the office when there was a knock on the door and the clerk ushered a lady in. It was Mrs Seeney.

'Mrs Seeney,' cried Amy in delight. The lady stared at Amy then light dawned on her face.

'Miss Arabella. I couldn't believe it when Ginny told me. I thought she was having a funny turn. What ever happened to you? And where have you been all these years?' Amy quickly gave her an update on her life, and then the three of them left the office, leaving Mr Coates a lot more confident that she was the rightful heiress.

It was a delighted Amy and Jane who danced round the kitchen table that night, whilst Geoffrey looked on bemused. It was not a moment too soon as Matron was expected back the next day.

The following morning, Amy braced herself for the showdown that she knew would happen. Matron came downstairs when Amy was already in the study, working on the duty rotas.

'What has being going on in my absence, Storm?' Matron bellowed as soon as she entered the room.

'Good day Matron, did you have a nice holiday?'

'Never mind that, I asked what was going on?'

'What exactly do you mean by going on?' Amy asked, stalling for time.

'Why are two patients working in the gardens? And I've just seen Payne carrying a bottle of Eusol? And I've heard Payne and Higgins using their first names to each other. Quite brazen they were. Really Storm, the whole place is a shambles. What have you been doing? I expressly told you to maintain the standards whilst I was away. It'll take me weeks to get them back to my standards.' Amy noticed that Matron was going puce coloured and worried for her state of health momentarily.

'Well, what have you to say for yourself, before I give you notice to quit?'

'Oh I don't think you can do that, Matron.'
'Oh yes I can, lady. I don't know who you think you are, but I will not tolerate insolence from the staff.' Amy took a deep breath and reminded herself to keep calm.
'Here is a letter from the Board of Trustees. Perhaps you should read it.'
'The Board of Trustees? What have they to do with anything?'
'They visited here in your absence and weren't happy at what they found.'
'Not happy? Not happy?' she screeched. 'I'll give them not happy. I've worked hard here in the middle of nowhere. I've got the patients and staff all obedient and biddable and they say they're not happy.'
'Perhaps you should read the letter,' Amy urged.
Matron read the letter and sank back into the chair, her breath coming in great gasps. Amy thought that she was going to have a seizure and offered to get her a drink.
'I want nothing from you, you snake in the grass. You've plotted this behind my back, just to get control of this place. I knew there was something fishy about you from the start. I suppose you're going to be Matron now?'
Amy was silent.
'Yes,' Matron continued, 'I bet that was your plan all along. Pick on a poor defenceless body who only tries to do her best and get rid of her, so that you can have the position instead. Oh, I've met your sort before. Come up from nothing and think you own the place.'
'Actually I do,' replied Amy.
'Do what?' Matron replied, a little lost at the way the conversation had turned.
'Own the place. I do own the place, Montague Hall,' replied Amy. 'I was on the Titanic and lost my mind. I have only just been able to prove that I'm the heiress to this house. So yes, I will continue to be Matron. I've decided to let the government continue using the house as a hospital. The Board of Trustees have agreed it all.'
'Well,' said Matron, for once unable to say anything else. But the fight all seemed to have gone out of her now and Amy even felt a little sorry for her.
'What will you do?' asked Amy solicitously.

'What do you care?' Matron shrieked back. 'I'm packing my bags now and I won't be back.' Jumping up out of the chair, Matron left the room and stalked upstairs.

As Amy left the room to see what was happening with the staff and patients, one of the maids arrived to say that the new doctor had arrived and wanted to see Matron, but she had just gone upstairs and ignored her. What should she do, the young girl wanted to know?

'I'll see him,' replied Amy. 'Show him in here, please.'

A tall man with ginger hair walked into the room, limping quite heavily as he walked. He gave Amy an engaging smile and said good morning.

'Er, good morning,' Amy replied. 'I'm the new Matron here, Amy Storm.' She held out her hand to him. A strong hand gripped hers and held on to it just a shade longer than was normal in courteous circles.

'Jonathon Threlfall at your service, Amy Storm,' he said, whilst continuing to gaze at her. Amy felt a blush stealing over her face and hurried to the bell rope to order tea, so that she could recover her composure.

'I'm here part time,' he continued. 'I have a practice in York but am to spend one day a week here. Apparently the last doctor left some months ago and it's been difficult replacing him. From the notes that the last doctor left, there seem to have been concerns about how the patients were being treated. Can you spill any light on that, Matron Amy?'

'I certainly can,' replied Amy, recovering her composure through talking about work. 'The previous Matron ruled with a rod of iron, both with the patients and staff. She has been on holiday and the whole place has changed now. Also, the Board of Trustees have dismissed her from the position and now I have taken over.' A loud bang of the front door interrupted their conversation. Amy cringed but said nothing.

'What was that?' asked Jonathon, 'someone sounded in a bad mood.'

'That was the former Matron leaving.'

'Oh, so it's that recent a change of Matron?'

'Yes, as of this morning,' replied Amy smiling.

'Well, that's a good omen. You and I both starting new positions together. I'm sure we're going to work very well together, aren't you?' Jonathon asked.

'I hope so,' said Amy, trying to be non-committal, yet desperately hoping they would work together well.

'And what great plans have you in store?' he asked.

'I've already made many changes whilst Matron was on holiday, but I've more plans.' A knock on the door heralded the maid with the tea tray and whilst Amy served them both, she outlined how the men and staff had been called by their surnames and had all suffered punishments that weren't warranted. She also told him about the men doing little jobs around the grounds to make them feel more useful.

'It's made a difference already. We've only used a quarter of the medication to calm the men down since the new regime was instigated.'

'That's admirable. I was really keen to come and work here. Having worked in France during the war, I know what some of the men went through.'

'Where did you work?'

'On one of the battlefield camps. It was hairy at times, I can tell you. The Hun thought nothing of bombing medical tents. That's why I have a limp. Roof came down on me in a makeshift operating theatre.'

'I worked in a casualty receiving station for most of my time in France,' replied Amy.

'Did you? Pity we never met,' he started laughing and then suddenly stopped. 'I do apologise; I have just noticed your wedding band. I assumed you were single, as most nurses are. I do hope that my behaviour hasn't offended you.'

'No, not at all, I am a widow. My husband was an ambulance driver and got killed in France whilst on duty.'

'I'm so sorry. Were you married long?'

'Less than a week. It seems like a dream now. But at least I got my little boy out of it, to remember my husband by.'

'How old is he?'

'Four. He's a good boy. He is as happy as the day is long. We live in a cottage in the grounds, with my friend Jane, who looks after him. Anyway, enough of my life, I'll take you round the patients and staff, if you are ready. The next thing I want to do is get rid of these bright blue hospital uniforms and let the men wear their own clothes. This way if you please.'

The two of them walked round the wards and grounds until Jonathon had met all the staff and patients. He adopted the new ethos of the place and asked to be called Jonathon by all the staff.

After he had gone, Nurse Payne or Margaret as she was now called, came to tell Amy that there was a phone call in the office. Amy hurried into the office and picked up the receiver.

'Hello, Amy Storm here,' replied Amy in her best Matron voice.

'Oh hello, Amy Storm,' mimicked a voice back to her. 'It's your old friend Molly.'

'Molly! Where are you?'

'We're in York. We've come for a short holiday and thought we'd like to visit you.'

'Where are you staying? Shall I come and pick you up?'

'If you wouldn't mind, that'd be great. We're staying in a tiny hotel on Walmgate.'

'Tell me the name and I'll come over. Will two o' clock suit you?'

'Yes, perfect. Oh Amy, I've a lot to tell you.'

'Same here, Molly. I'd better get the kettle on then, so that we can have a good chat.' The two girls made final arrangements and then Amy decided to go back to the cottage.

As she walked in, Geoffrey flung her arms round her and hugged her.

'Hello Mummy, is it teatime already?'

'No, son, but I've come to tell you something exciting. Do you remember Aunty Molly, who lived in Burnley?'

'No, I remember Mrs Smith in Burnley and my friends on Lansdowne Street.'

'Mrs Smith is Aunty Molly's mummy. Her husband is Uncle Edwin.'

'Oh the man who tickles me?'

'Yes, that's right. Do you remember them now?'

'Yes.'

'Well, they are coming to visit us today. Can you manage extra for tea, Jane?'

'Of course I can. By the way, who was that man you were walking round the grounds with earlier?'
'Oh, that's the other news. It's our new doctor, Jonathon Threlfall.'
'Jonathon, is it?' teased Jane.
'Yes, he wants to be known by his first name, to all the staff and patients alike. He seems to have a lot of new ideas. I think we'll get along well together.'
'Mm, I'm sure you will,' answered Jane, nodding her head wisely.
Amy was very excited by the time she got to the hotel. She bundled Molly, Edwin and little Emma into the automobile and drove back to Montague Hall. On the way, Amy told Molly all that had been happening to her since she arrived at the Hall. When they were almost there, Amy then told Molly about her real status and situation and that she had reclaimed her inheritance.
Molly and Edwin were awestruck by all the revelations.
'Why did you never tell me who you were Amy?'
'It was too painful to think about for a long time, and then we lost touch for a while when you were nursing in Portsmouth.'
'So what's happening now?'
'I'm the new Matron and at present I live in a cottage in the grounds. But now I've reclaimed my inheritance, I'm going to make a suite of rooms for us in the main house, in one of the wings. And what about you? What's made you come to York?'
'Edwin came for an interview in York.'
'Great, we can be together again,' enthused Amy.
'Fraid not,' replied Molly. 'He didn't get the job.' Having arrived at the cottage, they all went inside. Geoffrey was a little shy at first, but soon came round and took little Emma wandering off to see his playthings.
After a cup of tea, they sat together and Amy asked what plans they had next.
'We don't know. We'd pinned all our hopes on this position. We'll have to think again now.'
'What sort of position was it?'
'Bookkeeping,' replied Edwin. 'I found I'd an aptitude for sums when I was convalescing. I was good at sums at school but you know what it was like in Burnley. You either went down the pit or into the mill. There was no schooling past twelve for any of us.'

'Do you want work Molly?' Amy suddenly asked.
'Why? Have you got a job here?'
'Yes, you could help me be Matron. We could work half a week each and then have more time with our children.'
'But who would look after Emma whilst I was working?'
'If you speak nicely to Jane, and pay her a good salary, she may be inclined to help you,' teased Amy. Molly turned round to Jane.
'Would you Jane, would you help me?'
'Of course, and I wouldn't need a salary. I have no need of extra money. And besides, young Geoffrey will be going to school soon, so I'd have too much time on my hands.'
'Great, I'll take the position then,' beamed Molly. 'Oh it'll be great working with you again. I'm so glad we rang you up. But I've got a little problem.'
'What's that?' laughed Amy. 'You don't like the colour of the uniforms? You don't want to work with me? What is it?'
'You're going to be an aunty again.'
'Molly, you lucky thing. I didn't notice. Is it early days?'
'Yes, that's why we were hoping that Edwin would get this job, as I won't be able to earn anything for a time.'
'Your worries are over, then. I will pay you whilst you have your baby. At least I can be Godmother this time and no excuses. We seem to have missed the important events of each others lives in the last four or five years.'
'And what about me?' asked Edwin mournfully.
'You can be my bookkeeper and help with the men. I can keep you quite busy.' Edwin visibly cheered.
'That sounds great. All we need now is somewhere to live,' said Edwin.
'You can live here in this cottage,' replied Amy.
'And where are we going to live?' asked Jane quietly.
'Oh, I forgot to tell you. I've decided to take a suite of rooms in the far wing of the main house. We can live there quite comfortably. Besides, I want Geoffrey to love this house like I do. After all, he will inherit it eventually. It'll be up to him whether it stays as a hospital or not.'
'But what about his Storm inheritance?' asked Jane.

'Well, if it happens, it happens, but I'm not going to worry about that for now. Time enough later.'
'What Storm inheritance?' asked a curious Molly.
'One day, Geoffrey will be Lord Storm, but at the present, they are not acknowledging him or me. Some day, I'll fight for it but not yet. I'm happy as we are. Now, are you all going to stay here right away or do you want to go back to York?'
'We'll have to go back to York to settle up with the hotel, but then we'll send for all our clothes.'
'Where are they?'
'In Burnley, at my mums house.'
'Why don't we all go and collect them in the automobile? That way I could see your mum again and my other friends in Burnley.'
'What a good idea,' said Molly. 'Hey, Amy, why don't we try and find all our nursing friends and have a get together?'
'Better still, why don't we invite them and all their families up to Montague Hall for a holiday? We've plenty of rooms that aren't being used. Why, they may even want positions here, what do you think?'
'I know that Katie, Olivia, Sophia and Eleanor are still in Burnley. We could find out about the other ones later.'
The two friends continued making plans about the future, until it was time for Amy to take them back to York. On her return, she asked Jane if she minded moving into the Hall and she said no, she'd be happy wherever Amy and Geoffrey were.
'Because if ever you did want to leave, I've put the house on Lansdowne Street in your name, and all the rent money is going to your bank account. I always want you to have a place where you can go to, if ever you need it.'
Jane thanked Amy profusely, not without a few tears.
'I can't ever see me wanting to go from here, but thank you so much. It's a tremendous thought knowing that I have security for my old age.' Amy said that she would put Geoffrey to bed that night so Jane went to bed early.
As she was tucking Geoffrey up in bed, he excitedly told Amy all about the games that he was planning for Emma when she lived at Montague Hall. His excitement rubbed off and Amy was awake for a long time that night, thinking about the future. She was happy with

herself now. She remembered Jack's kind words of advice, that her sins were forgiven and knew that they had been a turning point for her.

She no longer felt that she was responsible for Lizzie's death, and the work that she had done for others was in some way a measure of being forgiven. Also, now that she was wealthy, she could give these men a better life. She could also take care of her friends, if they were in need, as they had helped her when she was in need. She might even send for Laura and Martha from the asylum. And she would write to Lord Storm and tell him where his grandchild was living, just in case they wanted to get in touch: she owed it to little Geoffrey and his father.

It could only get better, she decided. Molly and Edwin working for her; Geoffrey with a little playmate; a new baby to look forward to; and the staff and patients far more happy. Oh and yes, with all the excitement she had forgotten the new doctor. Jonathon Threlfall. His name lingered in her mind. How could she have forgotten him? She was certainly going to enjoy working with him, she thought, as she slowly slipped into sleep with a smile on her face.

A Pasty In A Pear Tree

Daphne Neville

ISBN: 978-0-244-34415-3

PublishNation, London
www.publishnation.co.uk

Other Titles by This Author

TRENGILLION CORNISH MYSTERY SERIES

The Ringing Bells Inn

Polquillick

Sea, Sun, Cads and Scallywags

Grave Allegations

The Old Vicarage

A Celestial Affair

Trengillion's Jubilee Jamboree

PENTRILLICK CORNISH MYSTERY SERIES

The Chocolate Box Holiday

The Old Tile House

Chapter One

December 2016

On a dull but dry afternoon on the second day of December, a small yellow car drove along the winding main street of Pentrillick, a village on the south coast of West Cornwall. As it neared the Crown and Anchor it slowed down, turned right into Long Lane and wound its way up the steep and narrow road. At the very top it stopped outside Primrose Cottage, the second house in Blackberry Way, and the female passenger in the front seat eagerly sprang from the vehicle. The double wooden gates creaked as she pushed them open and dried leaves which had gathered during the autumn months, scattered across the tarmacked front garden.

On the back seat, a Jack Russell terrier, sensing the cheery mood of the lady behind the steering wheel, leapt to his feet, looked from the window and excitedly barked as the car drove between the gateposts and parked in front of the up-and-over door of a garage. As the engine faded, the driver stepped from the car and glanced up at the word SOLD on the estate agent's board. With a broad smile on her face, she gleefully clapped her hands. "We did it, Lottie. I can't believe it. We really are here at last."

Hetty reached back inside the car where the keys to the cottage lay on the dashboard. "Let's have a quick look round before the removal men get here."

She closed the car door.

"But what about Albert?" Lottie asked, "Can't he come too?"

Inside the car, Albert's head was tilted to one side and as Hetty opened the door his tail wagged nineteen to the dozen. "Of course he can. Come on then, my love, I expect you're as keen to explore our new home as we are."

Hetty and Lottie were sisters and also twins. Lottie was recently widowed and Hetty who had never married, retired at the age of sixty two after a long career as a midwife. The sisters were now sixty four years old and each having sold their respective homes were moving to Pentrillick to begin a new chapter in their lives. They had chosen Cornwall and Pentrillick in particular because they had stayed there for a holiday earlier in the year.

The interior of Primrose Cottage was unfamiliar to them but they knew the house's location and so decided to rely on the pictures and details on the estate agent's website rather than make a special journey to view the property in person. Happy with what they had read and seen, they had then made an offer which was promptly accepted because although the house had raised much interest due to a murder having recently taken place there, no-one it seemed, other than the twins had any desire to make it their home.

The sisters were drinking tea having had the foresight to bring the kettle, mugs, milk and teabags in the car, when they heard the rumble of the removal lorry approaching. Eager to get their belongings indoors before darkness fell, they went outside to greet the removal men.

In less than two hours the lorry was unloaded and on its way back to Northamptonshire.

"Let's just make up our beds tonight and do the rest tomorrow," said Lottie, eying the bags and boxes stacked up on the living room furniture, "after all I daresay you're feeling pretty weary after the long drive."

Hetty shook her head. "No, I'm not really tired at all because I'm far too excited to even think about sleeping. A bit like a child really, I suppose. You're right about the beds though. Let's make them up now and then celebrate."

The cottage had three bedrooms; two large doubles on the front with views overlooking the village and out towards the sea, and a smaller one at the back on the opposite side of the stairwell to a large bathroom which had been converted from a bedroom in the nineteen fifties. As the doubles were almost identical in size, the sisters had no reason to squabble who had which as they might have done fifty years earlier.

When the beds were made they sat in the kitchen with an electric fire to keep them warm and then opened a bottle of wine and popped a pizza into the oven, already installed and part of the house purchase price.

"Will Albert be alright in here tonight?" Lottie asked, glancing down at the dog who had already made himself at home and was curled up asleep in his basket, after having explored every room several times over.

"Well, I suppose so. I can't see any reason why not. I mean, he has his own bed so should be fine. But if you're worried I'll leave my bedroom door open so that he can find me if he's disorientated."

Lottie smiled. "And I'll leave mine open too because I want him to get used to me."

"I think he already has, bless him. He's a very sociable dog. I can't believe someone was heartless enough to abandon him."

Albert opened one eye and looked at the two sisters instinctively knowing they were talking about him, and then after a quick wag of his tail he resumed his sleep.

"We must pop down to the charity shop tomorrow," said Hetty, reaching for the bottle of wine standing on the work surface to refill their glasses, "and ask Maisie or Daisy who they'd recommend for fuel. Having been empty for a while the cottage feels quite damp so we need to get the central heating going as soon as possible."

"Yes, but we ought to have it checked over first though," said Lottie, who was very safety conscious. "It won't have been used since last winter and so might be dangerous."

"Very true, we'll see if they can recommend someone to do that as well."

Lottie took a sip of wine and then stood the glass down on a box marked pots and pans. "It's nice to think we already know a few people. It must be strange moving to a new place when you don't know a soul. I mean, there is so much we need to find out as at present we don't even know which day the dustmen come."

"Well that shouldn't be a problem as I can look that up on the council's website. You've reminded me though that's something else we need to do. Get the internet, I mean. It's not good for my eyes to try and do everything on my phone."

Lottie leaned forwards, removed her shoes and rested her feet on the fluffy white top of a stool destined to go into her bedroom. "Ah, that's better. I think we ought to make a list of jobs that need doing. The important ones anyway."

"Good idea," Hetty reached for her handbag and pulled out a notebook and pen. "Well there's one thing for sure, we certainly won't be bored for the rest of the year, will we? Because on top of everything else we have Christmas to look forward to. I can't wait to see in the New Year here as I'm sure the atmosphere in the Crown and Anchor will be fantastic." She opened up the notebook.

Lottie agreed, "Yes and I'm also looking forward to visiting the Christmas Wonderland thing at Pentrillick House, if for no other reason than just to see the old house again."

The following morning dawned with grey skies and light raindrops trickling down the window panes of Primrose

Cottage, but despite the weather neither sister was enticed to stay in bed and so both were downstairs eating breakfast before the day was even fully light.

By mid-morning the drizzle had stopped and so Hetty keen to get a little fresh air went outside to clean the front room window and while out there, Tommy Thomas who lived a few doors away at Fuchsia Cottage, called over the front boundary wall.

"Good morning, gorgeous," he said, with a cheeky grin, "I heard on the grapevine that it was you and your lovely sister were buying this place. I'm glad about that as we don't want any old riff-raff up here."

Hetty stepped down from the chair and went over to Tommy and held out her hand. "Lovely to see you again. It's great to be back and we can't wait to see everyone. Is everything in the village okay?"

"Oh, yes. It's been very quiet since you and your family went home." He laughed. "No-one's been murdered, thank goodness, and I don't even think there have been any punch-ups."

"I'm pleased to hear it. And how's your mother?"

The smile disappeared from Tommy's face. "Sadly she died in October. She took a tumble and ended up in hospital with a few broken bones. Poor thing. After that she came down with bronchitis from which she never recovered."

"Oh, I am sorry," said Hetty, "so you're all alone now."

Tommy nodded. "Yep, just me and the dog," he patted the head of the dog sitting at his feet, "and this time of the year folks don't have their windows cleaned as much so I'm often at a bit of a loose end."

Hetty felt guilty that she was cleaning her own windows and had not called in Tommy, so quickly changed the subject.

"Who lives next door at whatever the house is called?" she asked, nodding towards a house surrounded by scaffolding with only half of the roof slated.

"It's called Hillside and Alex and Ginny live there. They own and run the antique shop in the village. They're a nice couple. You'll like them."

"Any children?" Hetty asked.

"Yes, but they're grown up and have flown the nest. I daresay Alex and Ginny must be in their mid-fifties."

"Lovely, I look forward to meeting them."

"Anyway," said Tommy, turning to continue his walk, "if there's anything I can do to help you, please give me a shout."

Hetty's eyebrows rose. "Well, actually there are one or two things you might be able to help us with. The central heating for one. The stove is multi-fuel and neither of us have ever had anything like that before as we both had oil. So, do you know anyone who services fires, flues and stuff like that?"

Tommy took a bow. "Yours truly," he said. "I worked as a heating engineer for a while before Mother and me moved to Pentrillick but I gave it up then and decided to clean windows instead because I was reaching retirement age anyway and I like to be outdoors."

"Really, that's music to my ears. We'd love to get it going before the weather turns colder, so if you'd have a look when you have the time we'd really appreciate it."

"No time like the present," said Tommy, as he made his way towards the gates. "As long as you don't mind Fagan coming with me."

Hetty looked down at the Yorkshire terrier close to Tommy's feet. "What! You've named him after the pickpocket in Oliver."

"No, he were Fagin not Fagan. Fagan is an Irish name and it means little fierce one. Isn't that right, boy?"

Fagan wagged his tail and looked anything but fierce.

Hetty opened the gate. “Fagan is most welcome, but I am mystified why a Cornishman would give his dog an Irish name.”

Tommy chuckled. “My maternal grandmother was Irish and so you see I’m an Irish Cornishman.”

“Really, what an interesting combination. Anyway, I also have a dog now and he’s called Albert so Fagan will have company. Albert is named after my father, Albert Tonkins.”

“And mine too,” said Lottie, standing on the doorstep having come out to see to whom Hetty was talking. She held out her hand. “Lovely to see you again, Tommy.”

By mid-afternoon a fire was burning in the multi-fuel stove and the radiators were steadily warming. Hetty and Lottie wanted to pay Tommy for his work but he insisted that he was only too happy to have helped.

“In which case,” said Lottie, “we must take you out for a meal. To the pub perhaps.”

“Now that sounds very nice and I should like it if we were to do that.” He chuckled. “Should impress the other chaps to see me out with a couple of lovely ladies.”

Hetty tutted. “Less of your cheek, Tommy Thomas. Lovely ladies indeed. We’re more than aware of the fact that we’re both on the wrong side of sixty.”

Tommy looked offended. “But I meant it. You are lovely ladies and I’m the wrong side of sixty too.”

Because Hetty and Lottie were eager to go to the pub, it was agreed they would all go out for a meal that evening. For being a Saturday, it should be quite busy and so they’d be able to see some of the villagers with whom they were already acquainted.

The Crown and Anchor, a seventeenth century, detached, granite built construction, lay on the southern side of Pentrillick’s main street just before a bend and near to the village junior school. Hence, the back windows of the building had sea views and its sun terrace accessed by French doors in the bar, partly stood on the beach. Alison and Ashley Rowe were the licensees and to the delight of Hetty and Lottie, both remembered the sisters' names and welcomed them effusively to their new home.

Rather than eat in the dining room where they would be tucked away from people out for a drink, they decided to eat in the bar and chose a table near to a roaring fire. But before they ate they decided to have a few drinks first.

"It's just as I imagined it would be," said Hetty, with enthusiasm. "The pub I mean on a winter's night. I think I like it so much more than in the summer."

"Hmm, I'm inclined to agree," said Lottie, "on the other hand I rather like the notion of popping out on a summer's evening while it's light and the sun is still shining."

"Like when we were on holiday," said Hetty, "Yes, I know what you mean but an open fire takes a bit of beating and with the Christmas decorations up it's quite breath-taking."

On one of the stools at the bar alongside a man who was a stranger to the sisters, sat Bernie the Boatman, a man in his fifties who took visitors out on fishing trips during the summer months. When he caught Lottie's eye he waved and gave the thumbs up sign. Lottie waved back.

"Bernie's beard seems bigger and bushier than ever," she said, "or perhaps it's my imagination."

"No, you're right," said Tommy, "he's grown it for the Christmas Wonderland. He's one of the Father Christmases, you see. He looks really good, but of course his beard has to be sprayed white to look authentic."

"Now, that I must see," said Hetty, "When is the Wonderland thing on?"

"It started last weekend," said Tommy, pausing to take a sip of his beer, "and goes on until twelfth night. It's open six days a week, Wednesday to Monday, and starts at eleven in the morning and closes at six in the evening on weekdays but stays open until seven at the weekends."

"Obviously closed on Tuesday then," reasoned Lottie, "and is the House open to the public at all?"

"Yes, but only twice a day."

"We must go as soon as possible," said Hetty. "It'll help get us in the Christmas spirit. Although seeing the lovely decorations in here is already having that affect on me."

When the person to whom Bernie the Boatman was talking got up and left the pub, Bernie picked up his pint and joined the sisters and Tommy sitting by the fire.

"I heard you were back," said Bernie, shaking hands with each sister in turn. "How's Bill?" He sat down.

"Fine thanks," said Lottie, "He rang this morning to see how we were settling in and said to tell you all he sends his regards. I got a feeling he half wished he was able to come down with us. Still, perhaps he can when he retires but that won't be for a few years yet as he's only forty two."

"I take it Bill's the son who you came down with in the summer," said Tommy.

Lottie nodded. "That's right. We were with Bill and his wife, Sandra and their three children. Quite a houseful."

Tommy turned to Bernie. "Simeon left early tonight. Is he okay?"

Bernie nodded. "Yeah, he's fine but he needs to be up early to get baking. The last few days have been really busy and so stocks are getting low."

Hetty and Lottie were both intrigued. "Who is Simeon?" Hetty quickly asked before the subject was changed.

"He's a patti…um...a French pastry chef," said Tommy, "and he's running the café at Pentrillick House for the Wonderland."

"Oh, a patissier," said Hetty, "how lovely. We must certainly pay him a visit."

“How come they’ve got in a French chap?” Lottie asked.

“The café closes during the winter months between November the first and the end of February,” said Bernie, “but the Wonderland Committee thought food should be on offer and so they asked Tristan if they could use the café. He agreed and the committee decided rather than do the same thing every year to invite in different nationalities to ring the changes. Last year we had an Indian chap called Sai and his curries were to die for.”

Lottie sighed. “We chose the right year to come then. I’m not one for spicy food so the pastries will suit me fine.”

“You’re such an old stick-in-the-mud, Lottie. Curries are gorgeous. I love them.”

Lottie ignored her sister. “So, are there any other strangers at the Wonderland or are the rest locals?”

“About fifty fifty,” said Tommy, “There are quite a few folks with the fairground attractions and several others with stalls who seem to go around the country from one event to another. They seem a nice lot anyway, especially Psychic Sid. In fact the whole Wonderland thing has a lovely atmosphere and so far is better attended than last year.”

Chapter Two

Sunday dawned bright and sunny but with a cold wind blowing. Lottie woke first and thought about going to church but decided against as there was still much to be done to get the house in some sort of order. Only the kitchen and the bathroom could be described as neat and tidy. The rest of the house was still littered with boxes and bulging black bin liners which needed to be unpacked. It was decided therefore when Hetty arose that each would concentrate on their own bedroom thus ensuring the bin liners would be emptied, as most contained items of clothing and bed linen.

By lunch time both front bedrooms were neat, clean and tidy.

"What now?" Hetty asked, as they sat down at the kitchen table with well-earned cups of coffee. "Shall we go to the pub for a roast or shall we go to the Wonderland thing?"

Lottie sighed. "I'd like to do both but I don't think I have the energy. What do you think?"

"I agree with you but I am feeling hungry so I think the pub has the greatest appeal. I mean, we can only have a roast on a Sunday whereas we can go to the Wonderland any day bar Tuesday. On the other hand it's nice and sunny today which is ideal for being outdoors."

"In that case we'll go to the pub and we'll walk there and back to get some fresh air. That way you'll be able to have a glass or two of wine as well. We'd have to take the car if we went to Pentrillick House because it's too far to walk. Too far for us anyway when feeling weary."

"That's settled then and we'll take Albert too. It's time he got to know his new homeland."

Albert sat up and crossed to the table when he heard mention of his name.

"Poor old thing, we've neglected you haven't we?" Hetty said, bending down to stroke the back of his soft, warm head, "But I promise once we're straight we'll take you for lots and lots of walks."

After the sisters had locked up the cottage they crossed the road and paused by a five bar gate to take in the view over the field and down towards the coast and the village.

"I still can't believe we're here," said Hetty, pulling on Albert's lead to stop him trying to run away with her. "And this view, well, I don't think I'll ever get tired of seeing it."

Lottie smiled. "Me neither and it's all just as we imagined it. You even have a dog. Isn't it funny the way things work out in life?"

"Yes, it certainly is and right now I think we have much to be grateful for."

Albert barked as though to endorse Hetty's sentiments.

At the end of Blackberry Way they turned into Long Lane which ran sharply downhill. The hedgerows were less dense than in the summer; blackberry brambles bore only a few withered leaves and there were no flowers to add a dash of colour.

Despite the fact that the weather was good they met no-one along the lane and when they reached the bottom of the hill which came out opposite the pub, they observed that the main street which ran through the village was devoid of traffic.

The Crown and Anchor as on the previous evening was busy with diners and drinkers and the smell of Sunday dinner hung in the air. The tables nearest to the fire were already taken and so the sisters sat at the far end of the bar near to a piano which stood in a dimly lit corner beside a Christmas tree part-hidden beneath coloured lights, baubles and strands of silver tinsel. Before they ordered their food they both had a small glass of wine and sat back to soak up the atmosphere. Albert, alarmed by the many pairs of feet, shuffled underneath the table and took a nap.

Every time the front door opened, Hetty and Lottie turned their heads, eager to see if they knew whosoever emerged through the door and to their amusement, shortly after their arrival, Vince Royale who owned a garage on the outskirts of the village, walked in.

Hetty giggled like a school girl. "I swear, Lottie, that Vince looks even more like a young Prince Charles every time I see him."

However, when he unzipped his jacket they were both surprised by his choice of clothing. For he wore a bright green, thick woollen knitted jumper with the face of a reindeer on the front and a large red bobble for as its nose. Alison, it seemed also shared their mirth for she laughed helplessly.

"I really thought you were joking, Vince," she said, reaching across the bar to flick the overlarge nose, "but it's good to see you've adopted a little Christmas spirit albeit the least subtle I'm sure of all the knitwear that Nancy and Neil had on offer."

Vince removed his jacket and did a quick twirl so that all might see the latest addition to his wardrobe.

When the chuckling died down he said, "Actually, I had to buy it and wear it because Bernie bet fifty quid that I wouldn't. I'm hoping he'll be in this lunchtime so I can see him put his money in the Roof Fund box."

In the afternoon the sisters, feeling sleepy after a huge lunch and two glasses each of wine, fell asleep by the fire in the sitting room. When they woke up it was half past three.

"Shall we go for a walk?" Lottie asked, seeing the sun was still shining. "Not far, perhaps just through the village and back."

"Okay, but can we have a cup of tea first?"

Lottie shook her head. "Better not as it'll be dark in less than two hours. Let's leave it until we get back."

The main street of the village was surprisingly quiet even for a Sunday in December. No-one was standing in the pub car park nor outside in the smoking shelter. On both sides of the road, cars were parked close to each other for, being a Sunday, most people were at home. The post office was closed and the fish and chip shop too until four thirty. No-one waited at the bus stop for a bus and Chloe's Café was closed for the winter. However, as they approached the church they saw confetti blowing around the lichgate in the light breeze.

"Must have been a wedding recently," said Lottie, reaching inside the gate and picking up a few pieces of the colourful tissue. "How romantic to marry in the winter. It reminds me of Mum and Dad. Mum often told us when we were kids how a few flakes of snow fell when they came out of the church on their wedding day."

"But that was January," said Hetty.

"Yes, but same thing. This confetti is fresh too so I think whoever got married did so yesterday."

As they walked round the bend, Lottie pointed to a car parked outside Sea View Cottage, the holiday let in which they had stayed during the summer.

"Probably someone down for Christmas," said Hetty, "and very nice too."

"It's a bit early to be here for Christmas, I would have thought. I mean, most people don't finish work until a few days before."

"Yes, I suppose so, although it might be someone who is retired."

Outside the antique shop they stopped and looked in the window to see what their next door neighbours whom they had yet to meet, sold.

"Pricey," said Hetty.

"Hmm, better to go to car boot sales and charity shops."

Next door was a hairdresser. Both sisters peered in through the window. "Looks nice and clean," said Hetty, "so I shall definitely have my hair done here when it next needs cutting."

"Me too. We must support small businesses especially here in the village."

Finally they reached the Pentrillick Hotel which said 'vacancies' on the bottom of its large name board.

"Let's go back now," said Hetty, "there are no more shops after the hotel and I'm longing for a cup of tea."

As they approached Primrose Cottage it was getting dark but so as not to have wasted the entire day, after cups of tea, they set to and tackled the dining room where boxes were stacked on and around the drop-leaf table which until a few days earlier had taken pride of place in Lottie's former home.

Chapter Three

On Monday morning, Hetty and Lottie were up bright and early for they had decided the previous day that they must go to the charity shop in the morning to see Maisie and Daisy, two ladies with whom they had made friends while on holiday during the summer.

As Lottie pulled back the living room curtains she saw a lady of a similar age to herself walking briskly along the lane in the front of the cottage. She turned to Hetty who was switching on the television to watch the news. "There's a woman walking by who I've seen a couple of times now. I wonder who she is."

Hetty joined her sister at the window just in time to see the stranger disappear from view. "No idea, but I suppose she might live up here somewhere. I mean, there are several houses along here that we don't know anything about yet and we've not even met or seen anything of our next door neighbours at Hillside."

"Yes, I expect you're right. We'll no doubt find out in time."

They left for the charity shop just after ten and took Albert with them on his lead. As Hetty locked the door, Lottie saw on the roof of their neighbour's house, Hillside, two young men kneeling on the roof fixing new slates onto the wooden battens.

"I bet it's chilly up there," she said, buttoning up her coat, "draughty too. Rather them than me."

"They're young," said Hetty, dropping the house key into her pocket, "I don't think young people feel the cold like we do."

"No, I suppose not although I well remember being cold when we were young."

"But that was in the Midlands," said Hetty, "The winters are colder up there."

As they approached the charity shop, the woman who had walked past their cottage earlier in the day, came out. She nodded her head and said, "Good morning," before walking off briskly through the village clutching a carrier bag.

Inside the charity shop, Hetty and Lottie were disappointed to find that Daisy and Maisie were not working as it was their Monday off and it was their new neighbour, Tommy Thomas who was behind the counter sticking price tickets on pieces of bric-a-brac.

"Well, hello," he said, as they stepped over the threshold, "have you settled in yet?"

"I think so," said Hetty, pausing in the doorway, "Is it alright if I bring Albert in here?"

Tommy nodded his head, "Yeah, that's fine as long as he's well behaved. I often bring Fagan with me now that Mum's not at home to keep him company but this morning he didn't want to come out."

"Oh, Albert is very well behaved," said Hetty, with enthusiasm, "aren't you, my sweetheart?"

"I suppose you expected Maisie and Daisy to be here," said Tommy.

Hetty nodded. "Well, yes, we were hoping they would be. Not that we mind seeing you," she hastily added.

"And we really only popped in for a chat and to say hello anyway," said Lottie, "although I daresay there are a few bits and pieces amongst your stock that we could do with."

"A chat and to find out the latest gossip," said Tommy, with a chuckle, "You know where to come. Not that there's been much to gossip about lately, although to be fair folks have been very cautious about what they say to me since Mum went. I suppose they don't want to be seen as indelicate."

"Yes that's understandable," Lottie agreed. "I found the same when my husband died."

"Out of curiosity, who was the lady who was leaving the shop as we arrived? Hetty asked, "I only wonder because we saw her walking past our cottage this morning,"

"Ah, that's Miss Vickery. She lives up Blackberry Way in the very last house."

"The one hidden behind an extremely tall privet hedge?" Lottie asked.

"That's the one. It's called Meadowsweet. You'll probably see her quite often as she's always out walking. In fact she walks for miles, doesn't drive and I've never seen her on a bus."

"Hmm, that must be why she's so slim," said Hetty, a little envious.

"What's her Christian name?" Lottie asked.

"Katherine, but those who dare call her by her Christian name know her as Kitty," said Tommy, with a chuckle.

"Dare," repeated Hetty, somewhat bewildered.

"She's very old school," said Tommy, "brought up strictly and to address her elders by their titles and for that reason she expects everyone to address her likewise."

Hetty frowned. "How old is she? I only ask so we know whether or not we must call her Miss Vickery or whether we'll be permitted to call her Kitty."

"Ah, that's a tricky one. I know she's in her sixties but that's about all. Best to ask Maisie or Daisy. They've known her all their lives, you see, as they all went to the village school here many moons ago."

The sisters went home for lunch after purchasing a vase and a brass coal scuttle. When they arrived back they found the postman had been and there were five envelopes on the doormat.

"How exciting," said Lottie, picking up the post. "I suppose they'll be Christmas cards and so will brighten up the mantelpiece nicely."

However, as she looked at the last envelope her face dropped. "Oh, I'm not so sure about this one as it'll no doubt be my provisional driving licence."

"Excellent," said Hetty, standing the coal scuttle by the fireplace, "I'll sort out the insurance later and then you can have your first driving lesson tomorrow."

"Well I'm not really sure it's a good idea having you teach me to drive. I mean, I know you're very good and all that but your car doesn't have duel control and so it might not be safe."

"No, you'll be perfectly alright, Lottie. We'll start off by driving up and down Blackberry Way so there's little or no chance of meeting any traffic. I'm pretty sure you'll get the hang of it in no time and as with everything, practise makes perfect."

"If you say so but I don't want to damage your car reversing and stuff like that."

Lottie opened the buff coloured envelope half hoping the DVLA had forgotten to enclose the licence. She scowled when she saw the picture of herself. "Ugh, I look hideous. If only they'd permit us to smile on things like this but I know they can't for mathematical identification reasons or something technical like that."

Hetty looked over her shoulder. "Hmm, but you don't look any worse than I do on mine. I really think we ought to dye your hair though. It'd take years off you. Anyway, pop it in your purse for safe keeping. I can't wait to teach you to drive."

"I think you might regret ever having offered as I'm sure I'll be rubbish."

"Of course you won't. Besides, you're a level-headed lady, Lottie Burton and I believe that you'll make an excellent driver. Anyway, I'll only teach you the basics for a week or two and then you must have proper lessons after Christmas to get you ready for your test. I reckon you'll be a confident driver by the summer."

They left for Pentrillick House just before four and on arriving parked in the car park. Excited to be back in the grounds of the lovely old house, they made their way across a gravelled area where fairground amusements were positioned at the top of the extensive lawns. Gentle music drifted from the speakers of a kiddie's roundabout, next to swing boats and a coconut shy. Further along, a bouncy castle shuddered with the movement of small feet alongside a stall tempting passers-by to 'hook the duck'. And at the end of the row, a machine to 'test your strength' sat in the shadow of the cone-shaped tower of a helter-skelter.

Once past the amusements, German style, open-fronted wooden huts provided selling space for retailers, each situated on either side of the avenue of trees bordering a track which ran down towards the lake. From the trees, strings of coloured illuminations were just beginning to glow in the fading light of day. While in the air, the pleasant smell of burning pine wood rose from glowing braziers behind barriers to prevent children from burning their fingers.

"That's a good idea," said Lottie, "somewhere to warm our hands."

"Talking of keeping warm, we could buy one of those," said Hetty, pointing to a stall where Christmas jumpers and other knitted items were for sale.

"That must be where Vince bought his. Shall we get one?"

Hetty thought for a moment. "I think not. I mean they're not very flattering so might be alright for you or someone skinny like Miss Vickery, but they'd make me look even fatter than I already am."

"You're not fat, Het."

"No, but I'm not skinny either and I could do with losing a pound or two."

"I'm a bit confused, Het. I mean, you wear leggings and jumpers most of the time so I would have thought one of those Christmas ones would have been right up your street. Although I must admit they are a little garish."

"And a little short, Lottie. I doubt they would successfully cover my bottom and that would look hideous with leggings."

To change the subject Lottie pointed towards Christmas trees with roots which leaned against the last few trees in the avenue near to Santa's Grotto. "Now, that we must have," she said, "I've not had a real tree for years and they do smell so nice."

"Trouble is they also drop needles everywhere."

"That's what Hugh used to say and so we always had an artificial tree. In fact we had it for years but I sent it to a charity shop when sorting out stuff before the move."

"In that case we'll get one. I mean it has to be said that we'll have all the time in the world over the coming months to vacuum up the needles."

As they passed Santa's Grotto they peeped inside to see if Bernie the Boatman was on duty, but Santa's chair was empty and a list of opening times for visiting him stated that he would be there between eleven in the morning until three in the afternoon on weekdays and eleven until six at the weekend.

"Missed him," said Lottie, "still never mind, we'll catch him next time we're here."

"I wonder where the reindeer and sleigh are." Hetty looked all around.

“That’s probably the sleigh over there,” Lottie pointed to a sheet of tarpaulin covering something large, “I expect as they use real reindeer the rides are only on busy days or when Santa is on duty.”

A large marquee stood at the bottom of the avenue to the right where the area was flat. And near to the lake, stood the café which was for the Christmas period a Patisserie and the home of Simeon Dupont the patissier for whom accommodation had been made in an adjacent room.

Keen to sample Simeon’s wares, the sisters headed for the café where they were overwhelmed by the mouth-watering display and especially the stack of multi-coloured macarons. Unsure what to order they finally settled on something they were familiar with and ordered two eclairs and two coffees. To their surprise, Tess Dobson, who they had met during their summer holiday was the waitress.

“Well, hello there,” she said, recognising the sisters, “I heard you were buying Faith’s place but didn’t realise you were here yet.”

Hetty’s jaw dropped. “It seems everyone we speak to knew we were the buyers of Primrose Cottage. Goodness only knows how.”

Tess smiled. “Maisie’s son, Brian, works for the estate agents who dealt with the sale.”

“Say no more,” said Hetty, gently shaking her head. “Anyway, it’s lovely to see you again, Tess.”

“And you too. So, when did you get here?”

“Last Friday,” said Lottie.

“Ideal, just in time for Christmas.”

By the time the sisters left the café, the lights in the trees were shining brightly against the dark sky and the air felt chilly. Keen to know what was inside the marquee they went to take a look. To their delight it was crammed full of Christmassy house plants and brightly coloured decorations.

Suddenly overwhelmed with a festive spirit they bought a poinsettia, two cyclamen and a bowl of hyacinths. They also bought a few decorations to add to ones each already owned and had brought with them to Cornwall.

Before they left they also bought a tree and as Hetty watched the netting process, Lottie noticed a small caravan over towards the maze.

"Well, look at that," she said, much amused by the large sign over the closed door, where a small queue was gathered, "Psychic Sid, Fortune Teller, extraordinaire. I wonder if he's any good."

Hetty squinted to read the sign. "Well, there's only one way to find out. We'll put him to the test next time we come up here."

When they arrived back at the cottage they found a small magazine on the doormat. Hetty picked it up.

"What's that?" Lottie asked, as she placed the box of plants on a table in the hallway.

"It says it's *The Pentrillick Gazette*," Hetty flicked through the pages. "Looks like a local advertising magazine. Should be interesting and could be useful for any jobs we need doing." She tossed it onto the table beside the plants and then went back out to the car to fetch in the Christmas tree.

In the evening, the sisters sat down by the fire and admired their handiwork. The Christmas tree, planted in a bucket, stood in the corner with twinkling white lights which reflected the numerous coloured baubles and strands of silver tinsel.

"Where did you put that village magazine?" Lottie asked, standing up to replace a strand of fine tinsel which had fallen onto the floor from the fleshy leaves of her aspidistra, "I'd like to have a look at it now."

"I think it's still on the hall table."

The magazine was the December edition, and Lottie gleaned on reading the first page that it was a non-profit making monthly publication financed by advertising which was distributed free to residents of the village and was on sale to others in the post office for the modest sum of fifty pence.

"The August one must have been around in the summer when we were here on holiday," said Lottie, "but I don't recall seeing it at all."

"Well I daresay the people who stayed at Sea View Cottage the week before us took it home with them and I should imagine it was in demand anyway if it mentioned the murder of poor Faith Trethewy."

"Hmm, it may well have done as there seem to be a few news items dotted here and there."

"So, is there anything exciting in it?" Hetty asked.

"Could be," said Lottie. "Lots of businesses have adverts here and are wishing patrons a happy Christmas and so forth. There are items for sale too and details of the Wonderland at Pentrillick House and church services over the Christmas period." She turned over the page. "Ah, and this looks like another news page."

She read through the articles and then laughed. "You're never going to believe this, Het, but there have been a number of robberies in the village and the surrounding areas but the same things have been taken from each. You'll never guess what."

Hetty frowned. "Christmas presents from beneath trees," she said, unconvinced.

Lottie shook her head. "No, all the things were taken from gardens."

"Garments from washing lines," said Hetty, with a chuckle.

"Nope, try again."

"Garden furniture."

"No,"

"Christmas wreaths from doors."

"No."

"I give up."

"Gnomes," said Lottie. "So far fifty three have been reported missing since the beginning of October and all were taken after dark."

"Gnomes," said Hetty, her tone one of disgust, "why would anyone take those horrid little things?"

"That's a bit harsh, Het. Some of them are rather sweet."

"Humph, well I hope you don't want any here. I can't abide the nasty little things. They give me the creeps."

"Well, each to his or her own," said Lottie, closing the magazine and standing up to put another log in the stove.

Chapter Four

On Tuesday morning, Lottie went into the garden straight after breakfast to gather greenery to make a wreath for the front door but as she looked up at the holly she saw that the branches bearing plump red berries were well out of her reach. However, in the garden next door a holly bush bore berries on much lower branches. She cut several strands of ivy and a little fir, picked up a handful of small pine cones, just visible in the long grass, and then returned indoors.

"Do you think I'd be out of order if I popped next door to Tuzzy-Muzzy and borrowed a few twigs of holly?" Lottie asked Hetty who was washing up the breakfast dishes.

"Borrow?" said Hetty, with an impish grin, "Would you be intending to return them after Christmas then?"

Lottie tutted. "Don't be pernickety, Het, you know what I mean. It's just that the bush next door has lovely red berries which I could reach whereas ours doesn't."

Hetty placed the last item onto the draining board and tipped the washing up water down the sink. "Yes, I noticed you were struggling; I was watching from the kitchen window."

"So what do you think?"

Hetty dried her hands. "I think if you're going next door then I'm going with you. I'd like to take a closer look at the place anyway and we know there's no-one there nor is there likely to be until the place is sold or whatever next year."

Tuzzy-Muzzy lay well back from the road at the end of a driveway. It was a detached house of considerable size and at one time had been run as a guest house. However, its current owner, an artist, had lived there alone and the house had been empty since she had gone away.

Having gained access to the grounds by way of gates at the foot of the driveway, Hetty and Lottie furtively walked around the perimeter of the gardens, admiring the landscaping, impressive even in the dead of winter.

"Poor house," said Lottie, gazing up towards the upstairs windows, "What it needs is a family to bring it to life. It's far too big for one. Rosie must have been lost in it."

"I agree and if it were mine I'd turn it back into a guest house."

Hetty paused beside a peach coloured rose. "That's something I've never seen before…a rose in December. Not growing in a garden anyway." She leaned forward to see if it had a scent. "Hmm, and it smells divine."

"And some of the fuchsias are still flowering too. And look at that camellia, it's massive."

Hetty looked at the tree to which Lottie was pointing. "Is that what it is? I had wondered. I must admit I'm looking forward to seeing what might come up in our garden next year. From what we know Faith had an interest in gardens so there could well be all sorts of fascinating things."

While Lottie cut several small sprigs of holly, Hetty wandered off and followed a path around a large pond and then back towards the rose garden.

"When you've finished, pass me the secateurs, please," Hetty was smelling the peach coloured rose again.

"Okay, but why?" Lottie handed over the secateurs and then laid the holly down on the path to tie a piece of string around it so that she could carry it without pricking her fingers.

"Because this rose is beautiful and I want to take it home. Besides it looks lonely here with no-one to admire it whereas I shall give it pride of place on one of our windowsills."

"But that's theft, Hetty. Honestly I don't think you should."

"Really?" Hetty cast a withering look at her sister and pointed to the bundle of holly she held by the string.

"Yes, okay. Point taken."

Later in the day, after Lottie had made the Christmas wreath and hung it on the front door, the sisters went again to the charity shop and to their delight found Daisy and Maisie were both there. After greeting each other, Maisie put on the kettle and insisted they join Daisy and herself for a cup of tea.

"We're so glad you came back," said Daisy. "We've talked about you both often, haven't we, Maisie?"

"Yes, and all of it good," Maisie grinned as she took four mugs from beneath the counter.

"The place seemed so quiet after you'd gone," Daisy continued, "Not that you made a lot of noise, it's just, well, you know, you added a bit of excitement to our lives."

"That's really sweet and I have to confess you've both been in our thoughts a lot over the past few months too." Lottie was moved by the words of kindness.

"So what's been happening here," Hetty asked, as she took a seat on a chair by the counter, "since we went home in August, that is?"

"Not a great deal," said Daisy, "nothing noteworthy anyway."

Maisie chuckled. "Except for the gnomes going missing, that is. Rum do that. I mean, who in their right mind would steal one gnome let alone dozens?"

"That's what I think," said Hetty, "Ghastly little things. There must be a madman in your midst."

"So, what's the story behind the thefts?" Lottie asked, feeling sorry for the garden ornaments.

Maisie shrugged her shoulders. "Search me. All we know is that they disappeared after nightfall over several weeks back in October and November."

"Probably turn up at a car boot sale next summer," said Hetty, dispassionately. "Might be worth a bob or two to folks who like geeky things like that."

Daisy nodded. "That's what I think."

"Hmm, yes, I suppose that is a possibility," Maisie agreed, "but it might be risky as I'm sure the police will be on the look-out."

Hetty frowned. "Humph, I very much doubt the police would allocate much time to a trivial crime like that. On the other hand, if there's not much going on, perhaps they might."

Lottie looked puzzled. "If I remember correctly I saw someone selling gnomes at Wonderland when we went there yesterday. He had quite a few garden items including miniature wooden wheelbarrows which rather took my fancy, I must admit."

"Ah, that would have been Jack," said Daisy, "He makes the barrows for use as planters and sells them on-line as well as at Wonderland. His gnomes are all brand new though and not second hand. He's a nice bloke and as straight as a die and the last person likely to go round nicking stuff."

"When we went for a walk the other day we saw a car parked outside Sea View Cottage," said Hetty, having just remembered. "Is someone staying there?"

Maisie handed out mugs of tea. "Yes, four young people who have stalls up at the Wonderland. Apparently they're staying there until the new year."

"In which case we probably saw them then," said Hetty, "as we were up there yesterday. What do they sell?"

"All sorts," said Maisie, as she sat down on a small sturdy table, "The two chaps are called Finn and Woody and they sell these video games that youngsters seem to like. The two girls are Shelley and Ginger and they sell jewellery, candles, perfume and stuff like that. They all seem really nice, especially the girls. I was chatting to them in the pub last week. I hope they do some good trade."

"We'll have a look at their stuff when we go again as we need to do a bit of Christmas shopping," said Lottie.

"I saw someone was selling designer clothes as well," said Hetty, "so I must give that a go. I'm a sucker for nice clothes even if my figure isn't great, nor ever has been."

"We're planning to have our fortunes told too," said Lottie, who thought designer clothes were a dreadful waste of money, "who knows what the future holds for us?"

Daisy laughed. "Well not Psychic Sid, that's for sure. From what I've heard he talks as his belly guides him but then I've never believed in that sort of stuff anyway."

"Me neither," Hetty agreed, "but it should be a bit of fun."

In the evening, the sisters, keen to get out and about and mix with people as much as possible, went to the village hall to play bingo. Neither won any of the games but much to her delight, Hetty won a box of chocolates in the raffle and after she had collected her prize, they decided as it was only half past nine to pop into the Crown and Anchor as they would pass it on their way home anyway. Inside they found a man of medium height, who was a little overweight, sitting at the bar talking to Bernie the Boatman.

"Ah, ladies," said Bernie with a huge grin, "allow me to introduce you to the Wonderland's star attraction."

Hetty frowned. "Well, we know you're not Simeon the Patissier so I'm a little mystified as to who you might be."

Lottie tutted. "Oh, Het, use your imagination. My money goes on this gentleman being Psychic Sid."

The star attraction slapped his thigh. "Spot on, my lovely. I am yours truly Psychic Sid. Please allow me to buy you and your delightful friend a drink."

"That's very kind," said Lottie, feeling pleased with herself for her correct assumption, "we'd both like a glass of red wine, if that's okay."

"Coming up," said Sid, beckoning Alison to assist him.

"Please allow us to introduce ourselves," said Lottie, unbuttoning her coat. "I'm Lottie Burton and this is my twin sister, Hetty Tonkins."

"Twins," said Sid, clearly surprised, "but you don't look anything like each other."

"Not all twins are identical," said Hetty, as Sid handed her a glass of merlot, "although at times when we were younger I wished that we were." She raised her glass. "Cheers and thank you for the drink."

"Hetty and Lottie have only recently moved to the village," said Bernie, "but they know quite a few of us already because they were down here in the summer for a family holiday."

"Very nice," said Sid, "and would that have been with your husbands?"

Lottie opened her mouth to answer but Hetty shushed her. "Don't say a word, Lottie. You'll no doubt be having your fortune told on our next visit to the Wonderland so you mustn't give away any secrets."

Sid chuckled. "Very wise but please do at least tell me how long you've been living here?"

"Less than a week," said Lottie. "We arrived here last Friday."

"Real newcomers then," said Sid, "Can't say that I blame you though. This is a lovely spot even in the winter and I wouldn't mind settling here myself."

"The ladies were here during the summer when police were investigating the murders I told you about the other night," said Bernie, "and even helped out in a funny sort of way."

"Amateur sleuths," said Sid with a chuckle, "that conjures up quite a comical image."

Chapter Five

On Wednesday morning, Hetty and Lottie drove down to Long Rock to shop for groceries and especially frozen goods to fill up the small freezer which Hetty had owned for several years. They also bought the ingredients needed to make a Christmas cake and a Christmas pudding. On the way back they called in at Vince Royale's garage for petrol. They were unable to establish whether or not he was wearing his Christmas jumper because his clothing was hidden beneath a dark green boiler suit. However, when they went into the shop to pay for the petrol, they saw the lady behind the counter was wearing a red Santa hat and flashing Christmas tree earrings.

Hetty was mesmerised. "Sorry, for staring," she said, "but your earrings…where did you get them? They're brilliant."

The lady was clearly pleased and pointed to a box on the end of the counter. "We sell them, my 'ansum. It was our Vince's idea. He's a sucker for Christmas gadgets and has been since he were a child."

"Are you and Vince related?" Lottie asked, "I ask because when you smiled then you looked just like him."

"A lot of people say that and you're right. I'm his mum. I help out in here from time to time as it makes a nice change."

Hetty shuffled through the box of earrings. As well as trees there were snowmen, reindeer and Father Christmases. "I must have a pair. How about you, Lottie?"

Lottie frowned. "They're not really me."

“Well, I shall buy two pairs and then if you change your mind you can borrow mine.” She selected the snowmen and the Christmas trees.

Afterwards they drove through the village and parked along the main street. They then walked down an alleyway beside the fish and chip shop which led onto the beach.

“Weird, don’t you think?” said Hetty, “the beach I mean, being cold and deserted. So different from when we were here in the summer.”

“I like it,” said Lottie, walking down to the water’s edge, “it seems more natural. No, that’s not the right word. It seems more welcoming. You know, like it’s pleased to see us.”

“Hmm, can’t quite follow your drift but I think I sort of know what you mean. It’s difficult to put into words but when we were on holiday it was as though we had to share the sea but now we can lay claim to it just a teeny weeny bit.”

“That’s right, the sea is part of our lives now and I love it.” Lottie picked up a piece of driftwood. “We must come down here beachcombing one day after there’s been a storm. I can imagine now that I’ve seen it in the winter what it will be like and all sorts of things must get washed up on the shore.”

“Yes, but sadly much of it will be junk. Still, it’ll be worth doing if for no other reason than to bin some of the rubbish.”

“Fancy fish and chips?” Lottie asked, looking towards the backs of the buildings which lined the street, “the smell is making me feel hungry.”

“I was just about to ask you the same question and so the answer is yes. We must make a move anyway as there is all that frozen stuff amongst the shopping.”

The sisters bought takeaway fish and chips and then drove home. In the garden of Hillside the two roofers were eating the contents of their lunch boxes.

“Would you two young men like a coffee?” Lottie called over the garden wall.

“Yes, please,” said one. The other agreed.

“Milk and sugar?”

“Yes, please. One sugar in each.”

“Coming up.”

“While Hetty quickly warmed two plates on top of the stove and then put the frozen items away in the freezer, Lottie made coffee for the lads which she took out to them on a tray.

“Put the mugs on the wall when you’re finished,” she said, “and I’ll collect them later. I must say you’re doing a splendid job, but rather you than me. I’ve no head for heights.”

“You’re very quiet, Lottie,” said Hetty, seeing her sister stare blankly into space as they sat by the fire in the evening, “are you alright?”

“What? Oh, yes, I’m fine. I was just thinking about poor Faith. I mean, she was murdered in this room, wasn’t she? Please don’t think me daft but I was just wondering if her spirit is ever in here, you know, watching us.”

Hetty shuddered. “Oh, my goodness, I do hope not.”

Lottie turned to face her sister. “But why not? I mean if she was here she wouldn’t hurt us, would she? In fact I’m sure that if she was she’d be really pleased to see that her cottage is loved again.”

“Yes, I suppose so but all the same it’s not something I like to think about. Anyway, if she was here I’m sure Albert would have noticed. I mean dogs are supposed to be susceptible to spirits and stuff like that, aren’t they?”

“True.” Lottie glanced at Albert who was fast asleep in his basket.

“Anyway,” said Hetty, “Faith’s murder case was successfully resolved and so there is no reason for her spirit to be here. The case is closed and best forgotten.”

“Yes, maybe, but there are times, Het when I wish I was clairvoyant. I mean it must be fascinating to see beyond the grave especially knowing that most people are unable to do so."

Hetty laughed. "Well, perhaps you ought to invite Psychic Sid over to have a poke around. He should be able to tell you whether Faith is here or not."

"You're mocking me," said Lottie, fully aware of the ridicule in her sister's voice. "Anyway, Sid's a psychic not a medium so he wouldn't be much help."

"I think my dear, Lottie, that Psychic Sid is a phony."

"Oh no, Het, I'm sure he's not."

"Want to make a bet on that?"

Lottie paused before she answered. "I'm not sure. I mean, I'm not really one for gambling."

"It's only gambling if it's for money," said Hetty, pretty confident that she was on safe ground with her suggestion of a wager, "so I declare that if any of Sid's predictions come to fruition then I shall make losing one whole stone a New Year's resolution and what's more, I shall stick to it."

Lottie's eyes twinkled. "Really? In that case you're on and I look forward to seeing you of a similar size to myself."

After a day at the Wonderland playing Father Christmas, Bernie was glad to get home, have a shower and wash the white snow paint out of his beard. After his dinner, he bade his wife who was watching television farewell and said he was just popping down to the pub for a couple of pints and to take part in the quiz with his mates.

A thick mist veiled the village as he walked the short distance from his home near the church to the Crown and Anchor and every sound seemed amplified as he walked along the quiet street. As he approached the pub he heard raised voices coming from the car park situated alongside the building, and in the shadows two people were just visible standing beside a dark coloured truck. Both were speaking in

French and so he assumed one to be Simeon Dupont. Curious to know who the other might be, he paused to listen but to his dismay realised it could have been anyone and as his French was poor to non-existent he was unable to understand the nature of the heated conversation. Rebuking himself for being nosy, he went into the pub, bought himself a pint of beer and then agreed to play a game of darts with Vince from the garage before the weekly quiz began.

On Thursday evening many of the villagers made their way to Pentrillick House for the junior school's nativity play and amongst them were Hetty and Lottie.

It was a beautiful evening with a clear, dark moonlit sky unevenly scattered with a mass of twinkling stars. And in the light of the moon, the sheets of clear plastic covering the fake snow on the rooves of the closed chalets, sparkled, giving the illusion that the synthetic snow was authentic. While down in the valley, the quiet lake shimmered in the moonlight tricking the eye into believing that it was covered in a thin layer of ice.

Rows of seating were rapidly filling up and at the end of the avenue of trees, Santa's Grotto had been converted into a stable. There was no sign of any children and Hetty wondered how the teachers were managing to keep them so quiet. The reason soon became apparent for the children were assembled inside Pentrillick House.

At seven o'clock the children processed through the avenue of trees singing 'Little Donkey,' each holding a lantern and dressed as shepherds, wise men and angels. And at the back of the procession, Mary sat on a real donkey, led by Joseph.

Hetty and Lottie were able to recognise a few faces amongst the considerable crowd but most were unfamiliar to them and no doubt they conceded, were parents and relations of the school children. However, when the performance was over they saw coming towards them a young woman waving who they recognised as Emma who worked in Chloe's Café during the summer holidays when she was not at college.

"Hello," she said, "I thought it was you I saw earlier. I heard you'd bought Primrose Cottage but didn't realise you were here yet."

"Tomorrow we'll have been here for a whole week," said Hetty, "and it seems to have flown by."

"And do you like it here in the winter?"

"We love it, don't we, Lottie?"

"Without question. I think it's the best thing I've ever done in my life. After getting married, having the children and becoming a grandmother, that is."

"That's nice to hear," said Emma, ""And how are Zac and his sisters?"

"Very well, last time I saw them," said Lottie. "Hopefully they'll be able to visit us some time in the summer. I know Zac in particular is keen to come and stay. He was over the moon when he heard we intended to move here."

"And we shall be glad to see him," said Emma, "Many a time we've said how we wished he was here to play on the pool team because he really was surprisingly good by the end of your holiday."

Lottie sighed. "Yes, and that seems a very long time ago."

As she spoke the little girl who had played Mary ran up to Emma's side and hugged her.

"This is my little sister, Claire," said Emma, taking the child's hand.

"Really," said Hetty, "I bet you had fun riding on the donkey and I'm pleased to see he didn't try and throw you off."

Claire giggled but didn't speak.

"He's Claire's donkey," said Emma, "so they are quite good friends."

As she spoke a voice called out, "Co-ee, is that you, Emma?"

Emma turned as a figure stepped into the light from the darkness. "Patricia, I heard you were here again and have been meaning to come and see you. How are you?"

"I'm fine, thank you, love."

Hetty and Lottie looked at the woman who had addressed Emma but quickly realised she was not someone with whom they were acquainted.

"How is Patrick? Is he here?" Emma gave a quick glance over the people milling around.

"He's fine but no he's not here. He's already gone to the pub with Steve."

"Steve?" Emma queried.

"He's one of the newcomers at the fair this year and runs a test your strength thing quite close to our set-up. He and Patrick have become great mates and needless to say Nativity plays aren't really their sort of thing." She wagged her finger at Emma. "We could have done with you last night, young lady because the three of us were in the pub for the quiz and we didn't do very well without you youngsters to help us. In fact we were rubbish and I daresay we came last."

Hetty tutted. "Of course, yesterday was Wednesday so it would have been Quiz night. Damn, I wish we'd remembered."

"I would have been there last night," said Emma, "but I had some college work to catch up with. Perhaps we can all get together next week and make up a team because the winners are usually the teams with the most members."

"Hmm, maybe." Patricia scowled and gave the impression that she wasn't keen to associate with Hetty and Lottie.

"So how come you all know each other?" Hetty was determined to find out all she could.

"Patricia and Patrick have an attraction at the fair and were here for Wonderland last year," said Emma, brightly, "Whenever possible I like to go to quiz night with my friends, but on a Wednesday just before Christmas last year, Kyle and I were the only ones in our circle of friends who didn't have a cold and so we joined up with Patricia and her husband who were on the next table to give us all a better chance. We didn't win but if I remember correctly we came a respectable third and just four points behind the winners."

Hetty nodded. "I guessed it must be something like that."

Patricia patted Emma's arm. "Hmm, well I best be off to the pub before Patrick has spent all of today's takings. Nice to see you again, Emma. Do pop along for a chat when you're next up here."

She gave a cursory glance in the direction of Hetty and Lottie but said nothing and walked away, head held high.

Chapter Six

On Friday morning, the sun was shining and there was very little wind. Keen to get outdoors, the sisters made a third journey to the Christmas Wonderland. Back in the summer when they had first visited the estate they had taken a tour of Pentrillick House but because they were preoccupied on that occasion, both agreed there was undoubtedly much they had missed and so in order to have another look around they booked a tour for four o'clock. To while away the half hour they had to spare, they strolled around the fairground amusements.

"Makes me feel quite nostalgic," said Lottie, sniffing in the sugary smell of candy floss. "In fact for old time's sake I'm going to hook a duck."

As Lottie approached the circular enclosure with Pat's Hook a Duck garishly painted three times around the top, she saw that the woman who ran the stall was in fact Patricia with whom Emma had spoken the previous evening. Without letting on she recognised Patricia, Lottie paid her fee and was handed a short rod with a hook on its end.

"Which one shall I go for, Het?"

"I don't expect it'll make much difference as none of the prizes look very exciting. Not for someone of your age anyway." Hetty was more interested in Patricia than she was in which duck Lottie should attempt to hook.

"Killjoy." Lottie watched the yellow plastic ducks bobbing along on the shallow water which ran around a central pillar where prizes were displayed on a peg-board. She had to confess that the ducks all looked the same until one came round with the orange paint partly worn off its beak. Convinced that he was the one to go for Lottie successfully plucked him from the water by the hook on its head with her rod.

Without a smile, Patricia looked at the number on the bottom of the duck. "Twenty two," she said, stifling a yawn, and handed Lottie a gaudy plastic gnome measuring less than six inches.

"Yuck," said Hetty, "still should suit you because apparently you like gnomes."

Lottie didn't reply and hurriedly dropped the gnome into her handbag. When she looked up, a man had appeared and he was clutching a paper bag. She watched as he opened up a small door into the Hook a Duck circle and joined Patricia.

"He still doesn't have any doughnuts, petal, even though I suggested he makes some, so I've bought you a couple of these."

"Still no doughnuts. That's ridiculous." She looked inside the bag. "What are they?"

"Chouquettes."

"What! Oh well, I suppose they'll have to do but I think it's daft having a French bloke here with all his fancy stuff."

"Philistine," muttered Hetty beneath her breath as they walked away.

"Come on, ladies. Test your strength," beckoned a heavily sun tanned man with bare arms and a mop of golden hair tied back with a thick black band.

"Aren't you cold?" Hetty asked, astounded that someone could be outdoors without warm clothing in December.

"No, I don't feel the cold, darlin'. Are you gonna have a go? I think you're probably stronger than you think you are." He winked at Hetty. "In fact, I saw you in the pub the other night so if you can make the bell ring I'll buy both you ladies a drink when I'm next in there."

"Okay, you're on" she said, always up for a challenge, "Hold my bag please, Lottie. She paid her fee and was handed a mallet which she grasped firmly with both hands. To her utter amazement and that of the blond-haired man too, as she crashed the mallet down on the solid base, the bell rang out loud and clear.

"Wow, blimey, I know a lot of blokes who can't do as well as that."

Hetty smiled sweetly. "That'll be two glasses of merlot, please, when you're next in the Crown and Anchor."

"Okay, yeah, it's a deal," said the blond man, "You have my word. Scouts honour and all that."

Lottie tutted. "Come on, Hetty, it's nearly four o' clock and we don't want to be late for the tour."

"No of course not." She nodded to the Test Your Strength man. "And I look forward to seeing you in the pub."

"Me too," said Lottie, as she waved goodbye.

They made their way back to the house where they were to meet their guide in the vestibule. To their delight they were greeted by a huge Christmas tree, perfect in shape, which stood at the foot of the grand staircase, its branches swathed in thick strands of tinsel, traditional decorations and colourful baubles. Beneath it, parcels wrapped in gold and red paper hid the tree's container from view while close by, a large cat slept in a chair with one eye open as though to keep guard.

The guided tour took the same route as before but this time their guide was a woman whose name was Cynthia. As they climbed the grand staircase where the reflection of brass wall lights shone onto the glossy leaves of holly branches tucked over pictures hanging from the wood panelling, Hetty half-wished the Christmas music playing quietly in the background were a little louder so that it might drown out the annoying voice of their guide. For although Hetty was certain that Cynthia was very knowledgeable when it came to spouting historical facts regarding the house and the Liddicott-Treen family, her voice grated and it made the headache she'd woken up with that morning seem considerably worse.

After the tour Lottie said she was keen to have her fortune told by Psychic Sid, but Hetty, who didn't want to let on she had a headache, said she'd prefer to stay outside in the fresh air. Lottie then joined the considerably long queue and Hetty knowing she had plenty of time to spare while waiting for her sister, browsed goods for sale in the wooden huts and bought a few items.

As Hetty wandered down to the lake she saw that the nativity stable had already reverted back to Santa's Grotto and Bernie the Boatman was inside along with a sack of mysterious items wrapped in Christmas paper, eagerly eyed by excited toddlers and young children.

On reaching the lake, Hetty sat down on a bench beside a clump of pampas grass swaying and rustling in the freshening wind. All was peaceful as she leaned her head back and watched swans and ducks gracefully gliding over the rippling water.

When it was Lottie's turn to enter Sid's caravan she was very surprised to find the psychic dressed as an elf. She bit her bottom lip to suppress the desire to laugh, for Sid was quite a large man and his light brown droopy moustache looked a little incongruous on the face of a supposed elf.

"I know, I know," said Sid, with a shake of his head which caused the bell on his hat to tinkle, "you think I look ridiculous. But there's a reason for my get-up. I like to fit in with the surroundings, you see. Soak up the ambience, so to speak and I couldn't be Father Christmas, could I? So I decided to be an elf."

"Oh, I see," said Lottie, "that's very good-spirited of you."

"Anyway, sit down, my lovely, and let's see what the future has in store for you."

Lottie sat down opposite Sid and rested her hands on her lap. "I shall be very interested to hear what you have to say for, since my sister and I moved here we've no idea how things might pan out."

"Well, you soon will," said Sid, with a hearty laugh, "you soon will."

After the fortune telling, Lottie walked down to the lake where she found Hetty still sitting on a bench. Hetty looked round as she heard someone approaching. "Ah, it's you Lottie. So how did it go?"

Lottie sat down beside her sister. "Fine, he's a really nice bloke and very likable." She saw Hetty had a carrier bag beside her, "Have you bought something nice?"

"Yes, a dress," said Hetty, taking it from the bag, "I thought it'd be ideal to wear for Christmas. What do you think?"

"Very pretty, lovely colour but it wouldn't suit me. Perfect for you though. Where did you get it?"

"From that bloke who sells designer clothes," said Hetty, "he's called Nick and is a real chatterbox. You, know, the sort as could sell ice to an Eskimo."

Lottie stretched out her arm and felt the dress fabric, "How much?" she asked.

"Enough," Hetty replied, "It's a Mimi Monfils apparently. I must admit I've actually never heard of that brand but Nick assures me it's very well thought of on the continent."

Lottie tutted disapprovingly.

"Anyway, that's enough about Nick and my dress because I don't know about you but I rather fancy a coffee and one of Simeon's delicious looking mille feuille."

"Oh definitely although I might go for a macaron."

"Hmm tempting, but first please tell me what Sid had to say?" Hetty folded the dress and returned it to its bag.

Lottie's face brightened up. "He didn't say a lot but then I think he was pulling my leg anyway. Well, I know he was. You see, he said there would be another murder in Pentrillick before the festive season was over and that you and I would be involved."

Hetty frowned. "You're joking."

"No, I'm not, he really did say that but I know he was kidding because he was having difficulty keeping a straight face."

"Looks like I'll be spared dieting in the New Year then," said Hetty, with a chuckle. "I must admit that's a relief. So, did he say anything else?"

"Yes, he said that I'd find happiness here in Cornwall and perhaps even after many years of being a spinster, meet a dashingly handsome man who'd sweep me off my feet."

Hetty threw back her head and laughed. "Bernie obviously told him a bit about us then and he's got us muddled up."

Lottie nodded. "Precisely. Silly Sid. Had I not been wearing gloves he would have seen my wedding ring and realised that I was the widow and you the umm…"

"…old maid," Hetty finished.

When they arrived back at Primrose Cottage, Hetty took a couple of aspirins to relieve her headache because she and Lottie planned to go out in the evening. She then hung up her new dress in her wardrobe and hid the blouse she'd secretly bought for Lottie as part of her Christmas present underneath her bed. Meanwhile, Lottie went into the living room, put a hook through the hat of her plastic gnome and hung him on the Christmas tree towards the back where he was less conspicuous.

It was drizzling with rain in the evening as the sisters stepped out from their cottage and so Lottie went back indoors to fetch two umbrellas. By the time they reached the pub the rain was quite heavy and so their lower garments were somewhat wet. For that reason they made a bee-line for a table near to the fire hoping to dry out long before it was time to return home.

Once coats were removed and umbrellas placed in a large pot by the door with several others, Hetty went to the bar. While waiting to be served she saw that she was standing next to one of the girls she'd earlier seen selling cosmetics and jewellery at Wonderland.

"Would I be right in thinking that you and your friends are staying at Sea View Cottage?" Hetty asked.

"Yeah, that's right. It's lovely, I wish we could live there forever."

"I know, we stayed there for a holiday in the summer and loved it too."

The younger woman looked surprised. "Oh, for some reason I thought you lived in Pentrillick."

"We do now," said Hetty, "we being my sister and I. We've only been here for a week though. My name's Hetty, by the way. Hetty Tonkins."

"And I'm Shelley. Shelley Blackmoor."

"Pleased to meet you, Shelley."

"Likewise."

"Who's next?" Landlady Alison asked, as she approached the two women.

"Shelley," said Hetty, waving her hand.

"Thank you. Two gin and tonics, please. One with no ice, both with lemon."

"I take it you're here for the Wonderland," said Hetty, as from the corner of her eye she saw Alison pick up two glasses, "I must admit it's quite an impressive set-up."

"Yes, and we came last year too," said Shelley, "but we stayed in a caravan then on a site further along the coast. It was nice but not a patch on the cottage. It was really windy one night when we were there and Ginger was scared the caravan would blow away."

Hetty frowned. "Why is your friend called Ginger when her hair is blonde?"

"Well, apparently it's because when she was a child she loved ginger biscuits. Her brother named her that." She smiled, "I'm not actually sure what her real name is but it might be Jackie or perhaps it's Jenny. It definitely begins with a J anyway."

"I see," said Hetty, casting a glance around the bar. "And are your boyfriends not here tonight?"

Shelley giggled. "They're not our boyfriends. We met them at a fayre in Devon and discovered they were coming down here for Christmas too, so we invited them along to share the expenses, which is working out really well. I think they've gone into Penzance tonight."

Alison placed two gin and tonics on the bar and Shelley handed her a twenty pound note.

It was Hetty's turn next and as Alison was pouring two glasses of wine, Hetty heard a voice from behind say, "I'll pay for those drinks, love."

Hetty turned round to see the Test Your Strength man from the fair.

"Really, you don't have to," she said, "it was all a bit of a laugh."

"No, I always keep my word." He handed Alison a ten pound note.

Hetty tutted. "In that case, thank you very much."

With drinks in hand, Hetty returned to the table where her sister was waiting. "These are with the compliments of the man at the fair." Hetty sat down.

"Oh no, he shouldn't have. He'll never make a living if he goes around challenging people like that." Lottie tutted.

"I agree and for that reason I shall put in for a pint of whatever he's drinking next time I'm at the bar."

"Good idea. Anyway, I thought you might like to know that I've just been chatting to Simeon," Lottie picked up her glass of wine, "and I told him how simply delicious his pastries are. Apparently he has a shop up-country somewhere in the South East, in fact it might even have been a district in London. Anyway, whatever, he likes to visit fayres and so forth to get himself out and about."

"I can't blame him for that," said Hetty, "it must get a bit tedious working in the same place every day doing the same thing." She took a sip of her wine. "That was one of the many nice things about midwifery…the getting out and about."

"Yes, and Simeon told me that with the shop he has to be up and baking at four in the morning to have everything ready for opening at nine whereas here the Wonderland doesn't open until eleven so he gets a lie-in."

"So, who's doing the baking in his absence?"

"He has a couple of very reliable chaps who are holding the fort for him."

As they spoke a tall, stockily built, bald headed man wearing a Manchester United T-shirt walked by carrying two pints of beer. He winked at Hetty. "Evening ma'am, not wearing your new dress, I see."

"Saving it for Christmas," she replied.

He raised his eyebrows. "Looking forward to seeing you in it."

"Who on earth was that?" Lottie asked, somewhat surprised.

"Nick," she replied, "the chap who sold me the dress."

"Of course, I should have guessed. The T-shirt put me off a bit though. I mean, designer clothes and football don't seem compatible. But then I don't like football. Never have and never shall."

"Lottie Burton, I distinctly remember you following Manchester United avidly and watching all their matches on television. Admittedly it was many moons ago but you were obsessed and even knitted a red and white scarf."

Lottie chuckled. "You're right, so I did. How could I have forgotten? But then it was only because of George Best. He was my hero and it was a very long time ago."

On a nearby table sat Patrick and Patricia who ran Pat's Hook a Duck stall at the fair and both were drinking pints of lager. As Hetty was about to point out their presence to Lottie, a waitress arrived with plates of food for the middle-aged couple.

"That's more like it," said Patricia in a very loud, shrill voice, "Pasty and chips. Better than that fancy stuff old poncey Simon sells."

"Simeon," corrected Patrick, "his name is Simeon."

"Simeon, Simon, it's all the same to me." She turned to the waitress. "Got any ketchup, love?"

"Just coming," said the waitress as another waitress arrived with a tray of cutlery and an assortment of condiments.

"The philistine nearly smiled then," Hetty hissed.

"Shush, Het, she might hear you." Lottie deliberately moved her chair so that she obstructed her sister's view of the fair people. However, it was Bernie the Boatman who, oblivious of Hetty's remark, successfully changed the subject as he passed their table on his way back from the pool table. "Had your fortunes told yet, ladies?" he chuckled.

"I have," said Lottie, "but Hetty is a non-believer."

"Oh, that's a shame." He stood aside to let someone pass by. "So did he say anything interesting?"

Lottie smiled. "He did and he didn't, but from what he said I'm pretty convinced that you or someone else primed him up a little about Hetty and myself."

"Oh, well maybe I did drop him a hint or two," said Bernie, attempting to look innocent and failing miserably.

"Hmm, the reason I say that is because he mentioned a turn in my love-life which was a little inappropriate." She smiled, "He also said that there would be another murder in the village before the festive season was over and that Hetty and I would be involved."

Bernie laughed. "Oh no, what a Charlie."

"That's what I thought, but the best thing is that if his predictions do come to fruition, then Hetty will make going on a diet her New Year's resolution, but I think she's on safe ground as that's hardly likely to happen. In fact I hope it doesn't because we don't want anyone dead, especially this time of the year."

"Yes, I agree with you there." He drained his glass. "Time for another, I think. How about you two ladies. Can I buy you a drink?"

"No, no," said Hetty, "let us get you one. I need to go to the bar anyway as I want to put one in for the strength chappie."

"Strength chappie?" Bernie was puzzled.

"Hetty's referring to the Test Your Strength man from Wonderland."

"Oh, Steve. I didn't know you knew him."

"We didn't until today," said Hetty, taking her purse from her handbag. She glanced around to see if she could spot him. "I can't see him anywhere. Is he still here?"

Bernie nodded. "Yes, he's playing pool with Nick."

"Nick, you mean the chap I bought a dress from?"

"Most likely as that's what he sells." Bernie handed Hetty his empty glass. "The two of them have just come to an agreement about accommodation, you see. Nick's currently staying in bed and breakfast but he's finding it a bit pricey so Steve who lives alone has offered him a bed in his caravan which of course is up at Pentrillick House so will be much more convenient. Nick's moving in tomorrow before Wonderland opens up for the day."

By half past ten, the sisters, feeling weary after having been in the fresh air at Pentrillick House, decided to head for home. When they left the pub, they found the rain had stopped, the pavement was dry and the sky was clear. As they stood by the kerb to cross the road into Long Lane, Simeon emerged from the pub car park on his bicycle. He waved as he passed by and then cycled off through the village whistling *Petit Papa Noel.*

Inside his caravan in the grounds of Pentrillick House, Sid Moore made himself a mug of hot chocolate and drank it in bed. He'd been feeling a bit under the weather since tea time and put it down to the meat pie he'd eaten for lunch which had been in his fridge for a few days longer than it ought. Still, he reckoned a good night's sleep should do the trick and that he'd be as right as rain in the morning. Which was just as well because Saturday would be a busy day at Wonderland and he'd no doubt have a queue of ladies desperate to hear words of wisdom from his lips. Sid chuckled as he contemplated the success of his new found career as a psychic. Until the previous year he'd been a tradesman, a plumber and he'd made a decent living. The trouble was, being a bachelor he'd not looked after himself properly; he ate too many takeaways and drank too much beer thus causing him to put on a considerable amount of weight. The excess weight made bending and contorting, often in unsociable conditions, difficult to say the least and so he'd decided after a particularly arduous job, to turn his life around. He sold his modest house and bought a caravan and then set forth to travel the country as Psychic Sid even though he was fully aware that he had not the slightest ability to see into the future.

When his mug was empty, Sid stood it on the floor beside his bed and snuggled down beneath the duvet. He sighed and felt a little cheated for Friday night in the Crown and Anchor usually had a good atmosphere and he'd had to give it a miss. Still, there was always the next week and he intended to stay in Pentrillick until Wonderland wound up in the New Year.

Chapter Seven

On Saturday morning, Tess Dobson left her husband standing on the upper rung of a ladder hanging icicle shaped Christmas lights from the facia board on the front of their bungalow near to the church. She then drove to Pentrillick House to work in the café. Simeon was usually in the kitchen putting the final touches to his latest batch of fancies when she arrived but to her surprise, he was not in the kitchen or the café. Confused she knocked on the door of the adjacent room where he slept and called his name. There was no answer and so she peeped inside. He was not there and his bed had not been slept in. Hoping that someone might know of his whereabouts, she walked up to the marquee and asked if anyone there had seen him. No-one had. She then walked to the wooden huts and asked the stall holders the same question but again the response was negative. She decided not to bother Psychic Sid for the curtains of his caravan were still drawn, and as a last resort she walked up to the fairground but no-one there had seen him since the previous day. Unsure what to do, Tess returned to the café. He definitely was not there nor had he been for the ovens were stone cold and the kitchen was tidy just as Simeon had left it when they had closed up on Friday evening. Wondering if his bicycle was around she looked behind the building and saw it leaning on the wall where he always left it. Tess was concerned. There were very few pastries left from the previous day and so it would not be possible to open up the café especially as, being a Saturday, trade was likely to be brisk. Feeling she needed to speak to someone she walked up to the house hoping to see Tristan Liddicott-Treen. She was in luck. Tristan was just leaving the house when she arrived.

"Is something wrong, Tess? You look perplexed."

She nodded. "Yes, I am. It's Simeon. He's not in the café, his bed has not been slept in, the ovens are stone cold and no-one has seen him today. Yet his bicycle is where he always leaves it."

"Are you sure?"

"Positive."

"Come on, let's go back down and have another look. He can't be far away."

Tristan's search was as unproductive as Tess's although he did establish from Shelley that Simeon had been in the Crown and Anchor the previous evening, and Nick, who sold designer clothes and had just dropped off a few of his belongings at Steve the Test Your Strength man's caravan, said that he had seen Simeon cycling along the road the previous evening when he was on his way back from the pub to the guest house where he was staying for the last time.

As Tristan and Tess stood outside the café, puzzling what to do, one of the groundsman walked by with finely chopped green vegetables to feed to the swans.

"Morning, Ben," said Tristan, "I don't suppose you've seen Simeon today, have you?"

Ben shook his head. "Sorry, guv, haven't seen him since I were down here this time yesterday."

"Okay, thanks."

"How about making us both a coffee," said Tristan, as Ben continued on his way to the lake.

Tess nodded. "Okay, would you like the real stuff or instant?"

"Instant will do fine, thank you. Not too strong and with milk but no sugar."

While Tess made the coffee, Tristan looked at the trays of pastries to weigh up what little there was left. Just as he was about to comment he heard someone shouting. Tristan went to the door and saw Ben running towards him frantically waving his arms.

"Come quick," said Ben, gasping for breath, "there's something in the lake."

Tristan followed Ben and Tess followed Tristan. When by the side of the lake, they saw something close to the island, floating and seemingly caught up in the overhanging foliage.

"Oh my God," screamed Tess, as her eyes filled with tears, "it's Simeon. I recognise his jacket."

Tristan ran to the boathouse and took out the small punt. He and Ben then rowed over to the island. When they reached the something in the water, Ben turned it over. Tess was right. It was Simeon Dupont and he was dead.

Psychic Sid, feeling much better after a good night's sleep, had just risen and was eating a late breakfast in his caravan when he heard the sirens of police cars. Wondering why the boys in blue were paying a visit, he rose from the table and looked from a window. To his astonishment there were two police cars, followed by an ambulance and all were heading down towards the lake. Sid opened the door of his caravan and went outside in his dressing gown to see if there were any obvious signs of anything wrong. He was staggered when he saw that several people who worked at Wonderland were gathered at the water's edge and more from the fairground were walking in that direction. Eager to know the cause of the gathering, he quickly threw on some clothes, picked up the remains of his bacon sandwich and went to join them.

Once Simeon's body was back on dry land, the police ushered away the spectators and asked that no-one leave the premises. A police board stating 'no entry' was placed at the entrance to Pentrillick House and they requested a notice be placed alongside it stating that the venue was to be closed until further notice. Meanwhile, more police cars had arrived along with scenes of crime officers. Everyone was then questioned to try and establish who might have been the last person to see the patissier alive, and where: a routine procedure even though there appeared to be no suggestion of foul play at that point.

Questioning revealed that all who had amusements in the fairground area also had caravans in which they resided on site but that no-one claimed to have seen Simeon at all the previous evening in the grounds of Pentrillick House. However, it transpired that several from the fairground and some of the stall holders had seen him in the Crown and Anchor on Friday evening and many said that he left the pub long before closing time as was always the case for he had to be up early in the mornings to begin his baking.

Hetty and Lottie were in the Crown and Anchor on Saturday evening when they first heard news of Simeon's death. It was Tommy Thomas who told them.

"I don't know," he jested, "the village has been trouble free these past few months but you've only been back a week and already we've had an unexplained death."

"Unexplained," said Hetty, "I thought you said that poor Simeon had drowned in the lake."

"Well, when I say unexplained it's because no-one knows yet what happened. I mean, why on earth would he fall in the lake? It's not as if he didn't know it was there. They'll know more of course when they get the results of the post mortem but I expect the cause of death will be drowning. Having said that, I suppose the poor bloke might have had a heart attack and fallen in because he was disorientated."

Hetty shook her head. "No, I can't believe he'd have suffered a heart attack because he looked a picture of health.

Poor Simeon, his pastries were out of this world, he'll be a great loss to Wonderland."

Lottie sighed. "Yes, he certainly will."

As Hetty lifted her drink, she glanced towards the window and the street outside. "We saw him leave here last night. He seemed very cheerful and was whistling. It's horrid to think that soon after that he was dead. Poor soul."

Tommy nodded. "I know. I was chatting to him earlier in the evening and he seemed fine. He said he liked the weekends because Wonderland was really busy. He was a hard worker, no-one can take that away from him."

"What will they do about the café when Wonderland is able to open up again?" Lottie asked. "I mean, it was quite an important part of the set-up, wasn't it?"

Tommy shrugged his shoulders. "Yes, and I've no idea what they'll do. I mean, it's a bit short notice to get someone else, especially this time of the year. We'll no doubt find out in due course though because Bernie is on the Wonderland Committee and so he'll be in the know when they get the go ahead to open up again."

"Do we know anything about his family?" Hetty asked. "I mean Simeon's of course, not Bernie's."

Tommy shook his head. "No, he never mentioned family at all, either in this country or France. But I do know he didn't have children because he said so when we were talking about Santa's grotto."

"Well, that's something, I suppose. At least no children have lost their father."

"And I'm glad he wasn't married," said Lottie, twisting around the wedding ring on her finger, "It would be horrid for a wife to have lost a husband that way. Or any other way for that matter and I speak from experience."

Finn and Woody, tired of hearing everyone talking about the death of Simeon Dupont while they were detained at Wonderland for several hours, decided rather than go to the Crown and Anchor in the evening where no doubt they would hear more of the same, to go to Helston instead. For they had been told by the couple of women that ran the children's roundabout at the fair that a pub in Helston called the Blue Anchor brewed its own beer. It was called Spingo and over Easter and during the Christmas period they made extra strong specials.

To help the lads out, Shelley agreed to drive them to Helston so they would only need to have a taxi home. She was happy to do so for Ginger also expressed the desire to try just one pint of the Christmas brew. Shelley knew she could not do the same and so instead would settle for a half of regular Spingo and then when Ginger was ready she would drive the two of them back to Pentrillick.

However, when they arrived at the Blue Anchor they found the death of Simeon Dupont was also the main topic of conversation there and when it was discovered that the four were not only staying in Pentrillick but that they had stalls at Wonderland too and had known the deceased then they were bombarded with questions. Needless to say, Finn and Woody were not amused, but the girls who liked a bit of gossip answered as many questions as they were able and it wasn't until they had been there for well over an hour, that talk of Simeon finally died down. This enabled Shelley and Ginger to make a quiet exit leaving behind the lads, who having consumed two pints each of the Christmas brew and were in the throes of buying their third, happy to stay, especially as they had found like-minded people to talk to.

Chapter Eight

On Sunday morning, Hetty and Lottie both woke up well before it was light and so rather than lie awake squandering time which could be put to good use, they both got up without even knowing the other was doing the same. However, once they were up and had eaten breakfast, neither had the appetite for menial tasks around the home and so instead they decided to go to church. For saddened by the death of Simeon Dupont they both felt in need of hearing something positive and church, they agreed, usually had that effect, especially during Advent in the lead up to Christmas.

To their surprise they discovered that Miss Vickery who also lived in Blackberry Way, played the church organ, and after the service, Daisy in attendance with her husband, introduced them to their near neighbour. However, having learned earlier in the week from Maisie that Miss Vickery was sixty eight years of age, they knew that to call her Katherine or Kitty would be quite unacceptable and so politely called her Miss Vickery.

Miss Vickery stood five feet eleven inches tall and because of her height she always wore flat shoes. For the morning service she was dressed in a green suit with a box pleated skirt. Her thick grey hair curled around the green felt hat that part-covered her hair. Her thin lips were coloured with a dark shade of pink lipstick and a pair of delicate pearl earrings dangled from her pierced earlobes.

After leaving the church, and still feeling subdued, Hetty and Lottie walked home for it was too early to go to the pub for a roast and they knew that Chloe's Café was closed during the winter months. When they arrived back they forced themselves to tidy up the spare bedroom and then had lunch at home rather than go to the pub.

"Since we've nothing else planned for today, I think you ought to have a driving lesson," said Hetty, as she put away the dishes having just washed up."

"Oh, but I don't know whether I'll be able to concentrate with all that's going on." Lottie, hoped her dispirited mood might spare her a spell behind the steering wheel.

Hetty tutted. "Come on now, don't make up excuses. Driving will take your mind off poor Simeon and serve a useful purpose too. You did really well the other day. I think you're a natural and you really want to have your test over and done with before the summer when the roads are much busier with visitors."

Slightly flattered by her sister's words, Lottie grudgingly agreed to the driving lesson providing they went no further than Blackberry Way.

Inside Sea View Cottage, Shelley and Ginger were busy cooking dinner: toad-in-the-hole with roast potatoes, fried onions, stuffed mushrooms, lots of vegetables and thick gravy. Had Wonderland not been closed then they would of course have been working and during breakfast they had agreed that because of the impromptu day off, they must enjoy it and go to the Crown and Anchor for lunch. However, practicality changed their minds; for on thinking a little deeper they realised the future was uncertain because every day that Wonderland was closed meant they were being deprived of much needed income. Hence they thought it wise to watch the pennies for a few days and eat at the cottage instead. Besides, they were pretty confident that neither Finn nor Woody would be too keen on a visit to the pub for it had been in the early hours of Sunday morning that the girls heard a taxi pull up outside the cottage, and from the racket the lads made as they climbed the stairs to their respective rooms, it was unlikely either would be feeling anything other than awful for the entire day.

Inside the grounds of Pentrillick House, police tape cordoned off the lake and the wooden chalets were closed and locked up. No Christmas lights twinkled along the avenue of trees and no-one ho-ho-hoed in Santa's grotto. The sleigh ride stood abandoned beneath a sheet of tarpaulin and the fairground amusements were eerily silent.

Psychic Sid, saddened by the sombre mood of the usually happy atmosphere of Wonderland, decided to drive into the village on Sunday afternoon and have few pints of Doom Bar at the Crown and Anchor where he hoped the jovial tone of the pub would lift his spirit. After putting on his coat because the day felt chilly, he locked up his caravan and walked across the grass, up through the avenue of trees and over to the car park where his estate car stood alone in its row. As he pulled the car keys from his pocket, he saw the forlorn figure of a young lad who he estimated to be in his early teens, sitting on a grass bank.

"Are you lost, son?" he asked. "You know that Wonderland is closed for a few days now."

The lad nodded. "Yes, I know. My father told me of Monsieur Dupont's demise. Very sad, not that I knew the gentleman."

Sid unlocked his car, dropped the keys onto the driver's seat and turned back towards the lad. "May I ask who your father is?" Sid felt the lad ought not to be on the premises and didn't want him to get into trouble.

"Of course. My father is Tristan Liddicott-Treen and I am his son Jeremy. My sister, Jemima and I arrived home from school last night."

Sid's shoulders slumped. "Oh dear, not much of a welcome home then, Master Jeremy."

Jeremy smiled. "No need for the master," he said. "Jeremy will do just fine."

"Jeremy it is then and may I ask how old you are?"

"You may indeed. I am thirteen years old and my sister, Jemima is fifteen."

Sid sighed. "Oh, to be so young."

Jeremy considered himself to be quite grown up but thought better of contradicting his elders. "And may I ask who you are, sir?"

Sid chuckled. "You may indeed. I'm Sidney Moore, better known as Psychic Sid. You've probably seen my caravan down by the maze."

Jeremy's face lit up. "Yes, I have and I must say that my sister was very impressed to discover that you're here this year. She'll no doubt pay you a visit before the holidays are over. She and her friends are always reading their horoscopes on the internet and in magazines and I've noticed how they manipulate the words to mean whatever suits them best."

"Oh, that'll be nice," gulped Sid, hoping it would be very near to the end of the holiday and preferably just before he was due to leave Cornwall, that Jemima called upon his services. "I shall look forward to seeing the young lady."

"Did you know Monsieur Dupont?" Jeremy suddenly asked.

"Yes, but not very well." Sid chuckled, "He never came to have his fortune told but I did sample a few of his wares as my figure probably tells you."

Jeremy smiled. "And who can blame you."

"So, is there any reason why you're sitting out here in the car park when you've acres of beautiful gardens you could be in?"

"Every good reason. I love cars and all modes of transportation. I'm a bit of a nerd, you see. Of course, there's not much here today but hopefully the Wonderland will be open again soon and the car park will be packed full of interesting vehicles."

As he spoke a girl with similar looks to the lad came running around the corner. "There you are, Jeremy," she said. "Mother sent me to look for you. Come on, we're going out on the horses."

Jeremy stood. "Okay, Jemima, I'm coming." He turned to Sid and shook his hand. "Goodbye, Mr Moore, it's been really nice talking to you and hopefully I'll see you again soon."

The grounds of Pentrillick House fell silent earlier on Sunday evening than it had for the first few days of the week. For the Crown and Anchor rang last orders just before ten thirty ensuring that most of the fairground people were back on site and tucked up in their caravan beds before midnight. All were hopeful of a good night's sleep and optimistic that the following morning they would hear that Wonderland was to be reopened very soon.

Inside Pentrillick House, the Liddicott-Treen family also slept, oblivious of the freshening wind whistling around the house and sending ripples across the dark waters of the lake. As the time ticked by the wind strengthened further and then suddenly in the early hours of the morning, Jeremy Liddicott-Treen was woken by a crashing noise deep inside the house. Curious as to what it might have been, he courageously slipped from his bed, put on his dressing gown and tip-toed into the long, dark passageway. At the top of the main staircase, dimly lit by wall lights on the old wood panelling, he sat and waited to see if the noise occurred again. Another crash and the sound of breaking glass caused him to jump, but not one to be frightened by the unknown, he crept down the stairs into the vestibule and from there proceeded towards the part of the house from which the noise had seemed to emanate. Inside the old kitchen which had not been used for many years he found a window wide open and shattered glass from a broken pane lying on the old tiled floor.

He tutted. How many times had he heard his mother remind his father that the faulty catch needed to be repaired? He leaned across and pulled the window to but left the glass for others to clear up in the morning and made a mental note that he must inform his father that Jenkins, the maintenance man, needed to repair the window promptly.

Rather than go back to his room by way of the main staircase he took a shortcut up the narrow back stairs which led to the now disused servants' quarters and because he had not been in there for some time he peeped into the old nursery simply because its contents always made him smile. Without switching on the light he went into the room, stroked the mane on the old rocking horse and crossed to the window which looked out to the south. In the distance the sea could be glimpsed above the trees in the valley and beneath large clouds that moved swiftly across the dark sky. Jeremy took in a deep breath…it was good to be home. A sudden flash of light amongst the trees on the far side of the lake caused him to squint. Knowing that there was no lighting in that area, he opened the window hopeful that his visibility would be improved. The light appeared to be moving through the trees near to the children's adventure area. Suddenly it briefly stopped and then began to move again but now in a changed direction. Jeremy frowned for if the light were a torch then someone was retracing their steps.

He continued to watch until he saw a figure emerge from the woods and onto the path which ran round the lake. It moved with haste but as it approached the old boathouse, the light went out and he saw nothing more.

Chapter Nine

On Monday afternoon, villagers learned that the results of Simeon Dupont's post mortem specified the cause of death, as expected, was drowning. It also stated there were excessive amounts of alcohol in his blood and it was unlikely that he knew much about his demise.

Hetty and Lottie learned of this from Bernie when they went to the post office for stamps to send off their Christmas cards to friends and family up-country.

"Are you sure?" Hetty asked. "About the excessive alcohol, I mean? Because Lottie and I left the Crown and Anchor at the same time as Simeon on Friday night and he seemed fine and not at all drunk. Isn't that so, Lottie?"

"Absolutely," Lottie agreed, "We watched him peddle off down the road without so much as a wobble and he was whistling too."

"Really," said Bernie, "I must admit I found the bit about alcohol rather surprising too. It's said he'd been drinking red wine and vodka, but I thought he only ever drank wine. At least that's what he drank when he was in the pub."

"Red wine and vodka. That sounds a pretty lethal combination. He must have been as drunk as a lord." Hetty looked puzzled. "Why would he mix drinks like that when he has to work the next day?"

Bernie nodded. "Exactly and it rather negates his reason for leaving the pub before closing time if he's going to carry on drinking back at the cafe."

"Hmm, definitely odd and I suppose with Wonderland being a crime scene it will be closed for a few days now so we won't be able to do any poking around." Lottie was clearly disappointed.

Bernie grinned. "And what, may I ask, do you think you might find if you were able to have a poke around?"

Lottie shrugged her shoulders. "I don't know, but I'd start by looking in the café to see if there are any empty wine and vodka bottles. Although on reflection I suppose the police will already have done that."

"I daresay they have," Bernie agreed, "what's more, when I saw Tess on my way here, I asked her if she'd ever seen any wine and vodka bottles at the café and she said definitely not. In fact Simeon had no alcohol at the café at all. He liked to go to the pub, you see. He was a sociable chap and wasn't one for drinking alone."

Hetty frowned. "Strange for a Frenchman. I thought they always drank wine with every meal."

"You can't categorise people like that, Het," chided Lottie, "It's a bit like assuming they all ride bikes, wear striped tops and berets and have strings of onions round their necks."

"But he did ride a bike," Hetty reasoned.

"I've just remembered, there's another thing you might be interested to hear," said Bernie, moving aside as another customer entered the post office, "The other day I heard a couple of blokes having a few cross words in the pub car park. I couldn't make out what they were saying because they were both talking in French, more's the shame. It was dark and misty too so I couldn't see them properly even though there's a lamp in the car park. I told the police about it, not that it'll be much help, but they thanked me all the same."

"So do you reckon one of them was Simeon?" Hetty asked, her imagination going into overdrive. "That's really interesting."

Bernie nodded. "Well yes, most likely. I mean, he's the only French bloke I know around here or should I say knew, poor chap."

"But what about the other person," Lottie asked, "I mean, haven't you any idea at all who that might have been? Take the fair people for instance. Are any of them French?"

"Not that I know of, but then I've not had much to do with them having no little 'uns to take up there. Oh dear, I wish I'd paid more attention now, but once I got in the pub I thought no more of it. I mean, two blokes having a tiff is hardly cause for concern, is it? And as far as I know it didn't result in fisticuffs because I saw Simeon the next day when I went for my usual croissant for my tea break and he certainly didn't look as though he'd been in a punch-up, in fact he was in a very good mood, if I remember correctly."

Hetty's face turned pale. "I've just had a thought. Do you think we ought to tell the police about what Psychic Sid said when you had your fortune told, Lottie?"

"No, don't be daft, it was said in jest and he was pulling my leg."

"But he wasn't in the pub on Friday night," persisted Hetty, "at least, if he was I didn't see him."

Bernie looked shocked. "You're not suggesting Simeon was murdered are you?"

Hetty shook her head. "No, no I'm not, but all the same I think it's only right that the police are given as much information as possible and Sid did say that there would be a murder in Pentrillick before the festive season was over."

Lottie sighed. "Yes, he did and as much as it goes against the grain, I agree we ought to report it if needs be. But we'll keep quiet for now and say nothing unless we hear that it was murder and that the police are seeking information. I mean, the chances are that it was just an unfortunate accident and I hope for all concerned that it was."

Early on Monday afternoon, Jeremy Liddicott-Treen left Pentrillick House and walked down towards the lake, happy in the knowledge that Jenkins had already replaced the broken glass in the old kitchen window and was currently looking in his workshop for a new catch. When he reached the police cordon he slipped beneath it after first making sure there were no officers in the grounds even though he knew that was unlikely for there were no police cars on the estate. An explanation to Jeremy's furtive behaviour was simple: he was eager to see if he could establish any obvious reason as to why someone would have been lurking around in the woods in the early hours of the morning.

Just past the café he stepped onto the path which ran around the lake and when he reached the boathouse he slowed down his pace in order to make sure that he missed nothing. With the area around the café being out of bounds he met no-one other than a family of ducks waddling along the path, water dripping from their feet and feathers having just stepped from the lake.

Inside the wooded area all was quiet bar the cawing of rooks from the tops of tall sycamore trees and the wind eerily whistling through the leafless branches. The adventure play area, usually noisy with laughter and excited chatter, lay silent as Jeremy, enjoying his adventure, slowly crept across the damp bark scattered around the children's activity apparatus. Continually looking from left to right he approached a group of old conifer trees and stood beneath the swaying branches, hoping to see anything that might justify his walk; for he knew he should not really have crossed the police cordon and for that reason had told neither of his parents nor his sister of that which he had witnessed during the night nor of his plans to explore the woods when he thought it safe so to do.

Convinced that he had walked as far as the torchlight had gone he turned around to retrace his steps and as he passed by a spindly sycamore sapling, he saw lying part-hidden amongst decaying leaves, a glove. He picked it up. It was black, quite large and made of leather. He turned it over in his hand and concluded it would have belonged to a man. But who had dropped it and when? Surely if it had been there when the police had scoured the area following the death of Simeon Dupont then they would have found it and taken it away. Which meant it was probably dropped by the person he had seen during the night and if so it was possible that person would return to the woodland to retrieve it because he too should not have crossed the police cordon. Eager to get back to the house, he tucked the glove inside a pocket of his jacket and hurried around the lakeside path; watching as he went to make sure that he was seen by no-one.

Patricia, who with her husband, Patrick ran Pat's Hook a Duck stall, decided to take her dog Tyronne out for a walk on Monday afternoon. Normally Tyronne would have been left in the caravan for much of the day and walked in the evening but with Wonderland closed Patricia had time on her hands and she was alone with the dog anyway because Patrick had gone to the Crown and Anchor with his new best mate, Steve.

She left the caravan after her lunch with Tyronne on his lead, and since time was plentiful opted to take a different route from the one she usually took. After weighing up the surrounding landscape she chose a rough path sheltered by a few leafless trees which ran near to the boundary wall of the estate alongside the lane leading to the main entrance.

After walking for less than ten minutes, she stopped and sat down on the trunk of a fallen tree and released Tyronne from his lead so that he could run off to sniff around in the undergrowth. From her pocket she took a packet of cigarettes and smoked one, glad that Patrick was not around to reprimand her. When the cigarette was gone she threw the stub onto dried fallen leaves and stamped on it to make sure that it was out. It was as she looked up and glanced towards the lake that she saw a figure emerge from beyond the police cordon. Knowing that area was out of bounds she stepped back amongst the trees and called Tyronne to her side. She then watched as the figure left the lake and walked up towards the avenue of trees. She was surprised and a little suspicious when she realised that the person in question was the Liddicott-Treens' boy. "What's he been up to?" Patricia asked Tyronne. "I dunno, these posh folks think they're above the law."

As Jeremy stepped over the police cordon, he saw from the corner of his eye, someone dart back amongst the trees. His heart began to race. Was the person hiding behind the trees the person who had lost the glove? Without bothering to investigate further he ran through the avenue of trees and into the house.

Early on Tuesday afternoon, Anna a receptionist at the Pentrillick Hotel was just finishing a cup of tea when a woman in her late twenties, dressed in flamboyant clothes, wheeled her pink suitcase into the reception area. After looking around and nodding with approval, the new arrival approached the desk.

"Hello," said Anna, with a welcoming smile, "how may I help you?"

"Hmm, do you have a room available, please? Single, double or whatever, I'm not fussy," said the stranger trying hard to disguise her broad Cockney accent.

"Would that be just for yourself?" Anna politely asked.

"Yep, I am quite alone."

Anna looked at the computer screen. "In which case, yes, we do have a single room available. It's on the front of the hotel on the second floor and has sea views."

"Yeah, sounds great."

"For how long would you be wanting to stay?"

"Oh, umm, I dunno. Three, four days, a week maybe. All depends."

Anna told the lady of the rates which were agreed as acceptable; she then asked the guest for her name.

"Misty," she said, "Misty Merryweather."

Anna looked up from the screen. "That's a pretty name. Unusual too."

Misty smiled. "Thank you. It's my professional name and the one I always use."

Misty was delighted with her room and once she had unpacked her case and put her clothes in the wardrobe and her toiletries in the en suite bathroom, she then sat for a long time by the open window, thoughtfully drinking coffee and looking at the sea over the roof tops of the cottages opposite. For Misty had only ever been to the seaside once before in her twenty nine years and that was for a day trip to Brighton in her junior school days; hence she was mesmerised by the calmness of the sea and the gentle lull of the tumbling waves.

"When I'm rich," she whispered, "well, if I'm ever rich, I think I'll buy a little house by the sea. Nothing grand, just somewhere to come and stay when I get tired of city life." She leaned her head back on the wall and looked to the skies, "ain't never gonna happen though, is it, my love. Especially now you're gone."

In the evening Misty wandered down to the Crown and Anchor. When she arrived she paused in the doorway and looked around wishing that she knew someone in Pentrillick who might offer her a hand of friendship. She was much surprised, therefore, when as the door closed behind her, she heard a familiar voice call her name from the far end of the bar.

"What the? I don't believe it. Misty Merryweather, what the hell are you doing here?"

Misty looked across the bar to where Finn sat with Woody, Shelley and Ginger. Her heart skipped a beat.

"Do you two know each other?" Ginger asked, as Finn rose to his feet and Misty walked towards the small group, her face a picture of disbelief.

"Not 'arf," said Misty, overcome with emotion on seeing a familiar face. "Blimey, Finn, it must be well over a year since I last clapped eyes on you. How are you doing, darlin'?"

"I'm all the better for seeing you." He gave her a quick hug and a peck on the cheek. "So what brings you down here in the depths of winter?"

"I could ask you the same," said Misty. Her eyes brimmed with tears.

"Are you alright, sweetheart?"

"Yes, yes, well perhaps not, it's just that well," she gulped, "I'm here to see where my dear husband lost his life." Misty took a tissue from the pocket of her faux fur jacket and dabbed her eyes. "Poor Simeon, I can't believe he's dead."

Finn sat down, his mouth gaped open wide. "What, are you talking about Simeon Dupont the pastry cook? I mean, surely he wasn't your old man."

Misty nodded. "Yes, he was."

"Good heavens. Well I never. So is he the bloke you left me for? I mean, I knew you'd gone after a French geezer called Simeon but never dreamt it was Dupont and I certainly didn't know you'd married although I've often thought of you and wondered what you're up to."

"That's sweet, Finn. I've thought of you too. I mean, we did get on well, didn't we?"

"Yeah, we did." Finn looked downcast.

"Come and sit down," said Shelley, shuffling along the seat to make room, "you're awfully pale and don't look too steady on your pins."

Misty sat. "Thank you, yeah, I do feel a bit shaky."

"Hey, what am I doing, where are my manners? Allow me to get you a drink, sweetheart," said Finn, rising, "What'll you have, love? Still a fan of whisky and dry?"

"Not really. Since I met Simeon I've become more of a wine drinker but right now I think I'd like a neat brandy, please."

"Coming up," said Finn as he headed towards the bar.

Lottie and Hetty missed out on the latest developments in the case of Simeon Dupont because they went to play bingo in the village hall on Tuesday night. To their surprise on this occasion, Miss Vickery was also there as were their next door neighbours, Alex and Ginny from Hillside.

"We meet at last," said Alex, shaking the hands of the sisters in turn just after they had arrived, "I've seen you on several occasions from our windows but we've never got round to making your acquaintance."

"And for that we apologise," said Ginny, likewise shaking hands. "We should have called when you first arrived. It was very remiss of us."

"I'm sure you've plenty to take up your time without having to make social calls," said Lottie, "I mean, what with running your antique business and having a new roof, there can't be enough hours in the day."

"Alex does driving lessons too," said Ginny, "but not full time because he thinks that might be too stressful."

"Well that's not entirely true," Alex clearly didn't want to give the illusion that he was unable to handle stress. "Much of it is about finding the time. I like being in the shop, you see, because I'm interested in history and antiques. I go to a lot of auctions as well because we have to maintain a good stock."

Lottie's jaw dropped. "Well, fancy that. The driving lessons bit, I mean. I'm learning to drive, you see and Hetty is teaching me but we've agreed I must have proper lessons too. So if you can fit me in I'd really appreciate it."

"No problem. Just say the word," said Alex, "I've two pupils taking their tests this month and I'm sure they'll both pass. Well, at least one will. So I'd be happy to take you out in the New Year."

"Ideal," said Lottie, "thank you."

"Have you been driving long?" Ginny asked.

"No, I only started a week ago just after we moved in and so far I've only driven back and forth along Blackberry Way to get used to the gadgets."

"But next time we're going to try reversing in and out of our driveway," said Hetty, "and then we might go a bit further afield."

Lottie felt her face flush with embarrassment. "But we'll make sure I do the driveway bit when you're down at your shop. I don't want you to have to witness my efforts from your windows and have it put you off teaching me."

After bingo during which neither sister won anything, they spoke to Miss Vickery and in order to get to know her better, they invited her to join them for coffee on Thursday morning.

"That's very sweet of you," said Miss Vickery. "I shall be delighted to call and I'm sure we'll have much to talk about."

Chapter Ten

On Wednesday morning, much to the delight of the stall holders and fairground people, the police agreed that Wonderland could reopen but that the lake and café must remain cordoned off until further notice. Hetty learned of this from Tommy who she met in Long Lane while out walking Albert. Excited by the news she cut short Albert's walk and returned to Primrose Cottage where Lottie was making curtains for the landing window.

"You're back early," called Lottie, from the sitting room as she removed pins from the floral fabric, "surely you've not been as far as you said you would in that time."

In the hallway, Hetty unhooked Albert's lead and hung it by the door. "No, we cut it short because we saw Tommy who said that Wonderland is to reopen today." She threw her coat on its peg and entered the room. "Have you nearly finished the curtains?"

"I've done one but not started the other." She laid down the curtain. "I assume by the look on your face that you're eager to make another visit to Pentrillick House."

"Absolutely. I want to get as near to the scene of the crime as possible to see if we can shed any light on Simeon's death and I'm sure you do too."

"Yes, I must admit I am intrigued." Lottie stood up and switched off the sewing machine plug in the wall socket. "I can finish the curtains later. But it's nearly half past twelve now so we ought to have lunch before we go as we'll not be able to eat anything at Wonderland other than candy floss and toffee apples."

"True, but let's make do with a sandwich because to cook anything would be a waste of precious time."

They arrived at Pentrillick House just after two and found they were not alone in their fascination with the death of Simeon Dupont for the Wonderland was already bustling with people and the organisers predicted it might well be the busiest day of the festive period so far. Several shoppers browsed the chalets, Father Christmas was surrounded by a group of small children, there was a long queue to hear words of wisdom from Psychic Sid and the sleigh which had concealed wheels inside the runners was slowly crossing the extensive lawns with the help of four reindeer.

After wandering around and accepting the fact they were unable to get anywhere near to the lake, Hetty and Lottie likewise browsed the stalls where they were surprised to see that Nick the designer clothes seller was wearing a Leeds United football T-shirt.

"Can't make his mind up who to support," said Hetty, waving to Nick after he had waved to her.

"Or trying to keep all of his customers happy," giggled Lottie.

"Yes, maybe, but I think with his bulky build he'd be more suited to wearing an England rugby polo shirt than a football shirt."

"Why England? I mean, he might be Welsh, Scottish or even Irish."

Hetty shook her head. "No, I don't think so. If you listen carefully you can hear the hint of a Brummie accent."

"I wish we could go down to the lake," said Lottie, as she glanced across the grounds, "perhaps we ought to take another tour of the house then we'd be able to see it from the upstairs windows."

Hetty turned up her nose. "No, I don't really think I could stomach listening to Cynthia prattling on again. She wasn't a patch on Christopher who did the tours back in the summer and her voice really grated on my nerves."

"Okay, so how about going on the helter skelter instead, there's bound to be a good view up there."

"Don't you think we're a bit too old?"

"No, come on, it'll be fun."

On arriving at the helter skelter they found quite a long queue as many no doubt had the same idea as the sisters. However, having all the time in the world they patiently waited their turn and then excitedly, with mats in hands, climbed up the spiral staircase.

"Wow," said Hetty when they reached the top, "look at that view although I can't see much of the lake."

"Move along please," said the attendant whose job it was to make sure riders were properly seated on their mats.

Hetty groaned, dropped her mat down, sat on top of it and pushed herself off.

The ride down the slide was quite exhilarating and Hetty found herself laughing when she reached the bottom.

"Come on, Grandma, up you get," said a young man who offered his hands to help her onto her feet.

"Cheeky," she chuckled and stepped out of the way just in time to prevent herself being hit by Lottie who came whizzing around the corner also laughing.

After the helter skelter they decided to do something a little more seemly and so opted to take the maze challenge. To enter, each person paid two pounds and their time of entry was recorded. The task was to find a basket of coloured balls hanging from the arm of a statue in the middle of the maze. To prove they had reached the centre each entrant must obtain a ball and then find their way to the exit. Anyone who completed the task in less than thirty minutes received a mystery prize which they would select from a bran tub where items worth ten pounds or more were wrapped in Christmas paper. Only twenty people were allowed in the maze at the same time and according to a 'winner's board' near to where the entry fees were paid, only seven people had mastered the challenge since Wonderland had opened at the end of November.

After coming up against one dead end after another, Hetty suggested, in hushed tones, that they follow a couple who had just emerged from somewhere as they sounded very confident. To their delight, the plan worked and they all found themselves by the statue holding the basket of balls. The young couple each quickly grabbed a ball and then with haste walked away from the statue. Hetty and Lottie also took a ball each but to their dismay neither saw in which direction the young couple had gone. Nevertheless, with ten minutes to spare before their thirty minutes ran out, they were confident they would be able to find their own route to the exit.

Five minutes later, they felt they were no nearer the way out than when they had left the statue, but still they persevered. However, luck was not on their side for as they quickly turned realising they were approaching yet another dead-end, Lottie's ball slipped from her hands and rolled away beneath the hedge.

"Oh, for heaven's sake, Lottie," hissed Hetty in exasperation, "we only have three minutes left. Pick it up quick."

Lottie bent down to pick up the ball but in haste lost her balance and fell down onto her bottom. Trying to suppress the desire to giggle and keen not to anger her sister further she quickly scrambled to her knees and reached out for the ball, but in doing so something inside the lower part of the hedge caught her eye. Intrigued to see what the something was she parted the foliage and gasped. "No way. Look, Het. Look what's in here."

Hetty impatiently crossed to her sister. "Whatever it is it doesn't matter. Come on, Lottie we've only one minute left."

"I don't think you'll care when you see what I've found," Lottie looked smug.

Hetty frowned and knelt down beside her sister. Inside the hedge were two empty bottles. One vodka and the other French red wine.

The maze was promptly cordoned off by the police when they arrived at Pentrillick House and the couple whose job it was to take money for the challenge were questioned, as were the gardeners who were responsible for the maze's upkeep. Lottie and Hetty, likewise were questioned and the police were very interested to hear the results of Psychic Sid's fortune telling which Hetty felt duty-bound to mention even though by doing so she clearly annoyed Lottie who thought it purely coincidental. For the officers having questioned Sidney Moore on the Saturday afternoon following the discovery of Simeon Dupont's body, knew that he was on the premises of Pentrillick House during the night on which the Frenchman had died. At the time he claimed to have heard nothing untoward as he had slept soundly throughout the night having felt unwell earlier in the evening. However, the fact that empty vodka and wine bottles had now been found in the maze which was very near to his caravan, gave them every reason to question him again.

Psychic Sid told fortunes from eleven in the morning until five in the afternoon. He found it was not possible to do more hours than that for it was a strain on his voice and his imagination. As the last person left on Wednesday afternoon he changed from his elf outfit into his normal clothes, and removed the rosy cheeks painted on his face while looking forward to a mug of tea. However, having heard a police siren in the grounds of Pentrillick House earlier in the afternoon and the loud chatter of excited voices close to his caravan while he was telling a bumptious blonde she would meet a wealthy billionaire on her next holiday, he knew that something must have happened to have brought the boys in blue back to the

Wonderland again. He assumed that meant there had been further developments in the case of Simeon Dupont. Therefore, before he put on the kettle to make a cup of tea, he glanced from the window above the sink to see if there was any obvious activity. To his surprise he saw that two officers were walking towards his caravan.

Sid opened the door before the police had a chance to knock.

"Good afternoon, gentlemen, and what can I do for you?"

"Mr Moore, we'd like to ask you a few questions regarding a recent fortune telling you did for a lady to whom you predicted a murder in Pentrillick before the festive season was over."

Sid groaned as his shoulders slumped.

Jeremy Liddicott-Treen anxiously watched the activity outside the maze from the drawing room window of Pentrillick House. Two police cars had been there for some time and he could see that the area was cordoned off. Several people had gathered to watch and a white van used by scenes of crime officers was parked alongside the police cars. Jeremy frowned as two of the police officers left the maze and walked towards the caravan belonging to Mr Moore the fortune teller. Why were they calling on Mr Moore? What had he done or what had he seen? Perhaps he was the owner of the lost glove and it was he that Jeremy had seen flashing the torch in the woodland in the early hours of Monday morning. Or worse still, perhaps Mr Moore was the person Jeremy had seen hiding beneath the trees when he had retrieved the glove and now he, Mr Moore, was about to report seeing Jeremy down by the lake on Monday afternoon.

"Don't panic," he said to himself, "you have done nothing wrong."

"But I have, I have. I crossed a police cordon and removed possible evidence and I really should have known better." He sat down. If only he had told his parents what he had seen then his conscience would now be clear. On the other hand, maybe he should do a little detective work of his own. After all he was not unfamiliar with police procedures because detective novels were his favourite genre of books and he read a lot of books.

Jeremy left the drawing room and ran upstairs. From the bottom of a drawer in his bedroom he pulled out the glove and tucked it beneath the waistband of his jeans; he then left the house. After making sure that the police cars were still outside the maze, he walked across the grounds, still busy with people, and over towards the car park. After checking that no-one was around, he hooked the glove on top of railings. For he concluded that if it was still there in a few days' time then he would know that it had probably been lost for some time and its owner was not looking out for it, meaning the fact that he had found it was of no consequence. On the other hand, if the glove disappeared quickly then the chances were that whoever had lost it would be glad to have it back and relieved that he'd not dropped it when on the wrong side of the police cordon in the middle of the night. And if that were the case then he, Jeremy Liddicott-Treen, would keep a watchful eye out for said person wearing the gloves which might then help him to fathom out why the mystery man had been in the woods in the first place. With a spring in his step, Jeremy happily returned to the house glad that the glove was no longer in his possession.

Chapter Eleven

On Thursday morning, the police were busy taking finger prints from all adults who lived in Pentrillick and visitors likewise but according to the village grapevine, none thus far had matched the prints on either wine or vodka bottles. It was, however, confirmed that because Simeon Dupont's prints were on the wine bottle the police considered them to be an important piece of evidence. However, it was thought unlikely that they would ever be able to establish to whom any other prints on either bottle belonged for it was obvious that both would have been handled by several people before and after their purchase and for that reason it was impossible to take prints from all retailers and wholesalers. However, it was, they believed, evidence to suggest that Monsieur Dupont might not have been drinking alone on the night that he died and, because the weather that evening had been cold there was every good reason to assume that the person with whom Simeon drank the red wine vodka combination had worn gloves. This meant there was justification to suspect foul play regarding the patissier's death as it was possible his wine had been spiked with vodka in order to get him inebriated. Consequently, the case was upgraded from unexplained to suspicious. This piece of information, leaked by someone who had heard the police talking, fired up the imaginations of many in the village, and especially so after villagers learned that licensees, Ashley and Alison Rowe had been questioned as to who amongst their clientèle were regular vodka drinkers. This latest piece of gossip was being discussed by several people in the post office and Miss Vickery, who was amongst them, passed on the news when she arrived at Primrose Cottage for coffee.

"Goodness me, I should imagine sales of vodka will drop dramatically in the pub then," said Hetty, as she placed a tray laden with a plate of chocolate biscuits and three steaming mugs of coffee on an occasional table. "After all most people will be keen to say they never touch the stuff and who can blame them."

Miss Vickery nodded as Hetty handed her a mug of coffee. "That is precisely what was said to Gail in the post office. Silly, I know but I've been racking my brains all morning trying to think of anyone I know who drinks vodka but I've drawn a blank. Not that I go in the pub very often. I'm not much of a drinker, you see, and often just drink tonic water."

"Very wise," said Hetty, as she lifted the plate of biscuits, "far too many calories in alcohol."

"And in chocolate biscuits too," said Miss Vickery, taking one from the plate offered by Hetty, "but they are my favourites."

"That's good to hear," said Lottie, "because we were going to make mince pies this morning but then found we had forgotten to buy mincemeat. Needless to say, had we gone out and bought some we would not have had enough time to make them before you arrived."

Miss Vickery laughed. "Probably just as well because to be honest I find pastry gives me indigestion so I try to avoid it."

"Oh dear, that is a shame," said Hetty, as she sat down on a chair by the window, "So I assume you weren't able to sample any of Simeon's delicacies."

"Oh but I did. I had macarons on two occasions. They were heavenly and melted in the mouth."

"Of course, silly me. I'd forgotten that not all of his wares are pastry based or should I say, were."

"Is that a gnome hanging on the tree?" Miss Vickery asked, as she squinted to adjust her vision.

Lottie nodded. "Yes, I won him at the fair."

"How long has he been there?" Hetty's mouth gaped open, "I hadn't seen him until Miss Vickery pointed him out."

"Since the day I won him. I wondered how long it would take you to notice and that's why I put him towards the back." Lottie looked smug.

"Humph, well I suppose since he's part hidden he can stay there. Horrid little thing."

"Oh dear, I take it you don't like gnomes," said Miss Vickery.

"No I don't and I reckon whoever stole them from the gardens around here must be stark staring mad."

The sound of a horse clip-clopping along the lane caused all to look towards the window. Hetty, who was nearest, stood up and peeped out through the glass panes where she saw a horse and rider passing by. "I wonder who that is," she said, "I've not seen horses in fields anywhere around here."

"That'll be either Tristan or Samantha Liddicott-Treen," said Miss Vickery, not bothering to stand. "Or it might be one of the children as I believe they came home from school at the weekend. The family often ride along here and then go over the fields and back to the house. I've always rather fancied the notion of riding but if the truth be known I'm a little afraid of horses. They're so big and powerful yet so graceful too."

"I totally agree," said Lottie, "I can never understand how such slim legs hold up their weight. And have you seen their teeth? They're enormous."

"I take it there are stables at Pentrillick House then," said Hetty, as she returned to her armchair. "I don't recall seeing them anywhere."

Miss Vickery swallowed her last piece of biscuit. "No, you wouldn't have seen them as they're well away from the house in an area not open to the public. If I remember correctly they have four horses but I may be wrong as I've never really taken much notice of them and so they aren't very high on my list of favourite things."

"So what is on your list of favourite things?" Lottie asked, "other than playing the church organ, that is."

"Knitting," said Miss Vickery, without hesitation, "I love knitting." She reached for a large bag that she had brought with her, opened it up and from it she took several knitted toys, owls, reindeer, black and white cows, snowmen, penguins and robins. "I knit these for Nancy and Neil to sell in their chalet at Wonderland. They're quite popular, I'm delighted to say."

"They're really cute," chuckled Lottie, amused by the face of a small owl. "I like to knit too but I'm not in the same league as you. I'm really impressed."

"Thank you."

Hetty's mouth gaped open. "But surely you're not going to walk all the way to Pentrillick House with them, it's quite a long way from here even for someone such as yourself who likes walking and I see there are spots of rain on the window now so it must be drizzling."

Miss Vickery shook her head. "Not too far for me, but no, I'll not be walking up there today as I have a key to Nancy and Neil's house which is only about half a mile or so outside the village. Nancy is my niece, you see, and so that's why I have a key."

"Oh that's nice. So do you knit their umm, err festive jumpers as well?" Lottie asked.

"Goodness me no. Much too time consuming. Nancy has a knitting machine to do them." She gave a sudden laugh. "To be honest, I don't think I'd be able to knit garments quite as gaudy as they are. Not much job satisfaction in something like that. Not for me anyway."

"I agree," said Lottie, "although for a brief moment the other day Hetty and I were tempted, weren't we, Het?"

"Yes, but we agreed that such voluminous garments would definitely make us look fat, well, me anyway as I'm quite bulky enough already."

"You should take up walking," said Miss Vickery, "I was rather chubby as a child but the pounds dropped off when I started walking and I've been lean ever since."

Hetty's face lit up. "Really, now that is interesting."

"We often see you walking by here," said Lottie. "Do you go out every day?"

"Absolutely and whatever the weather. In fact I quite like walking in the rain as long as it's not too heavy." She looked towards the rain splashed window, "Today's drizzle won't bother me at all."

Lottie drained her coffee mug and placed it on the tray. "I'm surprised we didn't see you when we were down in the summer for a holiday. We came up here once or twice because we liked the view over the village and out to sea. Still do, of course."

"I see, so when exactly were you here?"

"For three weeks during August but I can't remember the exact dates."

"I can," Hetty raised her hand as though at school, "because we came down the day after a wedding I attended and so were here from the sixth until the twenty seventh. It was Bank Holiday when we went home and the weather was absolutely glorious."

"I see, well in that case for most of it I would have been away visiting my cousin in Hunstanton. I go every year for two weeks."

After Miss Vickery had gone on her way, Hetty washed up and made herself and Lottie cheese on toast for lunch.

"I was just looking at the walls in the kitchen, they're looking quite shabby round by the back door. If we had some paint I'd give them a quick coat today since we're not going anywhere."

Lottie took the plate from her sister's hands. "Thank you, Het. Yes, I thought the same the other day. I'd like to decorate my bedroom too as the wallpaper in there is very faded around the window. But my Hugh always said winter wasn't a good time of year to decorate because the light isn't very good and it's often too cold to open the windows and let in the fresh air."

Hetty sat down. "Very true, and I suppose it's best to do the whole house properly rather than patch it up now. I shall have a new carpet in my bedroom too because it's well-worn in the doorway, and the one in here is quite stained in places so that will have to go as well."

Lottie's face looked alarmed and she pointed to the floor. "Oh, Het, that horrible stain over there. The one we've cursed. It's just occurred to me. I mean, do you think it might be blood? Faith's blood and the spot where she was murdered. I know blood is hard to get rid of."

"Ugh." Hetty put down her toast to take a closer look. "It might well be and that's not a nice thought. Perhaps we ought to buy a rug to cover it up until we get the room done."

"Good idea and I'm sure I saw a couple of rugs in the charity shop the other day. One of them would do as a temporary measure. We must pop down sometime and have a look."

By midday the rain had stopped and a few patches of blue sky had appeared amongst the grey, so in the early afternoon, Misty Merryweather rang for a taxi to collect her from the hotel and drive her to Pentrillick House, as she was keen to see the Wonderland that everyone was talking about and the place where her husband had died.

On arriving she walked straight down through the avenue of trees and on towards the lake. After stepping over the police cordon she sat down on a bench and watched swans gracefully swimming across the still water. The sight reminded her of Hyde Park and the many times that she and Simeon had walked hand in hand around the Serpentine and then sat, as now, watching the swans and ducks. With her thoughts far away she recalled the many happy times before and after the short time that they had been married. He had been and always would be the love of her life.

After leaving the lake she sauntered back towards the wooden huts hoping that speaking to Finn would lift her spirit, but he and Woody were both busy with customers as were Shelley and Ginger in the adjacent chalet. Not wanting to be in the way, she wandered off towards the maze where she saw a long queue of people outside a caravan which she observed was the workplace of someone called Psychic Sid. She smiled. The idea of someone looking into her future appealed greatly because she had no idea how her life would pan out with Simeon gone. And so without hesitation she joined the long queue; her time was her own and there was no-one to wonder or worry where she was should she be gone for some time.

When Misty took a seat opposite Sid, a puzzled look crossed his face. He wondered if he had seen the lady somewhere before but if he had he couldn't remember where and certainly not anything about her. If she were a complete stranger then he'd quite happily say the first things that came into his head but it was different with locals because he might bump into them after his predictions. As Misty placed her handbag on the floor beside her chair he noticed that she was wearing a wedding ring so at least he knew that she was married. She also spoke with an East London accent. His heart began to thump. Might she be one of the actors in the BBC soap, *EastEnders*? But then he never watched the programme so it was impossible for him to have seen her there. Feeling he must play it safe he span a yarn about her making new friends over the festive season but that one of them would disappear into the night leaving a gaping wound in her heart.

After leaving Sid's caravan, Misty went back towards the chalets. As she reached Santa's Grotto she paused and peeped inside. The children looked so happy, so content. She sighed. How nice it would be to be a child again and to recapture the magic of Christmas.

Leaving the laughter behind, she walked back towards the chalets where she saw that trade had quietened down. Glad to see a familiar face, she went to speak to Finn, happy to have someone with whom she could pass away the time. She chuckled as she recalled Sid's prediction. For Finn, Woody, Shelley and Ginger were all new friends. Well, not Finn actually because she'd known him for some time, but the others were and so already Psychic Sid was correct in his prophecy, for her new friends would certainly all disappear into the night when Wonderland closed. She laughed. But whether or not that would leave a gaping wound in her heart remained to be seen.

Early on Thursday afternoon, at the Pentrillick Hotel, as Anna was saying goodbye to guests who were going out to look around Falmouth, an elegantly dressed lady in her mid-thirties wheeled her designer suitcase into the reception area and stopped at the desk.

Anna smiled sweetly. "Good afternoon, how may I help you?"

"Do you have a room, please?" she asked in broken English.

"Would that be for one?" Anna asked.

The lady nodded. "Yes,"

Anna looked at the computer screen. "Yes, we have two rooms available now. A double on the front of the hotel with sea views and a single on the back which looks to the open countryside. Both are on the second floor but we do have a lift."

"The double sounds perfect, thank you."

"And may I ask for how long you would be wanting to stay?"

"I don't know. Three, four days, a week maybe. It all depends."

Anna told the lady of the rates which met with her approval and then asked her name.

"Aimée," she said, "my name is Madame Aimée Dupont."

Chapter Twelve

News of Aimée's arrival in Pentrillick went through the village at break-neck speed but it was not until the evening that the news reached Misty Merryweather. At the time she was in the Crown and Anchor being showered with drinks by sympathetic well-wishers, Finn and Woody amongst them. It was Shelley and Ginger who broke the news when they arrived later in the evening.

"Umm, have you heard the latest?" Shelley casually asked, looking at Misty, trying to establish if she really was who she claimed to be.

"News," said Misty, crossing her long legs, "what news?"

"About Madame Aimée Dupont."

Misty shrugged her shoulders and frowned. "And who might this Aimée woman be?"

Shelley cleared her throat and smiled weakly. "She says she is Simeon Dupont's widow."

Misty's face froze in a look of utter confusion. Her jaw dropped and she banged her glass down on the table. "But she can't be. I'm his widow. We got hitched in Hackney back in September." She flashed her wedding and engagement rings as if to prove her point. "She must be an imposter who's after his bleedin' cake shop."

Finn looked at Shelley. "Are you sure, Shell? I mean, might you have got your wires crossed? She could be his sister or something like that."

Shelley shook her head. "No, she's definitely his wife, well, his widow. I heard it from Tess Dobson. You know who I mean: Tess, the woman that was Simeon's waitress. She was up at the Wonderland today helping in the marquee while they sort out the café problem. I saw her when I popped in for a holly wreath for our door. Poor soul seems a bit lost with no café to work in. Anyway, she'd only just heard the news from a mate who'd sent her a text. She doesn't know any details other than that Aimée Dupont arrived in the village this afternoon and claims to be Simeon's widow."

Finn shook his head. "Well, it's news to me. Can't believe we didn't get wind of it while we were up there today. Having said that, neither of us had a chance to go for a wander because we were surprisingly busy, I'm pleased to say."

Ginger felt slighted. "Well, we were busy too but I knew Shell was keen to get a wreath so I held the fort on my own. You know, us women we can multi-task and so forth."

Finn opened his mouth to retaliate but couldn't find the right words.

"You alright, Misty?" Ginger asked. "You've gone awfully quiet."

Misty's face was flushed. "Yeah, I'm alright, Ginge, but do you know where this French woman is staying? I mean, I think I need to have a word with her, don't you?"

Ginger nodded her head. "Yes, you do but I've no idea where she's staying."

"I'm pretty sure it's The Pentrillick Hotel," said Shelley.

"What! I do hope so then I'll see her at breakfast. Any idea what she looks like?"

Shelley shrugged her shoulders. "Sorry I don't. All I know is that she's French and arrived today."

Meanwhile at the other end of the bar, as Sid was enjoying a drink with Bernie who was celebrating his birthday, he spotted Misty.

"Who's the smashing looking bird sitting with Finn, Woody and the girls?" he asked. "I ask because she was up at Wonderland today and had her fortune told by yours truly."

Bernie smiled. "Yes, she's a beauty, isn't she? She's called Misty something or other and what's more she's Simeon Dupont's widow. She arrived here a few days ago. Tuesday, I think it was and according to my missus she's staying up at the hotel."

"She's who? Oh no, I hope I didn't put my blooming great foot in it," said Sid, trying hard to remember what he'd said to Misty. "I didn't know who she was, you see. I mean, I thought her face seemed familiar but couldn't place it. In retrospect, I realise I must have seen her in here if she's been around for a couple of days but for some reason it hadn't registered. What an idiot I am."

"Don't worry, I daresay she won't have remembered much of what you told her anyway," said Bernie, standing and taking a ten pound note from his trouser pocket. "She looks a bit of an airhead to me. Another drink, Sid? I'm going onto the whisky now. Care to join me?"

Sid nodded. "I shouldn't as I've got to work tomorrow, but yes, go on, count me in."

Chapter Thirteen

On Friday morning, Psychic Sid was woken after a late night drinking with Bernie to hear the sound of knocking on his caravan door. Rubbing his aching head, he slid out of bed and peeped through the curtains to see who was there. To his surprise, three people, two men and a woman, stood outside chatting excitedly amongst themselves. Intrigued as to the reason for their early morning visit, Sid opened the door, clutching the front of his dressing gown as he tried to fasten its sash.

"Mr Moore?" asked the pretty, young female.

Sid nodded. "That's me."

"If we may, we'd like to interview you."

Sid then listened in utter amazement. The woman was a reporter from a local newspaper and the two men were members of the team who published *The Pentrillick Gazette*. The reason for their visit was because all had heard of his uncanny predictions regarding a murder in Pentrillick before the festive season was out. Sid was flabbergasted and flattered too as they sang his praises and asked if they might take his picture for the articles they wished to write. The young woman then added that they were particularly eager to learn from which of his parents he had inherited his extremely psychic skills. Realising there was money to be made from good publicity he invited them all inside his caravan, made them tea and offered them jammy dodger biscuits before excusing himself while he dressed in order to give himself time to think. He then span them a yarn about a grandmother who had been brought up by gypsies, all the time with his fingers crossed, hoping that his ancestors were not able to listen in to his blossoming fabrication. By the end of the interview Sid was hailed a celebrity and promised a large spread on the newspaper's website as well as in print.

Meanwhile, down by the lake, two police officers removed the cordon to enable the area to be used again and then later in the day, the café was to reopen. During a meeting of the Wonderland committee earlier in the week it had been agreed they would ask Chloe whose own café in the village was closed during the winter months, if she would help them out as there was insufficient time to advertise and get someone for what little time there remained of the season.

Tess Dobson, who had worked briefly as Simeon's waitress, was delighted to be employed again for the money earned in the café would go a long way towards the extra expenses brought about by Christmas. Furthermore, it was agreed that Emma, the student who worked at Chloe's café during the summer holiday, could also be employed, because the college she attended was due to break up for Christmas that same day, so she would be free then to work full-time until Wonderland closed on twelfth night.

This news was welcomed by everyone, especially Patrick and Patricia who ran Pat's Hook a Duck stall, when they learned that Chloe had a very good reputation for her Cornish pasties and that she even made her own doughnuts.

On Friday evening, patrons of the Crown and Anchor were surprised to see Aimée Dupont and Misty Merryweather walk into the pub together. They were even more surprised when it became apparent that their attitude to one another was anything but hostile. The two women had met during breakfast at the hotel when Misty had introduced herself. Aimée at first had been shocked and asked for time to get her head round the bizarre situation. They then met again in the afternoon on very amicable terms and during the conversation which ensued, Misty suggested they go to the pub in the evening to discuss the situation further in a more relaxed atmosphere.

"Are you feeling a little better now?" Misty asked, trying hard to tone down her broad Cockney speech which sounded harsh against Aimée's attractive, soft French accent.

Aimée nodded. "Yes, thank you. I am composed again now but it was a dreadful shock to learn who you are."

Misty smiled. "Yeah, same for me. You could've knocked me down with a feather when I heard you'd turned up."

"So tell me again. How long had you and Simeon been married?" Aimée asked, "For some reason my brain seems unable to retain the facts."

Misty took a sip of her wine. "It's just over a couple of months now because it was back in September. It wasn't a big do, just us and a few friends. We got married at the registry office and then afterwards had a bit of a do in a nice hotel." She shook her head. "I càn see now why Simeon only wanted a small wedding. He said it would be a lot of hassle to get his family over from France and of course I believed him."

Aimée smiled sweetly. "So where did you meet?"

"In his shop. I liked his posh cakes, you see, and got to know one of the ladies who worked there. One day Simeon was actually in the shop and the lady introduced me. I was gobsmacked, but we sort of hit it off and he asked me out."

"Oh, I see."

Misty smiled. "What about you? "When did you and Simeon get hitched?"

"Hitched?" Aimée queried.

"Married." As the word faded on Misty's lips, her smile vanished and her brows puckered into a frown. "It's only just struck me," she muttered, "but Simeon must have come over here and left you on your own in France. Why on earth did he do that? I mean, it wasn't very gentlemanlike, was it?"

Aimee nodded. "I'll explain." She cast a glance at the rings on her left hand and then took in a deep breath. "We were married fifteen and a half years ago in Paris just after my twentieth birthday on a beautiful sunny day in May. For a while everything was good but sadly it didn't last. You see, shortly before the wedding, with the help of an aunt, I had started up my own business and because I was eager to see it succeed, it took up a lot of my time and I must admit that it was the root cause of our marriage failing. Of course Simeon had his own business too and it has to be said that he was passionate about baking. Inevitably, all too soon the novelty of being married wore off for both of us, simply because we were far more interested in, and preoccupied with, our own work than we ever were with each other. Sadly the situation did not improve and eventually it became so bad that we mutually agreed it might help save our marriage if we took a break from each other for a year or so. I knew Simeon was keen to open up a patisserie in England and so that seemed to be the perfect solution. He left Paris for London about eighteen months ago. We frequently kept in touch but our correspondence was more business-like than intimate." She half-smiled and her voice softened. "But he always put a kiss at the end of every email."

The colour drained from Misty's face. "Fifteen and a half years. Cor blimey, I feel really bad now. If only I'd known."

Aimée reached out and stroked Misty's hand. "Don't feel bad, ma chérie. It was not your fault."

"Thank you, but…I mean, blimey, I'd never have married him if I knew he already had a wife." Misty twisted the rings on her fingers. "I hardly dare ask, but did you have any nippers?"

"Nippers?"

"Sorry…kids, children."

Aimée shook her head. "No, when we first married we both agreed that children must wait and so it never happened because the time was never right."

"Good. I mean, I'm glad that no children have just lost their dad."

"Yes, so am I."

Misty drained her glass. "So how did you learn that Simeon had, you know, died?"

"I was informed by the police. You see, amongst Simeon's belongings at the Wonderland place was his laptop and so your policemen here checked his emails and established that I was his wife. They notified the French police who came and told me the news. It was a great shock."

"Yeah, I bet it was. Silly, but it never occurred to me that I'd not been told officially. I learned about it from a mate, you see, who read about it on a news website. I should have smelled a rat because in retrospect the cop…cop…police always tell the next of kin when summat like this happens."

Aimée smiled. "If the police had known about you, they too would have smelled a rat. I find it hard to believe that Simeon was a bigamist. He was always so law-abiding. At least he was while in France."

"Simeon would never talk about France." Misty's eyes misted over, "Whenever I asked him of his past he said he preferred to talk of the present and the future. I wish I'd had the nous to suspect a reason for that."

"Had he told you anything of his past then you could have found out a lot about him. His father was a famous chef, you see, and had restaurants all over France and two in Paris. Simeon inherited his love of cooking from his father but much preferred the baking side and so with his father's help he started his own patisserie. Had you known the name of his father you could have Googled him. There is much to be read about him on the Internet. But sadly he is no longer with us. He died three years ago and left everything to Simeon who was his only child. Simeon sold his father's restaurants and I think that's when he first expressed the desire to come to England. I know he owns two prestigious houses in London in which he has tenants who are regarded as celebrities."

Misty's jaw dropped. "You mean to say he was loaded?"

Aimée smiled sweetly. "Oui."

Misty sighed. "And I suppose because our marriage was illegal, I'll get sweet F A."

"Wow, that's tough, babe," said a voice from behind.

Misty turned around to see Finn perched on a bar stool near to where she sat.

"Sorry," he said, "but I couldn't help but overhear what was said. Looks like you should have stuck with me."

Misty scowled.

"Sorry," said Finn, "that was a stupid thing to say. But you know me. I always manage to put my foot in it."

Misty nodded. "Yeah you do." She turned to Aimée. "Aimée," she said, "this blo…person is Finn. I knew him several years ago and he's in Cornwall now because he and his mate have a stall at the Christmas Wonderland."

Aimée held out her lightly tanned hand. "Delighted to meet you, Finn."

"Likewise," he said, and kissed the back of her hand.

Catching a glimpse of the watch strap on Finn's wrist caused Misty to frown. "I've just remembered something. Simeon always wore a Rolex watch. I mean, naturally I assumed it was a fake which he'd bought from some dodgy source but now I realise it was probably the real deal."

Aimée nodded. "Oh yes, it was genuine. I bought it for him for his fortieth birthday a couple of years back. I'm glad he still wore it but wonder where it is now."

"The cops must have it," said Misty, "I expect they'll hand it over eventually."

"But they have already given me the clothing that Simeon was wearing and everything he had about his person when he died and that included the signet ring he always wore on his little finger."

"What! So where the devil is it then?"

"Perhaps someone pinched it." Finn suggested. "Although having said that I daresay it wouldn't be much good anyway after being in the lake for a while."

Aimée scowled. "It was waterproof and so should have been fine."

"On the other hand," said Finn, "someone might have taken it from him before they did him i…i…I mean umm, before he died. In which case it wouldn't have got wet anyway. I mean, we know he was drinking red wine and vodka with someone, so that someone might have nicked it."

"Drinking red wine and vodka!" Aimée gasped. "Simeon never ever touched spirits other than the occasional small glass of brandy if he was feeling unwell."

Chapter Fourteen

On Saturday morning, when Hetty came in from hanging out washing on the line at the bottom of the garden she told Lottie that it looked as though the Hillside roof was finished and it was looking really nice. "Shows ours up, in fact," she said as she pushed the empty laundry basket inside the pantry.

Lottie, standing at the kitchen table dribbling cream sherry onto the surface of the Christmas cake she had made the previous day, nodded her head. "Well, I suppose we could have a new one sometime but it hardly seems worth it as this one doesn't appear to leak."

"Ah, that's reminded me of something I've been meaning to do for a while," said Hetty, "Look in the attic, that is."

Lottie pulled a face. "Ugh, rather you than me. I bet there are lots of spiders and things up there."

"Yes, and probably woodworm too. Not having had a survey done when we bought the place there might be a few nasties lurking amongst the dust, not that that's the reason I thought of going up. My purpose really is to see if there's much headroom. The roof seems to be quite steep when looking at it from the outside, don't you think, and so it might be possible to do a loft conversion and make another bedroom or two."

Lottie's face lit up. "Really! Oh that would be wonderful because if it were possible then Bill, Sandra and the children could all visit us at the same time."

"That's what I thought and we do have some money to spare after the sale of our respective houses. I'd go up there now but trouble is we don't have a ladder and I'm not nimble enough to get up there by way of a chair because it is too high."

Lottie replaced the lid on the sherry bottle and then lowered the cake into an empty biscuit tin. "We must mention it to Tommy when next we see him. He must have some ladders for cleaning windows so I'm sure he'll help us out."

"Good idea. Fancy a coffee?" Hetty reached for the kettle.

"Yes please, but before you make it go and have a look at the rug. It was dry so I've put it down over the horrid stain. "

Hetty crossed the hallway into the sitting room and Lottie followed. "Oh yes, that looks much better and it's cleaned up really well. You've done a good job."

"Thank you. I'm so glad we bought it and next time we're in the charity shop I'll buy the other one if it's still there as I think it would look nice in my bedroom."

In the evening, Lottie looked out her favourite outfit and Hetty put on the new dress she had bought at Wonderland and also her flashing snowman earrings. She offered her sister the Christmas tree earrings to wear but Lottie declined saying the green would clash with her dress but in reality she was self-conscious and didn't want to draw attention to herself.

Once they were ready, they locked up the cottage and walked down to the Crown and Anchor where the Pentrillick Players, the village's amateur dramatic group, were holding their Christmas Dinner and party. According to Maisie and Daisy with whom they had chatted in the charity shop when they bought the rug, this annual occurrence always made for a memorable night. For over the past few years the evening had followed the same pattern; once dinner was eaten and the players were out in the bars and mingling with the rest of the villagers, a local male voice choir would sing favourite Cornish songs. And then afterwards, to round off the evening,

Christmas Carols would be sung by all accompanied by Miss Vickery at the piano.

They arrived at the pub just after seven thirty to find the bars busy and the sound of jovial voices ringing out from the dining room. Maisie and Daisy, in with their respective husbands, beckoned the sisters to join them at a large table near to the French doors.

"Oh, it's lovely and warm in here," said Hetty, removing her coat and hanging it on the back of a chair. "It's quite nippy out." She picked up her handbag from the table where she'd put it. "Right, can I get you all a drink?"

"That's very sweet," said Daisy, "but we've only just got these." She held up her near-full glass. The rest of the foursome did the same.

"Okay," said Hetty, "perhaps later then." She turned to address her sister. "Red or white, Lottie?"

"Red, please, Het."

Miss Vickery was at the far end of the bar along with several members of the church choir who were also members of the male voice choir. However, according to the chat inside the pub, she was reluctant to play the piano for the carol singing later in the evening because that morning she had tumbled on her front doorstep and sprained her wrist. The injury was not serious but it was painful and Miss Vickery was keen to rest it hopeful that it would be a lot better the following day for playing the organ at the Sunday services.

"I can play the piano," said Hetty, on hearing of Miss Vickery's misfortune from Daisy, "and I'd be very willing to help."

Lottie nodded. "She's good too because she can play by ear or by reading the music."

"I didn't know you were a pianist," said Tommy, who had joined the party round the table, "I envy you. It's something I've always wanted to do."

"I think to call me a pianist might be a bit of an exaggeration," said Hetty, much amused, "but as regards you playing, Tommy, it's never too late to learn."

"Well, I dunno about that. I reckon it's not easy to teach an old dog new tricks."

Hetty tutted. "Old dog indeed. You're as young as you feel, Tommy, and to be honest you look ten years younger than you really are."

Tommy ran his hand over his thin grey hair. "Do you think so? Thanks. Anyway, that's enough flattery. I'll go and have a word with Miss Vickery and the choir and see if they're happy to let you tinkle the old ivories."

"Thank you," Hetty looked pleased.

"So how long have you been playing?" Daisy asked, as Tommy left the table.

"Since I was a girl. We both had lessons, didn't we, Lottie? But I was the only one who took to it."

"I'm more the practical type," said Lottie, not wanting to be outdone. "You know, sewing, mending, cooking and suchlike. To be honest, a sheet of music is mumbo-jumbo to me."

"Same goes for me," said Maisie. "So do you have a piano at Primrose Cottage?"

Hetty shook her head. "Sadly no. I had one back home but gave it to Bill and Sandra because their daughter, Kate, is keen to learn. I have a keyboard now but it's not the same so I shall enjoy playing later if it's alright with Miss Vickery."

Miss Vickery was delighted to hear that there was a willing substitute for her services for she knew that without the piano several would struggle to keep in tune for the carol singing, especially after a few too many drinks. To celebrate the fact that Hetty had come to the rescue, she ditched the tonic water for a large glass of mulled wine which she carried to the table by the French doors in order to thank Hetty for offering to help.

"Will the Liddicott-Treens be amongst the party goers in the dining room?" Lottie asked, amused by the raucous laughter coming from said area. "If I remember correctly they are members of the drama group."

"They came last year but can't make it this year," said Miss Vickery, having seated herself at the table, "because they have another function to attend which I daresay will be a little more sedate than this." As she spoke a mighty crash emanated from the dining room followed by peals of laughter and a round of applause.

"Sounds like they're having a smashing time," said Nick, who was sitting at the next table with Patricia and Patrick who ran Pat's Hook a Duck stall and Test Your Strength Steve.

To Hetty's surprise she observed that Nick had abandoned his football T-shirts for the evening and was wearing a crisp white shirt and bow tie. Psychic Sid who was leaning on the bar, was also looking smart although the shirt he wore did look a little on the tight side.

"Nice to see you dressed up," said Hetty, when Sid pulled up a chair and joined everyone around the table.

Lottie agreed. "Yes, you look very dapper."

Sid grinned as he placed his glass on a beer mat. "Thank you, Hottie and Letty, you're both looking lovely too."

Tommy, standing nearby talking to Bernie the Boatman, slapped his thigh. "Hottie and Letty. I like it."

Sid chuckled. "I didn't mean to say that but it is a bit of a tongue twister especially when drinking cider."

Hetty frowned. "Hmm, so which one am I, Hottie or Letty?"

"Hottie," said Bernie, patting her cheek, "definitely Hottie, especially in that dress." As he spoke Aimée Dupont walked by on her way to the Ladies; she paused momentarily and gave Hetty a quizzical look before continuing on her way.

"She thinks I'm mutton dressed as lamb," said Hetty, somewhat down-hearted, "and plump mutton at that."

"Nonsense," said Tommy, "and that French woman is far too skinny anyway."

"You old flatterer," said Hetty, secretly delighted.

"Anyway, you'll be slim soon because old Sid here came up with an accurate fortune telling for Lottie here: didn't you, Sid?" Tommy nudged Sid with his elbow.

"I certainly did. I'm probably one of the best fortune tellers Cornwall has ever seen, or heard for that matter." His tongue was firmly in his cheek.

"What do you mean? What did you get right?" Hetty squirmed in discomfort.

Lottie tutted. "Oh come on, Hetty. You can't have forgotten that Sid said there would be a murder in Pentrillick before the festive season was out and that you and I would be involved. After all, that's why he's regarded as a celebrity all of a sudden. Isn't that so, Sid?"

Sid took a huge gulp of cider and grinned.

"Oh, but that's silly because we don't know for sure that it was murder," said Hetty, horrified at the thought of a diet strict enough for her to lose a whole stone, "and even if it was, you and I aren't involved, Lottie, nor are we likely to be, so that bit was definitely wrong."

"I found the wine and vodka bottles," persisted Lottie.

"Quite right," said Maisie, "and that's why Simeon's death has gone from unexplained to suspicious."

Tommy laughed and rubbed his hands together. "Two weeks to go then till New Year resolutions come into effect."

"You must take up my advice then and go for a nice long walk every day of at least five miles," said Miss Vickery, who now having drunk two large glasses of mulled wine was standing in order to go to the Ladies.

"Five miles!" Hetty looked horrified.

"That's an excellent idea," agreed Lottie, "I must get you a nice strong pair of walking shoes for Christmas, Het. Thank you, Miss Vickery for reminding us."

Miss Vickery cheeks glowed as she wagged her finger to everyone gathered around the table. "No more Miss Vickery," she chuckled, "I insist that you all call me Kitty."

Shortly afterwards, members of the village drama group and their partners emerged from the dining room with glowing cheeks and party popper streamers caught in their hair. They left behind a mess far worse than a children's party for the waiting staff to clear up which included two broken wine bottles knocked onto the flagstone floor earlier in the evening which had been the crash heard by drinkers in the bar.

As soon as the party-goers had refilled their glasses, the male voice choir began their recital with the 'White Rose' which slightly raised the decorum of the Pentrillick Players who stood quietly and listened.

Aimée and Misty, also in the Crown and Anchor, were enjoying a drink with Shelley and Ginger. As the singing progressed, Misty became more and more overcome with emotion.

"Simeon liked this tune. I dunno what it's called but he had a CD of a Cornish male voice choir. I think that's part of the reason why he wanted to come down here for Christmas. He had a nice voice too and used to sing along with some of the songs."

"I hope you don't think me indelicate," said Ginger, "but that's something I've been meaning to ask you about for a while. I mean, why didn't you come to Wonderland with Simeon? It's just that if you'd not been married for long it seems odd that he came down here without you."

Misty smiled. "I was gonna come with him but then a job came up that I really wanted to do. I'm a model, you see. I don't do nothing fancy and take the work when it comes up and the job that came up paid well so I'd have been a fool not to have taken it. Simeon was all for it because he wanted me to still have a career and so we decided that I would join him as soon me job was done which funnily enough was the very day I learned of his death. Bless him, he said that he'd shack up in the café until I got down here then we'd find a nice hotel or even rent a cottage for Christmas and we'd choose it together. Poor soul. It grieves me to think that had I not stayed up there for the job, he'd still be alive today because he wouldn't have gone out boozing without me, that's for sure."

"No, possibly not, but the police are treating his death as suspicious now," said Ginger, "and I don't want to be insensitive but if he was murdered then I daresay there's nothing you could have done to have prevented it."

Misty sighed. "Yeah, I guess you're right. The rotten bastard who did it would just have found another way. I don't think he was murdered though. I mean, he was much too nice a bloke and wouldn't hurt a fly."

"I agree," said Aimée, "he was far from perfect but had no enemies as far as I know and I said as much to the police. But I do have my doubts now especially since discovering his Rolex watch is missing. The police assure me he was not wearing it when they pulled him from the lake and it would have been impossible for anyone to have taken it from his wrist during that process because there were several witnesses."

Ginger nodded. "Yeah, Shelley and I were amongst them as were most of the stall holders, and even the fair folks who were further away came down to see what was going on when they heard the police sirens."

Misty shuddered. "It must have been horrible seeing poor Simeon's lifeless body being pulled from the lake."

Shelley, keen to divert the talk away from such a morbid subject and back in line with the party spirit surrounding them, said, "Ah, it looks like the choir have finished their Cornish stuff and everyone's going to start singing carols now. That woman, Hetty has just sat down on the piano stool. I don't know about you lot but I quite fancy a bit of a sing-song."

Ginger scowled. "Yeah well, each to their own, I suppose. I've never been into singing carols so won't know any of the words."

Misty's face brightened. "I will because I was in the church choir when I was a kid and I really like singing, especially carols. I've always loved them because they meant it was Christmas and Christmas meant presents."

"You weren't," said Ginger, unconvinced. "In a church choir, I mean?"

"I bloomin' well was. I'd show you some pictures of me in all the clobber but I can't because they're all in me mum's photo albums and she lives in Battersea."

Shortly after the singing got underway, Aimée's phone rang and the call was from a number she didn't recognise.

"Excuse me," she said, rising, "better take this outside. Might be important and it's much too noisy in here."

She left the pub by the main entrance and leaned on the front of the building beneath the coloured lights hanging from the fascia board.

"Hello," she said, glad to have answered before the ringing stopped.

"Hello, Madame Dupont. You don't know me but I have news for you regarding the death of your husband."

Aimée frowned. "News, what sort of news?"

"I don't want to tell you over the phone but I have a room at the Pentrillick Hotel and so if you could meet me here I'll be waiting for you in the bar."

"Okay, yes, but how will I recognise you?"

"I'll be sitting at the bar on a stool and I'm wearing black trousers and a red shirt."

“Right, I’ll be there in ten minutes then. I just need to collect my handbag from inside the pub and to say goodbye to my friends.”

“Of course, I understand. There’s no rush as I shall be here all evening.”

“Lovely, goodbye then.”

“Goodbye.”

Misty frowned when Aimée told her of the phone call. “Sounds a bit odd. Would you like me to go with you? I mean, you’ve no idea who he is and he might be dangerous.”

“No, no, there’s no need for that, you stay and enjoy the singing. Whoever he is sounded very nice and there will be plenty of people in the hotel and especially in the bar so we’ll not be alone.”

“Yeah, that’s as maybe,” said Shelley, her face set in a scowl, “but where did he get your number from?”

Aimée frowned. “Oh, oh, I don’t know. I hadn’t thought of that. Perhaps someone at the hotel gave it to him.”

“No, I wouldn’t have thought so,” said Ginger, “that’d be really unethical.”

“Well, it doesn’t matter, does it? If I’m honest I have given my number to several people including all of you. So he could have found out from almost anyone.”

She quickly put on her coat, threw her silk scarf round her neck and picked up her handbag.

“See you in the morning for breakfast, Misty. Goodbye everyone and enjoy the rest of the evening.”

She then hastily left the Crown and Anchor leaving her new friends to join in with the singing.

“Right,” said a choir member with whom Hetty was not acquainted as she finished playing ‘Hark the Herald Angels Sing,’ “time for ‘The Twelve Days of Christmas,’ I think.”

"I hope you mean the Cornish version," said Tommy, having just had his glass refilled, "we haven't sung that since last Christmas."

"Of course that's what I mean," said the choir member," whose voice was very deep, "start playing, maid."

Hetty looked confused. "Okay, but what exactly is the Cornish version of 'The Twelve Days of Christmas? I mean, I've never heard of it. Is it the same tune?"

Kitty giggled. "Yes, it is, Hetty, so you've no need to worry. It's our very own version. We wrote it this time last year."

"You wrote it," said Hetty, hoping she looked more enthusiastic than she felt.

Bernie nodded. "Yes, we decided to put our own words to it, you see, and so to make it fair twelve people were each allocated a number between one and twelve and had five minutes to come up with a line which related to Cornwall."

"Only five minutes," chuckled Lottie, "that's not very long."

"Long enough," said Tommy, "anyway, we only did it for a bit of fun."

"It's really silly," said Kitty, "so please don't judge us harshly."

Vince from the garage chuckled. "No, please don't because back then, like now, we'd all had a drink or two."

"Okay, so will someone tell me what the words are?"

"I'll quickly sing it to you starting with twelve," said Kitty, "No need to accompany me though as I'm very familiar with the tune."

Kitty cleared her throat.

"On the twelfth day of Christmas my true love sent to me -
Twelve bagpipes wailing,
Eleven mermaids dancing.
Ten piskies chanting.
Nine boats a fishing.
Eight kilts in tartan,

Seven shirts for rugby,
Six pies of pilchards,
Five…rum and shrubs,
Four saffron buns,
Three hevva cakes,
Two Newlyn crabs
and a pasty in a pear tree."

"Bagpipes," said Hetty, not sure whether to laugh or cry, "surely they belong to Scotland not Cornwall."

"Yes and no," said Alex from Hillside who was into history and had written the line for bagpipes, "You see they were common in Cornwall during the nineteenth century and are also mentioned in Cornish documentary sources dating from eleven fifty to eighteen thirty. So I think we can lay claim to them as well."

"Oh," was all Hetty could say.

"I can play the bagpipes," said a slightly inebriated voice.

"Lovely," said Alex, with enthusiasm. "Do you have them with you?"

"No, they're back in me caravan. I'll bring 'em with me next time I'm in though."

Lottie muttered beneath her breath, "Mrs Hookaduck playing the bagpipes, that's all we need."

It was well after midnight when Misty left the pub along with Shelley and Ginger all with arms linked to steady each other. As they stepped out onto the pavement to the sound of 'Deck the hall with boughs of holly,' they were surprised to see Aimée's scarf lying just a few yards away near to the car park entrance. Misty unlinked her arms and picked it up.

"She was in a hurry, wasn't she? Not to have noticed she'd dropped this, I mean."

Misty folded up the scarf and placed it in her handbag. "Still, never mind, I'll give it to her in the morning when I see her for breakfast."

"And when hopefully she'll have some interesting news to tell you," said Shelley, "although I really can't see what it might be and whoever the bloke is he ought to go to the police if he knows something useful."

"I agree totally," said Misty.

"You off already?" called a voice from the car park. It was Finn out in the smoking area with Woody.

Shelley sighed. "Yes, we have to work tomorrow. Remember?"

"Yeah, I know and we'll be back soon too. Got to get the old beauty sleep. We only came out for a fag, well, and to get away from the carol singing. Not really our scene."

"Oh, we rather liked it. Anyway must go. See you in the morning."

"Yep, goodnight, ladies."

Chapter Fifteen

When Misty went down for breakfast on Sunday morning she was surprised to find that Aimée was not already in the dining room, for being a dedicated business woman she had said during breakfast the previous day that to rise early every morning was her golden rule. Assuming that she might have had a later night than usual talking to the mystery man and had for that reason overslept, Misty draped the silk scarf across the back of the chair in which Aimée usually sat and then ordered her own breakfast. Half an hour later and with breakfast eaten there was still no sign of Aimée. Misty was confused and a little alarmed and so when she caught the eye of the young waiter she asked if Madame Dupont had already been down for breakfast.

The waiter shook his head. "Sorry, but I've not seen the lady at all this morning."

"Okay, thank you."

Misty picked up the scarf to return to her room. She took the stairs because she didn't like the way the lifts jolted when they stopped. When she reached the first floor where her room was located, she paused and then decided to go up another floor to knock on Aimée's door. She knocked twice and there was no reply, so she rang Aimée's phone. No-one answered. Misty returned to the stairwell and slowly made her way back down to her own room where she sat on the bed with her legs crossed. Something was wrong; she could feel it in her bones and felt compelled to do something about it. Without further ado she left her room again and went downstairs to the reception desk.

"Good morning," said Anna, brightly, "how may I help you, Ms Merryweather?"

"I was just wondering, have you by any chance seen Aimée, you know, Madame Dupont this morning?"

Anna shook her head. "No, but then I only came on duty a few minutes ago. May I ask why you want to know?"

"Oh yes, of course, it's because I'm worried. She hasn't been down to breakfast, you see. She's not answering her door either or her phone. I haven't seen her since last night when we were in the pub and that's why I'm anxious. You see, last night Aimée got a phone call from some bloke who said he was staying here and that he had information about the death of her husband, you know, Simeon Dupont. He asked her to meet him here in the bar and she agreed. I think something might have happened to her."

Anna frowned and called to the porter who was lurking near the doorway. "Keep an eye on the desk for me, please, John. I won't be a mo, just need to check something out."

John nodded as Anna took a key card from under the desk. "Come with me," she said to Misty, "We'll go and take a look."

Inside Aimée's room it was evident that her bed had not been slept in that night nor had the shower or bath been used. Yet her clothes still hung in the wardrobe and her toiletries were in the bathroom.

"Oh my god, I don't think she came back here at all last night," said Misty, feeling goose-pimples prickle her arms. "Her handbag is not here and neither are the shoes and coat she was wearing when we were with her in the pub."

"Most odd," said Anna, "I think I'll give the police a ring and ask their advice. Were it not for the fact that she was supposed to meet someone here last night I wouldn't be too concerned, but as it is it seems most perculiar."

Misty nodded. "I agree and Aimée's hardly likely to have done a runner to avoid paying the bill because she's loaded."

The police were puzzled by Aimée's disappearance and questioned Misty to ascertain the details and nature of the phone call that she had received. They then sent out a team of officers to make door-to-door enquiries in order to try and establish whether or not anyone had seen her leave the Crown and Anchor on Saturday evening or indeed if anyone had seen her since then. Meanwhile, Misty prepared to go to the pub when it opened at midday to ask everyone there with whom she was acquainted if they'd seen Aimée, but before that she phoned Shelley to tell her and Ginger that Aimée was missing, knowing that they would be at Wonderland as it was half past eleven and so the venue would have opened up for the day.

"I knew it," said Shelley, after she had passed on the news to Ginger. "I thought it sounded dodgy last night. She should never have gone."

"What's that then?" Finn asked, hearing the distress in Shelley's voice as he pinned a poster for a new video game on the chalet door.

"Aimée's disappeared. Some bloke phoned her when we were in the pub last night and told her that he had news about Simeon's death. He asked her to meet him at the hotel and she went. It appears she's not been seen since."

Finn left Woody to man their retail outlet and stepped into the girls' chalet. "Really, that sounds a bit fishy. I mean if the bloke had news he should have told the cops."

"Exactly, she should never have gone." Shelley was close to tears.

"Was the bloke who rang her French or was he English?" Finn asked.

Shelley shrugged her shoulders. "No idea because Aimée didn't say, but that's a very good question. All we know is that she said he sounded very nice."

"But obviously wasn't," Ginger muttered.

"Stupid woman," Shelley hissed. She wanted to shout but knew it would be unwise with customers browsing, "Misty offered to go with her last night because none of us liked the sound of it but she was confident that she'd be alright because there would be plenty of people around in the hotel bar."

"Hmm, but it sounds like she never even got as far as the hotel," said Finn.

"Yes, that's the impression I get too," Shelley, sat down on a stool to steady her legs. "Poor Misty she sounded distraught. Naturally she's called the police. Well, actually the hotel did that, and it appears that no-one at the hotel recalls seeing her at all last night. What's more, there are only ten men amongst the hotel guests staying there and they've already been questioned and all have alibis for the entire evening so it looks like the bloke who rang was lying through his teeth and wasn't at the hotel at all."

Ginger frowned. "Yes, it certainly seems that way, but why?"

"Search me," said Shelley, "but I hope to God that she's okay."

Having spent the daylight hours at home tidying up the back garden of Primrose Cottage and burning dead twigs and brambles on a bonfire, Hetty and Lottie knew nothing of Aimée's disappearance until they went to the service of Nine Lessons and Carols in the church on Sunday evening. It was Miss Vickery who told them after the service which came as a shock for the service had been heart-warming and filled them with the Christmas spirit, hence the sisters were instantly deflated when they heard the news.

"It appears the lady left the pub while we were all singing carols and has not been seen since, but her scarf was found by her friends lying out on the pavement outside the Crown and Anchor when they left. No-one is saying so but I fear the worst bearing in mind what happened to her poor husband."

Hetty frowned. "But why would anyone want to hurt Aimée? I thought her very likable even if she did think my dress was more suited to someone younger and slimmer."

"You don't know that she thought that, Het," tutted Lottie, "I reckon it's just your conscience punishing you because it cost too much. Anyway, as you say, what possible motive could anyone have for harming her? But then on the other hand as yet we know of no motive for the death of poor Simeon and he was very likable too."

"True enough," said Miss Vickery. "I do hope this is all resolved soon or I fear it will put a damper on Christmas. Not to mention the fact I feel a little nervous living alone. It's not nice knowing there is a murderer in our midst and I find myself looking over my shoulder far more than I used to and I even look under my bed every night, which is really silly."

Hetty scowled. "Well, in spite of what everyone else might think I don't believe that Simeon was murdered at all. There's not a jot of evidence to back that up. I mean, the fact his fingerprints are on an empty wine bottle proves absolutely nothing. He could have sat alone in the maze and had a skinful because he was unhappy about something."

Lottie tutted. "Oh, Het, you're just saying that because of the diet threat and don't forget Tess said she'd been told by Shelley that Simeon always wore a Rolex watch and it's now missing. Besides what could have bothered Simeon so much that it would have caused him to drink large quantities of red wine *and* vodka? Everyone says it's a lethal combination."

Miss Vickery nodded. "I have to agree and what's more, I should imagine if one were to drink that much then one would be ill for days."

Hetty remained obstinate. "The watch could be anywhere. He may have lost it before his death. And as regards the bottles, who's to say they were full when he started drinking that night anyway? He may have been an alcoholic and hidden them in the maze so that Tess wouldn't find them. I know she kept his room in the café tidy so he wouldn't have risked hiding them under the bed. On the other hand, he might have been having a drop every night since Wonderland opened and liked sitting in the maze for some reason but on that last night he overdid it because he was feeling low and then fell into the lake on his way back to the café."

Miss Vickery thoughtfully nodded her head. "You've both made some very good points and in defence of your sister, Lottie, I think the fact that Simeon knew he'd committed a crime by having two wives might have been enough to turn the man to drink in excess. I mean, had he been caught he would have found himself up before the magistrate and then no doubt been sentenced to a few years in prison."

Hetty nodded smugly. "Precisely and so it was an accident."

A few days earlier, when Jeremy Liddicott-Treen had overheard his father tell his mother that Monsieur Dupont's death had been upgraded from unexplained to suspicious and that the police had told him confidentially that it was likely the French patissier was murdered, he was devastated. For it seemed obvious to him then that the person whom he had seen skulking in the woods in the early hours of Monday morning might well have been the murderer and for some reason he had returned to the scene of the crime. Because of this piece of information Jeremy now checked daily to see if the glove was still on the railings where he had placed it, for he knew it was very important that he discover to whom the glove belonged. However, on Sunday because he had not been able to slip away he thought he would give the glove a miss, but then during dinner that evening, his father mentioned that Monsieur Dupont's widow had mysteriously disappeared. Hearing this caused Jeremy to lose his appetite for he knew it was imperative that he check for the glove before the day was out. And so much later in the evening when he knew his father was in his office attending to some paperwork, he told his mother who was reading, that he was going up to his room to play the new video game he had bought the previous day at Wonderland. He then slipped from the house and walked up towards the car park.

Visibility was poor as Jeremy approached the area where the fair people had their caravans, for the only illumination was from the caravan windows. Not wanting to be seen, he kept well away from the shafts of light and when he saw Patricia, who ran Pat's Hook a Duck stall with her husband, Patrick, standing in the doorway of their caravan, he hid behind a tree and listened. Patricia was telling Patrick that she was going to take out Tyronne for a quick walk around the car park before she turned in for the night.

Jeremy cursed, realising they would both be going in same direction, but knowing that he dare not be away from the house for too long, he followed Patricia by keeping in the shadows. That way, once he had established whether or not the glove was still there he would be able to return home before he was missed.

There were three lampposts in the car park and so Jeremy was able to see clearly where Patricia was and to his dismay he saw her walking very near to the railings, humming as she went and with the occasional word to Tyronne. With his eyes fixed on the fairground lady, Jeremy, walked on in the semi-darkness, stumbling occasionally and not looking where he was placing his feet. When he stepped on a twig, he smothered a gasp. The twig snapped noisily and Patricia stopped walking near to where the glove was hooked on the railings.

"Is there anyone there?" Patricia called, a tremor in her voice, as she glanced over towards the area where Jeremy, desperate not to be seen, crouched behind a parked van. There he waited, holding his breath until he felt that it was safe to move on. When he finally stood there was no sign of Patricia and Jeremy was relieved to hear her chatting to the dog over in the direction of the caravans. Assuming that she had returned to her home, Jeremy quickly stood and dashed over to the railings. When he saw the glove was no longer there, his heart skipped a beat. But to make sure that it had not fallen or been blown from the fence, he carefully looked through the adjacent grass and checked the entire car park, but the glove was gone. Jeremy looked over towards the fairground. Had Patricia taken it? And if so did it belong to Patrick? His heart raced excitedly. He had to find out.

Chapter Sixteen

Sitting on a cold tiled floor, Aimée Dupont shuffled her legs from beneath her bottom to her side. To say she was uncomfortable would have been an understatement; every joint in her body ached and her throbbing head burned with fear and worry. Tired through lack of sleep and frustrated by not knowing where she was, she felt helpless and had no idea how her seemingly pointless ordeal might end. All she knew was that she was in a cold but spacious bathroom in an unidentified building. Her feet were tied together with coarse rope and her wrists were bound in front of her with several layers of gaffer tape. She laughed. But at least her captors had had the decency to hold her prisoner in a bathroom so that she was able to use the loo, albeit with great adversity due to the gaffer tape.

Feeling that her legs were going numb she struggled to stand and the blanket she had wrapped around her shoulders fell to the floor. She was only able to shuffle her feet a short distance because the end of the rope that bound her ankles was tied around the pedestal of the wash basin. This meant that she was unable to reach the small window and call for help or to see what lay on the other side of the frosted glass.

Aimée sat down on the side of the bath and listened. Living in Paris she was used to the sound of traffic and for that reason she knew that wherever she was must be in the countryside somewhere for all was quiet in the outside world and only occasionally did she hear the muffled hum of a car passing by.

She looked to the floor where within her reach stood a jug of water and a plastic beaker. Alongside it were three packets of custard cream biscuits, six packets of cheese and onion crisps and a cold takeaway margarita pizza, conveniently sliced in its box of which she had eaten half. Her captors had said that she must help herself to sustain her strength until she was free to go. But they had not said when that might be or why she had been taken from the Crown and Anchor, and she had no idea who her captors were because she had been forced to wear a blindfold for the duration of the journey to her temporary prison.

Aimée looked at the miserable food on offer and cursed. All those calories. Had she not frequently castigated Simeon because he was always bringing his fancy pastries home? Fattening fancy pasties while she was constantly trying to watch her weight. Men! They were hopeless and that included her half-witted English captors.

On Monday morning, Neil, who with his wife, Nancy had a retail chalet at Wonderland where they sold knitwear including the popular festive jumpers, went to the car park of the Crown and Anchor to pick up his van. Nancy had dropped him off on her way to Pentrillick House and once he had collected the van Neil intended to join her there for a day's work.

The van had been in the car park since Saturday night; he had left it there and taken a taxi home due to the amount of alcohol he and Nancy had consumed at the Pentrillick Players' Christmas party. Normally he would have picked up his vehicle the following morning but because he hadn't been feeling too good, partly because he'd drunk too much and partly because he had a cold, Nancy had attended to their stall at Wonderland alone on Sunday. And because he had stayed in bed for the best part of the day and the van was not needed, he saw no reason to make any effort to collect it.

As Neil approached the van he sensed that something was amiss. For a start it wasn't in the corner where he usually parked it but over near to the recycling bins. Furthermore, the van was unlocked. Assuming that his usual place must have been taken by someone else when he'd parked on Saturday night and that he had forgotten and likewise he must then have forgotten to lock it, he scolded himself for his memory being a blur and climbed into the driver's seat. But as he put the key into the ignition and started the engine the radio came on, on a station that Neil never listened to. Neil frowned and then he sniffed. Could he smell smoke? Instinctively he looked in the ashtray. The squashed butt of a cigarette lay in the bottom. Neil was baffled. He didn't smoke and neither did Nancy.

"I reckon someone's attempted to steal you, my old beauty," said Neil, fondly patting the dashboard. "They must have picked the lock on the door but then couldn't drive you away without the key so they just sat here and had a fag instead." But then he frowned. Without a key, they whoever they might be, would not have been able to switch on the radio either.

"Oh well, not to worry, you're still here and that's all that matters but we won't tell Nancy or she'll tell me to get a better van which is more secure and we don't want that, do we?"

Before he started up the engine he opened up the glove compartment and felt around inside for a packet of biscuits. He cursed as his hands touched nothing other than a few sheets of paper; mostly old MOTs, petrol receipts and stuff like that. Confused, he leaned across the passenger seat and looked inside. "I don't believe it," he muttered, "the thieving swines have nicked me custard creams and me crisps. Is nothing sacred?"

Inside her hotel room, Misty Merryweather sat on her bed worrying about Aimée. She had slept very badly during the night instinctively knowing, as did Shelley and Ginger, that something was very wrong. To keep herself alert, she made a third mug of coffee and then sat down by the window. The sea was grey as was the sky. Misty sighed, "Much like my mood," she whispered.

Leaning her head back against the white wall, she racked her brains wishing it were possible to seize some telepathic signals from Aimée to alert her as to where her new friend might have gone. As she sipped her coffee, she sighed. How wonderful it would be to have psychic skills especially at a time such as this. With sudden alarm she sat bolt upright and set down her coffee mug on the window sill. The words uttered by Psychic Sid when she'd had her fortune told, came back to her crystal clear. He had said that a new friend of hers would disappear into the night leaving a gaping wound in her heart. Misty's heart began to race. Shocked by the accuracy of the prediction she reached for her handbag and took out her phone. With trembling hands, she called the number given to her by the police to ring should she remember anything at all that might help them find Aimée Dupont.

Psychic Sid was in his caravan painting on his rosy cheeks ready for another day's work. The radio was on and playing a tune from the nineteen eighties which reminded him of his teenage years. Feeling in a particularly happy mood he joined in with the song and was surprised to find that he could remember most of the words. His make-up was finished at the same time that the song ended and during the chat of the talkative DJ he changed from his dressing gown into his elf outfit.

Five minutes later the DJ bade everyone farewell and the news came on.

"Eleven o'clock," said Sid, "and all is well." He looked from his window and saw that already the first of the day's visitors were walking towards the avenue of trees.

Sid reached up to the shelf where the radio sat and switched it off. In the silence which followed he heard the wail of a police siren which sounded as though it were in the grounds of Pentrillick House. Feeling curious he went to the window to see where the car might be going. To his dismay it was driving towards his caravan and when it stopped, two officers stepped out.

"Now what?" said Sid, as he opened the door before the police had a chance to knock.

"Mr Moore. We'd like to ask you a few questions regarding a recent fortune telling you did for a lady whose new friend has mysteriously gone missing."

Sid groaned. "Oh no, not again."

Jemima Liddicott-Treen was in very high spirits because she had a friend whom she'd known since she had started primary school coming round in the afternoon so that they could look around Wonderland together. Over the course of several text messages earlier in the day they had agreed that both must have their fortunes told by Psychic Sid after they had looked at everything else. When the friend arrived both girls left the house, chatting excitedly with arms linked.

Thinking back to her own teenage years, Samantha wistfully watched them go and wondered where the years had all gone. She then turned towards the kitchen as she needed to finish decorating the Christmas cake; not that she minded: cake decorating was a hobby at which she was very talented. However, as she passed a table in the passageway, she saw that Jemima had left behind her shoulder bag. Aware that without it her daughter would have no money, she picked it up. As she walked towards the door, she saw Jeremy with a pair of binoculars hanging around his neck.

"Be a sweetheart, please, Jerry and take this bag to your sister. She's gone for a look around Wonderland with her friend but has left it behind."

Jeremy eagerly took the bag, glad of an excuse for a wander around the grounds. "Of course, Mum. No problem at all."

He left the house and walked quickly towards the fair area which he assumed would be the girls' first destination. He was right, they were standing beside the coconut shy watching and cheering on a contemporary of theirs who was trying to win a prize.

Jeremy held up the bag. "Mum thinks you'll need this, Jem."

Jemima tutted. "Oh dear, yes, silly me. Thanks, Jerry."

"That's okay. Have fun."

Jeremy turned away as though to walk back towards the house but he deliberately made a detour so that he would pass by Pat's Hook a Duck stall. He was keen to see if Patrick, his prime suspect, had large hands for Jeremy was confident Patricia had taken the glove from the railing knowing it belonged to her husband. But to his dismay, Patricia was working alone and so he continued on towards the Test Your Strength high striker hoping that Patrick might be chatting to Steve. He was not there and Steve was busy with a group of young people all determined to prove themselves stronger than their contemporaries. However, as he passed by Steve's caravan, something lying inside on the window ledge, caught his eye and the something looked very much like a pair of gloves. With a quick glance around to make sure that neither Steve nor anyone else was looking in his direction, he moved closer, stood on tip-toe and peered into the window. He placed his hand over his mouth to stop himself shouting with delight, for there on the ledge lay a pair of black leather gloves with a swirly pattern on the back, identical to the one that he had found by the lake.

Chapter Seventeen

On Tuesday, Wonderland was as usual closed for the day and so in order to relax, Nick the designer clothes seller, went to the pub as soon as it opened and to the amusement of Sid who had also made the Crown and Anchor his destination, Nick was wearing an Aston Villa T-shirt. Nick looked up from a December copy of *The Pentrillick Gazette* as the psychic took a seat at the next table.

"Do you get to watch much football?" asked Sid, carefully placing his pint glass on a beer mat. "I mean, you must like the game as you've an extensive wardrobe of shirts."

Nick looked a little sheepish as he laid the *Gazette* down on the table. "Not really. All told I have shirts for twelve different teams but I only wear them because I like to think they attract a bit of attention. That's why I keep chopping and changing teams. It gets the blokes to stop for a chat, you see, and while they're chatting their wives or whatever, often browse my clobber and buy something. Cunning, eh?"

"Yes, very. So I'd be wasting my time chatting to you about the game then."

Nick wrinkled his nose. "Not entirely. I mean, I like to watch the home teams play in the big events like the World Cup but I don't support a local team or anything like that but then that's probably because I'm always on the move. How about you? Do you like football?"

Sid picked up his pint. "Very much so. I went over to France for a couple of days in the summer to watch England play in the European Championship. Had a fantastic time but it's a pity they lost."

"Oh no, not the match against Iceland?"

"Yep, the very one. Took me a couple of days to get over the shock. Still, these things happen and both teams can't win, can they? It certainly gave everyone something to talk about though."

"Yes, it did that alright and the press had a field day with it," Nick took a sip of his beer, "I've never been abroad. Silly, I know but I don't like the idea of flying nor going anywhere by boat. I suppose that makes me a bit of a wimp."

"I don't know, I think there are lots of folks with similar phobias. Have you never thought of going across to France by way of the Channel tunnel?"

Nick turned pale. "That's even worse. I mean, the thought of being under all that water terrifies me. When I'm up in London I think it's pretty scary going under the Thames on the underground and that only takes a few seconds."

"Yeah, I'd never really thought of it like that and the water must weigh a fair bit but then engineers know what they're doing especially today with all the technology and stuff."

"True, very true."

"I've been popping over to France for as long as I can remember so think nothing of it," said Sid, "My mother's half French, you see and she still has family over there."

"Oh, I didn't know that. So I suppose you speak French."

"Yes, like a native. I was taught to speak both languages from a very early age," He smiled, "I was able to have a chat with Simeon a while back about football, would you believe. Needless to say the discussion got a bit heated as we were both determined to stand for our respective countries even if we weren't entirely happy with their performances."

"And now he's dead, poor bloke."

"Yep, now he's dead."

"But at least France got to the final in the European Championship."

Sid chuckled. "Yeah, and they beat Iceland."

"So, what about your dad. Where's he from?"

"Newcastle," said Sid.

It was Nick's turn to chuckle. "Hence your difficult to identify accent. A cross between French and Geordie. Very interesting."

Hetty and Lottie decided to go into Penzance on Tuesday morning to do a bit of Christmas shopping. However, they didn't take the car but instead went by bus so that they could alight in Marazion and walk into Penzance by way of the coastal path. It was a route the sisters had discovered during their summer holiday and both were keen to tread the path again.

A fresh wind was blowing as they stepped from the bus causing both ladies to zip up their jackets and pull up the collars.

"Too chilly for ice cream today, eh, Het," said Lottie, as she tucked her hands inside her pockets.

"Absolutely, but the sea air is good for our health, Lottie, even if it is a little bracing."

The tide was in as they reached the path after crossing a car park and they could feel the damp spray on their faces. As the walk progressed the wind seemed to get stronger which made talking difficult as it was hard to be heard. But not ones to be thwarted, the sisters relished the fresh air and even sat down for a while on giant boulders to watch the thundering waves as they crashed onto the shore.

Once in Penzance they looked for suitable gifts for Kitty Vickery and Tommy Thomas. For both had accepted the sisters' invitation to dinner on Christmas Day. At first Hetty and Lottie had proposed just to cook for themselves but when they learned that Tommy would be alone for the first time in his life, they asked him to join them and then Kitty too for she also lived alone.

After a brief look around they settled on a pair of diamante earrings for Kitty and for Tommy they bought a dark green fleece top for such a garment seemed to be his favourite item of clothing. They then went in search of a café or pub in order to have some lunch.

To their surprise, as they passed a tattoo parlour, Shelley and Ginger stepped out onto the pavement.

Lottie tutted. "You've not spoiled your lovely bodies with nasty ink I hope."

"Lottie, the girls must do as they please," Hetty rebuked, "after all it is a free country."

"We've only had little ones done," said Shelley. She lifted the leg of her jeans to reveal a small butterfly on her ankle.

"And I've a flower on my shoulder," said Ginger, "but it's too cold to show you out here."

"Very nice," said Hetty. "Not too intrusive and being small they should still look good when you're old and wrinkled, like us."

"You're not old and wrinkled," said Shelley, "I think you're both amazing."

"Hmm, well, yes, that's as maybe," said Hetty. "Anyway, more importantly is there any more news of Aimée's whereabouts?"

Ginger squirmed as she resisted the temptation to scratch the new tattoo which itched. "Sadly not. In fact to be honest, we've come into town today to try and forget about it for a while. It's keeping us awake at night, I must admit, and the same goes for poor Misty. She's really worried and we're worried about her as she's been through a lot lately."

Lottie tutted. "Wherever can Aimée have gone? It can't be far if she's not taken her belongings."

"We don't think she's gone anywhere of her own free will," said Shelley, pushing a strand of hair behind her ear which was being tousled by the wind. "Having said that, I can't believe that she's been kidnapped by the man who made the phone call or anything like that because there have been no ransom demands."

"Yes, and after two days there would have been by now if that were the case," Hetty agreed.

"I hate to say this," said Shelley, "but there are rumours that as Wonderland is closed today the police might be going to drag the lake but I hope it's not true."

Hetty gasped. "Oh no, surely they don't think she's taken her own life?"

Shelley shook her head but Ginger answered, "No, we don't think anyone suspects that at all. But from what we gather the police believe it's possible that someone may have had cause to hold a grudge against both her and Simeon and for that reason she might have gone the same way."

After a couple of pints in the Crown and Anchor and sausage and chips for his lunch, Sid wandered along the main street in Pentrillick wondering how best to spend the rest of the day. He didn't want to go back to his caravan as he knew the police intended to drag the lake looking for Aimée Dupont. Sid shuddered at the thought. As he reached the bus stop a double decker bus pulled up and its destination board said Penzance.

"Fate," said Sid, and hopped on board. He'd never been to Penzance but liked the thought of a quick look round.

After wandering along the sea front he walked up towards the town. As he passed a charity shop he saw a bright yellow highly patterned shirt in the window which greatly appealed to him, for he reasoned that it was like the sun and therefore would be a happy shirt. Hoping that it was his size he went inside to enquire. The elderly gentleman in the shop was very obliging and took the shirt from the window to check the label. To Sid's delight it was extra-large and so he bought it. With shirt inside an old supermarket carrier bag, he turned to leave the shop, but before he reached the door, he saw two garden gnomes standing on the floor next to a basket of plastic flower pots. He chuckled for one of them had the name Sid on his green pointed hat. Sid picked him up. "You look a bit like me, mate when I'm wearing my elf get-up. I think I'd better buy you." And then being an old softie he bought the other one, too, feeling it would be unkind to separate them.

Once back at Pentrillick House, oblivious of the gnome thefts in the area, Sid stood the two gnomes on either side of the steps leading up to his caravan. Pleased with his purchases, he gave them the thumbs up. "Now you'll be able to give the ladies who queue to see me something to coo over."

On Tuesday evening it rained but Hetty and Lottie went to bingo for no other reason than to see if there was any news regarding the whereabouts of Aimée Dupont. They took the car and also a prize for the raffle which they put with other donations when they arrived.

To their dismay there was no news of Aimée but they did learn from their next door neighbour, Ginny, that the lake at Pentrillick House had been dragged that afternoon and that thankfully nothing was found.

Just before play commenced at eight o'clock, Patrick and Patricia from the fair arrived. Both were dressed smartly and Patricia seemed unusually subdued.

"What do you reckon's up with Mrs Hookaduck?" Hetty hissed, "She's even talking quietly."

"Goodness knows, and I must admit I'm rather surprised to see them here."

"Me too, but then they were probably just bored and wanted to get out. It can't be much fun being stuck in a caravan on a wet evening and I don't suppose they want to go to the pub every night as it'd cost a fortune."

"True."

"Having said that, they're probably quiet because they witnessed the lake being dragged today. That wouldn't have been a very nice experience."

"I think that's unlikely as I'm sure the police wouldn't have allowed them anywhere near the lake and they certainly wouldn't have been able to see anything from their caravan." Lottie reached into her handbag and took out her reading glasses. "It's just a thought, but I wonder if she looks glum because she's feeling guilty for some reason."

"Guilty." Hetty looked puzzled, "What are you talking about?"

"Well, I'm keeping my options open but if you remember, Mrs Hookaduck was no fan of Simeon as we witnessed on a couple of occasions and so perhaps she had something to do with his death. She might even know where Aimée is."

Hetty shook her head. "Don't be daft, that's ridiculous. I mean, not liking his pastries is hardly a motive for murder, is it? Anyway, you know my thoughts over the poor bloke's passing. I think it was an accident and you'll never sway me from that."

"But they live on site," Lottie persisted, "and so would have been at Pentrillick House on the night that he died. They could easily have pushed him into the lake."

"Yes, they live on site but so do all the fair people. Anyway, they would have been questioned by the police and no doubt have an alibi. I think you're barking up the wrong tree, Lottie, and it's best to say no more."

With a sulky face Lottie glanced over towards the fairground people. When something caught her eye she sat up straight and then pulled a tissue from her pocket. To Hetty's surprise, Lottie then stood up, walked over to the rubbish bin and dropped a tissue inside. As she walked very slowly back she glanced down at the Hookaduck's table.

"What are you up to?" Hetty asked as her sister sat back down.

"I just had to check something out," said Lottie, excitedly, "You're never going to believe this, but Mr Hookaduck is wearing a Rolex watch."

Chapter Eighteen

On Wednesday morning, half an hour before Wonderland opened for the day, Jeremy Liddicott-Treen sat on the grass bank which overlooked the car park at Pentrillick House hoping to see some rare or interesting cars amongst the day's visitors. He was happy to be alone for it also gave him time to think and there was much to think about. However, when a yellow Vauxhall Corsa drove in and stopped well away from the cars already parked, all thoughts slipped from his mind, for he was intrigued not by the car itself but by the fact it had parked so far away from all other vehicles. It remained on the same spot for several minutes with its engine ticking over and then suddenly it moved forwards and slowly drove towards the nearest row of cars. To Jeremy's amazement, it then made several comical attempts at parking in a huge gap between a Land Rover and a green mini. He was mesmerised, for the occupants of the car appeared to be elderly. At least one, the driver, had grey hair, the other lady's hair was dark brown. Jeremy looked at his watch in order to see how long it took the driver to park. To his amusement, it took fifteen minutes and countless attempts. He chuckled to himself and wondered if George, the head groundsman, was right in his claim that women were inferior drivers, although he had to confess that his mother was very competent and probably an even better driver than his father. It wasn't until the car pulled out of its parking slot and drove away that Jeremy noticed the L plate on the back.

Shortly after the Corsa left, a white transit van drove in which Jeremy knew belonged to Nick who sold dresses which his sister and her friends drooled over. As he stepped from the van, Nick spotted Jeremy and waved. Jeremy waved back and watched as Nick walked away towards the chalets whistling the tune of the 'Twelve Days of Christmas.'

The next vehicle Jeremy saw was Steve from the Test Your Strength challenge. Jeremy sat bolt upright and watched as from the back of his van Steve took a cardboard box. Jeremy couldn't see what was in it but it jangled as Steve walked across the car park and so he assumed it was bottles.

"Bottles!" Jeremy whispered as Steve disappeared from view. Without waiting to see more vehicles he sprang to his feet and made his way over towards the fair. For the previous day he had heard the girls that sold candles and cosmetics talking about the death of Monsieur Dupont. They had mentioned the possibility of the red wine that he had been drinking in the maze on the night he died, being laced with vodka.

In the early afternoon, Tess Dobson took a short break from her waitressing job in the café and walked up to the fairground to deliver pasties to fair people who ordered them daily.

"Thank goodness," said Patrick, who had left Patricia to manage the Hook a Duck stall on her own and was chatting to Steve, "I'm famished because Patricia dropped the last couple of eggs this morning and the dog ate them before we had a chance to try and rescue them. So all I had for breakfast was a slice of toast because we ran out of bacon yesterday."

"Yeah, I know what you mean," said Steve, "my stocks are getting low and I can't be bothered to go shopping after I finish here. Although to be fair, Nick has offered to do some shopping later because he wants to take his jacket in to get it dry cleaned."

"Just as well we're here then," reasoned Tess, handing them each a pasty, "at least you can be guaranteed lunch."

"True enough and you're a godsend," said Steve, opening the paper bag containing his pasty and taking a sniff, "Hmm, heavenly, and tell Chloe if ever she decides to ditch her old man that I'm first in the queue to marry her."

"Will do," said Tess, who was used to the cheeky chat of the fairground people.

On her way back to the café she glanced over towards Sid's caravan to see how many ladies there were in his queue. When she spotted the two gnomes standing at the foot of the steps she stopped dead in her tracks. Knowing of the mysterious disappearances of gnomes in the area she thought it only right that she should investigate and so went to take a closer look. To her amazement she saw that one of the little men held an umbrella and he looked very much like the gnome which had been taken from her friend, Gail's garden at the end of November. Her first thought was to ask Sid from what source he had acquired them for she was pretty sure that they had not been there for long and certainly not when she had had her fortune told during the first week after Wonderland had opened. However, rather than confront him herself, especially when he had a queue of eight ladies waiting to see him, she decided it would be best for the authorities to question him and so she went over to a quiet part of the grounds and called the local police.

Sid was counting out the money he'd made that day when he heard the sound of a car approaching his caravan. Knowing no cars other than emergency vehicles were permitted to drive over the grass, he pulled back a curtain to see who his visitors might be. His shoulders slumped when he saw it was the police again but he was relieved to see there was only one officer and that he had not put on the sirens and alerted everyone on the site.

Sid went to the door and opened it completely baffled as to why the police were about to call yet again, for as far as he was aware he had not made any other predictions regarding death and disappearances. In fact since he'd been questioned about his prophecy for Misty Merryweather he'd kept his forecasts on more mundane matters such as travel, love and prosperity and he had been particularly careful when he had told the fortune of Miss Jemima Liddicott-Treen.

"Good afternoon, officer," said Sid, with a forced smile, "and what can I do for you today?"

"Good afternoon to you, Mr Moore," replied the young officer, as he tried to keep a straight face, "I'd like to ask you a few questions if I may regarding this little fella with the umbrella." He pointed to the gnome in question. "We have reason, you see, to believe he may have been stolen from a property in the village."

Sid opened his mouth to reply but for once in his life he was speechless.

Early on Wednesday evening, Hetty slipped out through the back door of the cottage to put two glass jars into the recycling box in the garden shed. It was December the twenty first and the shortest day of the year. While outside she paused to look up at the clear night sky. The fading moon was shining brightly and surrounded by millions of twinkling stars. There was not a breath of wind and the stillness of the early evening seemed to be gripped in a mystical aura.

"Look at that," she said to Albert who had followed her outside. "It's skies like that that make me feel glad to be alive. It almost feels like I should be hearing angelic voices singing 'Silent Night.'"

Feeling chilly, Hetty then turned to go back indoors, but when she reached for the handle, she heard the sound of a car on the track which ran alongside Tuzzy-Muzzy. Hetty frowned.

It was too late for the farmer to be going to his fields and there was no-one living in the house.

Inside the sitting room, Lottie reached for the box of matches hidden behind the clock on the mantelpiece so that she could light the candles on either side of the fireplace. She paused when she saw the puzzled expression on her sister's face.

"What the matter, Het?"

"I'm not sure but I think there might be something fishy going on next door. Tuzzy-Muzzy that is, not Hillside. And when I say next door I actually mean the track that runs alongside it. I just heard a car, you see."

"Well, I expect it's the farmer," said Lottie, opening up the match box.

"At this time of night and in the dark. No, it can't be and no-one other than the farmer would have reason to go up there because the track only goes as far as a five bar gate."

"Hmm, I suppose you're right and there are no animals to care for anyway, just cauliflowers and you don't cut them in the dark."

"Precisely."

"So what do you reckon?"

"I don't know but I feel uneasy so I think I'll pop round and have a quick look. It won't take a minute."

"Well, you're not going on your own in the dark so I'd better go with you." Lottie closed the matchbox and dropped it into her pocket.

"Okay, but you must stay here, Albert," said Hetty. "We'll be back in a jiffy."

She switched on the television so that he would not feel lonely and then without bothering to put on their coats the sisters left their warm cottage and went to investigate the vehicle Hetty had heard. They didn't bother to lock the cottage door and to save time they took a short cut through the gardens of Tuzzy-Muzzy, for the farm track ran by the side gate of the empty old house.

"We should have brought a torch," said Hetty, rubbing the back of her hand scratched by a spiky berberis, "although now that my eyes have adjusted to the dark I think there is just about sufficient light from the moon to see by."

"I've got matches in my pocket," said Lottie, in a reassuring manner, "so if we need to look at anything in detail they should give enough light. It would be foolhardy to have a torch anyway if there are likely to be any dodgy folks around here."

"True and I suppose in case there is anyone here we ought to keep our voices down."

Tuzzy-Muzzy was in total darkness as they crept up its driveway and crossed in front of the house and over towards the side boundary beyond which ran the farm track.

"Where's the gate?" Lottie whispered, as she followed Hetty along a garden path part-hidden by leaves that had fallen from a large horse chestnut tree, "I can't see it."

"I can, we're nearly there."

Everything was quiet as they slowly opened the gate and looked out into the muddy lane where to their surprise, they saw a van parked nearby in the shadows.

"I wonder who that belongs to," whispered Hetty.

"Could be anyone," said Lottie, wishing she was safely back inside Primrose Cottage, "I mean as yet we don't really know who drives what. Not that I'd be much help anyway. My recognition of cars and whatnot doesn't go much beyond colour."

"Yes, same for me although I'm pretty good at recognising registration numbers but that one means nothing. Come on, there's no cause for concern, let's go home."

As Lottie closed the gate, Hetty looked up at the house. She squinted and reached for her sister's arm. "Look up at that small window, Lottie. Am I imagining it or is there a dim light shining from inside?"

Lottie looked up. "Well, yes, it looks like there is. Do you think there might be someone in there?"

Hetty shuddered. "That's what I'd like to know but I don't think I want to hang around and find out. On the other hand, perhaps it's left on for security reasons."

Lottie shook her head. "No, if that were the case they'd leave lights on at the front of the house rather than round the back."

"You're right. Come on, since we're here anyway, we'll just creep round to the back door and listen out for voices. If we hear nothing then we can then go back home." She shivered. "I wish I'd put a coat on though because it's quite chilly out here."

"I agree but I daresay some of the cold is being caused by fear."

"Fear," repeated Hetty, "there's nothing to be frightened of."

"If you say so." Lottie was unconvinced. "You lead and I'll follow."

They followed the path around to the rear of the house and there listened carefully by the back door. All it seemed was quiet and so they then moved along towards the kitchen window and peeped inside. There was no light in the room and no sound either.

"There's no-one here. Come on," said Lottie, "let's get back to the fire before we freeze to death."

But as they turned they saw a small, dim, red light glowing in the darkness, like the end of a lighted cigarette.

"You're going nowhere," said a voice in the darkness. And before they had time to run each were grabbed by a strong arm and pushed inside the back door of Tuzzy-Muzzy.

Chapter Nineteen

"Shall we pop down to the pub for something to eat?" Shelley asked Ginger. "There's nothing on the telly that I want to see and I'm feeling quite peckish."

"Yeah, so am I. Those microwave meals were pretty small, weren't they?" She tossed her tablet to one side. "But what about the blokes?"

"We'll leave the key under the old plant pot so there's no need to worry. Better leave them a note though to let them know where we are. Not that they'll care."

"Okay, but I don't really see why we should as we've no idea where they are half the time."

"True." Ginger looked at her phone for the time. "Better get a move on as they stop doing food at nine."

From an upstairs window of Pentrillick House, Jeremy watched through his binoculars as a taxi pulled up just beyond the fair area and into it stepped Steve, Nick, Patrick, Patricia and the two young men who looked after the helter skelter. He assumed, as was the case with many who owned fairground attractions and who ran stalls that they were going to the Crown and Anchor. Jeremy wished that he too could go and be a fly on the wall but knew it was out of the question for his parents only ever went to the pub for specific occasions, usually fund raising events and so there was no way he could suggest to them that they all go to the pub for the evening.

Steve was the last to get into the taxi, he wasn't wearing the gloves or even a coat. Jeremy sighed. Since the day that he had seen the gloves in Steve's caravan, he had, whenever it was possible, observed his movements, but to his dismay he had done nothing at all suspicious and never once had gone anywhere near the lake. And as for the bottles that he had bought the previous day, they all contained beer for Jeremy had seen them as he had casually walked by the caravan where the box stood on the ground as Steve had unlocked the door.

As the taxi pulled away, he picked up the latest detective novel for which he had gone to the room in the first place and made his way down to the sitting room.

Inside Tuzzy-Muzzy, Hetty and Lottie sat on the floor of a bathroom. Both had their legs bound together with gaffer tape and likewise each had their wrists tied at the front with coarse rope; their hands rested on their laps. Another rope ran from their ankles and was knotted to the base of the wash basin pedestal.

"Humph," said Lottie, as they heard two doors slam shut on the van beyond the back gate, "at least they've left enough slack on the rope so that we can use the loo."

"But not enough for us to get to the door or the window," Hetty said in frustration.

They heard the sound of an engine start up. "Good, they're going, now we can figure out how to escape." Lottie tried to free her hands from the rope.

Hetty laughed. "I doubt if Houdini could get out of this pickle."

"Oh, no, Het, you're wrong there, he'd have seen this as a piece of cake."

"Really, I'll leave you to work out the escape plan then, clever clogs."

As Hetty finished speaking both heard the sound of tapping.

"What's that?" Hetty was alarmed.

Lottie quickly glanced around the room. "I don't know but I don't like the idea of us being in this old place in the dead of night. It's spooky even though they've left the light on."

"Spooky, my foot, that sound wasn't made by a ghost, spook or whatever you want to call it and it came from over there." She nodded her head towards the interior wall and then still sitting she shuffled across the floor and with her cuffed hands knocked against the cladding. Instantly someone knocked back.

Hetty jumped. "Cripes, who's that?" she stuttered.

"Shout louder and ask."

"Okay." Hetty cleared her throat. "Who's there?"

"Aimée Dupont," came a faint reply.

Lottie gasped. "Aimée. She must be in another bathroom then and it was the light from that room that we saw from outside."

"And she's alive," said Hetty, "Thank goodness for that."

"Amen, but if she's been trussed up like us for the last few days, she must be in a bad way."

"You're right," Hetty knocked on the wall again. "Aimée, we're in the bathroom next to you and we're trying to work out how to escape."

A knock in return was followed by Aimée's voice. "Who is we?" she asked.

"Hetty and Lottie, we've never been introduced but you'll have seen us in the pub on a few occasions. Don't be frightened, we'll sort something out." She turned to Lottie. "Well, have you thought out how we can escape yet?" she asked, a hint of sarcasm in her voice.

Lottie nodded. "Oh yes," and in her cuffed hands she held up the box of matches which she had taken from her pocket. "I'm going to burn through the rope around your wrists."

After choir practise, Kitty Vickery locked up the church and dropped the cumbersome key into the pocket of her jacket. She then walked through the village to return to her home. As she passed by the Crown and Anchor she peeped in through one of the windows which ran with condensation. Visibility was poor but she concluded by the noise coming from inside that people were already getting into the festive spirit. She paused. A mulled wine would slip down a treat but she resisted the temptation and went on her way.

It was dark as she crossed the road and turned into Long Lane for there were no street lights to light her way. From her bag she took out her torch and walked on up the hill behind the beam of light, quietly singing the anthem the choir had learned for Christmas.

All seemed eerily still as she passed by the closed gates of Tuzzy-Muzzy but inside Primrose Cottage the lights were on and she could hear the signature tune of a popular television programme. Suddenly she stopped. The hairs on the back of her neck rose. She sensed that something was wrong but had no inkling as to what or why. Without a second thought she opened the gates and knocked on the cottage door. No-one answered but Albert barked and she could see his shadow through a stained glass panel in the door. She knocked again but still no-one answered. She looked behind to where Hetty's car was parked on the tarmac. She paused to think. Perhaps the sisters had walked to the pub for a drink, but deep down she knew that was not the case. She clasped the door handle and gently pushed it down. The door was not locked and so she knew the sisters must be at home. With the door slightly ajar she called out, "Hetty, Lottie, are you alright?"

No-one answered. She pushed the door wide open and stepped inside. Albert jumped up at her legs barking wildly.

"Down boy," she said, "you'll leave hairs on my skirt."

Albert obeyed but he continued to bark as she closed the door.

"Quiet, quiet, please," she commanded.

Albert's bark ceased and then he began to whine.

"Where are Hetty and Lottie?" Kitty asked, glancing around the hallway.

Albert's tail wagged on hearing the sisters' names.

"I must check all the rooms," she said, brushing past the dog.

Albert followed as Kitty went from room to room but there was no sign of the two women anywhere. Back in the hallway she reached for Albert's lead hanging from a coat peg and clipped it onto his collar.

"Find Hetty," she commanded, "find Lottie."

Once outside, Albert ran towards the gates dragging Kitty behind him. He allowed her no time to close the gates nor time to switch on her torch and to her surprise he ran only a few yards and then stopped by the gates of Tuzzy-Muzzy where he leapt up barking nosily and hitting the latch with his paws.

"But they won't be in here," said Kitty, opening the gates nonetheless. "The house is quite empty because no-one lives here. Silly boy." She groaned. "Oh dear, I hope you don't think we're chasing cats because I know Ginny's cat, Snowy, treats all of the gardens along here as his own."

But Albert was not interested in cats, he was following a scent and knew he was on the right track. Once through the gates he dragged Kitty along the driveway, then around the side of the house and on towards the back door where barking excitedly, he scratched at the paintwork, his tail wagging non-stop. Kitty shook her head, clearly puzzled by the dog's behaviour.

Meanwhile, inside the bathroom of Tuzzy-Muzzy, Hetty and Lottie heard the welcome sound of Albert barking. For although they had successfully freed themselves from the ropes that had tied their hands and the gaffer tape that had bound their feet, they were unable to leave the room because their captors had placed a large wardrobe in front of the doorway to prevent them getting out.

Hetty, intrigued to know how Albert had managed to leave Primrose Cottage and find his way round to Tuzzy-Muzzy, flung open the window and looked down to the garden below. Kitty had now switched on her torch and was flashing it over the back of the house.

"Who's there?" Hetty called, unable to see the face behind the torch.

"It's me, Kitty Vickery. Is that you, Hetty?"

"Yes it is."

"Where are you?"

"We're in the bathroom."

Albert stopped barking on hearing Hetty's voice and looked up at the window. Kitty's jaw dropped in surprise.

"What are you doing up there?" she asked, flashing the torch across the bathroom window.

"Long story. Come and rescue us, please. We're locked in the bathroom, you see, and can't get out because a damn great wardrobe is blocking the doorway."

"A wardrobe." Kitty was nonplussed but nevertheless she tried the back door. It was locked. "But how can I get in without a key?" she asked.

"Break the kitchen window," said Hetty. "No-one will hear."

Kitty flashed her torch across the garden. A brick sat on top of the dustbin to prevent the lid from blowing away. Without hesitation, she picked it up and smashed the glass near to the catch. As the glass shattered she put her hands over her ears as the shrill sound of an alarm rang out through the clear, still night.

Chapter Twenty

Inside the Crown and Anchor, Finn and Woody nervously sat with pints of beer, puzzling how they could resolve the hopeless mess they found themselves in.

"If only we could turn back the clock to Saturday," said Woody, "I wish I was anywhere but here."

Finn scowled. "Well we can't turn it back, can we? So we must use ours brains instead. I mean, there must be a way out of this muddle."

"Yeah, well you better think of one. I mean it was you that got us into it in the first place."

"You thought it was a good idea as well at the time," scoffed Finn.

"Yeah, but ideas often sound good when you've had a drink or two. Can't believe we were so daft." Woody winced as he picked up his pint glass of beer.

"Is the hand still hurting?" Finn asked.

"Yes, it is and so would yours be if it had been smashed against the wall by a damn great wardrobe. God knows why you thought it necessary to do that."

"Because there were two of them," Finn growled, "which meant in time they might have managed to free each other and the last thing we want is them escaping and telling the old Bill what we've been up to."

"Don't really see that as a problem. I mean, if they did try to escape the alarm would go off and that'd give us plenty of time to scarper."

"The alarm. You mean, you set the alarm?" Finn was flabbergasted.

"Yeah, of course."

"You numpty. How do you reckon we'd hear it down here in the village?"

"Because those things are deafening and we'd certainly hear it if it went off in the middle of the night."

"Yeah, and so would all the folks as live in Blackberry Way. They'd have the cops up there before we'd have the chance to get dressed."

"Well, that's as maybe but it isn't likely to go off anyway, is it?" Woody looked at his hand. "Not with that damn great wardrobe there."

"You're right, I suppose." Finn sighed. "If only we'd never met the girls, then things might have gone a lot differently." He pulled a cigarette packet from the pocket of his jeans and placed it on the table. "I could do with a fag but can't be bothered to go outside. I wish they'd never brought in the stupid smoking ban."

"Why do you wish we'd never met the girls? I mean, they have nothing whatsoever to do with all this."

"Dunno, but I gotta blame someone."

Finn and Woody had met Shelley and Ginger at a fayre in Devon during which the girls told them that the Christmas Wonderland in Pentrillick would be their final destination for the year. By sheer chance, Finn and Woody had also booked a pitch at Wonderland and so when the girls told them of their planned stay at Sea View Cottage, it was agreed that the men would share the girls' accommodation in order to keep down their expenses. For Finn and Woody knew they could not admit as to where they would otherwise have stayed, that being to squat at Tuzzy-Muzzy. For Finn had access to the house due to the fact that someone whom he had met and befriended while serving a prison sentence for GBH had offered him the loan of an illicit set of duplicate keys.

After the fayre in Devon they went their separate ways vowing to meet up again towards the end of November ready for the opening of Wonderland on November the twenty sixth.

When Finn and Woody arrived in Cornwall they were unaware of any other trades people with pitches at Wonderland other than the girls and so it wasn't until the day before it opened that they learned that Simeon Dupont was to run a patisserie there. Finn was intrigued, for a year or so earlier, his then girlfriend, Misty Merryweather, had left him for a French patissier called Simeon and it crossed Finn's mind that it might be possible they were one and the same person. Although after their parting, he'd heard nothing more of Misty or Simeon and certainly had no reason to believe the couple had married. However, after Wonderland had been open for a few days it became apparent that Simeon was in Cornwall alone and because he never mentioned having a wife or even a girlfriend, Finn assumed that they were not the same person; besides, Simeon no doubt was a commonplace name in France. It was therefore, a genuine shock to Finn when Misty appeared on the scene a few days after Simeon's demise in a state of some distress and declared herself to be Simeon Dupont's widow.

Finn was delighted that Misty seemed genuinely pleased to see him and for that reason thought that if he were to play his cards right then perhaps they might be able to resume their relationship and rekindle the affection they had felt for one another before Simeon Dupont came onto the scene. There was after all a cake shop in London to consider which Finn knew would be worth a bob or two and should go to his poor widow, Misty. But what no-one was prepared for was the arrival of Aimée Dupont thus causing him and everyone else to realise that Simeon Dupont was a bigamist. Hence the dilemma. For Finn having learned from Aimée that Simeon's wealth went far beyond one cake shop, had with Woody's help kidnapped the French lady, hoping by doing so that Misty would inherit Simeon's entire fortune. And if that were the case then some of it would certainly come in Finn's direction if he were able to marry Misty in due course. The problem was the kidnapping was done on impulse after a few pints of beer. It had been on the night of the Pentrillick Players' Christmas party when drinks had flowed like water. The plan was a simple one; ring Aimée and tell her that they had news regarding her husband's death and then when she emerged from the pub, bundle her into the back of a vehicle in the car park - preferably a van - which Finn would break into. Starting the vehicle would not prove a problem because Finn was a past master at stealing cars. Once done, Aimée Dupont would be out of the way and tied up in one of Tuzzy-Muzzy's three bathrooms and they would be back at the Crown and Anchor before they were missed. They put the plan into action. It worked and Aimée Dupont was bound and gagged with ropes and gaffer tape which they had found in a Tuzzy-Muzzy shed.

However, on waking up on Sunday morning and remembering what they had done they realised it had been a ridiculous idea and were clueless as to what their next move should be. If Aimée were to die in circumstances that looked anything other than accidental then their plan could unravel. The problem was neither Finn nor Woody had a thirst for murder anyway. Dodgy deals yes and minor offences but murder wasn't their scene. And then as if things were not already bad enough, the two old dears from Primrose Cottage had poked in their noses meaning that all three ladies were now locked up in Tuzzy-Muzzy's bathrooms until they could come up with a plausible plan.

"Oh for God's sake, no. Look the girls are here," groaned Woody, as Shelley and Ginger walked into the bar, "better try and behave as though everything's normal, I suppose."

"Ah, there you are," said Ginger, unzipping her jacket as Shelley went to get their drinks and order some food. "We left you a note at the cottage to say we were coming here." She frowned. "Why do you both look so glum? Were your takings poor today?"

"No, they were brilliant," said Woody, with an obvious false laugh, "In fact today was probably the best day we've had so far." He tried to look cheerful.

"That's alright then. So where have you been all evening? We haven't seen you since we got back."

"What? Oh, here and there. In fact we've been here for quite a while now?" Finn was finding it hard to be sociable.

"Just as well because we couldn't be bothered to cook anything tonight and so made do with microwave meals. Trouble is we're still hungry so we've popped in here for some cheesy chips. Hope you've had something to eat. You shouldn't drink on an empty stomach, you know."

Woody scowled. "Stop nagging, Ginge. We're alright because we each had a pasty from the café before we left and a couple of doughnuts."

"Oh good. Anyway, I better go as we're going to have a game of pool, so see you later." She walked towards Shelley who held two pints of lager in her hands.

"Oh for God's sake, Woody, what are we gonna do," said Finn, with a deep sigh of exasperation. "We can't leave those sodding women locked in the bathrooms for ever, especially the French woman. She's been there for four days now and must have long ago eaten the pizza we bought for her and the biscuits and crisps we found in the van."

"That was the whole idea of going up there today, to give her some doughnuts."

"Yeah, I know and she'd have got them as well if the two old biddies hadn't turned up." Finn groaned. "I wish it was January then we could scarper."

Woody's face brightened. "Yes, of course, that's the answer. We must do a runner now before the women are found. I mean, what's to stop us from getting our clobber from the cottage and then driving up to Pentrillick House and grabbing our stuff from the chalet. If we did that we could be out of the county by the time anyone was up tomorrow morning."

"But we've been drinking and so are well over the limit."

Woody snorted. "I think that's the least of our worries."

"Yeah, okay, but what about the three women? I mean, if they're never found they'll all die and I couldn't live with that on my conscience."

"We'll ring the police anonymously when we're safely away from here," said Woody, "it shouldn't be a problem. We'll ring from a phone box in Devon and will be miles away before they've traced the call."

"Okay, what you say makes sense, but if we do it that means I won't have a chance to say goodbye to Misty."

"Humph, I think that girl's caused us more than enough trouble already, don't you?" He drained his glass and banged it down on the table. "Come on, drink up, Finn. It's time to get out of here."

"Yeah, alright, I suppose so."

As Finn lifted his glass to finish his beer, he saw two police officers over its rim. He froze as the officers spoke to the landlord, glanced around the bar and then walked towards their table.

"Don't try and make a run for it," said one of the policemen, seeing Woody reach for his jacket, "I've more men outside. Quietly stand, please, and come with us. We've a few questions we'd like you to answer regarding the kidnapping of Madame Aimée Dupont, Mrs Charlotte Burton and Ms Henrietta Tonkins and also the murder of Monsieur Simeon Dupont."

Chapter Twenty-One

Tommy was in a very good frame of mind on Thursday morning as he cleaned Kitty's upstairs windows. She had agreed to his offer of doing them as she was unable to clean them effectively herself, being afraid to climb a ladder. Hence, for years she had cleaned them from the inside by leaning out, which meant there was always a corner on each pane that her cloth couldn't reach. Tommy on hearing this had said his work would cost her nothing. It was to be an act of kindness to someone he considered to be a friend, especially since that evening in the pub when she'd allowed him and a few others to call her Kitty.

After he finished the two windows on the front and was descending the ladder in order to move it round to the back of the house, he spotted Hetty and Lottie walking along the garden path below with a huge bunch of flowers for Kitty.

Tommy waved. "I've been hearing all about you and your Tuzzy-Muzzy adventure this morning from Kitty. I've nearly done here then I'll be down to hear what you have to say."

"Okay," said Lottie, "but you be careful. Seeing you up there makes me nervous. You're not as young as you were, Tommy."

"Yes, and don't I know it."

While Kitty invited the sisters into the house, Tommy moved his ladder round to the back garden to finish the windows. The first one he did had frosted glass and so he assumed it was the bathroom. The second was on the landing and the last appeared to be a spare bedroom for there were several boxes on the bed and numerous objects all over the floor. When the glass was clean, Tommy put his face close to the window to see what the objects on the floor were. He nearly fell from his ladder when he realised they were gnomes. Dozens of them standing in rows.

Kitty, sitting downstairs in her living room drinking coffee and chatting with Hetty and Lottie suddenly remembered the gnomes. With haste she excused herself and flew up the stairs to draw the curtains but it was too late. Her heart sank when she saw Tommy's face peering in the window, his expression one of disbelief.

When Tommy walked into the living room at Meadowsweet, he found Kitty sitting in an armchair in floods of tears. Hetty and Lottie were trying to console her but had no idea why she was crying. Without being asked, Tommy sat down opposite her.

"Kitty, please don't cry," he said, "I don't know why you did it but please talk to me and see if I can help you."

"Did what?" asked Hetty and Lottie together.

"Gnomes," said Tommy, as Hetty and Lottie returned to their chairs.

Kitty stopped crying and sat up. A tear dripped from her chin as she reached into her pocket for a handkerchief. "It's not what it seems," she said, drying her eyes. "Honestly, I'm not a thief."

Lottie gasped. "Thief. You mean, you took the gnomes?"

"Shush," said Tommy, "it looks that way." He took Kitty's hand. "So, why did you do it, Kitty?" he asked.

Kitty tried to smile but failed miserably. "It all began back in the summer when I was out walking on a route I'd not taken before and in the garden of a small cottage were a couple of gnomes near to the garden gate. They had cheeky little faces and seemed to be looking at me as I passed by and so I wished them good day and after that did the same every time I saw them." As she spoke she kept her eyes focussed on the floor to avoid looking at her friends.

"Go on," urged Hetty, her voice tinged with embarrassment as she recalled saying on the morning Kitty had called in for coffee that whoever took the gnomes was stark staring mad.

"Yes, of course, sorry." Kitty continued. "Anyway, as the summer went on the gnomes began to look a little careworn. Both were covered with dry grass which I assumed had flicked onto them when the lawn was cut and one had bird droppings on his little green hat. Poor things, I began to feel sorry for them. And then one day I saw that one had toppled over and his arm was chipped and what's more there was heavy rain forecast and the weather was getting colder. It was October by then."

Lottie bit her bottom lip. "So you picked them up and brought them home with you."

Kitty nodded. "Not straight away. I didn't want to be seen, you see, so I waited until it was dark and then crept back. Once back here I gave them both a bath, mended the chip with Polyfilla and touched up their paint. But it was never my intention to keep them. I shall return them soon."

"And all the others?" Tommy asked.

"After taking the first two it seemed that there were gnomes everywhere. Admittedly, I looked out for them and they all seemed the same, downcast by the impending cold weather."

Tommy chuckled. "So you started to go out in the dead of night and bring them all back here."

Kitty smiled. "Yes and they've all been cleaned and repainted. I sort of see myself as having given them a home for the winter. It's not theft…I'm just caring for them until springtime when I shall put them back in their rightful places."

"But how will you know which go where?" Hetty asked, "I mean, it sounds as though there are rather a lot of them."

Kitty nodded. "I've stuck a label on the base of each one and on it is written the address from which it was taken and whereabouts in the garden it had stood."

"You old softie," said Tommy, beginning to laugh, "There's a lot more to you than meets the eye, Katherine Vickery."

Kitty smiled. "You don't think ill of me, do you? All of you, I mean. I should hate it if you did."

"Absolutely not," said Lottie, "and in a funny sort of way I admire you. I mean those little chaps are often quite heavy so it must have been a real labour of love."

"Yes, and it took me a fair while to gather them all in as I could only ever carry two at once."

Tommy leaned forward in his chair. "Well, it'll be a lot easier when it's time to take the little fellas back to their homes because I shall help you."

"So shall I," said Hetty.

"And me," Lottie added, "because I like gnomes and always have done."

"Of course you know poor old Psychic Sid got a visit from the old Bill over a gnome he bought in a charity shop in Penzance, don't you?" Tommy chuckled recalling Sid's account of the police visit told to him while in the Crown and Anchor.

"Did he?" Kitty looked shocked.

"Yes, but fortunately, the gnome in question failed to be identified by its owner. Its umbrella was the wrong colour or something like that."

"Oh dear," said Kitty, "poor Sid, I shall have to make it up to him somehow without him knowing why."

"Well," said Tommy, "it looks as though all of Pentrillick's mysteries have been solved at once. We know where the gnomes are now, not that we'll tell anyone, Aimée Dupont has been found and the police have the blokes who murdered poor old Simeon."

"Oh no they haven't," said Hetty, "I don't think for one minute that Finn and Woody killed Simeon or anyone else for that matter. Certainly they're guilty of kidnapping his widow and tying us up like trussed chickens, but from what we've heard this morning they're denying all knowledge of Simeon's murder if indeed murdered he was. Remember, we still don't know for sure. It's pure speculation."

"Well, the police must think that he was or they wouldn't be questioning Finn and Woody about it, would they?" persisted Lottie, "And don't forget Simeon's Rolex watch is still missing as well."

Hetty shook her head and tutted noisily. "Yes, and I hope for your sake, Lottie, that the Hookaducks never find out that it was you that told the police Patrick had a Rolex."

Lottie giggled. "Okay, so it was fake but it could easily have been the real thing. And then of course there are the empty vodka and wine bottles. As far as I'm concerned they're solid proof Simeon that was murdered."

Hetty remained obstinate. "Humph, the bottles mean nothing. It seems to me that were it not for Sid's silly predictions then there would be no reason at all to doubt his death was anything other than an unfortunate accident."

Before Sid opened up for another day's fortune telling, he forced himself to tidy out the cupboard beneath the seating in which he chucked everything that he didn't want lying around. Much of it was of no use like receipts and packaging, a radio that no longer worked and his old mobile phone. There were also a few pairs of shoes, stuff that needed mending and a collection of old newspapers.

Sid put the shoes in the bottom of the wardrobe where they belonged. The receipts and packaging he placed in a heap for recycling along with the old newspapers. The items in need of repair he put back in the cupboard along with the radio and his old phone. After finding the old carrier bag in which he'd brought back his shirt from the charity shop in Penzance, he picked up the newspapers and packaging and dropped them inside, but as the last one slid into the bag the name Mimi Monfils caught his eye. Sid pulled out the newspaper; one he had bought while in France for the football. He sat down. The article told of the theft of designer clothing from a warehouse in Paris amongst which were dresses by French designer, Mimi Monfils.

Chapter Twenty-Two

Standing in front of their chalets before Wonderland opened up for the day, Nick was avidly listening to Ginger and Shelley tell how Finn and Woody had been taken in for questioning the previous evening in connection with the kidnapping of Aimée Dupont and the murder of her husband, Simeon. However, both girls were emphatic that their acquaintances were in no way guilty of murder and were willing to provide alibis when asked so to do to prove the point. For on the night that Simeon Dupont died, Finn and Woody were in the Crown and Anchor with the girls and all four returned together to Sea View Cottage where they ate pizzas and watched a late night film on television which finished at two twenty five; an hour after the estimated time of Simeon's demise.

"So they're off the hook," said Nick, "that's good because I rather liked them."

"What, even though they appear to have kidnapped poor Aimée?"

"Well, yeah, I suppose that wasn't very nice. Any idea why they did it?"

"Not very nice?" Shelley was appalled by Nick's flippant response.

"They tied up the two old dears as well," said Ginger, "apparently they live next door to the house where Aimée was hidden but we don't know any more than that at present."

"And to answer your question, Nick, no we don't know why the boys kidnapped Aimée either," said Shelley, "but no doubt an explanation will be doing the rounds pretty soon."

As Nick opened his mouth to ask another question, a police car drove into the grounds.

Shelley frowned. “Oh no, they’re not visiting poor old Sid again, are they?”

Everyone stopped what they were doing and watched as the police car drove past through the avenue of trees and pulled up outside the fortune teller’s caravan as on three previous occasions.

“For God’s sake,” said Ginger, “what’s the poor bloke supposed to have done now? I wish they’d leave him alone.”

“Dunno,” said Nick, as he fumbled with the lock on the double doors of his chalet, “but Sid’s porkies certainly seem to get him in a lot of trouble.”

The police were with Sid for less than half an hour and to everyone’s relief they left without the fortune teller as on the three previous occasions. Sid even stood on his doorstep and waved to the police as they left; one officer driving, the other speaking on the car radio.

“Thank goodness,” said Shelley, watching as the car disappeared round a corner, “for a horrible moment then I thought they might have found another reason to think he’d murdered poor old Simeon which is daft because Sid wouldn’t hurt a fly.”

“Why do you think that?” Nick asked.

“Because he has a heart of gold. You see, he bought the gnomes that got him into trouble recently from a charity shop in Penzance. He really only wanted the one with Sid written on its hat. But being kind-hearted, he bought both because he couldn’t bear to leave the other on its own because it might have been lonely.”

“Really,” said Nick, “what a nutcase.”

Shelley scowled, annoyed by his jibe.

Ignoring the comments of Shelley and Nick, Ginger thoughtfully glanced down towards the lake. “I don’t know about you two but it gives me the creeps knowing that Simeon's death is still unsolved. I mean, we know for sure it wasn't Finn or Woody so whoever it is, is still at large and since there appears to be no motive he might be a serial killer who will strike again."

"Tosh. I reckon it was an accident," said Nick, as he pulled back the chalet's doors and spread out his racks of clothing. "I mean, as you say, no-one appears to have a motive and none of the locals knew him until he turned up down here, did they? As for him being a serial killer, it's unlikely as Simeon's death lacked gore and brutality."

"Ugh, that's gross." Ginger was repulsed.

Shelley nodded. "I'm inclined to agree with you, Nick."

"Okay," said Ginger, "good point and I hope you're both right. I mean it would be horrible to find out it was someone we knew from up here." She looked towards Finn and Woody's closed up chalet and sighed. "I wonder if we'll ever see the lads again."

"We might do," said Shelley "if they're let out on bail."

"You two certainly keep some dodgy company," said Nick, with a laugh, as they watched the first of the day's visitors emerging down the avenue of trees. But to Ginger's surprise she noticed the laughter didn't reach Nick's eyes and that his clenched hands were shaking.

After their visit to Kitty at Meadowsweet, Hetty and Lottie, having fully recovered from their ordeal in the Tuzzy-Muzzy bathroom thought it would be a good idea to go out especially as the weather was fine and sunny. After brief deliberation, Lottie agreed to have a driving lesson, for the fact that she had been able to free them from the ropes binding their wrists the previous evening had left her with new found confidence and she felt ready to tackle anything.

Meanwhile, back at the Wonderland, in less than ten minutes after it had opened up for the day, Nick suddenly left his chalet and ran across the grounds of Pentrillick House and disappeared from view.

"Where's he off to," said Ginger, opening up a new box of scented candles to put on display, "can't be the loo because he didn't ask us to look after his stuff."

Shelley stepped outside and looked to her left. "Weird! Look, he's locked up as well and put 'closed' on the door."

Ten minutes later he re-appeared with his white transit van.

"Everything alright?" Shelley asked, as he jumped from the van and unlocked the doors of his chalet.

Nick shook his head. "Afraid not. My old man just rang. Me mum's had a fall and so I have to go and see her."

"Oh dear, I am sorry. So are you taking all your stuff with you?" Shelley asked, as he grabbed clothing and bundled it into the back of his van.

"Yeah, it's unlikely I'll be back before this all winds up, you see. So I've got to take it with me." He paused for breath. "Care to give us a hand?"

"Of course," said Shelley. "Do you want it done in any particular order?"

"No, just bung it in as it comes. The van's clean inside and I'll sort it later."

"So have you told Steve you're going?" Ginger asked. "I mean, he'll wonder where you are if you just suddenly disappear."

"Yeah, I have. I had to grab my things from his caravan, you see. I didn't have time to chat much though because he had several customers." Nick paused and pulled three twenty pound notes from his wallet. "When you next see him, please give him these. I owe him twenty for rent and the rest can be for a drink on me."

"Of course," said Ginger, as she tucked the money inside a pocket of her jeans. "I'll make sure he gets it before the day is out."

Jeremy and Jemima Liddicott-Treen, with time on their hands until their mother was ready to take them shopping for new shoes, wandered through the attractions in the fairground where they rode in the swing boats and bought toffee apples. After four goes each on the helter-skelter, Jeremy challenged Jemima to see who would be the most successful when it came to testing their strength. Jemima accepted the challenge for as a keen gymnast she knew that the muscles in her arms were strong.

As they made their way towards Steve and his apparatus, they heard the shrill sound of the bell on his striker.

"Someone's done it," said Jeremy, "I often hear the bell though so it can't be too difficult."

"Good morning," said Steve, as he saw the young siblings approaching. But Jeremy was too shocked to reply for Steve was wearing the black leather gloves.

"Good morning," said Jemima, brightly.

Conscious that her brother had not returned the greeting she elbowed him in the ribs.

"What, oh yes, good morning, Steve," Jeremy muttered, "I see you wearing gloves today. You must be feeling the cold."

"No not at all, young sir. It's just I cut my hand yesterday and so I'm wearing the gloves to make sure the plaster doesn't come unstuck. Plasters don't seem to stick like they did when I were a kid. I remember me mum having to rip them off my legs when I'd been in the wars and it damn well hurt."

"Oh, I see, very wise. Wearing gloves that is." Jeremy wanted to ask questions but realised he had none of his detective heroes' skills when it came to gleaning information.

However, Steve inadvertently divulged the information he sought without him having to utter a word.

"It's really good of Nick to let me keep them as it's a lot colder up-country than it is down here so he might wish he'd kept them once he gets up there."

"Nick, up what, where?" Jeremy tried to make sense of what Steve had said.

"Yeah, these are Nick's gloves, they're really nice and must have cost a fair bit." Steve chuckled. "He's lucky to have them both though because he lost one a while back but fortunately Patricia found it when out walking Tyronne."

"Oh," was all Jeremy could say.

"Never mind about who found the silly glove," said Jemima, the expression on her face looking anything but happy, "what's this about Nick going up-country?"

"He's got to go home because his mum's in hospital." Steve looked concerned.

Jemima squealed and stamped her feet. "No, but I haven't had time to persuade Mum to buy me the dress I like yet. It's a gorgeous Mimi Monfils and I wanted it to wear for Christmas."

But Jeremy couldn't speak. Too many thoughts were rattling round in his head.

Inside the police station, the two officers who had visited Sid, believed, after they had been in touch with their colleagues across the Channel, that they had sufficient evidence to question Nick Roberts regarding his possible involvement in the theft of goods which were stolen from a Paris warehouse back in the summer. Indeed their investigations revealed that several men were already serving time in a French prison for said crime but the stolen garments had never been traced and recovered. However, while there was no evidence to suggest that Nick Roberts was involved with the actual theft, there was more than enough evidence to suggest that he was in possession of stolen goods with the sole intent of selling them to the unsuspecting public.

Nick had already left the grounds of Pentrillick House when the police arrived with a list of the stolen garments and so were unable to examine his stock. When Shelley and Ginger told the officers that he had gone home because his mother had taken a fall, they suspected that he knew that they were onto him and had therefore gone on the run.

"Any idea where his mother lives?" The taller of the two officers asked going along with Nick's story.

Shelley and Ginger both shrugged their shoulders. "Sorry, haven't the foggiest," said Shelley, "and I never thought to ask."

Having made sure that he was able to hear all that was being said, Jack, who sold garden ornaments and made miniature wheelbarrows, called out from his nearby chalet. "He told me a while back that his parents were both dead. I remember it clearly. His dad died when he was a teenager and his mum passed away just last year."

"Hmm, that doesn't surprise me," said the police officer, as the second officer opened up a notebook.

"Why do you want to talk to Nick?" Ginger asked.

"At this stage I can't say." The police officer glanced around at the ever increasing crowd, "Right, can anybody here give me a good description of the vehicle Mr Roberts drives and if possible the registration number."

"I can," said Jeremy Liddicott-Treen, who along with his sister had arrived breathlessly after hearing the police siren. He then proceeded to give the make, the model and the full registration number of Nick's van.

Chapter Twenty-Three

The screeching of brakes on the forecourt of his garage brought Vince out from his workshop to see who was responsible for the noise. From a white transit van, Nick from Wonderland jumped out his face red and his hands trembling as he reached for the pump hose. As Vince wiped his hands on an oily cloth he watched as Nick filled up the vehicle, ran inside the shop to pay for the fuel and then drove off as quickly as he'd arrived.

Vince tutted and then returned to the workshop.

With his tank filled up with petrol, Nick drove through the village and headed back in the direction of Pentrillick House. Half a mile before the main entrance, he pulled into the gateway of a field, jumped down from his van and without bothering to lock the doors climbed over the five bar gate and into the field where daffodils were just coming into bloom. Not wanting to be seen crushing the flowers, he ran along the edge of the field where he was hidden from the road by an overgrown hedge. In the valley at the bottom, he paused to catch his breath and then leapt across a stream and ventured into the back of the woodland area which ran behind the lake in the grounds of Pentrillick House.

In the adventure playground, a group of children were surprised to see a man appear from inside the woods. He said nothing and didn't look in their direction but they watched silently as he furtively walked towards a large conifer tree. After quickly glancing across the lake and up into the area where Wonderland bustled with people, he pushed his hand into a neatly concealed crevice in the tree's decrepit trunk and from it he pulled out a small bag. With haste he opened the bag and took out something bright and shiny which he slipped onto his wrist. The bag he screwed up and tossed to the ground amongst dried pine needles. He then ran back through the trees and disappeared from view.

Lottie was feeling very pleased with herself. With Hetty by her side she had just driven all the way to Helston and back along the main road. However, as she turned into the lane which led down into Pentrillick she became a little more uptight for the road was narrow and in places it was not wide enough for two vehicles to pass by one another.

Back in his van Nick looked at his phone to see if there was a route out of Cornwall along country lanes for he was keen to avoid all main roads. To his dismay, he realised that for the first part of his journey he would have to travel along the A394 for several miles. Tossing his phone on the passenger seat, he started up the van's engine and then proceeded towards the quiet lane which led up from Pentrillick to the main road.

Lottie meanwhile found it hard to concentrate for she was distracted by a police helicopter flying low overhead and zig-zagging close to the lane.

"Never mind about the helicopter, keep your eyes on the road," said Hetty, aware of her sister's erratic steering, "or we'll end up in the ditch."

Conscious that she was over-heating and her hands were shaking, Lottie focused on the winding road ahead but as she approached a particularly narrow stretch of the lane, a white van came flying around the corner travelling much too fast. Lottie screamed, slammed on the brakes, stalled the engine and blocked the road.

The van driver shook his fists in anger.

"It's Nick," said Hetty, dumbfounded, as he jumped from the driver's seat of the van, "but where on earth is he going? He should be at Wonderland today."

As Nick left the van and scrambled over a large metal gate, a police car pulled up behind Hetty and Lottie's car and at the same time another police car stopped behind Nick's van.

"What the…?" said Hetty, as the helicopter hovered over the field into which Nick had run. Two police officers jumped from each car, leapt over the gate and gave chase.

In the field, a strong wind caused by the helicopter blades stopped Nick in his tracks. He raised his hands and put them over his face as protection against the dust, dry earth and stubble.

Desperate to see what was happening, Hetty and Lottie sprang from the car just in time to see the first two police officers grab Nick from behind, pull him to the ground and snap handcuffs around his wrists behind his back. As one of the officers waved to the helicopter it turned around and then disappeared from view. Meanwhile, back in the lane, two more police cars arrived.

Misty Merryweather looked a sad figure as she sat in the Crown and Anchor on Thursday evening with Shelley and Ginger. The death of her illegal husband, the kidnapping of his real wife, Aimée, and the discovery that her old friend Finn was responsible for said kidnapping had destroyed her faith in human nature. She felt there was no-one in whom she could put her trust as the tears in her red eyes seemed to emphasise.

"So, what exactly happened today?" Tommy, who had just arrived at the pub, asked Bernie the Boatman, after he had bought a pint. "I heard someone had been arrested for selling stolen goods, but know no more than that."

Bernie nodded to a table by the fire where sat Hetty and Lottie. "Let's go and sit by the sisters as they were in on some of the action."

"I might have known," said Tommy, with a chuckle.

"Poor Misty," said Hetty, as the two men sat down, "poor Aimée too. What a terrible time they've both had."

"It's been a shock to all of us," said Lottie, who had an extra-large glass of wine, "and I think it will be a while before I feel confident enough to drive again."

"So, what exactly happened today?" Tommy asked.

Hetty, with Lottie's help told of the outcome of the afternoon's driving lesson.

"So, you mean to tell me that the cops sent out a helicopter just to catch a bloke who was selling stolen goods? What a waste of money." Tommy was shocked.

"It appears so," said Hetty.

"No, no, there's more to it than that," said Bernie, removing his cap due to the heat of the fire. "You see, it's not just because Nick was selling stolen goods that he was arrested. It was because he's the bloke who murdered poor old Simeon Dupont."

"What!" All three uttered the same word in response to Bernie's brief statement.

"So, how come? I mean, why?" Tommy asked.

"Well, we assume Simeon recognised some of the dresses that Nick was selling and knew that they'd been stolen. And if that were the case and Simeon approached Nick then it wouldn't have gone down too well, would it? I mean, we know that Simeon drank red wine and vodka on the night he died and it's now assumed that Nick was the mystery person with whom he was drinking and that he laced Simeon's wine with vodka. Simeon certainly wouldn't have done it himself because he didn't like the stuff."

"And then you reckon that Nick followed Simeon back to the café and drowned him in the lake knowing he was too drunk to put up a fight." Tommy looked shocked.

"That's the theory, yes."

Hetty shook her head. "No, I don't believe a word of it. I liked Nick. He was a bit rough but he was a nice bloke and always most courteous."

"Yes, it does seem odd," Lottie agreed, "I mean, if Nick and Simeon had fallen out as you suggest then it seems unlikely that Simeon would have agreed to go drinking with Nick especially in the maze of all places. And what did they drink out of? Obviously not the bottles because the police would have checked them for DNA so they must have had glasses and so where are they?"

"That's a good point and yes, they must have had glasses for Nick to have slipped vodka into Simeon's wine. But they could be anywhere. There are rubbish bins all over Wonderland which are emptied several times each day and the police had no reason to search them when Simeon was found in the lake because it appeared to be an accident."

Lottie nodded. "Yes, and of course the glasses would have had traces of Nick's DNA, so he knew they had to be disposed of."

"Exactly," said Bernie, "whereas there was nothing to link the bottles to Nick so he shoved them in the most convenient place."

"I still don't think he did it." Hetty was po-faced.

Bernie folded his arms. "Well, whether you like it or not he is guilty because I've been told by a very reliable source that he has confessed."

"He's confessed." Hetty was flabbergasted.

"Who said?" Lottie asked.

"I can't say, but I can tell you that Arnold is the one who holds the key. You know Arnold, don't you, Tom?"

Tommy nodded. "You mean the chap who works up at the big house?"

"That's the one, Arnold Pascoe. Been a groundsman up at Pentrillick House for goodness knows how many years."

Tommy looked confused. "But Arnold's not here. He and his missus are away on holiday. Gone for a cruise if I remember correctly."

"That's right but they got home early this morning. It were a bit of a shock for them when they heard what had been going on because of course they knew nothing about it as neither he nor his wife have mobile phones and so they would have been completely in the dark. But as it turns out Arnold knows the answers to quite a few of the questions that have puzzled us for a while." Bernie paused and shook his head as a strand of tinsel fell onto him from one of the beams above.

"Carry on," said Lottie, grabbing the tinsel, "we're all ears."

"Right, well Arnold went off for his holiday on December the third which I believe was a Saturday."

"It was," said Hetty, "because we moved down here the day before on Friday, December the second."

"Good, anyway, Wonderland opened a week before Arnold went away and so whenever he could he chatted to a few of the folks who were selling their wares and the fair people too but it was Nick that he got on best with. You see, Arnold and Nick were both fascinated with the maze and so one morning before Wonderland opened up for the day, Arnold showed Nick a clever way to find the exit. It was something he'd worked out which I'm told is quite logical if you're in the know. Apparently Nick was fascinated and said that if the opportunity ever arose he'd get someone to go into the maze with him, they'd both have a few drinks and then they'd see who could find their way out first. They'd do it at night time too, with only the moonlight and maybe a torch to help find the way out. Apparently Arnold thought that was hilarious."

"And you think that's what Nick did? He challenged Simeon to do that on the night that he died?" Tommy half-heartedly took a sip of beer.

"Most likely. Anyway, that's not all. Because they got on so well, Arnold and his wife invited Nick over for dinner one night and with him he took a bottle of vodka. After their meal, Arnold joined Nick in a few glasses but Deidre, Arnold's wife, said she couldn't face drinking it and she told Nick how when she was younger a friend of hers had put vodka in her wine. She said the wine tasted much the same and so she drank her usual three glasses. By the end of the third though she was legless and remembers nothing more of that evening. She well remembers the next day though and said she's never been so ill in her life."

Lottie's face was pale. "So you think Nick enticed Simeon into the maze for a drink and the challenge of finding his way out, and then laced his wine with vodka to get him drunk? The sole purpose being murder?"

"Well, yes, after all his livelihood was at stake and as we all agree, Nick was a charmer and so probably got round Simeon with some rigmarole or another," Bernie sighed. "It's almost the perfect crime."

"And you say he's confessed?" Hetty felt downcast.

"Yes, he's confessed."

"What a terrible waste of two lives," said Lottie.

"Two?" Hetty queried.

"Yes, Simeon of course and now Nick because his life isn't going to be much now, is it? And it's certainly true that crime doesn't pay."

No-one spoke for a minute or two while they all digested information received.

"By the way, it was Sid who tipped the police off about Nick," said Bernie, finding the quiet unnerving, "he came across an article about the robbery in an old copy of a French newspaper which he'd picked up back in the summer when he was over in France for the football. He told me that when he read the article he recalled you, Hetty, saying that your dress was a Mimi Monfils and that brand was amongst the ones listed in the paper as stolen, so Sid put two and two together and rang the police."

"That makes sense," said Tommy, "but I wonder how Simeon knew that the dresses were nicked. I mean, I wouldn't have thought he'd have been into fashion and stuff like that."

"Well, that's simple," said Bernie, glancing at the door of the pub through which Aimée Dupont had just entered, "You see, Mimi Monfils is Aimée Dupont and so he was familiar with the dress label and knew a batch had been stolen back in the summer."

Hetty's mouth gaped open. "Aimée is Mimi!" she screeched.

"Yes," said Bernie, "apparently Monfils was her maiden name and her younger sister called her Mimi when they were kids. Sort of makes sense, doesn't it?"

"Yes, goodness me," said Hetty, taking a large swig of wine, "no wonder Aimée gave me a funny look when she saw me wearing one of her frocks. She obviously recognised it."

"But was probably too stressed to really care where you got it from," said Lottie.

Hetty shook her head. "I can't believe that I'm in the possession of stolen goods. I'll never be able to wear that dress again which is such a shame because I really like it."

"Don't be silly," said Tommy, "it looked great on you and you bought it in good faith."

"But it had been nicked," Hetty exclaimed.

"And you bought it from Nick," chuckled Bernie, "The chap certainly lived up to his name."

Chapter Twenty-Four

"I've just seen Tommy walking by with Kitty," said Lottie, on Christmas Eve morning as she opened door number twenty-four on the Advent calendar, "That's the second time I've seen them together over the last couple of days. They seem very chummy all of a sudden."

Hetty looked up from the floor where she knelt sweeping up pine needles from beneath the Christmas tree. "Funny you should say that because I saw them laughing and chatting in the pub last night and Kitty was drinking Guinness."

"Guinness," said Lottie, "surely not by the pint?"

Hetty nodded. "Yes, by the pint. I meant to say something to you last night but got distracted for some reason or other. But then that's hardly surprising because there's been so much happening lately."

Lottie shrugged her shoulders. "There certainly has, and as regards, Kitty and Tommy, I suppose they've known each other for donkey's years."

Hetty shook her head. "No, if you remember, back in the summer either Daisy or Maisie told us that Tommy has only been in the village for a year or eighteen months or something like that. Before that he lived at Lamorna. At least I think it was Lamorna. It was definitely West Cornwall anyway."

Because neither had any reason to leave Pentrillick with any urgency, Aimée and Misty both agreed to stay on for the Christmas weekend to keep each other company. For in a funny sort of way, because both had married the same man, they felt as though they were related, even though Simeon's marriage to Misty was illegal.

"We must put all the bad behind us," said Aimée, as they sat together for breakfast at the hotel, "What is done cannot be undone and we must look to the future. Tonight, I suggest we go to the Crown and Anchor and celebrate Christmas with the locals who have been very good to both of us." She brushed a tear from her eye, "In a funny sort of way I think it's what Simeon would have wanted and he must have loved you, Misty."

The Crown and Anchor was very busy on Christmas Eve. For as well as it being Christmas and a time when many had several days off work there was also much to discuss and discover about the events which had dominated village gossip throughout much of December.

Many of the Wonderland's workforce were in the pub too for the attraction was to be closed on Christmas Day.

"Are you two staying here for Christmas then?" Shelley asked Aimée and Misty as they sat near to the fire in the pub drinking champagne.

Misty nodded. "Yes, we are and I think it's going to be rather special yet unusual at the same time. I mean, if you'd told me two months ago that I'd be spending Christmas in Cornwall with someone who would be my husband's real wife, then I should have thought you crazy."

Aimée smiled. "And the same goes for me."

"So will you be having Christmas dinner at the hotel?" Ginger asked.

Misty shook her head. "I'm afraid not. It's strictly a bookings only event as they don't normally do lunches and sadly it's been fully booked since September. Anna, who works on the reception desk said that she'll see what they can do but I don't hold out much hope unless someone cancels at the last minute due to illness or something like that."

"Then you must come to us," said Shelley, her voice raised excitedly. "We bought a frozen turkey a while back and took it out of the freezer this morning. Of course when we bought it we were expecting Finn and Woody to be with us too but that's obviously not to be and so there's far more than we'll ever be able to eat. Not only that, we'd love you to join us."

Misty looked at Aimée who nodded. "Are you sure?" she asked.

"Yes," squeaked Shelley and Ginger in unison.

"Then we'd love to join you," said Misty.

"I can think of nothing I'd like more," Aimée agreed.

"What about Sid?" Misty asked, glancing in the direction of the psychic who was sitting in the corner eating ham, egg and chips. "Where will he be tomorrow? Surely not all alone in his caravan with no-one for company but his gnomes."

"I believe he's been invited to dinner with Father Christmas and his wife," said Shelley.

Misty scowled. "Are you pulling my leg?"

"She means Bernie," said Ginger, "he plays the part of old Santa at Wonderland and very authentic he looks too."

Christmas Day dawned grey but at least it was dry. After they arose, Hetty and Lottie prepared the vegetables for dinner and put the turkey into the oven, they then changed their clothes in order to go to church for the morning service which was at a more leisurely time of eleven rather than the usual nine o'clock.

They decided not to open their presents before they went but instead to save their small pile for after dinner so they could open them along with Kitty and Tommy for whom they had bought modest gifts.

The church bells rang out loud and clear as they walked down Long Lane and into the village where everyone they met, including strangers, greeted them with smiles which seemed only to occur at Christmas. The service was well attended, the

Liddicott-Treens were amongst the congregation and the atmosphere was thick with joy as everyone heartily sang the carols so well known and loved. After the service, feeling full of Christmas cheer, Hetty and Lottie went to the Crown and Anchor for a quick drink. To their surprise Kitty, who had played the organ in church, arrived shortly after with Tommy who had also been at the service and was looking very smart.

"My Sunday best, as our mother would have said," chuckled Tommy when Hetty complimented him on his attire.

"What time shall we arrive for dinner?" Kitty asked, as Tommy handed her a small glass of wine.

"We were thinking of eating around two," said Lottie, "but come round whenever you're ready. We've only popped in here for a quick drink so shall be leaving soon."

"I shan't be staying here long either," said Kitty, "How about you, Tom?"

"I'll probably stay till Ashley and Alison chuck me out but that won't be late as they ring last orders at ten to one and like everyone gone by a quarter past. I need to pop home first to collect a few things too but don't worry I'll be there well before you dish up."

Kitty arrived at half past one with a carrier bag of presents which she placed under the Christmas tree and much to the delight of the ladies, Tommy was there soon after also with a bag of gifts which he placed alongside the others.

They ate in the dining room which they barely used. To brighten it up, Lottie had lit a small fire and had made artistic decorations for the table. After their meal, the ladies washed up. Tommy offered to help too but they insisted he sit down in the sitting room where they'd bring him a cup of tea once the chore was finished.

"Right, time for presents," said Lottie, as she sat down on the floor beside the tree so that she could distribute them.

No-one opened their presents until all were handed out and Lottie was back seated in her favourite armchair.

Kitty loved the earrings given to her by Hetty and Lottie and promptly removed the pearl ones she usually wore and replaced them with her gift. Tommy likewise was impressed by the fleece top he received and promised he would wear it when he went to the Crown and Anchor on Boxing Day. Lottie received a silk scarf from Kitty and a box of chocolates from Tommy. Hetty received a gift box of various nail varnishes from Kitty and to her amusement a book on dieting from Tommy.

"I hope I've not offended you," said Tommy, looking a little sheepish, "it seemed a good idea when I bought it but I don't want to get in your bad books."

Hetty shook her head. "I'm not at all offended, Tommy because I always keep my word. I said losing a stone will be my New Year's resolution if Sid's predictions came true and so lose a stone I shall."

"You're a good sport then," said Tommy, "because everyone knows Sid said it for a laugh."

"There's no doubt about that," Lottie agreed, "and I think if the truth be known Sid can no more see into the future than the rest of us, but he's been good fun and I shall miss him very much when he's gone."

Inside Number Four Honeysuckle Close, Bernie the Boatman sat beside an open fire with his wife, Veronica and Psychic Sid, all full after a very large lunch.

"What'll you do, Sid, after Wonderland closes?" Bernie asked.

Sid sighed. "I don't really know. The fair folks are all off to Wales in the New Year but I'm not sure whether to go with them or not."

"Why's that?" Veronica asked.

Sid sighed. "I suppose I'm getting a bit tired of travelling around and to be honest I've really enjoyed my stay here even if my fortune telling has got me into a bit of bother here and there."

"You could always stay then," said Bernie, "you seem to be footloose and fancy free so there's nothing to stop you putting down roots here."

"No, but what would I do? I mean, I wouldn't be able to make a living telling fortunes especially now everyone knows I'm rubbish."

"So have you always been a fortune teller?" Veronica asked.

Sid chuckled. "No, before that I was a plumber. I did a good job too. I gave it up though when bending became too much of an effort. I mean, look at the size of my stomach."

"So are you a qualified plumber?" Bernie asked.

"Oh yeah, got all the right bits of paper and so forth."

"Then stay for heaven's sake. Plumbers are always in demand and difficult to get hold of. You could make a very good living here."

"But what about this?" he said, wobbling the flab.

Bernie chuckled. "Hetty Tonkins is going on a diet in the New Year and you could do the same. She's going to lose a stone but I reckon you'd need to lose two. We could make a big thing of it and weigh you both in the pub on a selected evening. Be something to look forward too during the winter months. We could even sponsor you both and raise money for a good cause."

"Excellent idea," said Veronica.

"I can see it all now," said Bernie, "and I can hear the clapping when you've both reached your goals."

"But…what…where?"

"And you can put your caravan in our driveway," said Veronica, as though reading his mind, "until you get sorted out."

Chapter Twenty-Five

On Boxing Day morning, Tommy arrived at Primrose Cottage with a step ladder.

"I bet you thought I'd forgotten about looking in your loft, hadn't you?"

"Well, the thought had crossed my mind," said Hetty, as she closed the front door after he had entered into the hallway, "but there's no rush with most places being closed for Christmas and the New Year."

"Would you like a coffee and a slice of Christmas cake before or after you've taken a look?" Lottie asked.

"After, would suit me best. Once I've had a piece of that lovely cake I won't want to move."

With the ladder in place on the landing, Tommy pushed up the hatch and climbed into the attic. "Hmm," he said, "it certainly is a good size and surprisingly clean. Come on up and have a look. The floor's boarded so you'll both be perfectly safe."

The sisters, keen to see for themselves did as he suggested.

"And plenty of headroom," said Hetty, touching a rafter, "I reckon there's more than enough space for a couple of modest bedrooms, especially if we had dormer windows and probably even room for a loo and washbasin as well. What do you think, Tommy?"

"Could be, but you'll need room for stairs as well. I daresay a good architect could sort that out for you though with no problem at all."

“And do you know any good architects?” Lottie eagerly asked.

“Actually I do. Patrick Mannering. He lives in the village and is a really nice bloke.”

Hetty frowned. “Oh, I’ve not come across that name before. Does he go to the pub at all?”

Tommy nodded. “Yes but not a lot. He’s a smart looking chap in his mid to late forties. Clean shaven, dark hair and wears glasses. His daughter is young Emma who was friendly with your grandchildren, back in the summer, Lottie.”

“You mean Emma who goes to college and works in Chloe’s café during the summer holiday?”

“That’s right, and currently she’s helping Chloe out in the café at the Wonderland.”

“Brilliant,” said Lottie, rubbing her hands with glee, “please point him out to us next time we’re all in the pub and then if he’s willing to take on the work we can ask him about the procedure.”

On Boxing Day evening, Aimée announced to patrons of the Crown and Anchor that she and Misty were leaving Pentrillick on Thursday for Paris to make arrangements for and to attend Simeon’s funeral at the beginning of the following week.

“We shall miss you,” said Shelley, with sincerity. “We admire the spirit of both of you, and we should all take a lesson from the way you’ve behaved towards each other.”

“I’ll second that,” said Kitty, “you’ve behaved impeccably.”

“So what will you do then?” Ginger asked Misty. “I mean, will you return to London after the funeral?”

“Eventually,” she replied, “but not until we’ve sorted things out.”

“I’m taking Misty under my wing,” said Aimée, “after all she deserves to be taken care of. I intend for her to model some of the garments in my latest collection and then we are going into partnership. As Simeon's legal wife I shall inherit his wealth but I want to share it with Misty."

Misty blushed and looked a little embarrassed. "Aimée already has a Mimi Monfils shop in Paris and we're planning to open another one in London and if I feel capable, then I shall manage it. I'm really excited but apprehensive too."

"You'll be fine," said Hetty, "you're as sharp as a needle."

"The Lord moves in mysterious ways," said Lottie as she raised her glass. "Good luck to you both."

"Amen to that," said Kitty.

The Crown and Anchor was packed on New Year's Eve and many of its patrons wore fancy dress as was the case every year. To see out 2016, the chosen theme was television and film personnel from the nineteen sixties.

Many people chose to hire costumes from a shop in Penzance, the rest made use of the village charity shop amongst them Hetty and Lottie, who eventually with the help of Lottie's sewing machine, transformed themselves into two of their favourite characters from the chosen era. Hetty as Hattie Jacques playing matron in the Carry On films and Lottie as Emma Peel in *The Avengers*. Initially, Lottie had been a little apprehensive about wearing a tight black leather cat suit which was actually synthetic, but Hetty insisted she looked fantastic in it and so Lottie agreed to wear it. Furthermore to achieve the right look she also agreed to have her hair dyed a dark shade of brown in dye which Hetty assured her would wash out after eight shampoos. Pleased with their results, Hetty took several pictures on her phone and then sent them to Lottie's son, Bill, and Sandra his wife, along with every good wish for their happiness in the New Year during which they hoped the family might visit them for a holiday in Pentrillick once the loft was converted.

When Hetty and Lottie arrived at the pub they were greeted by a vast selection of identifiable characters. Bernie the Boatman with the help of a little padding was Captain Pugwash. His wife, Veronica, was Hilda Ogden from *Coronation Street*. Tommy Thomas was Robin Hood and Kitty was Maid Marian. Behind the bar, Ashley and Alison were Bonnie and Clyde. Maisie and Daisy were Bill and Ben but their husbands refused to make fools of themselves. Psychic Sid was Friar Tuck and Shelley and Ginger were Cilla Black and Dusty Springfield, two of their parents' favourite singers from the past.

As the pub began to fill up, Tommy introduced Hetty and Lottie to Bert the chimney sweep in *Mary Poppins* who in real life was Patrick Mannering, the architect. He agreed to help them with a loft conversion and said he would call round on Tuesday morning.

The evening was a huge success but probably the most unexpected happening occurred shortly before midnight when Tommy announced that he and Kitty were to be married in the spring.

"Well, you're a couple of dark horses," said Hetty, hugging Kitty and Tommy in turn, "I can't believe you came to dinner on Christmas Day without giving out any signs that you were a unit, as youngsters put it these days."

Kitty blushed. "I've had a soft spot for Tommy ever since he moved to Blackberry Way but of course being me I kept my feelings to myself."

"And likewise, Kitty here took my fancy too," said Tommy, "but I did nothing about it because Mother was my main concern. But of course now she's gone things are different."

"So how come you've finally learned of your affection for each other?" Lottie asked.

Kitty and Tommy both chuckled.

"I think it was probably when…umm… you know, when Tommy found certain persons in my spare bedroom," smiled Kitty.

"It's nearly midnight," shouted Ashley, as he turned up the radio and ran around from behind the bar with Alison and two other members of staff. Everyone then placed their glasses on the nearest available surface and linked arms for Auld Lang Syne.

Half an hour into the New Year, after all had watched a firework display on the beach, Hetty stood alone outside on the terrace, her hands gripped onto the railings as she listened to the sea gently tumbling onto the shore. A cool breeze tousled a loose stand of her hair which had slipped out from beneath the matron's cap she wore.

"A penny for your thoughts," said Lottie, as she joined her sister on the terrace.

"I'm bewitched," she whispered, "I'm bewitched by the sea. I love the smell, the sound, in fact I love everything about it."

Lottie cast her eyes to the shore where the waves were just visible in the outside lights of the Crown and Anchor. "No regrets then?"

Hetty smiled. "No, none whatsoever."

From inside the bar, Patricia Hookaduck, dressed as Wonder Woman, sat in the corner near to the fire quietly playing Auld Lang Syne on the bagpipes. The mournful sound drifted out to the terrace and into every corner of the pub, momentarily causing the revellers to cease their chat and listen until the very end of Patricia's impromptu performance. Some were even moved to tears.

"Let's have a sing-song," said Tommy, inspired as the last haunting notes of the bagpipes faded.

A chorus of yeses rang throughout the pub.

"Shall I play the piano?" Hetty asked, as she emerged through the French doors, open to let in some fresh air. "I mean, we mustn't split up the love birds." She glanced towards Kitty and Tommy.

Kitty nodded. "Please do."

Hetty took a seat on the piano stool. "Right, what shall we start with?" She asked the merrymakers as they gathered around her.

"The Twelve days of Christmas," shouted Ashley from behind the bar, "our Cornish version. A Pasty in a Pear Tree."

THE END

Lightning Source UK Ltd.
Milton Keynes UK
UKHW02f1102041217
313847UK00005B/632/P